9 780821 746349

50399

0-8217-4634-0

A ZEBRA REGENCY ROMANCE

Covington's Folly

Cindy Holbrook

Author of *A Daring Deception*

*A penniless heiress,
she hoped to find hidden
treasure...not to lose
her heart!*

ZEBRA 0-8217-4634-0 /CANADA $4.99 US $3.99

Covington's Folly
Cindy Holbrook

ZEBRA BOOKS
KENSINGTON PUBLISHING CORP.

ZEBRA BOOKS are published by

Kensington Publishing Corp.
850 Third Avenue
New York, NY 10022

First Printing: July, 1994

Printed in the United States of America

ZEBRA REGENCIES
ARE
THE TALK OF THE TON!

A REFORMED RAKE   (4499, $3.99)
by Jeanne Savery

After governess Harriet Cole helped her young charge flee to France — and the designs of a despicable suitor, more trouble soon arrived in the person of a London rake. Sir Frederick Carrington insisted on providing safe escort back to England. Harriet deemed Carrington more dangerous than any band of brigands, but secretly relished matching wits with him. But after being taken in his arms for a tender kiss, she found herself wondering — *could* a lady find love with an irresistible rogue?

A SCANDALOUS PROPOSAL   (4504, $4.99)
by Teresa DesJardien

After only two weeks into the London season, Lady Pamela Premington has already received her first offer of marriage. If only it hadn't come from the *ton's* most notorious rake, Lord Marchmont. Pamela had already set her sights on the distinguished Lieutenant Penford, who had the heroism and honor that made him the ideal match. Now she had to keep from falling under the spell of the seductive Lord so she could pursue the man more worthy of her love. Or was he?

A LADY'S CHAMPION   (4535, $3.99)
by Janice Bennett

Miss Daphne, art mistress of the Selwood Academy for Young Ladies, greeted the notion of ghosts haunting the academy with skepticism. However, to avoid rumors frightening off students, she found herself turning to Mr. Adrian Carstairs, sent by her uncle to be her "protector" against the "ghosts." Although, Daphne would accept no interference in her life, she *would* accept aid in exposing any spectral spirits. What she never expected was for Adrian to expose the secret wishes of her hidden heart . . .

CHARITY'S GAMBIT   (4537, $3.99)
by Marcy Stewart

Charity Abercrombie reluctantly embarks on a London season in hopes of making a suitable match. However she cannot forget the mysterious Dominic Castille — and the kiss they shared — when he fell from a tree as she strolled through the woods. Charity does not know that the dark and dashing captain harbors a dangerous secret that will ensnare them both in its web — leaving Charity to risk certain ruin and losing the man she so passionately loves . . .

Available wherever paperbacks are sold, or order direct from the Publisher. Send cover price plus 50¢ per copy for mailing and handling to Penguin USA, P.O. Box 999, c/o Dept. 17109, Bergenfield, NJ 07621. Residents of New York and Tennessee must include sales tax. DO NOT SEND CASH.

"I am giving you three different choices. Never say I am not generous. Give me the box, accept ravishment, or choose death."

The fiend was laughing at her. She could see it in his brilliant eyes! Chantel's red-headed temper steamed to the boiling point. "Very well," she said sweetly, "I chose death!"

He stopped smiling. "Good God, what an idiotic answer. You would actually be so goosish as to chose death over dishonor?"

She flushed angrily. "I am not goosish. For if I am not mistaken, a man of your stamp just might stick at murder. That is a gallows affair."

"With the authorities in this area? Come now."

"Indeed," Chantel was forced to admit, "they are bumbleheads."

The man smiled, his gray eyes dancing appreciatively behind his black mask. "With that in consideration, do you wish to choose a different option?"

"No. I promised Teddy to protect that box."

The stranger put his pistol away. Hope flared in Chantel until he clamped two large hands upon her shoulders and gave her a swift shake that rattled her teeth. She thought, inconsequentially, that she preferred the pointed gun over his touch, for the moment his hands clasped her shoulders a stunning shock coursed through her nerves, unsettling her even more than the weapon had . . .

Chapter One

"Take that, you odious monster," Chantel cried, stabbing the poker wickedly into the flickering fire. Not half an hour ago, it had flamed into a raging fury, bellowing and belching smoke into her bedroom. She'd fled to the balcony doors in response, throwing aside the burgundy brocade curtains, now worn to a color she preferred to think of as antique rose, and swinging wide the doors to air the room. Now, the perverse fire had sullenly died down to embers, leaving the room airy, but cold.

"Very well, beast," Chantel muttered, slamming the poker back among the irons. "Have it your own way." She turned to scamper back to her waiting bed. A slight movement from the balcony doors caught her attention. She pivoted to face them, and froze.

A large man, shrouded in a gray cape, stood quietly within the entrance; Chantel's eyes traveled up his towering, fear-inspiring form until she stared into compelling dark eyes, which watched her with detached calm from behind a concealing black mask. Moonlight glinted off mahogany hair. A chiseled chin and firmly sculptured lips were bold beneath the mask. Chantel opened her mouth in preparation for screaming the rafters down.

The stranger gently shook his head and raised a cautionary finger to his lips. A deadly-looking pistol slid out from beneath the folds of his cloak. His eyebrows quirked above his mask in an almost humorous dare. Chantel prudently clamped her mouth shut.

"I knew you would see it my way," he drawled confidently as he stepped into the room.

"Indeed." Voice cool, Chantel feigned calmness, though her heart had migrated to the pit of her stomach. "What do you want?"

The man slowly appraised her from the tip of her bare toes to the top of her head, and smiled. Chantel, fidgeting, refrained from straightening her unruly red hair, but she did wrap her arms around herself, hoping to hide her frayed cotton nightgown.

"Why not step into the candlelight?" the man said abruptly.

Lud, Chantel thought, *he's probably an escaped bedlamite.* The candlelight shone behind her as she hastened to the fireplace. "Will this do?"

His gaze fell on the irons, not three feet away from her. "No. Step over toward the bed."

Chantel paled, and cast a longing glance at the poker; how unfortunate that the man was such a wary bedlamite. Reluctantly, she crossed over toward the bed, praying he would not prove lecherous as well as clever. "Here, then?"

"Much better," he said with a smile. "Now, I would advise you against any foolish moves if you value your life." He must have sensed the rebellion flaring in

Chantel, for he went on, "Even if you do not care for your life, do but consider the lives of your staff, if you cause a commotion that brings them here. It is always unwise to reduce your serving staff at this time of the year. Good help is so difficult to come by."

"True." Chantel had only three on her staff, and she shuddered at the thought of her octogenarian butler, Mr. Todd, charging into the path of flying bullets. Then she thought of her maid. "I do have one servant though . . . If I pointed her out to you, do you think you could, perchance, shoot her rather than the others?"

He chuckled. "I can't oblige. My regrettable aim, you see."

"I quite understand. Indeed, it was too much to ask." Chantel bit her lip. What was she saying? She swallowed hard. "If you're hoping for money from me, you are definitely beside the bridge on that head; the silver was pawned ages ago, and our pockets are to let." She snapped her fingers. "I have it! You must be looking for a different residence! Only state your requirements and I will direct you."

"No, this is the correct address." The man's deep voice was filled with amusement. "I am not in the way of making such glaring mistakes, I assure you. Especially when it pertains to entering a lady's boudoir; that could prove fatal to a man."

"Then what do you want?" Perplexity pushed her fear back.

"You are in possession of a certain strongbox that I am desirous of obtaining."

"A strongbox?"

"Yes, your brother gave it into your keeping. I would imagine it was approximately a week ago."

"Teddy?" Chantel asked, surprised. Then the light dawned, and her eyes widened. Teddy had indeed given her a black, locked strongbox, telling her to guard it at all costs. She'd accepted it, dismissing his words as overly dramatic. Evidently she'd been wrong.

Her eyes wavered, uncontrollably eager to stray to the box's hiding place. She quickly regained control, however, and kept her gaze resolutely trained upon the stranger. "I have no earthly idea what you are talking about. I have no box."

"Very good, my dear, but it won't fadge. I know you have it. There is no use in denying it, Chantel." A tingle raced down her spine at the sound of her name on the masked intruder's lips. "Yes, I know your name. As I told you, I do not make mistakes. Now give me the box." He stepped closer.

"I can't," Chantel stammered, holding her ground with the greatest effort. "I—I don't have it anymore . . . I had it, yes, but Teddy took it back."

"You make a terrible liar. Now get it."

"No."

"Get it, Chantel." His voice was low.

She shook her head. He stood still for a moment, then trod slowly, insidiously up to her. A master of intimidation, Chantel thought hazily, when he stopped but an inch away from her. "Do you know what is in the box?"

His dark-seeming eyes, she realized, were gray, and he was even taller than she had thought; she grew even more insecure contemplating the way he dwarfed her petite stature.

"Ah—let's see, Teddy's memoirs?" He growled; despite her resolve, she pedaled backward in retreat. Her back hit the knarled post of the Jacobean bed, once considered the epitome of fashion, now considered worthy of a museum. She squeaked. "No, no of course not. That wouldn't interest you—or anyone else, for that matter. Perhaps his gaming vouchers? He owes you money?"

"No. It is something far more vital."

"More vital?" Chantel couldn't imagine anything more vital than money.

"And I want it now."

A sudden thought crossed her mind and her eyes narrowed. "Don't tell me you are one of Teddy's idiot friends. Do you say you aren't looking for the treasure too."

"Treasure?" He sounded bemused. "What are you talking about?"

She studied him. "No, you wouldn't be the type."

"What treasure? I thought you said you were poor."

"We are, but rich in family lore." A cynical twist curved her lips.

He hesitated a moment and then shrugged his broad, imposing shoulders. " 'Tis no moment to me. All I want is the box."

"And if I don't give it to you?" Chantel asked, challenging him.

"You'll regret it very, very much."

"I . . . have no doubt."

The stranger suddenly erased the remaining distance between them. This time, with the bedpost bolstered against her back, Chantel could not retreat. She cricked her neck, unwillingly to look into those steel-gray eyes. "I fear I cannot give it to you."

"You mean you will not give it to me."

" 'Tis the same thing," Chantel snapped. "I do not consider that an option."

The dark eyes examined her for one nerve-jangling moment. A wicked gleam slowly surfaced from their depths. "Very well, I will give you two other options. You can either give me the box—"

"I won't."

"—or face, let's see . . ." he drawled out slowly with a perverse smile, "ravishment or death."

She gasped. The man was touched in his upper works! "I beg your pardon?"

"I am giving you three different choices. Never say I am not generous. Give me the box, accept ravishment, or choose death."

The fiend was laughing at her. She could see it in his brilliant eyes! Chantel's red-headed temper steamed to the boiling point. "Very well," she said sweetly, "I choose death!"

He stopped smiling. "Good God, what an idiotic answer. You would actually choose death over dishonor?" He snorted. "Faith, I should have guessed. Your puritanical nightgown should have warned me."

She flushed angrily. Clutching her favorite muslin nightgown with poet's sleeves edged in the Belgian lace she had so patiently darned, she sputtered, "Now see here, sirrah, you may come in here and brandish that pistol all you want, but you have no right to comment upon my personal attire. That is the outside of enough!"

"A thousand apologies," the man said ironically,

"but would you be so goosish as to choose death over ravishment?"

"Yes, I would," Chantel said tartly. "And I am not goosish. For if I am not mistaken, a man of your stamp just might stick at murder. That is a gallows affair."

"Whereas I would not stick at ravishment? Thank you." He bowed mockingly. "But you are wide of the mark if you think murder a gallows affair. With the authorities in this area? Come now."

"Indeed," Chantel was forced to admit, "they are bumbleheads."

The man smiled, his gray eyes dancing appreciatively behind his black mask. "With that in consideration, do you wish to choose a different option?"

"No. I promised Teddy to protect that box."

"He might forgive you under the circumstances."

"Perhaps. But I wouldn't forgive myself."

"Faith, woman, you don't even know what you are doing." Suddenly angry, he put his pistol away; hope flared in Chantel until he clamped two large hands upon her shoulders and gave her a swift shake that rattled her teeth. She thought, inconsequentially, that she preferred the pointed gun over his touch, for the moment his hands clasped her shoulders a stunning shock coursed through her nerves, unsettling her even more than the weapon had. "Stop this and give me the box!"

"No. I keep my promises," she said weakly, steeling herself for another jolt.

It didn't come. "Do you know you protect a traitor?"

"A traitor?" Chantel gasped in amazement. She

struck at his hands, attempting to break away. "Don't be ridiculous! Teddy could never be a traitor. He is a fool, yes, but a traitor? No, impossible."

"But he is." The man's voice was as adamant as his grip was iron. "You must give me the box."

"I will not! Now let me go."

He looked at her in apparent frustration, then his eyes became stern. He slowly slid his hands from her shoulders to her neck, his thumb brushing the pulse point at the hollow of her throat, then resting there. "Give me the box, Chantel."

"No." She knew he could feel every erratic beat of her heart through that tender point.

"I could strangle it out of you," he said softly. Chantel felt faint, though his thumb did not leave the hollow of her throat, nor did it increase in pressure.

"Very well," Chantel said, closing her eyes. "Strangle me."

"You little fool!" His voice was rough. His hands did not enclose her neck, but moved to her shoulders to give her a swift, aggravated jerk, rattling her eyes open. "You would die to protect a traitor?"

"He's family . . ." she said weakly in the face of his rage.

He dropped his hands in exasperation. "I'm not going to kill you."

Chantel's sigh was tremulous. "I was hoping you wouldn't."

He looked at her speculatively. "How could you have risked it? I could have been a natural killer."

Chantel's smile was bitter. "I'm a natural gambler. I come from a long line of gamblers."

"Why didn't you think I would kill you?"

"You don't look like a man of unnecessary actions . . . or waste."

"You read character well." His voice was devoid of emotion. "I only wish you were as perspicacious in other areas." Reaching into his cloak with a sigh, he pulled out a piece of rope.

"What is that?" Chantel asked warily.

"If I can't force you to tell me where the box is—and, as you have divined, I will not kill without need—I will simply have to incapacitate you another way, and find the box myself."

"You—you're going to—to—"

"Tie you up, of course."

There was no "of course" to it! Chantel spun swiftly upon her heel and darted for the door. Her would-be captor followed directly behind, grabbing for her. She ducked and twisted away to the side. Slipping past his guard, she ran to the bed, snatched up a pillow, and threw it in his face. She rolled swiftly over the bed, putting it between them.

"Give it up, woman! I do not wish to chase you around this damned bed all night long."

"Something you are probably highly accustomed to!"

The man started, then laughed. "No, madam, most women get into the bed willingly."

"Conceited coxcomb!" Chantel watched him warily.

The man groaned in exasperation and lunged. He almost caught her, even from across the bed, but Chantel pulled out of his clasp. She sped toward the balcony doors, but didn't reach them; he caught hold of her nightrail and dragged her to a dead halt.

Chantel twisted in her voluminous gown and boxed his ears, hoping they rang as strongly as her hand stung. The brute merely grabbed her wrist. Air flew from Chantel's lungs as he jerked her up against the granite hardness of his body. He caught her other flailing arm and clipped both hands behind her back. Breathing hard, she tried to lean backward, away from him.

"Shall we proceed, Chantel?" The blasted man wasn't even winded! Chantel stifled a scream as he scooped her off her feet and carried her to the bed. As soon as he plunked her down upon it, she scrambled into a sitting position, no longer able to control her fear.

"Lord, woman, don't look at me like that! I stick at ravishment as well. Now, give me your feet."

She let them peek out from underneath her gown. "No," he said more gently, "they must be at the foot of the bed."

She flushed and scooted awkwardly down to the end of the bed. He reached into his cape and pulled out another length of rope. Did the man never run out of nasty things to bring forth from that cloak? He leaned over to grasp her right foot; his cape fell open, and she saw his pistol secured in his belt. Biting her lip, she lunged for it.

Pain shot through her arm as he turned swiftly and clenched his fist around her elbow. Her fingers but a touch away from the pistol, she struggled, tears of frustration stinging her eyes. The man growled as he clutched her shoulders, shoving her back to the mattress, where he pinned her with his full weight. "Do you never give up, woman?"

"Let me go." She tried desperately to writhe out from under him. "Let me go!"

"For God's sake, stop squirming!" He had an odd note in his voice that made him sound as desperate as she felt. "Stop it, Chantel—before I lose all vestiges of being a gentleman."

"Gentleman! Hah, you bast—"

He clamped a rough hand over her mouth. "Stop, lest I forget you're a lady!" He was breathing hard, as hard as she. Chantel looked into his eyes, and suddenly all the fight drained from her.

She lay deathly still, numbed by the expression in his eyes. She couldn't say why, but she felt that if she moved, whatever unknown emotion he held at bay behind his gaze would be unleashed. And whatever he felt was dangerous. She could feel fear shuddering through her, taking her breath away, leaving her weak with heated chills. "What—?" she whispered, then stopped, swallowing hard. She didn't even know the question she wanted to ask him.

"Don't ask me to explain," he said softly. "I just might." She only stared at him. "Now, whatever you do—" his voice sounded ragged, "don't move, don't fight me. There's only so much a man can withstand."

Frozen with fear, Chantel didn't even nod her head. Slowly, gently, he lifted his body from on top of her; she closed her eyes, feeling a flush run across her whole body wherever his had lain. She kept her eyes tightly closed as his hands touched her feet, warm where her skin felt so cold. His hands moved to her wrists and she closed her lids even tighter as he pulled her hands over her head and tied them to the bedpost.

The bed sank under his weight as he sat beside her. "Chantel, open your mouth."

Chantel's eyes flew open at that. "Why?"

"I must gag you."

"No! Don't—please don't!" She couldn't help it; that would be the last indignity, and she couldn't face it.

"I must, I am sorry. I cannot have you alerting everyone." She turned her head away, holding back the tears. He gently tugged her head back toward him, softly running his hand up her cheek. "Let me do this, Chantel, and I will be on my way."

"You will? Promise me."

"I do."

"Good!" Her spirits rose. "Because I want you gone. I hope I never see you again."

"I fully understand. It is a wish I shall endeavor to satisfy."

Without another word, Chantel opened her mouth. The man studied her a moment, then shook his head slightly. He slipped the material between her jaws, and she gritted her teeth as he tied it behind her head. "Is that too tight?"

She shook her head and turned her face away again. He sighed, then his weight disappeared from the bed. She listened intently as he prowled the room . . . reached her armoire . . . damn, he was thumping at the lower drawer! The cabinet-maker had sworn no one would discover the secret enclosure. How many customers had he told that same story to? The masked monster must have been one of them if he'd guessed the secret.

The man returned and sat beside her; she turned and

stared into his eyes—coldly, for he flaunted the black box in his arms. "I believe you truly do not think your brother is a traitor, but he is. Or at least, he is involved with traitors and, perhaps, unaware how far over his head the waters have risen.

"Don't let your loyalty drag you down with him as well. I don't think he can be protected, but if he can, I will try to aid him." He sighed at her silent, stoic gaze. "Good night, Chantel."

He rose, pulling the blanket up and around her, tucking her in at the sides as if he were a loving father. The brass of the man! He blew out the candle beside her and vanished, leaving Chantel staring into the darkness.

"Good morning, mum," a cockney voice caroled cheerfully.

Chantel came awake, stiff and unable to move— literally. Lord, it hadn't been a nightmare. It had been as real as the ropes that bound her. Sometime during the night she had finally fallen into an exhausted sleep, dreaming of the intruder until she'd ceased to believe him real.

She heard her maid, Juliet, cross over and rustle at the fire, humming. Juliet always hummed. Chantel had decided the noise filled the otherwise endless void that should have been occupied by her brain. She waited impatiently, teeth sawing on her gag in frustration, while Juliet continued to clank and thump at the fireplace. How long before Juliet noticed that her mistress was gagged? Chantel started counting.

"There, the fire be started," Juliet sang out. *Ten, eleven, twelve* . . . Chantel attempted to force a muffled croak through her gag, hoping to attract Juliet's vacuous awareness. "What, mum?"

Chantel lifted herself off the bed, but the stranger had done his rigging well. She squirmed beneath the covers and growled through the gag again. "Did ye have a bad night of it then?" Juliet responded. "I know, you'll be wanting your tea, I'll be back in a winking."

Chantel thumped her head against the pillow in frustration. Faith, she had let that beast bully her and tie her up, merely to protect the others in the household. She should have shouted the house down when the intruder had entered, then Juliet might have been the one to arrive and he could have disposed of her with Chantel's blessings!

If Juliet didn't reappear soon, Chantel decided exasperatedly to perform the homicide herself, if she ever got out of her bonds. Visions of being bound to her bed for days teased at her fraught mind. Yet, finally, she heard Juliet's hallmark humming again; the maid entered, laden with a large tea service. "Here ye go, mum." She came to the bed and set the tray down upon the bedside table.

Chantel pinned Juliet with a penetrating glare and howled as loudly as she could through the gag. Juliet's cornflower-blue eyes widened, and she gaped at her gagged mistress. Chantel rolled her eyes to heaven, huffing through her gag. In delayed reaction, Juliet screeched and flung up her hands in horror, dropping the tea service so that the crash of crockery made a counterpoint to her yowl. "Ohhhh, miss! Wot 'as 'appended? 'Ow did ye get like that?"

Chantel wagged her head furiously, hoping to

prompt Juliet to untie the gag. Juliet fired off several more questions before it occurred to her that her mistress couldn't answer through the gag. Finally, she reached over and undid the knot.

Chantel inhaled deeply. "Now, untie my hands and feet."

"Ye be tied as well?"

"Of course, else I could have undone the gag myself," Chantel snapped. "Nor would I be lying here awaiting your tender attentions. Now do hurry!"

"Ooo, yes, mum." Juliet attacked the bonds, perplexity marring her beautiful, bovine features. "Cor, mum, I can't do it. Should I get Mr. Todd?"

"No!" Chantel barked. She thought of her dear but very elderly butler and what could happen to his heart if he saw her this way. "No," she repeated firmly, "you must go and get a knife . . . and don't you dare disturb another soul on this matter, not a word to anyone. If I hear this become gossip, I shall know it was from you, and I shall have your head for a washing that you'll never forget, do you understand?"

Chantel, though much smaller than the buxom maid, could be intimidating upon occasion. The fear in the maid's eyes caused Chantel a twinge, but until she could make sense of everything, she did not want it to become common knowledge that the mistress of Covington's Folly had been found tied to her bed. The maid shuddered as Chantel purposely slitted her eyes and made a fierce face. "Now go."

Juliet only nodded. Chantel noticed she made the sign of the cross as she scurried from the room. Long, frustrating moments passed, then she jumped as Juliet finally rushed back into the room, a wicked carving

knife held high in her hand and a wild look in her eyes.
Perhaps, Chantel thought, she had overdone her act
. . .

Juliet waved the knife madly as she drew closer. "Be
careful!" Chantel gasped. Fortunately, Juliet attacked
only the ropes. The maid sawed at them nervously,
babbling incoherently to no one in particular during
the process, sometimes swinging the blade terrifyingly
close to Chantel's wrists. Juliet jerked the knife a final
time and the ropes split.

"Very good, Juliet." Pulling her hands free, Chantel
quickly unburdened her maid of the deadly weapon.
"Now, I want you to send a messenger to Teddy's
town house in London." Clutching the knife, Chantel
freed her feet.

"Yes, mum." A quick frown marred Juliet's forehead. "But will you be taking breakfast with him
downstairs?"

Chantel's fingers froze tightly upon the knife hilt.
"Teddy is downstairs?"

"Yes, mum. He came in sometime last night."

The carving knife shook in Chantel's hands, and her
knuckles turned white. "He did, did he?" She flung the
knife down and sprang from her bed. "The knave
. . . ouch, ouch!" She hopped from one foot to the
other as circulation returned to her feet with a ven-
geance. "Forget the message," Chantel muttered as
she hobbled to the door, her green eyes flaring. "I'll
deliver it myself."

"Teddy!" Chantel wrenched open the door to the
shabby breakfast room. The room had once been a
charming breakfast retreat adorned in rose, garden
greens, and sunny yellows, housing a fine collection of

English countryside paintings as well as a complete sideboard of Limoges china, lovingly rendered in the famed pattern of the Covington Rose. Now, the walls bore decorations in a cacophony of shades and shapes gathered from all corners of the Folly. The prized collections had become someone else's collections. Chantel strode toward her brother as he consumed the large breakfast before him with gusto. *There goes the larder,* she thought fleetingly. "Teddy, I must talk to you immediately."

"Morning, dear." Teddy Emberly forced the words through a mouthful of grilled kipper, watery hazel eyes widening as he looked at her. "I say, Sis, you ain't dressed. Not the thing, is it?" Confusion crossed his broad, freckled face. "You all right?"

Chantel sighed at her stepbrother, as far removed from her as her father had been from his. The charming, reckless ne'er-do-well who'd sired Chantel had met his Maker when his curricle careened into a dray cart, not only ending his life, but failing to beat the record time from Bristol to London. The family had lost a monkey on that one.

Less mercurial, Teddy's father had cared nothing for horses or wild bets, only cards. His well-known amiability had only been surpassed by his lack of luck at the tables. His intelligence, unfortunately, had matched his luck and not his amiability. Death had claimed him in his bed, after he'd choked on a chicken bone, and Chantel's mother had followed soon after, fever-stricken, leaving a seventeen-year-old girl to raise her young stepbrother.

Mama's heritage lay in her children's looks. However, where her mother's glorious titian hair and green,

green eyes had run true in Chantel, the color had weakened to a muted, rusty red with indeterminate hazel eyes in Teddy; where Chantel's creamy skin had escaped the freckling common to redheads, Teddy's had not.

"Teddy, a man came for the black box last night," Chantel said urgently, alighting on the mismatched chair next to him.

"Black box?" Teddy echoed, nonplussed.

"The black box you entrusted to me last week!" Teddy stared at her blankly; a sick feeling descended upon her that her words weren't even registering. Lud, she had risked her life for a black box he didn't even remember. "Think! You gave me a black box last week. You told me to guard it with my life, for goodness sake!"

"I did?" A frown marred his face. Then slowly, he showed signs of enlightenment. "Oh yes, I did. Who was the man?"

"I don't know," Chantel replied, clutching a napkin and wadding it up nervously. "He was masked and did not introduce himself."

"And Mr. Todd admitted him?" Teddy yelped. "That's it Chantel, he's got to go. I told you he was touched in the attic."

"Mr. Todd didn't let him in," Chantel explained as patiently as she could. "He came through my balcony doors last night into my bedroom. He must have climbed up."

"Egad! Now that ain't proper, ain't proper at all. You can't tell me it is!" What little Teddy knew, he knew well.

"Of course, it wasn't," Chantel said, assuringly. "Nor, of course, was his holding a gun on me."

"Well! What a total rudesby!"

"Yes, he was a monster. Now, Teddy, what was in that box that was so important?"

Teddy shook his head. "It stumps me. I don't like this, not by half." Suddenly, his hazel eyes focused and Chantel caught her breath—he must have remembered!

"You don't suppose he's after the treasure, do you? Rot his soul, he'd better not be."

Chantel's hope deflated. "No, Teddy, I am sure he wasn't. He said so. Don't tell me that was what was in the box. Please, please tell me it wasn't a—a—treasure map or some such fustian!"

"Ain't fustian," Teddy said stoutly. "You know it's the truth. Mother told us so."

Chantel shook her head wearily. "The man didn't seem to care about that, anyway."

"Better not. He'll catch cold at it if he is," Teddy said slyly. "Me and Neddy have the map hidden right and tight."

"You know there never was a map!"

"Wasn't, but there is now. Me and Edwin's been working it all out and we've put it on a map. We'll have the Covington treasure before long."

"Dearest, that was only a legend!" Chantel's hand clasped Teddy's sleeve gently. "An old family story. Besides, Great-great-Grandmother Genevieve swore no man would ever find it—only a female heir, remember?"

"What would she know? She was only a woman, after all!"

"The woman who supposedly hid the treasure. Denied to the Covington men for all time, so Mother put it."

"But—"

"No male of the line has found it yet."

"Yes . . ." For a second, Teddy looked dejected, then a grin crossed his face. And when Teddy grinned, it was a rare person who could be unkind to him; it would have been very much like kicking an innocent St. Bernard puppy. "But it's still out there. Ain't no woman found the treasure yet either!"

"That's why I think it nothing but a farradiddle," Chantel said firmly, meaning the words. From childhood she had grown up with the family legend, dreaming, like every Covington girl, of uncovering the treasure and breaking the family curse. Only with age and wisdom had she realized things would not be so ordered, and she doubted, indeed, that the Covingtons would ever be rid of their curse.

And a curse it was, a fatal flaw at the heart of every Covington. Gaming fever ran in the blood; the daring Covington men would bet on a fly crawling upon the wall, while the Covington women burned with fire, wit, and an unerring knack for marrying gamblers. As a result, the family fortunes had known a great influx of wealth . . . and a great outflow.

Make no mistake, the Covingtons had ties to some of England's finest and wealthiest families; the Covington men were as attractive as the women, and prone to marry heiresses. They had to, if only to stay out of debtor's prison.

Indeed, Chantel was sure it would have been a national concern if anyone had ever discovered and documented exactly how many of England's finest family fortunes had staked the Covington's excesses. Lady Genevieve Sinclair's family had been such a one. A green-eyed vixen with flaming red hair, she'd been rumored to be a witch, for she seemed to have a compelling power rarely found in women.

The rumors hadn't frightened Sir Alex Covington, a premier gambler who boasted it made the odds more intriguing. The dashing blade married her after a whirlwind courtship, then returned to the tables with her great fortune at his disposal.

Lady Genevieve, however, did not possess the Covington women's infamous tolerance for such conduct. She took great exception to her husband's squandering her fortune, especially after the birth of her first daughter. Therefore, one night, while Sir Alex was out, her ladyship had taken action.

She had stripped the household bare of all its finest treasures; the silver from the pantry, the famous heirloom jewelry, even the great artwork from the gallery. To do so in a single night must have been no mean feat, for Sir Alex's time had been one of those rare periods when the Covingtons were more than flush. Nevertheless, Lady Genevieve had taken and hidden it all; where and how had never been discovered, but witchcraft was suspected.

Her drunken husband had come home to a barren establishment. Lady Genevieve swore to him that night, or so the family tale would have it, that no Covington male would ever recover the treasure. She decreed that it would only be found by a woman of the Covington line, and then, only when the time was right and the taint of gambling had been wiped from the family's soul.

When he learned what else his wife had done, Sir Alex swore even more vehemently than she, calling her not only a witch, but a bitch. Lady Genevieve had created an iron-clad entail upon the family's country seat, Covington's Folly (which he had just renovated with her money), so that it could pass only to the women of the family, along with all the possessions within. Lady Genevieve also insinuated she'd hidden the family treasure within the mansion's depths.

Thanks to Lady Genevieve's machinations, Chantel was now owner of Covington's Folly, as her mother and grandmother had been before her. Covington fortunes rose and fell, properties and chattel changed hands across the tables, Covington men and women married or were taken in marriage, but the family seat remained, the one constant in all their lives.

No Covington man, even if he'd bet his last shirt— as many had—would have let the taxes fail upon Covington's Folly, or let it be taken from the women, for they all steadfastly believed that within it lay the treasure. Not a Covington woman inherited the Folly without cherishing it and taking care of its upkeep for to them it *was* the treasure, the only security for a Covington woman and her children.

Even Chantel, disbelieving in the treasure, blessed Lady Genevieve and her legend; gazing at the worn woodwork and the pale, slick marble of the breakfast room fireplace, a warmth filled her. Like her mother before her, she'd scrimped and saved to maintain Covington's Folly, for it remained her pride. The treasure? A myth. The curse? Well, she doubted she could lift it, but she'd certainly never succumb to it. If she never married, she couldn't align herself with a gambler. But Covington's Folly? She loved the place.

She shook herself. Nothing would save the Folly, not even Lady Genevieve's treasure, if the family were branded traitors. "Teddy, listen to me." Her hand clutched tightly around his wrist. "You must think. What was in that box that was so important? He said you were a traitor."

"What!" Teddy wheezed, dropping his fork into his eggs. "'Tain't true—I'd never be traitor! You know I wouldn't. Don't have the brains, for one thing." One of Teddy's saving graces was that he knew his own faults.

"I know, dear—so what was in the box?"

Teddy ruminated for a moment, then his eyes bulged. "Now I remember. This chap gave me the box, asked me to keep it safe, and said he'd send someone for it." He brightened. "Maybe the masked fellow was the someone."

"I doubt it. Who was the man who gave you the box?"

"Some foreign chap. Can't exactly remember his name. A sharp at the cards, though."

With Teddy, everyone was a sharp at the cards, even a six-year-old. "You took a box from a man and you don't even remember his name?"

Teddy had the grace to look shamefaced. "Truth is, we'd breached the fourth bottle of port that night. Can't recollect it all, but he held a few of my vouchers. He'd been called away from the table . . . came back looking as queer as Dick's hatband. Pulled me aside and said I wouldn't owe him anything if I'd only take this box he was holding and keep it safe. Told me to bring it here, and he'd send a man for it in a few weeks."

She stared at him as if he had two heads. "Teddy, are you bamming me?"

"No, wouldn't do that."

"Do you mean he told you to bring the box here— to Covington's Folly?"

Teddy nodded. "Didn't see any harm in it. I mean, he tore up my vouchers! Knew you'd like that."

"Just so you would keep this box?"

"Thought him balmy, but wasn't going to look a gift horse in the mouth. Besides, he was foreign, you know. They don't act the same as us."

"I . . . see."

"Truth is, forgot about the whole thing, till now."

"But, of course," Chantel said dryly. "You palmed the box off on me. Did you see what was in it?"

"Of course not, 'twas locked when he gave it to me. Besides, he told me not to try and open it."

"Yes, naturally." Teddy was perfect that way; he religiously did whatever he was told. She flushed. Hadn't she done exactly what Teddy had told her to do? What did that make her? She refused to follow that train of thought. "It simply makes no sense. Why would the man tell you to bring it to Covington's Folly? How would he even know of it?"

Teddy puffed up. "I'm a man about town, you know. Of course he knew my family seat."

Chantel bit her tongue and stifled her obvious retort. "I think we need to talk to Chad about this. Perhaps he can make some sense out of it."

"That's the ticket. He's clever, no flies on *him.*" He frowned. "That mean Aunt Beatrice will know?"

"This is serious business, Teddy. Aunt has the right to know that the family is threatened." Teddy's face fell. He loved their cousin Chad, but lived in deathly fear of Aunt Beatrice. But then, men far braver and wiser then he went pale in dread of Aunt Beatrice. Their Uncle Uriah had been one of them until he had slipped the leash twelve years ago and passed on to his reward. "Are you positive you can't remember the man's name?"

"I was rather cast away that night, Sis. It was French, though . . . I think."

"I want you to go back to town this day and inquire at the club who he was."

Teddy flushed red behind his freckles. "Wasn't at the club. We wanted to try this new hell—er, place."

"Then go to that place and see what you can find out." Chantel rose from the table, her mind spinning. She'd managed to pull Teddy out of his many scrapes all his life . . . but treason? Her heart sank; this imbroglio frightened her for some reason she could not define. She hoped it was not a premonition. The stranger had said Teddy was beyond help. She mentally shook herself, and straightened her shoulders. This was no time to be weak-willed or missish. Her small chin jutted out. She would be damned if she'd let that masked monster hurt Teddy or ruin her family. He just didn't know who he was dealing with. Well . . . he'd soon find out.

Chapter Two

"Chantel," Chad Tabor said, walking into the parlor where Chantel anxiously awaited him, "What is this all about? Your note said it was urgent."

Chantel looked up to view her cousin as he entered. A man of medium height, light brown hair, and bright brown eyes, his dress was impeccable and his carriage one of quiet confidence.

She rose and offered her hands to him. He clasped them and gave them a squeeze. His brows rose as he studied her. "Tell me, Coz, you look fair upset."

"I fear Teddy has thrown us in the briars again."

His face relaxed and he laughed. "Is that all? That is nothing new."

"No," Chantel said, shaking her head vehemently. "This time it is worse than ever before."

"It must be, to frighten you."

"The boy's a knock-in-the-cradle," Aunt Beatrice pronounced baldly in a low, gruff voice as she entered behind Chad. She promptly went to the best chair in the room and seated herself.

Chantel refrained from comment. It never ceased to

amaze her that Chad Tabor had sprung from the womb of her aunt. Beatrice Tabor was a grim, no-nonsense woman who had very few sensibilities and did not see why others should have any either. She was a short woman, almost squat, who dressed in black, gray and brown. Iron-gray streaked the red hair that framed her square, boldly cut face.

"Yes, Mother," Chad said gently, his eyes remaining upon Chantel. "But he has a good heart. Now, please, Chantel, tell me what has happened. I'm on tenterhooks."

Chantel drew in a deep breath. "I'm afraid Teddy has become embroiled with traitors."

"What?" Chad's voice was incredulous, his eyes wide with consternation. Then he laughed loudly and fully. "Chantel, you minx. You shouldn't roast us in such fashion."

"I'm not," Chantel said desperately, for Chad was still studying her with a humorous eye. "He is!"

"Very well, if you say so," Chad said. "But let us sit down and you can explain this fantastical notion you have that Teddy could . . . no, never. No self-respecting traitor would deal with him."

They moved to the sofa and sat. "I—" Chantel shook her head hopelessly. "I know it sounds ridiculous—but some foreign man gave Teddy a black strongbox and told him to keep it for him. Teddy did, of course."

Chad's smile disappeared and he stared at her. "He took a box? What possessed him to do so?"

"The man held vouchers of his. He said he'd tear them up if Teddy would only keep the box for him until someone arrived to pick it up."

"Oh Gads! The dunderhead!" Chad exclaimed.

"When isn't he? You know Teddy—he thought he was so clever in getting his vouchers torn up, he didn't stop to think why this man would give him a strongbox."

"Did Teddy see what was in the box?" Chad asked.

"No, it was locked—besides, he didn't keep it long, but gave it over to me."

"Oh, God! Even worse!"

"Yes, and I kept it, thinking it was some foolish stuff about the treasure Teddy might be hiding."

"The boy needs to be locked up," Aunt Beatrice said firmly.

"So he is still after the treasure?" Chad asked quickly, before Chantel could respond sharply to Beatrice. "I thought he would have outgrown that."

"Never," Chantel's eyes brightened for a moment. "Though he has left off knocking about the cellars at night."

"That is a comfort," Chad laughed.

"He still swears it was not him at all. He has Juliet scared out of the few wits she has, for he swears it must be the ghost of Lady Genevieve returned to tell us where the treasure lies."

"Poppycock," barked Aunt Beatrice.

"Indeed," Chantel agreed, "but now he say's he's devised a map to find the treasure."

"Impossible!" Beatrice shook her head pugnaciously. "What is he thinking? The legend says only a woman of the line can find the treasure."

"Then that leaves only you and me, does it not?" Chantel teased. "Have you been visited by Great-great-Grandmother Genevieve lately, Aunt?"

Beatrice's face took on a mottled hue that did not sit well with her severe black bombazine. Her jet earbobs shook as did the massive hematite brooch at her boned velvet collar, as she vehemently exclaimed, "No, I haven't, and it's all tommyrot!"

"Indeed," Chad said soothingly before the ladies could square off. "However, we are not here to consider Lady Genevieve's shade, but something of more importance."

Beatrice's fulminating eyes turned on him; amazingly, the anger drained away. "You are right. As usual." One thing that could not be doubted about Aunt Beatrice was her total, complete love for her son. Chantel sometimes wondered if Beatrice had ever loved anyone or anything else.

"Chantel, please continue," Chad said, frowning. "If neither of you looked into the box, why do you think its content was traitorous?"

"Because the masked stranger told me so."

"Masked stranger? What are you talking about?"

"A masked man came to retrieve the box last night."

"How?"

"He came into my bedroom through the balcony doors."

"He broke in?" Chad asked, shocked.

"No, I—" Chantel flushed. "I had opened the balcony doors."

"Tottyheaded thing to do," Aunt Beatrice remarked.

"I had only opened them long enough to air out the room. The fireplace flue had backed up."

"You need to repair that," Aunt Beatrice grumbled.

"You could burn the whole Folly down if you don't. You don't take care of this place as you should."

Chantel held her temper by counting to five. "When I find spare money, I shall have it repaired." She felt certain she heard a disdainful sniffle from Aunt Beatrice as those scornful brown eyes gazed at the threadbare patch in the Aubusson rug, arranged beneath a curio in an effort to minimize its condition.

Chantel then realized that the Folly was the one other thing Beatrice Tabor loved. She'd grown up in the Folly with Chantel's mother, but Mama, as the elder sister, had inherited it, then passed it on to Chantel, a reality Aunt Beatrice never seemed to take seriously.

"Chantel, what about this man?" Chad said urgently. "What did he do?"

"He demanded the box. I denied him, so he—he tied me up, hunted for the box, and found it."

"He tied you up! Damn him, how dare he!" Chad exclaimed, surprising Chantel with his vehemence. Chad was usually the even-tempered peacemaker within the wildly unconventional Covington family. His eyes pierced hers. "He did not hurt you? He did not touch you?"

"No," Chantel assured him quickly, flushing. "No, he didn't. But what are we to do? He told me the information in the box was traitorous, and that Teddy was involved. He said he would protect him if he could, but doubted it would be possible."

"The unmitigated gall of the man! As if Teddy could be a traitor or you would need a stranger's protection." Chad's shoulders stiffened and his brown eyes were the sternest she had ever seen them. "You must not stay here. You must come with us to our house."

"What? Why?" Chantel exclaimed.

"I want you safe until we can clear up this confusion. I don't want you here alone if that man comes back."

"He won't, I am sure. He's got his infernal box, after all."

"Please, Chantel, come and visit us. Just until we can discover what kind of scrape Teddy has tumbled into. I promise I'll try to find the foreigner who gave Teddy the box, but until we discover more, you'll be much safer at our house."

Chantel sighed. "Very well, but don't think I will stay long, even if this matter is still unsettled."

"I will settle it," Chad said confidently, his mood lightening again. "You have my word on it."

"Let us be going then." Aunt Beatrice rose briskly. "Chantel, you must pack. I shall inform the staff of the change in plans."

"I can take care of that," Chantel objected.

"Nonsense! No reason to waste extra time," Beatrice said briskly as she made toward the door. She stopped for a moment and gazed at a large portrait of the infamous Lady Genevieve.

At a quick glance one would have mistaken the lady in the portrait for Chantel, since her hair was flame red and her eyes green. But the painted eyes were far more imperious, and she wore a golden ball gown—her panniers wide, the fashion of another time. The artist had captured the Lady as if she were walking straight toward one, a fan unfurled and held flirtatiously before her. About her neck she wore the famous Covington jewels, a collar of perfect diamonds and emeralds. Its matching accessories were on her ears and fingers, flashing fire, even from the canvas.

"Humph," Aunt Beatrice said. "This painting needs a good cleaning."

Chantel bit the inside of her mouth in aggravation. "I intend to see to it when I can."

"Good," Aunt Beatrice grunted, and sailed from the room.

"You know, Mother loves you, despite her manners," Chad said.

"I am sure," Chantel said, her tone disbelieving.

He laughed. "Ah, my shrew. She truly does. As I do also," he said more softly.

Chantel flushed. "Chad, please . . ."

"I know, no embarrassing proposals." He grinned wryly. "But if you married me, you could clean that portrait and repair that backed-up fireplace to boot. Wouldn't you like that? You could put Mother's nose out of joint, at that."

Chantel laughed and reached to put a hand upon his. "Do not tempt me. I am far too fond of you to saddle you with Teddy and Covington's Folly."

"I wouldn't mind. Teddy I can handle, and I have enough money for Covington's Folly."

"No, dear." Chantel rose swiftly to her feet. "I thank you, though, from the bottom of my heart."

"At least allow me to lend you money enough to repair that fireplace. This house is falling down about your ears." He rose. "It's all in the family, after all."

She looked at him, shaking her head in amazement. "It never ceases to surprise me that one branch of the Covington line has escaped the curse and isn't in dun territory." Chad's eyes darkened and he stepped toward her. Before he could speak, she raised a silencing hand. "No, I will not take any of your money, Chad. Guard it and guard it well! I like having respectable relations."

"Very well," he sighed. "But if you ever change your mind . . ."

"You will be the first to know," Chantel said, laughing. She heard Aunt Beatrice's voice raised in command. "Now, I had best pack."

"Indeed. And I will go and help Mother." He started to leave, then turned, his eyes searching hers. "You are all right, aren't you?"

"Of course I am." Chantel forced a smile. She didn't wish to leave the Folly, yet the thought of facing the coming night alone in her room, even with the balcony doors shut and barred, frightened her. Chad was right, she would be safer at his house. The masked stranger wouldn't pursue her there. After all, he had what he wanted. All she needed to do was forget the ugly memory and move onward. Pretend it had never happened. Yes, she'd erase the man from her memory. She was safe now, and she'd never have to see that masked man again!

Squire Peterson's ball was crowded. A polished socialite would have claimed it a "squeeze." Indeed, Elisa Peterson, the jolly hostess, was heard to employ the term repeatedly in her boisterous voice.

Squire Peterson only called it "damned hot and damned noisy." He asked Richard St. James, the Earl of Hartford, if he would care to slip away and blow a cloud. Richard thought to decline, until he noticed Elisa Peterson weighing anchor and heading toward them with a giggling, freckle-faced debutante in tow. St. James, newly arrived to the area and considered very eligible, could not doubt her purpose. He accepted Squire Peterson's offer with alacrity.

"Come then, we must be quick about it," the squire chuckled. "Elisa's ogling you and dragging that Singleton chit along with her." He shook his head. "Damn fine woman . . . my wife that is, not the Singleton chit—she's a featherbrain—but my wife fancies herself a matchmaker, which she ain't."

Richard laughed. From the beginning of their acquaintance, Squire Peterson had treated him with an honesty and openness rare in such a new friendship. Richard's laughter died, however, as a petite, red-haired lady danced by, dressed in a fetching but outdated sapphire faille gown. Her vibrant locks were coiffured into an elegance that sat regally upon her small head, yet errant tendrils escaped to tease her slender neck and Richard's imagination.

"Damn," he murmured. What was she doing here? She was supposed to be safely away, visiting relatives. "Excuse me, Squire, do you know anything about the lady dancing over there?" He found it impossible to take his eyes from the woman. What did her being here mean?

"Heh?" The squire looked about and then chuckled. "Got an eye on you, my boy. That's Chantel Emberly of Covington's Folly. A beauty, in my opinion. That red hair is something, ain't it?"

"Does she attend these functions often?"

"No, more's the pity. She only came because Elisa badgered her. She was staying with her aunt—now there's a fright. Knew she would be having a dull time of it, so we invited her. Didn't let her say no. Gal doesn't get out enough."

"She doesn't?"

"Not by half. Ain't married either, and she four-and-twenty." The squire shook his head sadly. "Problem is, Chantel's too serious for her own good. Not like her mother—now there was a charmer! Light-hearted, always ready for a lark. She and Elisa were great friends—strange, that.

"But can't blame Chantel, after all. She's got that old barracks of Covington's Folly crumbling about her, and her brother making an ass of himself in London, trying to become the dandy without the brass to support it. Ain't no wonder she's a little sharp-edged."

"She is?" Richard stifled a laugh. The squire's watered-down description didn't seem to match his memory of the flame-haired woman he had accosted one night.

Peterson's smile became mischievous. "Truth is, the young bucks call her a shrew." His laughter rumbled within his barrel chest. "She's a feisty bit, no doubt about it; sad fact is, she ain't got much use for men. She treats them all the way she does her brother, and since he's an addle-pate that don't help. Now me, I like a woman with backbone. She ain't a milk-and-water miss . . . nimblewitted, too." The Squire studied Richard as if he were a joint of meat, ready for the carving. "Care to meet her?"

"Yes," Richard said. He ignored the large, satisfied grin that slowly crossed the squire's face. The squire promptly led him in her direction. Richard experienced a frisson of apprehension as Chantel Emberly looked up at him. Her green eyes were bright and sparkling, unshadowed by the fear he had seen in them at their first meeting; her piquant face was open and welcoming, not stiffened in rage. Would she recognize him? He sincerely hoped not. He wasn't ready for the engaging creature before him to vanish.

"Chanty!" The squire's voice rumbled with pleasure. "Allow me to introduce Richard St. James, Earl of Hartford. He's bought the Remington house, so he's somewhat a neighbor of yours." He laughed. "Well, somewhat."

"Indeed?" A smile twitched at her lips. "It is a pleasure to meet you . . . neighbor."

Richard bowed and smiled as winningly as he could. "I saw you across the floor and knew I must meet you."

Her fine brow arched. "Did you, my lord? Then you have met me." She was obviously amused by his compliment, but not overly impressed; evidently his title did not affect her, nor his flattery.

"May I have this dance?" he asked, bowing.

She cocked her head slightly, confusion entering her eyes. "I am certain I've never met you before, my lord, but you remind me of someone." She frowned. "But who?"

Richard kept a smile plastered to his face. "I do not know, but I hope it's someone you wish to dance with."

She laughed, but he could tell she was unsatisfied. Fortunately, the elderly lady she'd been chatting with spoke up. "Oh, for goodness sake, Chantel, do go and dance with this charming young man and stop dithering. He'll begin to think you a skitterwit."

The squire coughed. "Indeed, the musicians are

about to strike up and I believe it's a waltz. Must leave you now." The squire departed, hurrying in the direction of the orchestra. Chantel's elderly companion melted away just as expertly.

Richard laughed. "It seems they have abandoned you to my mercy."

"I fear, my lord, it is the other way around." Chantel observed the squire talking to the conductor and smiled.

"I beg your pardon?" Richard's brow rose.

Her eyes returned to his, filled with laughter. "I fear the squire has bagged you for me. He's now asking the musicians to play a waltz, which Elisa didn't intend to play until much later, after the more sober contingent had left."

"And the squire said Elisa was the impossible matchmaker," Richard said with amusement.

Chantel smiled. "They both are, but he far outstrips her in ruthlessness."

Richard bowed. "You see me, his offering, set before you. Do say you shall dance with me." She smiled again, but he could tell she still held reservations. It was an odd experience for him, as most females were not only prompt to accept but ecstatic at the chance to dance with him. "The squire will be quite disappointed in us, otherwise."

She laughed and rose. "Very well, I would not wish to hurt him."

"Ah, me," Richard said quietly as he took her slim hand within his and led her to the dance floor. "I know I am but the bagged quarry, but do you not have a shred of sympathy for me as well?"

"Should I, my lord?" Her eyes were disconcertingly

direct, and her manner lacked any resemblance to flirtation. Her words were more of a challenge than anything else.

Richard could see very well why Chantel frightened the local boys. He, however, was not a local boy, and hers was a challenge he would not deny. "Yes, you should," he returned, as he gazed into twin sparkling emerald pools reflecting the myriad of candles in the chandeliers above. He swung her firmly into the dance. "I would offer you my credentials, but I would not wish to appear to be puffing off my own consequence to you."

"I see. Then modesty is one of your qualities?"

"Indeed. But let us not talk of me. Let us talk of you instead."

"Me?" she asked pleasantly. She smiled. "Please, I do not wish to bore you."

"Now who is being modest?" he teased, slightly amazed that she did not care to list her virtues or impress him as many debutantes were wont to do when claiming his attention in a dance.

"I am not being modest. I lead an immensely dull life and possess no rare talents or qualities."

"Do you not?" Richard asked. A thread of amusement escaped him. "I do not believe others would agree with you."

Chantel Emberly's brow rose and she grimaced. "Now who's been gossiping about me? If it was the squire, I know he's an honest man; I'm sure he did not paint me as a paragon!"

Richard grinned. "He says you are a woman with backbone."

"My goodness!" She feigned surprise. "And you still wanted to dance with me?"

"Women with backbone do not frighten me." He caught her gaze and unconsciously held her closer. "I enjoy a good fight."

She stiffened. "Whereas I do not."

"Do you not, Chanty?" Richard teased. He liked the way the name rolled off his tongue.

"Don't call me that!" Her eyes darkened to a deep verdant hue and a becoming flush painted her cheeks.

Richard knew he was mad, but something drove him onward. Miss Chantel Emberly had been holding him at a distance, and he did not like being treated as a stranger. He did not feel like one with her, after all. "Why not?"

"Only the squire calls me by that name," she said coolly. "You, sir, do not know me and certainly have no right."

"And if I were to get to know you?"

Her small head rose imperiously, though it but came to his shoulder. "You still could not call me that."

Richard laughed. "Then I will call you Chantel."

She missed a step, then stared up at him with a stunned expression. Damnation! Without a doubt, he realized that Chantel Emberly had now recognized him. He could feel it in her body, read it in her touch. "Tell me," he said swiftly. "Do you stay for the house party?"

"No, I do not. Why?"

Richard shrugged. "I was hoping that you might; it looks to be fun. Could I not persuade you to?"

"No."

"You intend to return home, then? Perhaps I could escort you?"

"No," she said with unflattering promptness. "No, thank you. Squire Peterson will do so."

"I see," Richard said stiffly. They both fell silent. He could tell she was waiting impatiently for the dance to end. When it did, she swiftly left his arms, with no more than a perfunctory thank-you.

He watched her go to the squire and say something. He didn't need to hear what it was; he knew, without doubt, what Chantel was doing. She was bolting for Covington's Folly, the last place he wanted her to go. Blast and damn the woman!

Richard strode from the dance floor and went directly to the room reserved for cards. He entered and walked up to one of the players at a card table. "Edward, I would that you could spare me a moment."

The man he addressed looked up. His eyes were an angelic blue, his face mobile, and his hair glinted blond in the candlelight. He cast a glance at his cards and then grinned. "Be glad to give you a minute—four or five, in fact. Haven't had a decent hand all night."

Edward made his excuses and walked into the hall with Richard. "What is it? We still have four hours, don't we?"

"Chantel Emberly is here tonight."

Edward's blue eyes widened. "But she's supposed to be at her aunt's."

"She isn't," Richard said tersely, "and she's going home to Covington's Folly tonight."

Edward whistled. "That means she's in on it."

"No, not necessarily. But she needs to be stopped, and we don't have much time."

Edward rolled his eyes. "Good luck if you think you'll stop Chantel!"

Richard studied him. "You sound as if you know her well."

"Did when we were young. Used to be great friends, in fact." Edward appeared to flush.

"What happened?"

"I tried to kiss her and she pushed me into a pond."

"And that was it?" Richard asked, stunned.

"I was young! She hurt my pride."

Richard stared at him for a moment and then said, " 'Tis no matter. We're wasting time. She has to be taken care of before tonight's raid. If she's innocent, I don't want her walking into the middle of it; if she's not, I don't want her tipping them off."

"Why would she do that?"

"Because I am certain she recognized me."

Edward groaned. "Famous. We'll not get near her."

"Yes, we will," Richard said grimly.

"And what are we going to do then?" Edward asked, incredulous. "Kidnap her?"

"Yes. And then you are going to take her to my house and lock her up for safekeeping."

"You must be bamming me!" Edward exclaimed.

"I'm not," Richard said evenly. "Now listen carefully. We must get her before she leaves here . . ."

Chantel stood in the quiet library, waiting for the Squire's men to bring the carriage that would take her home. She stretched shaking hands out to the small fire in the grate; she was cold, cold with shock and fear.

Richard St. James, the Earl of Hartford, was the

man who had been in her bedroom. When he had approached her, she'd thought her confusion and nervousness odd; men rarely affected her, rarely unsettled her. And when he took her in his arms, a shiver had run through her—how could she not have known? But she hadn't. Not until he'd said her name. She could never have forgotten that voice speaking her name. She trembled recalling the sound.

Even she knew of Richard St. James; his family was a proud and powerful one, and he held an important seat in the House of Lords. And *he* was the man after poor, incompetent Teddy. What was she going to do?

The door opened; she turned swiftly, expecting the squire's servant. She stifled a gasp, for Richard St. James stood in the doorway, a crystal cup of punch in each hand. He crossed to her, obviously grimacing at a stuffed boar atop a massive glass and mahogany case filled end to end with an ancient Chinese sword. Chantel herself felt no appreciation for the squire's decor, yet perhaps the sword might come in handy if one could get past the boar.

"The squire said you were not feeling well, and that he's having his carriage brought around. He also sent me with refreshment. Perhaps it will soothe you."

"No, thank you." She turned back to the fire.

"I truly believe it could help you." Suddenly, St. James' voice came from directly behind her. She spun, and found him standing not a foot away. Even the weak firelight could not soften the angles and planes of his chiseled face. He raised a cup. "You don't want to disappoint the squire now, do you?"

She studied him. He blocked her path solidly, and seemed intent on getting his way. "Very well," she said stiffly, knowing she must not act oddly or give herself away. She forced a smile and took the punch cup.

He raised his. "To your health."

"And to yours," She drank swiftly, then handed the cup back to him. He took it, the expression on his face unreadable. "There, my lord, now if you will excuse me?"

"I thought I would keep you company."

"I do not need company," she returned curtly, trying to brush past him.

"Chantel, stop!" She halted a moment. "Are you running away?"

His voice was low, challenging. She turned. "No, of course not. It is simply improper to be alone with you."

"Is that the only reason?" St. James was watching her intently. She felt like a rabbit with a hawk hovering overhead.

"It's a good enough one." She waved a shaky hand in an attempt at nonchalance.

"But not the real one?" he parried. "Could it be that you don't trust me?"

"Trust you?" She was beginning to feel odd. "No, I do not."

"Why not?"

"You're a man, that is—sufficient." Her knees were shaking. Lud, it felt like they were turning to water. She started to sway, and then she knew. Spinning, she tried to make it to the door, but the hawk caught her first, turning her to face him.

"No, not again—" she said hoarsely, as he reached into his pocket and pulled out a handkerchief. Before she could turn her head, he placed it over her nose, smothering her with a sickly-sweet scent. "Why—"

His lips moved, but she heard nothing. She clutched him and knew no more.

Richard and Edward sat in the drawing room, enjoying their first cup of tea of the day. Morosely, Edward reached for the brandy bottle and poured a healthy amount of its contents into his cup. Richard raised an eyebrow.

"Oh, it don't taste that bad," Edward said quickly. "Besides, I have to have something to chase the blue devils away. Gads! I thought we'd catch our man for sure last night. The department won't be pinning any medals on us for nabbing a crate of smuggled French brandy and twenty bolts of silk."

"No, to be sure they won't."

"Fact is, they're getting downright testy over this," Edward grumbled.

"Our friend's leaking too many secrets." Richard shrugged. "At least we can tell them we're on his trail."

"Huh! We are on the trail of the infamous Teddy Emberly, a bumbler if you ever saw one. Certainly not up to our traitor's weight."

"Indeed." Richard absently poured brandy into the rest of his own tea and sipped it obliviously. "We know the black box was involved with our man. The information in it guarantees that, and even if we didn't catch him, at least we saved our own agent. What I cannot deduce is his connection with Teddy Emberly and Covington's Folly."

"It seems to me he must be framing Teddy." Edward shook his head. "But that makes no sense. Teddy Emberly as a great spy? No one in his right mind would swallow that clanker. Now if it were Chantel behind it, I could believe it."

"Why do you say that?"

"Because she's got the brains in the family, that's why. It could also explain why the drop-off was aborted last night. She wasn't there. We had her."

"Is she still secure?" Richard asked.

"Locked up right and tight in the gold bedroom. Out to the world, as well."

"How much laudanum did you give her?"

Edward grinned. "Enough for an elephant."

"Why? She's only a slip of a thing. Are you sure you aren't just getting revenge for her pushing you into the pond all those years ago?"

Edward raised a brow in disdain. "Of course not. But it wasn't you that had to get her back here and tuck her into bed. I know Chantel, and I didn't want her waking up on me." St. James only chuckled. "Well, it could have been the very devil—she can be a hellcat when she wants to be!"

"No need to tell me," Richard said dryly, then frowned. "Yet it can't be her. She's known to stay here, doesn't visit London that much, or anywhere else for that matter. Our man runs his operation from London. Besides, she didn't even know what I was talking about when I took the box from her, of that I am certain."

"Stumps me."

"Somewhere, however, Covington's Folly and Teddy Emberly are involved. Even if it is only as dupe and decoy for our man." St. James nodded to himself. "It doesn't matter, we still have that lead on him."

Edward sighed. "Blighter's probably just playing with us."

"I know. But the tables will be turned one day, and then it will be we who play with him, make no doubt of it."

A knock at the door interrupted the conversation. The earl called for entrance and his butler, Reed, appeared. "My lord, Mrs. Jasper, the vicar's wife, and the two Randall sisters are here to see you. They say they wish to welcome you to the community."

"I see," Richard grimaced. "Permit them to enter." The butler bowed and exited.

"Welcome you to the community," Edward grinned, "and hope you'll welcome them to your deep pockets for their charities."

"All too likely. Yet there is no better way to earn the locals' loyalty or hear their gossip. And that is why we are here."

A short, plump matron entered, bookended by two tall, gaunt women, their thin faces very much alike. The matron's face was truly kind and welcoming, but the two sisters could have frozen the Thames in August.

"Yikes!" Edward exclaimed, sotto *voce.* "What we don't do for God and country."

"Welcome, ladies." The earl rose.

"My lord," the plump woman nodded. Her gaze fell upon the silver-laden tea cart, which bore an assortment of almond cakes and cardamom biscuits. "Ah, you are having tea."

Richard's gray eyes glinted mischievously even as

Edward unobtrusively lowered the brandy bottle from the cart and hid it. "Yes, we are having tea, won't you please join us?"

Chantel slowly, very slowly, surfaced from the void that engulfed her. Her mind felt as though it were padded with lamb's wool, as did her mouth, but she forced her gritty eyes open. She wasn't in her own home, obviously; this room, with its appointments in soft golds and champagnes, was far too elegant. She glanced toward a dainty French escritoire draped in a spidery silk hairpin lace, upon which sat one of the loveliest cloisonné vases she had ever seen. A bouquet of golden day lilies and pearl-hued Peace roses graced the bedside stand. No, it definitely was not her room, but then whose room was it?

Suddenly, steel-gray eyes arose in her memory and she knew where she was. She lay in the masked man's power, in Richard St. James' power. She sat up, flinching when her head objected. She sighed. At least she wasn't locked in a dungeon or some such uncomfortable place. She held no charity with rats or mold, though she would have to admit that she had spotted both at Covington's Folly.

She shook her head, impatient to clear it, then pulled back the bedcover and gasped. She sported nothing but her shift, so thin from wear that it was close to gauze. She looked about frantically. Her dress was nowhere in sight, nor were her shoes. The beast!

Rising as quietly as a cat, Chantel padded to the door. She tried it without much hope, and sure enough it was locked. Chantel swore softly; she was locked in a room, heaven (or Richard St. James) only knew where, with hardly a stitch on, and in the hands of a man she knew had drugged her. It was not a heart-warming prospect. After a moment of thought, she knelt and peeked through the keyhole. Hah! Incompetents! They had left the key in the door. After raising Teddy through childhood, Chantel deemed she could escape from any room or fortress, and this made it child's play for her. Even Teddy's capers had been more imaginative.

She turned and surveyed the room, spied a stiffened doily, and pulled it from the bureau. Returning to the door, she slid it gently out along the floor, until she'd positioned it to her satisfaction. Smiling, she pulled a pin from her hair and jabbed it into the keyhole. A felicitous clink sounded; the prized key lay neatly upon the doily. A perfect job. Chantel pulled the key back in and snatched it up; clutching it close, she scanned the room. It was disgustingly void of any possible weapons. Shrugging, she stripped the sheet off the bed and wrapped it around herself like a toga.

Ahhh . . . she grabbed up the water pitcher beside the bed and gave it a practice swing; an unwieldy weapon, but better than nothing. Approaching the door with renewed confidence, she unlocked it and quietly slipped out into the hall. No one in sight; she scampered down the hallway until she came upon a staircase. Peering over its open banister, she saw the foyer at the foot of the stairs. Freedom! Thank heaven the house had a simple floor plan, and wasn't a maze like the Folly.

She trod softly down the stairs, her draperies trailing behind, her eyes intent upon the foyer and the double doors leading outside. Suddenly, a door from across the foyer opened. She froze, still six steps away from the foyer's floor. Richard St. James (that fiend) and four other people came out into the foyer. One was Edward Keller, whom she'd known in childhood. Then she gulped, for the others were Mrs. Jasper and the Randall sisters, the greatest tabbies in the shire.

"Flee," her mind screamed. She daren't be caught by the likes of the Randall sisters. She pivoted upon her bare toes to run, snagged herself on her sheet, became hopelessly entangled, and toppled over. Screeching inelegantly, she thumped and bumped to the bottom of the stairs. She landed with a somersault on the polished marble floor, smack on her bruised derriere, legs sprawled and her hand clutching nothing but the broken handle of the pitcher. Shards of it lay scattered on the stairs behind her; so did her sheet.

When her eyes cleared from the daze, the first figure in view was the composed, elegantly clad, figure of Richard St. James. "Fiend!" she spat. "Damn you!"

"Oh my heavens." Mrs. Jasper's hand flew up to patter upon her plump bosom.

"Here now, madam," Edward Keller said, rushing to support the wheezing Mrs. Jasper. "Don't faint." He sounded amazingly jolly.

Chantel turned her eyes to skewer him. She failed to command his attention, however, for his eyes were trained upon her chest in bemusement. That was when Chantel realized her chest felt decidedly chilly. She looked down and gasped; she wasn't totally exposed, but close. Far too close to be displaying herself to two gentleman of no relation, the vicar's wife, and two dour spinsters. Desperately she attempted to tug the shift back into place—and in response, the worn material surrendered up its last threads. It rent, and Chantel found herself much chillier.

"Good gracious!" Lavinia Randall's face tightened into a shape resembling a prune.

"Saints preserve us," exclaimed Divinia Randall, her lips pursing as if she'd just bitten into a lemon.

"Pardon." St. James calmly walked over and swept up Chantel's sheet from the stairs. All watched him, mouths agape, as he silently draped it about her, while her hands were overly employed in covering herself. "Here you are . . . Miss Bountiful," he added in a low voice as he knelt beside her.

His hands efficiently arranged the sheet around her. Enraged, Chantel slapped at them. The other three women gasped in concert, for the sound of the blow rang through the foyer. "Leave me be, you rogue, you—"

"Tut, tut, darling." St. James all but lifted her to a standing position. "You might give these ladies the wrong impression. Ladies, you must forgive my fiancée." The earl smiled kindly and slammed Chantel up against his side. The air flew from her lungs, but whether from his clinch upon her or from the term "fiancée" she could not have said.

"Fiancée!" the Randall sisters screeched in unison like twin harpies.

"Why, yes," St. James said smoothly. "My fiancée." Every woman there, including Chantel, stared at him as if he were three-headed and cloven-hooved. "It was a mad, whirlwind courtship."

"Mad! Yes!" Chantel said. "And yes, you could say he knocked me off my feet, but—"

"Swept, darling. You mean swept you off your

feet." His tone was indulgent and his eyes laughed down upon her.

"Yes, and he drugged me—"

"Ah yes, sweet passion is a drug. I feel the same way as my dear Chantel." The other women stared, confused. "You see, ladies, Chantel fell very ill last night at Squire Peterson's ball."

"Yes, with a very strange sickness," Chantel muttered, attempting to break from St. James' iron hold, but to no avail.

"I was so worried about her that I brought her here immediately rather than return her to Covington's Folly. You know the Folly is so much farther away and I did not wish to risk her traveling."

"Was that it?" Chantel asked through bared teeth.

"Indeed. And my staff is far larger and, I thought, possibly more capable in a crisis."

"How dare you insult my staff!"

"You can understand, Mrs. Jasper." St. James' eyes pleaded with the vicar's wife. He prudently ignored the Randall sisters, who appeared ready to foam at the mouth. "I—I could not worry over proprieties with my poor love's safety at stake."

"No, no, of course not!" Mrs. Jasper, to Chantel's indignation, almost reached out her hand in sympathy to the deceiving, conniving man.

"Thank you," he said warmly. "I knew you would understand. After all, it is the spirit of a deed that must be considered. Now, I fear that Chanty—"

"Chantel!" she corrected, rustling irately beneath her sheet.

"Yes, Chantel—must be getting back to her bed." Without further ado, he lifted her into his arms.

"Put me down," Chantel snapped. She could hear the women respond like cackling hens, and realized she now appeared as the villain. "Put me down . . . darling! I—I am sure I can walk, I certainly don't wish to go to my room again."

"But you cannot get well that way," Richard said with great solicitation, carrying her up the stairs. He turned on the fourth step. "Ladies, do excuse us; you are all invited to our wedding, of course. It shall be in . . . two months time."

"What?" Chantel sputtered.

"So soon?" chorused Lavinia and Divinia.

"But of course," Richard smiled. "I find I cannot be parted from my love for much longer than that." His love squirmed and growled under her breath. "Edward, could you please show the ladies out? I must get darling Chantel settled."

"My pleasure," Edward caroled, looking like a happy collie as he herded the stunned, bleating ladies to the door. Inexorably, St. James carried Chantel up the stairs and nearer to her dungeon. She could hear Edward touting himself as the very man who had introduced the loving couple.

"Rot!" Chantel exclaimed.

"Quiet," St. James said. "Edward will work wonders. He'll have those ladies turned up sweet in no time."

"You mean he's a liar just like you." Chantel's voice hissed with spite as he carried her into the gold room. She observed his jaw clench. Then he dropped her so hard on the bed that she bounced.

"I am no liar!"

Chantel scrambled for decorum when she had

stopped bouncing, pulling her sheet about her desperately. "Yes, you are. And a kidnapper, and a housebreaker—"

"Enough." St. James raised his hand curtly, appearing so angry that Chantel flinched, half-expecting that hand to land upon her. It stayed raised a moment, then he ran it through his dark locks, upsetting their arrangement. As Chantel stared at him, he began to pace; it was as if she watched a panther in a cage. "God save me!" he exclaimed, turning to face her, frustration clearly marring his features. "We needs must marry, and all you can do is call me names!"

"M-m-marry?" Chantel's mouth suddenly felt dry. "B-but I thought you were hoaxing them. Why must we get—get—"

"Get married? Need I truly explain? You have been found unchaperoned in my house without a shred of clothing—"

"I had a sheet on!"

"Oh, yes—until you rolled on down the stairs to greet Mrs. Jasper and the Randall sisters *sans* sheet, *sans*—"

"Don't say it!" Waves of embarrassment and rage heated Chantel. "You act as if this were all my fault. It was you who drugged and kidnapped me! I didn't ask to be here! And it was you who locked me in this room with naught but my shift on—"

"And it was here you should have stayed, dammit!" he growled. He resumed his pacing.

"Stayed here?" Chantel's tone let him know she thought him demented. "Stayed here for what? So that you could ravish me . . . or kill me?"

St. James halted in his stride and stepped menacingly close, his hands fisted. Chantel leaned back in the bed as he bent over her and spoke through clenched teeth. "If I have refrained from such acts to date, Miss Emberly, you can deem it a surety that I will continue to refrain. Though I resist the latter of the two only through great discipline!"

"Then—" Chantel looked away from the anger in those gray eyes, nonplussed. "Then wh-who undressed me?"

"My housekeeper, evidently."

"And where are my clothes?"

"If I know Mrs. Innes, she already has them washed and pressed for you."

"I—I see." Chantel clenched her hands together, feeling very stupid. "Then why did you bring me here?"

St. James remained silent, and her eyes flew to his. "Why? I brought you here because we raided Covington's Folly last night."

"Raided? What for?" Chantel exclaimed. It was the last thing she had expected him to say. "Why would anyone raid the Folly?"

"We thought to catch the spy we are looking for. He was to exchange information last night at the Folly. Our operative intercepted a note that said as much."

"And—and what happened?" Sudden fear rose in Chantel's throat, but St. James' eyes gave nothing away.

"We did not catch him."

She breathed out in relief. She hadn't realized she was holding her breath. Angry with herself for allowing him to scare her, Chantel lifted her chin and cast a disdainful look upon him. "I could have told you.

Teddy is no spy, and nothing like that would ever occur at Covington's Folly."

Chantel inched to the edge of the bed and stood as gracefully as one could when enveloped in a sheet. St. James didn't move, and she was forced to crick her neck to look at him. "Now, if you will please excuse me, I would like you to return my dress."

"We have not settled our marriage yet."

Chantel's mouth dropped and her hand shook as she clutched the sheet to her bosom. "You cannot be serious about that still?"

"I am." His tone was implacable.

Chantel's heart sank; the steel in his eyes was also unwavering. "This is preposterous," she sputtered, her mind balking at the thought. "I refuse to marry you!"

"But you shall," he said firmly. His stance was autocratic. "Your reputation and mine are at stake."

"Reputation be hanged!" Chantel said, stalking past him. "I will not marry a conniving, lying, drugging, kidnapping . . . *ooff!*" St. James caught her sheet and dragged her up against him.

"Silence!" His two hands caught Chantel at the sheet's edges. Gracious, they were such large hands. "That is no way to talk to your future husband," he said, his tone thunderous.

Chantel gulped, and forced herself to meet St. James' blazing glare. She ran her tongue nervously over her lips; his fierce eyes followed the movement. Suddenly, Chantel found it almost impossible to speak, for an odd, breathless feeling had entered her. She forced herself to say, "I—I told you, we do not need to get married."

"You may not think so, but evidently you do not

care for your reputation. Nor, I am sure, does your family," he sneered. "I, however, have a reputation to protect; my family is one of honor—"

"Oh, and mine is not?" Chantel asked indignantly.

"—and I will not allow its name to be dragged through the mud," St. James continued, as if applying himself to her question was unnecessary. "Nor will I allow you to endanger my political standing in the House with such a scandal."

Chantel tried to pull away, but St. James held her wrapped in the sheet like a cocoon. The heat radiating from him seared through the cloth and into her skin. "You cannot force me to marry you!" Chantel persevered, shutting her eyes to block out the demanding earl and his assault on her emotions.

"Yes I can." His voice was low, deadly confident. Chantel's eyes snapped open and she looked at him warily. "In our raid on Covington's Folly we found a crate of smuggled French brandy and some bolts of silk. That is still a criminal offense. I will bring your brother up on charges if you do not comply."

"Blackmailer!" Chantel exclaimed, appalled.

"Mine is not the crime," he countered swiftly. Both stood frozen. Chantel tried to think, tried to ignore the strange and frightening feelings coursing through her. Her instinct was to run; her instinct was to refuse St. James. Yet Teddy, her brother, would be brought up on charges if she did. She could never permit that. Her head lowered. "Could not we merely act engaged, and then break it off a month from now? Would that not suffice as well?"

"No." His breath whispered upon her hair. A shiver ran through her. "It would not serve."

Nervous tears stung Chantel's eyes. "Very well, I have no choice." She raised her head, lifting pain-filled eyes to him, and she stilled. The look in his eyes stunned her.

Her heart pounded as he leaned closer, bending to her infinitesimally. His lips hovered above hers. Chantel drew in a ragged breath and lifted her chin slightly; her eyes fluttered shut of their own accord. Lord, he was going to kiss her, she knew it for a certainty.

Then, suddenly, his hands were not upon hers, his body was not aligned to hers. She opened her eyes, bewildered and stunned; St. James stood across the room from her. How had he moved over there? Only a moment ago, he was—she shook her head dazedly.

"It can be a marriage of convenience," he said in a stiff, cold voice. She gazed at him stupidly. "A marriage in name only. After six months we can obtain an annulment."

"An—an annulment?"

"Yes. One can have an annulment as long as the marriage is never . . . consummated."

Chantel swallowed. "Oh . . . I see. Th—that is good."

"Yes. That will work," he said, his voice taking on strength. His eyes were an impassive fence in front of his thoughts. "Well, I shall go and get your dress."

If the idea weren't so ridiculous, Chantel would have thought him embarrassed. She flushed. It was she who was embarrassed. "Thank you," she nodded, shaking herself and raising her chin. His might be the great family, but she had her own pride.

He did not note this display, however, for he left without another look in her direction. Chantel walked to the bed and sat down numbly. She stared off into space, seeing nothing, but feeling everything. Good Lord, what had she gotten herself into? She was to marry a man who frightened her more than a little. She was to live with him for six months, until an annulment was obtained. Slowly, she toppled back upon the bed. How, oh how, was she to survive this incredible turn of events?

Chapter Three

"Miss Chantel!" Mr. Todd exclaimed, his aged voice cracking with emotion as he opened the door upon her. "We've been that worried about you! Where have you been? We . . ." His failing sight finally noted that she stood before him in her ballgown from the night before, albeit pressed. "Miss Chantel, you are still wearing . . ." His Adam's apple bobbed and he choked as Richard St. James strode up to stand behind her, grim visaged. "And with a man!"

"Mr. Todd, this is the Earl of Hartford," Chantel said, flushing red. "I—I shall explain it all later."

"Good morning, Mr. Todd. I am Chantel's fiancé," St. James said smoothly. Chantel flinched as poor Mr. Todd teetered.

"I see," said the ancient butler. His voice creaked like an unoiled hinge, but he managed to right himself before St. James could reach out and aid him.

"I am sorry, Mr. Todd," Chantel said, spinning to glare at Richard. "We did not mean to surprise you like that."

"No, miss. It is quite all right." Mr. Todd suddenly

gathered himself into the dignified personage that Chantel had revered since childhood. "Do allow me to congratulate you." He bowed. "And you also, my lord."

"Thank you, Mr. Todd."

The butler surveyed the man before him. He nodded slightly. "Miss Chantel is a fine lady, my lord. I am sure you will be happy." His rheumy eyes turned upon her. "Master Teddy is in the parlor, Miss, as well as your aunt and cousin, I fear."

"Oh no," Chantel groaned.

"Excellent," her future husband of six months said bracingly. "I look forward to meeting them." The man was not human!

"Right this way, my lord," Mr. Todd nodded approvingly. Chantel preceded the men, feeling like a helpless sheep with two herding dogs at her heels.

As they entered the parlor, they discovered the family well settled in to their tea. Chantel stopped, a flutter coursing through her. What to say?

Mr. Todd took the decision from her by stepping before her and announcing, "Miss Chantel and Richard St. James, the Earl of Hartford." Mr. Todd's voice had taken on a deep, important note. He stepped aside, no longer her shield.

And still Chantel could not muster the words. She stared at her family and her family stared back. Richard St. James approached from behind and rested a hand upon her shoulder.

"G-good morning," she finally squeaked, forcing a brightness. "How are you?"

"How are we?" Aunt Beatrice questioned in a rasp. "You ask how are we? We have been up since dawn wondering where you have been. We rushed here the instant we heard that you were missing and had not returned home last night."

Chantel pinned Teddy with a glare and he squirmed in his chair. "I didn't know what to do. Juliet came crying that your bed hadn't been slept in. Got scared. I mean, thought it was that queer duck again, you know, that masked fellow that . . ." Chantel winced as St. James' hand contracted upon her shoulder.

"Teddy, you are rambling," Chad said, his frown of concentration focused upon Chantel. "He sent a message to us, dear, in case you had returned to our house after the ball."

"Only right and proper," Aunt Beatrice approved. "We are your family, after all." The look she then directed at St. James made it clear what she thought of his unsanctioned presence. "We did not know you were out gallivanting with this . . ."

"Mother," Chad said swiftly. "Permit Chantel to explain please."

"I—I," Chantel looked desperately to Chad, who studied her with concern. Her hand went out to him. "I-I don't . . . I—I don't know what to say . . ."

"Except that I am her fiancé," St. James said urbanely.

Chad stiffened and turned white. Aunt Beatrice made a sound somewhat like a snort and Teddy yelped like a kicked dog.

"Fiancé!" Teddy exclaimed. He shook his head in refusal. "Can't be. Chantel never said anything about you. Must be a hum."

"No, Teddy, it isn't," Chantel said gently.

Teddy's mouth hinged open and shut in rapid succession. It appeared, however, that he had gained some divine inspiration from this exercise, for his jaw finally settled, and pursing his lips, he directed a dark, suspicious frown toward St. James. "I know why he's marrying you, Chantel! Bet a monkey he's after the treasure! That's what! Don't marry him, Chantel. He's got an eye to the treasure."

"I assure you," St. James said, his voice sounding harsh to Chantel's ears, "I am not marrying her for a treasure. Far from it."

"Indeed, Teddy," Chad said. "Your notion is highly unflattering to Chantel. As if Lord Hartford would only marry her for that. Marriage to Chantel is a treasure in itself. Furthermore, the Earl is quite wealthy in his own right." He glanced toward St. James, who wore the *de rigueur* attire of rust jacket and buff unmentionables of the proper gentleman country caller. The shine on his boots, constructed by Hoby, could only have been reached using a blacking mixed with champagne.

"Thank you for acquitting me of fortune hunting . . . or treasure hunting, shall I say." The earl's voice seemed arrogant and Chantel refused to turn and look at him. She trained her eyes straight ahead.

"Then why are you marrying her?" Aunt Beatrice asked baldly.

"I fear we must marry or Miss Emberly's reputation will suffer."

"Is this true, Chantel?" Chad asked urgently, rising to cross to her. He picked up her hands, his clasp warm. "Tell me, dear."

Chantel stood, torn. Richard St. James' cold, restraining grip rested upon her shoulder, while Chad's hands held hers tenderly. The hurt in his face pierced her. "It isn't what you think," she said swiftly. "It was totally innocent, but yes—I—I fear we were found in a compromising situation."

"Then let *me* marry you," he said urgently. "You know I love you."

"Yes, marry Chad," Aunt Beatrice said. "No need to involve this outsider."

"I am sorry to be the outsider," St. James said, amazing Chantel by laughing. "But I fear it must be me and no one else that Chantel marries. No one else but I can save her reputation."

"You mean your reputation, don't you?" Chantel spluttered. His arrogance enraged her. She spun on him angrily. "Don't try to play the hero! Because you aren't! You base, low—"

"Hartford, I'm calling you out!" Chad's voice cracked like a whip through her monologue.

Chantel gasped in shock. Her eyes widened and she watched St. James with bated breath. His eyes had darkened dangerously and she could tell he was barely restraining himself. He looked down at her and she mouthed the word "No" pleadingly.

He smiled. His brow quirked and he said, "Now who's playing the hero?"

Chantel breathed again. She turned to Chad, her hand reaching out to rest on his chest. "Please, Chad. Don't do it. The Earl is right. I must marry him if we are to stop a scandal. The whole town will know of our engagement within the hour; it cannot be changed. I . . . well, I was discovered in a compromising position at Lord Hartford's house this morning by the Randall sisters."

"Yikes," Teddy shouted. "The Randall sisters! They're bad, very bad." The Randall sisters had never missed a chance to treat Teddy like a wantwit and just the mention of them would set him to shivering as he was now. He grabbed his teacup and gulped its contents, only to find it was the sugar bowl. He choked and spluttered, coating the front of his jacket and cravat. Absently, he dropped the dish to the Bombay butler's table at his side, breaking the brass handle that Chantel had recently adhered with a mixture of beeswax and crumbled paper promoted by *Miss Berthwell's Home Companion* as an "economical yet sturdy means of reparation."

"So you see," she said, smiling wryly to Chad, "I really must marry him. Please let us not have a fight in the family."

"Very well," he said softly. "I will do as you wish." He glared over at St. James. "And only because you wish it."

"Thank you," Chantel said. She doubted she could handle any more without breaking down. She turned to the earl. "I am sure you have things you must do, my lord. Permit me to walk you to the door."

The room was extraordinarily silent as they left. Chantel was equally silent as she walked with St. James through the hall and to the door. "Goodbye, my lord," she said formally as she opened the door.

He turned to look at her, a fierce expression upon his face. "You fear marrying me, when you have a family like that? I would think you would jump at the chance to escape them, even if it is for only six months."

"They are my family," she said defensively, "and they love me."

"Do they?" he asked softly. He said it so gently that Chantel could only stare, arrested. His eyes became hooded, his face stern. "Make sure you don't tell them anything else about this all."

"Why not?"

"Because your cousin is foolish enough to want to call me out, and Teddy simply can't be trusted. You wouldn't want either of them killed would you?"

"No, I wouldn't," she said. "I'd rather see you killed instead."

He enraged her even more, for he only laughed. "I have no doubt, but that is not the way it would happen, so keep your relatives out of this."

"I will." She pulled a smile over bared teeth. "If anyone is to kill you it will be me."

He only laughed again. "Good afternoon, my sweet." He brushed her cheek, and she drew back sharply. "Don't cry too much while I am away." He turned and took the steps, whistling!

"Ohh!" Chantel raged impotently. She slammed the door so vehemently that it seemed all of Covington's Folly shook with the force. The sound reverberated through the rafters and resounded within its bowels.

Richard turned away from the floor-to-ceiling bay window through which he had been peering and looked at the pile of books and ledgers that were strewn across the embossed leather top of the mahogany desk before him, awaiting his wandering attention. Facts and figures, however, paled compared to the prospect of marriage to Chantel Emberly. He

hadn't seen that small package of volatility for almost
two weeks. He had thought to give her time to adjust
herself to the idea. Their marriage truly was the only
way. She'd be an outcast in her world if they didn't
wed, for he had seen it in those two old spinsters' eyes
when she'd tumbled down the stairs. And though he
believed he might outface it in his own world, he must
think of his family, a very proud and proper one. They
would not be able to handle such gossip and ostracism
with aplomb.

He shook his head ruefully. He had received neither
note nor word from his spitfire fiancée during the past
weeks. While he made arrangements, he still did not
know whether she would be present at the wedding or
not. A mirthless laughed escaped him. At least he did
not need to fear that his wife would be a clinging vine.
He might have to fear that she would strangle him, but
not that she would smother him.

He picked up a paper, only to set it down again.
Faith, what a damnable situation. He was about to
marry a little shrew who would rather see him dead
than beside her at the altar. Her family was far beyond
hostile, the cousin wanting Richard's future bride for
himself, her brother eccentric enough to think him
after some family treasure.

Sighing, he reached down to open the desk's lower
drawer. Suddenly a loud crack sounded, glass shattered, and the whine of a bullet pierced the air. The
ball embedded itself high in the wall across the room
from him. Instinctively, he rolled from his chair to the
floor. A second pane of glass shattered. Richard was
knocked hard upon the shoulder with a heavy missile.
It ricocheted off him and rolled away with a thud.

Turning over, he spied a dirty rock. A paper was wrapped around it, tied with twine. He grabbed it up and tore the strings away, uncreasing the grimy note. "Marry and you die."

Richard's jaw tightened and the paper ripped as his hand clenched it. He rose from the floor. A low, primal growl escaped from his lips. He stalked from the room.

A winded, alarmed Edward met him at the study door. "My God, what has happened?"

"Nothing," Richard gritted out as he strode past him. "Simply nothing."

"But I thought I heard a shot!"

"You did," Richard threw over his shoulder as he crossed the foyer and tore open the front door.

"Where are you going?"

"To strip the hide off of Mistress Emberly!"

It was wash day. The morning had dawned so bright and fair that Chantel had decided to tackle washing the faded drawing room curtains. She now peered at the gray-green mass floating in the sudsy water of the large washtub that came well nigh to her waist. It didn't appear that the curtains were going to benefit from their dunking. They would never be the rich bronze-green jacquard shot with petite gold *fleurs de lis* in gold metallic thread that they had been. Now these same gold markings had tarnished and corroded to resemble nothing so much as a multitude of dark brown houseflies. She swiped in exasperation at a damp curl that teased her forehead. Perhaps if she washed them again they would improve.

The sound of approaching hooves distracted her from her domestic contemplations. She spied Richard

St. James galloping toward her at breakneck speed.
Her heart sank. He would catch her out in her oldest
work dress, wet sleeves rolled up to her elbows, with a
crumpled, damp apron wrapped about her. She would
definitely appear at the disadvantage. Chantel's mouth
hardened. What did it matter! She didn't care a fig for
what the cursed earl thought. It was not as if she
wanted to marry the odious man—not even for six
months.

The earl drew rein directly in front of her, his large
black stallion snorting and pawing at the ground. Both
man and horse seemed to be in a stormy mood.

"Good afternoon," Chantel smiled sunnily, wiping
her hands upon her apron. The man was definitely up
in the boughs over something. His gray eyes were like
molten lava.

"What did you think you were doing?" he snapped.

"Doing? I am washing curtains."

"Cut line. Did you think you would frighten me? Or
did you truly mean to kill me?"

Chantel's jaw dropped. "What are you talking
about?"

"Did you personally shoot at me or did you hire
out? Either way, the shot went glaringly abroad!"

Chantel's hands came to her hips in exasperation.
"What the devil are you blathering about, my lord?"

"Did you, or did you not, shoot at me this morning?"

"Shoot at you?" Chantel exclaimed. "No, of course
not. How could you even ask such a question?"

"You said you intended to kill me. I just didn't
think you would take action, and so very promptly."

"Well I didn't! If someone shot at you, it must be

one of your other enemies. I make no doubt the world is littered with them. After all, your habit of drugging and kidnapping woman is not exactly a felicitous one."

"You, Miss Emberly . . ." he gritted the words out slowly, "are the only woman I have ever done such to."

"Oh? What a distinction for me. I know I should feel honored, but forgive me if I wish you would honor someone else."

"Do not stray from the subject. You cannot throw me off the scent that easily. I know you were behind it."

"And why?" Chantel asked indignantly. Anger was swelling within her. Evidently the man did not care how much he insulted her, for he was accusing her of attempted murder! "You seem to be up to your aristocratic neck in various intrigues . . . chasing after strongboxes and whatnot. Why choose me as the would-be assassin?"

He dismounted from his horse slowly and Chantel watched him warily. He was such a large, imposing man. He walked slowly up to her and Chantel glared at him in sheer dislike of his ability to overshadow her. "I choose you, my dear, because only you would send such a note."

"Note?"

"Yes. 'Marry and you die.' Come, Chantel. You are usually far more verbose than that. No names, no insults?"

Chantel stared at him. "You mean there was a note saying that?"

"It was wrapped about a rock and thrown through the window after the shot."

Chantel turned swiftly from him and buried her hands in the sudsy water, gripping the wet material. Her mind worked fiercely. The thought that occurred to her frightened her, which only made her angrier.

"Well?" St. James demanded from behind her. She refused to look at him. "What have you to say?"

"I would say," Chantel said, attempting to be calm, "what I have said before. Someone else did it. Someone who does not wish you to marry me. Look to the people you know, for it was not I." She lifted a dripping mass of curtains up in wet display. "I've been here working. I am innocent."

St. James stepped closer. "I see that now." She smiled in relief. "Who did you hire?"

"Hire!" Chantel exclaimed in exasperation. The man was a bulldog! "I hired no one, you stupid man. What, pray tell, would I pay my would-be assassin with? We are on queer street, for goodness sakes. Paying an assassin to rid myself of you would be an impossible luxury for my slim pockets. Look somewhere else for your killer. Stop insulting me and mine."

She turned back and wrung the material the way she wished she could wring St. James' neck. She plunged it fiercely into the sudsy water, imagining it was his head she was submerging rather than the curtains. "Perhaps it was another woman you know who does not wish you to marry. A jealous *inamorata,* perhaps?" Chantel turned to watch the effect of her slur upon him.

St. James stiffened, and his brow arched haughtily. "I have never aligned myself with the type of female who would consider such an action. Not until . . ." He halted suddenly, but the final word hung between them in the bright afternoon air.

Chantel supplied it. "Not until me?" she purred. "Well, my lord, it is not as if I wish to align myself with you either. You are not the man of my dreams, I assure you. Let us cancel this farcical wedding. Surely we can outface the gossipmongers."

"No," he retorted, his face stiffening. "We shall simply move it forward . . . to four days from now."

"What!" Chantel exclaimed. "Is your attic to let?"

He smiled grimly. "Did your little plan backfire, Chanty?"

"It was not my plan you blasted, stubborn man! And don't call me Chanty! I had nothing to do with this affair. Why make me suffer?"

His eyes narrowed. "I do not intend to allow anyone to take random shots at me during the coming weeks. We will marry in four days and have this all done with. That is final."

"Have you thought this all through, my thick-skulled lord?" Chantel asked, trying to rein in her wild anger. "If we marry in such haste, it would only cause the scandal you wish to avoid. You know what the gossips will think of such a havey-cavey affair. Then where will your fine family name be?"

St. James waved her objection away. "They will stop once we have proven them wrong."

She gulped. "You mean when we get an annulment in six months?"

He nodded imperiously.

"But, but . . ." Chantel thought quickly, hunting for anything to stay the wedding. "But your family won't be able to attend at such short notice. Surely it would help to have them present."

"They will be there," St. James said curtly. "They know what is necessary to protect the family's honor. As for your family," he shrugged negligently, "if they cannot attend, it is of no moment."

"Why you arrogant, top-lofty . . ." Red flared before Chantel's eyes and words failed her. St. James's expression was smug and condescending. Her anger wasn't even affecting him! Her eyes narrowed. She'd wipe that self important expression off his face. See if she didn't!

Chantel lifted the sodden mass of curtains she still grasped and threw it directly at his irritating grin. The curtain hit his face with a smack and slid slowly down his chest, leaving a sodden trail. The smug, obnoxious look was gone but the thunderous expression that replaced it was no better. Indeed, it was frightening.

"You stay away from me," Chantel warned, snatching up the remaining curtains from the water. She lifted them threateningly. "Stay away, do you hear me?"

St. James came at her and she let the mass fly. The soaking missile hit him fully in the chest, spattering suds across his silk vest.

St. James didn't stop. He grabbed her by the wrist. Chantel tried desperately to jerk free. "Let me go." He caught the other wrist before she could swing it. Swiftly, he hefted her up high.

"Put me down," Chantel cried, flailing out futilely. "Put me down, dammit!"

Splash! He'd put her down. Right into the tub of soapy water now cooled to an uncomfortable chilliness, the suds residue coating the surface resembling nothing so much as pond scum. "You monster!" Chantel cried, as she felt the cold water seeping through her petticoats to her bare skin. Furious and spluttering, she clutched at the tub's sides, attempting to pull herself up. Just as she had acquired a slippery leverage, St. James ruthlessly pushed her back in. Water splashed everywhere. Chantel surfaced, spitting out water.

"Stay there," St. James commanded, his eyes dangerous even as suds slid down his face. "Perhaps the water will cool your temper."

"I hate you!" Chantel fumed, the bitter and disgusting taste of soap in her mouth.

St. James grasped the tub on both sides of her and leaned into her, his eyes implacable. "No matter, we shall be married four days hence. And madam, I warn you! Once I am your husband, never, ever, dare to raise your hand to me again, or dare to throw so much as a drop of water upon me. It will be far the worse for you than this. Is that understood?"

Chantel's chin trembled. "Remember, my lord, you shall not truly be my husband. Do not think you can command me so."

"For six months I shall, madam," he retorted.

"Six months that I shall abhor!"

St. James growled at that. Without warning, he reached beneath her arms and dragged her from the tub. He drew her sodden body up against his and kissed her, roughly, passionately. She could taste the soapy water upon his lips, feel his hands beneath her arms brush the sides of her breasts. She shivered, a sudden heat flushing her cold, wet skin. A warmth spiraled to the core of her.

He tore his lips from her. His eyes were dark, perhaps as stunned as hers. He moved suddenly away from her. Without his support, Chantel fell directly back into the tub of water.

"Four days hence, madam, in my chapel." St. James spun away from her and swiftly mounted his horse. He galloped off, never looking back.

Chantel sat, plunged up to her armpits in sudsy water. Amazingly, she was grateful for the cold water surrounding her, cooling her. She closed her eyes in embarrassment. Imagined or not, she could swear the heat from her body was causing steam to rise from the tub!

Three hours later, in the salon, Chantel sat dried and dressed in her favorite peach muslin. It was tea time. She looked up hopefully as she heard footsteps approaching. Her hopes died a quick death as Chad entered the room. It was Teddy who was Chantel's quarry, not Chad. It was Teddy she intended to put through an inquisition to surpass the Spaniards.

"Chantel, have you seen Teddy?" Chad asked as he entered.

"No," she said, reaching for a biscuit. She attempted nonchalance. "Wasn't he with you today? I thought you two were to do something together."

"We were," Chad said, sitting and surveying the tea tray with interest. "We planned to go and look over Petersham's breakdown this morning, but Teddy never arrived."

"I see." Chantel choked on a crumb that perversely

lodged itself in her suddenly dry throat. She coughed loudly. Chad looked to her in concern. "Are you all right?"

"Oh, yes," Chantel said weakly, taking immediate recourse in her tea. "I wonder what detained him."

Chad grinned. "I am sure we shall find out soon. Teddy never misses tea. 'Tis one of the few certainties in life."

"Yes," Chantel said morosely. "He never does. I suppose we must just wait."

Chad studied her. "What is the matter? You look fairly moped."

Chantel laughed nervously. "Oh no, 'tis nothing."

"You don't have a migraine or anything?"

"Yes, I do," Chantel sighed. "But perhaps he will arrive soon," she added under her breath.

"Have you had it all day?" Chad asked compassionately.

"No, only since three hours ago," Chantel said truthfully. "I . . . it has . . ." She halted as atrocious, off-key singing drifted to them. The singing became louder and even more off-key, if that were possible. Then Teddy appeared in the doorway. He was a Teddy much the worse for wear. His nose shone red and his clothes hung on him askew.

"Hello, everyone," he greeted, waving a hand proudly to the entire room, even into the four corners of it. "Came to tea." He nodded, a great beaming smile splitting his freckles. He proceeded to meander with unsteady steps to a chair. He crumpled into it, sending it squeaking across the floor. He squinted at Chad and Chantel, as if they were a far distance off rather than six feet from him. "Oh, hello Chad," he said in happy surprise. "Glad you're here. Wish to apol—apol—er, sorry 'bout this morning."

"That's quite all right old fellow," Chad said, eyeing him in amusement. "It appears you had better plans."

"No," Teddy shook his head vehemently. "Just trying to think, was all." He hiccupped solemnly. "Thinking's not in my line, you know. Tis a devil-lil-ish hard thing to do. Th—thirsty business, what!"

"So it appears," Chad laughed.

Chantel, however, did not find it one whit amusing. She trained stern, suspicious eyes upon her inebriated sibling. "And what were you thinking about, Teddy?"

"You," Teddy said simply. His watery eyes suddenly blurred with tears. "Don't think you want to marry this St. James fellow. I ain't got much in me cockloft, but I can tell that. I'm your brother, you know."

"Yes, Teddy, you are," Chantel assured her grieving sibling.

"Don't want you to marry the chap if you don't want to—will figure a way out for you, promise," Teddy swore faithfully, leaning forward so earnestly that he almost tumbled from his chair.

Chantel could no longer ignore her fears. It was obvious. Teddy had taken that shot at the earl. "Oh Teddy," she moaned, "you didn't! I was praying that it wasn't you!"

"Wasn't me?" He burped loudly. "What wasn't me?"

"Oh, Teddy, how could you have done such a thing!" Chantel said, beside herself. "How could you have!"

"Done what?" Chad asked in confusion, for Teddy was hiccuping soundly.

"Yes," Teddy nodded when he could. "Done what?"

Chantel looked to Chad in exasperation. "He shot at Richard St. James this morning and threw a note through the window warning him not to marry me."

"He what!" Chad exclaimed, stunned.

"I what?" Teddy exclaimed, stupefied.

"You heard me," Chantel said irately, shaking her finger at Teddy. "You shot at Richard St. James and threw a note through his window."

"I did?" Teddy asked, amazed. He thought for a moment and sat up more proudly. "Damn, what a good notion. Clever, very clever. I'll do it, that's what!"

"It wasn't clever Teddy," Chantel cried in exasperation. "It only made things worse!"

"Did?" Teddy asked, then sighed heavily. "Then won't do it. Shame. Sounded like a capital notion."

"Teddy?" Chad asked patiently, for Chantel was now looking daggers at him and her hand was balling up into a fist. "Let us get something clear here, did you or did you not shoot at St. James this morning?"

Teddy looked at Chad suspiciously. He ruminated for a full minute and then shook his head. "Didn't. Wish I had," he said on another voracious burp. "B—bounder com—compromised Chantel. He's after the treasure too, what?"

Chad looked to Chantel, whose eyes had widened at Teddy's declaration. "He evidently didn't do it, Chantel. Now," he said more sternly, "could you please tell me what happened before I am driven to join Teddy at the bottle."

"Can't," Teddy said sadly. "Drank it all. No more. Got to order some, Chantel."

"Chantel! Would you please explain!" Chad said in exasperation.

"All I know is that someone shot at Richard St. James this morning, and then threw a note in through the window warning him not to marry me or he'd die," Chantel shrugged. "Who else would do such a queer thing but Teddy?"

"Didn't do it," Teddy said glumly. "For you I would have. Would do an—anything for you. But didn't think of that . . ."

"Well, I am glad you didn't," Chantel said. "Very glad, for it only made things worse. Now St. James has decided to advance the wedding. I am to marry him within four days, or so he says! Four days, mind you!"

"Wh—what?" stammered Teddy.

"He says he won't wait to be shot at anymore," Chantel said, fuming. "Neither will he call the wedding off. He has set his mind upon it and has issued me the decree. The man is insufferable!"

"B-bb-lighter," Teddy growled. "I-ll call him out, that's what!"

"No. I will call him out," Chad said softly.

Chantel looked from Teddy's hazy but devoted eyes to Chad's cooler and more determined ones and she shook her head frantically, her own eyes stinging at their obvious championing of her. "You are both dears and I love you for it, but no! Neither of you will call him out."

"Must," Teddy said resolutely. "Can't have you marry a b-b-lighter."

"Please, Teddy don't even think of it," Chantel asked.

"Can't have you suffer at the hands of that f—f-iend," Teddy continued, now totally consumed with gallantry as well as liqueur. "Damn, will call him out. If I botch it, Chad can call him out next."

"No, no!" Chantel exclaimed, struck with fear. "Please, Teddy, don't do it—it will only be for six months, I can survive that, really." Then her voice faltered, and she swallowed nervously as she discovered both men observing her with expressions of utter bewilderment.

"What do you mean, Chantel?" Chad asked very slowly and evenly. "What do you mean—for only six months?"

"Right," Teddy added, "m—marriage is for life." He hiccupped. "Death do part—and all that fr-right-ful s-stuff."

Chantel flushed. She had fallen in the broth now. Both men were eyeing her expectantly, their faces taut with suspicion. She realized she couldn't hold back any longer. "Very well, I wasn't supposed to tell you . . . he made me promise . . . but St. James and I intend to annul the marriage within six months." Chantel looked pleadingly toward Chad, who had a frozen look upon his face. "I'm sorry. Truly I am. As I said, St. James made me promise not to tell you. I wanted to so desperately, but he made me promise."

Chad's face finally thawed, and a slow, deep smile replaced his frown. "Faith, Chantel, I don't care about that. I am just so glad to know that you won't be truly married to him."

"Annulled?" Teddy said in wonder. "In only six months?"

"Yes, Teddy," Chantel said, relieved that she had finally confided in them. Hang Richard St. James and his ridiculous demands. Teddy, however, was still gazing at her in confusion and no small bemusement. "You see, Teddy, St. James and I can obtain an annulment as long as . . . well, as long as we don't *act* like husband and wife. This way the gossip will die down and his name will be protected. He-he didn't think a mere engagement would have sufficed. But if we get married, and later—after the scandal dies—annul it . . ."

Teddy was frowning, shaking his head as if he couldn't clear it. "But you'll have to not—er, act like man and wife . . . Th-think you can do that?"

"Of course," Chantel scoffed, amazed that this was the notion that bothered Teddy. "After all, it isn't as if St. James and I love each other. In fact, I hate the man, I absolutely abhor him! I detest him . . ." Chantel stopped to draw in a breath between her invectives against the Earl of Hartford. Before she could lengthen and broaden the scope of her diatribe, Mr. Todd entered the room.

"Delivery for Miss Chantel," he announced in an odd, choked voice. He then stepped aside, and a line of men, all dressed in the St. James livery, proceeded into the room, each bearing a stack of boxes encased in ivory velvet and tied with a posy of Irish lace ribbon and white violets. Each man set his offering down before a speechless and wide-eyed Chantel and bowed to her with proper ceremony. When the last box was placed and the last servant gone, Chantel was but a small, hidden figure amongst the towers of ivory froth. Mr. Todd bowed, his rheumy eyes bright. "Miss." He turned and left. Chantel could have sworn she heard a chuckle from him, but the old fellow was safely out of the room before she could be certain of it.

"Well," Chad said, his brows arched as he surveyed the sea of presents. "Just what do we have here?" He leaned over and dragged a box from the stack. He lifted the lid and a whistle escaped his lips. He withdrew a long, gossamer white veil. "I think we know who this is from," he said wryly.

"B-bounder," Teddy said, nodding. He rose from his chair unsteadily and stumbled across the room to grab up a box, his expression very much that of an expectant child at Christmas. He tore off the lid quickly and in an expansive gesture, pulled out the box's treasure.

It so happened to be the very sheerest of pantaloons, trimmed with the finest of lace. "Gads!" Teddy squeaked, slamming it back into the box, supremely horrified. "Don't look Chantel, ain't proper!"

Chantel had looked, however, and a deep red hue suffused her skin. She did not deem it embarrassment. It was sheer, unadulterated rage. How dare that odious blackmailer buy her such intimate apparel? How dare he take such liberties with her dignity? The memory of that afternoon's kiss entered her mind and she flushed an even deeper shade of red. If he took such liberties now, what would he do after their marriage?

Her chin jutted out pugnaciously. Well, she'd nip

such intimacies in the bud immediately. She would just see what the cad had to offer and then she would send the whole offensive lot back to him! "I will return it all," she vowed. "See if I don't!" Grimly, she snatched the lid off the largest box next to her and ruthlessly delved her hands into it. A gasp escaped her, despite her resolve. Her heated hands had contacted the coolest and smoothest satin. Slowly, Chantel withdrew from the box a gleaming white wedding dress, encrusted with small delicate seed pearls nestled amongst leaves woven of diamante. It was the most glorious dress Chantel had ever beheld in her entire lifetime. She looked at Chad and gulped.

" 'Twould be better standing up in that than your shift," Chad said in amusement.

Chantel instinctively and possessively clutched the dress to her. Just holding the exquisite creation made a woman feel wonderful. She could not meet Chad's knowing eyes. "Yes—yes, I suppose you are right."

"Still abhor the man?" Chad's voice was soft.

Chantel's eyes flew to his at that. "Of course, I do. He is detestable. I won't return the dress since it is he that demands I marry him with such disgraceful haste."

"I am glad you are being so reasonable," Chad said, still too irritatingly wise.

Chantel's eyes narrowed dangerously. "Do not think I am taken in by all this folderol. I'll not be so easily deceived. St. James had to have commissioned these garments weeks ago—he was that confident I would marry him." Chantel's stomach suddenly lurched at the thought. "The man is a Machiavelli, always getting his way no matter what! He is too arrogant by far!" Chantel looked down at the silken dress in her hands. Her stomach churned once again. "He is too, too arrogant by far!"

Chapter Four

Chantel attempted to sniff discreetly. She blinked watery eyes and squinted them, trying to focus upon the squat minister before her who was delivering an oratory on the solemnity of marriage. The gauze of her veil made him appear a frightful vision. Chantel stifled a sneeze, her nose tickling from the horrendous cold she had acquired from the very man the minister was now asking that she swear her love, honor, and obedience toward. She shook her head in an attempt to clear the fog from it. The watchers in the pews behind her gasped loudly and murmurs and hisses arose. Chantel suddenly realized it appeared to the onlookers that she was denying the oath the minister was requiring. Oh, if only she could!

"I—I do," she croaked quickly. The hissing died down. Gracious, were St. James' relatives a clutch of snakes? That was what they sounded like—or perhaps angry hornets. Yes, angry wasps!

Chantel's nose twitched. She desperately needed to sneeze, yet she daren't in front of the august personages assembled. The groom's side of the chapel was filled with the most polished and distinguished people, truly distinguished. Chantel had been grateful when the Prince Regent had sent his regrets.

On the bride's side was Chad, her aunt (who had not seen fit to throw off her black attire even for the wedding), and merely all the townspeople, come to gape and watch an Emberly of Covington's Folly marry into the noble line of St. James.

The tickle in her nose evolved into a tingle. Chantel shifted restlessly, screwing her eyes shut tightly in an attempt to control her sneeze. It was amazing. She was wedding a total stranger who had abducted her and was blackmailing her into a false marriage, and at the moment, the only thought in her mind was that she dare not sneeze and disgrace herself! Chantel knew she should be trembling with fear, but she was far too occupied trembling with the effort of diverting a sneeze. Still twitching her nose, Chantel heard St. James say something, and then the minister said something. His tone sounded terribly solemn and final. St. James turned to her and lifted her veil. Oh dear, Chantel thought in alarm, they were at the part where he was to kiss the bride!

St. James' gray eyes were cool and unemotional. He was leaning toward her. Yes, he was going to kiss her! Chantel panicked and lost the fragile control she held over herself. She sneezed, loudly and fully! The violence of the long-denied sneeze snapped her head forward and she cracked St. James' jaw soundly. Her veil flew forward and covered her face. She blinked wildly in both pain and mortification.

The crowd muttered and growled. After a stunned moment, St. James lifted the veil again. Chantel focused upon him and glared at him as defiantly as she could. Surprisingly he smiled, a soft, amused smile. He leaned close and his words were only for her as his lips tickled her ear. "Good, 'tis only a cold. I was afraid you were crying."

"I never cry," Chantel retorted, even as her eyes teared.

St. James merely chuckled and then leaned over and kissed her fully on the lips. His were stunningly warm for a man who had appeared so disgustingly cool and collected throughout the ceremony. Hers were merely frozen in shock.

St. James straightened and a look passed between them that Chantel could not explain. It caused a warm glow in her heart, yet at the same time her stomach did a somersault. "You'll catch my cold," was all she could whisper.

St. James looked away first, breaking the spell. " 'Tis lucky there is no real honeymoon, then," he said quietly as he turned them toward the congregation.

Chantel gulped. Now there was the reception to withstand. She was supposedly Lady St. James. She looked out upon a sea of faces. On the groom's side they were prim and disapproving. On the bride's side, the townsfolk looked on with rather gleeful interest. Except the Randall sisters; their faces were tortured. Indeed, as she scanned the crowd, the only face she saw that looked honestly happy was that of Squire Peterson. He was beaming fit to burst the buttons off his Sunday best. Chantel moaned imperceptibly. Being Lady St. James even for a short time was going to be a terrible experience!

* * *

"Chantel, permit me to introduce you to my mother, Lady Esther," Richard St. James said as a tall, regal woman with chestnut hair approached them. Her dress was of orchid satin and her gray eyes were arctic as she looked at Chantel. Indeed, the woman perused Chantel very much as if she were unacceptable merchandise found at a bazaar.

"I am pleased to meet you," Chantel said, attempting a polite smile. There was no reason to fight this woman, after all; she could keep her precious son. Chantel would be gone in six months.

"You do know," Lady St. James said coolly, even as she looked about and waved with an artificial smile at an acquaintance in the distance, "that my son only married you to protect the family name."

"As I married him to protect my family name," Chantel returned solemnly.

Her words wiped the smile from Lady St. James' face and she glared at Chantel. "This will not be a real marriage, mind you, and during that time I do hope you will refrain from the excesses that you Covingtons are so famous for."

"And what are those excesses, pray tell?" Chantel asked sweetly.

"Ladies, I suggest you do not start this," Richard said softly, his face cold.

Lady Esther looked at her son, a look that expressed exactly what Chantel felt—that he was an interfering male who had best stay out of the fray. Lady Esther turned taunting eyes back to Chantel. "The Covingtons are known for their intemperance, gaming, and spendthrift ways."

"I practice none of those . . . virtues," Chantel said, smiling a wide smile.

Lady Esther's eyes narrowed. "Do not think to play the innocent with me, my girl. You will not succeed in cozening Richard into making this a permanent arrangement. He will never enter into such a misalliance. He knows what is due his name."

"Mother," Richard St. James said stiffly, "you need not lecture Chantel. She is fully aware of the unsuitability of this marriage and shares our feelings completely."

His mother glanced at him witheringly. "Fie, Richard. Do you really think this chit will just pack up her bags at the end and leave without a fight? I doubt it! She'll not whistle an earldom away."

Chantel had tolerated enough. She pursed her lips together and began softly to whistle a merry little tune.

Lady Esther's face stiffened and she drew in her breath so indignantly that Chantel thought the woman would surely burst. "Impudent hussy," Lady Esther hissed. She turned glacial eyes upon her son. "I will not tolerate this, Richard. I will not stand beside you and this . . . this female. I will not lend countenance to this designing minx—"

"That is enough, Mother," Richard said quietly. "If you will not join us in the receiving line, so be it. But you will conduct yourself with dignity and you will not say anything against Chantel. Otherwise the very purpose of this marriage will be destroyed."

Lady Esther turned an alarming shade of purple. It was difficult to decide where her orchid dress stopped and she began, Chantel decided rather maliciously.

Without another word, Lady Esther spun on her heel and sailed away.

"That was totally uncalled for," St. James said rigidly.

"I know. Your mother truly went beyond the line," Chantel said sweetly.

"I meant you," Richard said in an undertone. "She is . . ." Richard was not permitted to finish his statement, for suddenly three more people stood before them. Since Chantel did not recognize them, she knew they must be more of the St. James brood.

"Ah, Aunt Lillian," Richard said, his voice formal, "and Uncle Thomas and Alicia, I am so glad you could come."

The woman was a shorter version of Richard's mother. "Of course we would come. Never think we would not stand by you in this time of trial."

Chantel rolled her eyes. The St. James family certainly did not hide their teeth. "Hello," Chantel smiled. "I'm the trial."

"Aunt Lillian," Richard said before the woman could formulate the answer that her mobile face was working over, "permit me to introduce you to Chantel. Chantel, this is my Aunt Lillian, her husband Thomas, and this beautiful young lady is Alicia, their daughter, and my cousin."

Sir Thomas was a gruff-looking man who appeared not at all interested in the interactions about him. The daughter, Alicia, was petite, with sandy brown hair and large brown eyes that were demure and hesitant.

"Hello, Alicia," Chantel said, smiling. "That is a lovely dress." The dress, however, was truly a monstrosity, adorned with row upon row of white lace and pink flowerettes. It looked very much like the wedding cake that had been prepared for the celebration.

"Thank you," the girl said softly, her eyes still upon the ground.

"Here you are, Chantel," Teddy's voice came from behind her. "Thought you might need some victuals. Know I do," he said, stepping into the circle. He held two plates mounded high with every sort of delicacy imaginable. It was apparent that Teddy had done some excessive raiding of the buffet table.

"Teddy," Chantel said, forcing a smile. "I would like you to meet the earl's Aunt Lillian and Uncle Thomas. And this is Alicia, their daughter."

"Pleased to meet you," Teddy nodded, his eyes still trained upon his heaping rewards. But then he glanced up. His eyes widened and locked upon Alicia. His freckled face turned first white, then pink, and finally red. As if in a trance, Teddy stepped slowly, ever so slowly, toward the girl until he stood but an inch away from her.

Alicia had looked up at Teddy as well and her brown eyes had widened alarmingly. "Oh my," she whispered. "Oh my."

"H-h-ello," Teddy stammered, and promptly performed a courtly bow. He had forgotten, however, that he balanced two plates of food. As he bent at the waist, the plates tipped with him and the food slid directly onto Alicia's dress. Lobster patties and sweetmeats and fruited pastries all hung within the lace of Alicia's gown, each upon its own tier.

"Look what you have done!" Aunt Lillian shrilled as raucously as any fishmonger.

" 'Tis nothing, Mama," Alicia said raptly, an ardent smile of pleasure turned upon Teddy.

"Forgive me," Teddy said, breathing hard. "Wouldn't have done it for the world." He fearlessly dropped the plates and gallantly knelt before Alicia to begin plucking off the various delicacies. Alicia merely stood, beaming fondly down at him.

"My stars, get up young man, get up!" protested Aunt Lillian.

"Here now, get your hands off my daughter," Sir Thomas finally spoke, his voice shocked.

"Truly, you should not kneel before me," Alicia breathed as she reached down for a strawberry tart at the same time as Teddy reached up. Their hands clasped together, the tart caught between them. "Please rise," Alicia whispered.

"I'd kn-neel at your feet anytime," Teddy said, standing at her command.

Their hands were still interlocked, the tart's strawberry glaze slowly seeping out between their fingers. It made no difference. Man and woman stood frozen, gazing into each other's eyes with bewitched and idiotic expressions upon their faces.

"Alicia, stop this. You are making a spectacle of yourself!" Aunt Lillian whispered angrily.

"Teddy, dear," Chantel said, hoping for better success with Teddy, since the rapt Alicia was not responding to her mother's commands in any manner. "Do go and bring me another plate. That—that strawberry tart looks delicious." It seemed she heard a choking sound from Richard but when she glanced at him his face was stern. "I will help Alicia."

"Do not!" Aunt Lillian said, her face mottled with

indignation. "You Emberlys have done enough. I will help my daughter. Come, Alicia." Alicia still stood gazing into Teddy's eyes. "Alicia!" Alicia remained a blissful statue. "Oh, for heaven's sake, Alicia, come on," Aunt Lillian said in exasperation. She clutched Alicia's arm and jerked, pulling her daughter's hand from Teddy's.

The tart that had been captured in the infatuated couple's clasp gained freedom—and flight. The mangled pastry splattered onto Aunt Lillian's chest, one oversized strawberry oozing down into her cleavage.

"Oh, my Lord!" Aunt Lillian exclaimed, a shocked expression upon her face. Her hand flew to her chest reflexively, only crushing the sticky tart to her all the more. Chantel barely stifled a giggle. Aunt Lillian glared venom at her and stalked off. Uncle Thomas added another steely look and followed his dishevelled wife.

"Y-you'd better go," Teddy said to Alicia.

"Yes, yes—goodbye," Alicia stammered, and rushed after her parents.

"Isn't she the most beautiful woman you have ever seen?" Teddy said in a reverent tone, his hazel eyes following Alicia's disappearing form with worship.

"Er-yes, dear," Chantel said soothingly. "But I do think you should go and wash your hands."

Teddy looked down at his red-glazed hands and his eyes widened in surprise. "What-ho. How did that get there?" Without another glance at Richard or Chantel he wandered off, still musing at his hands.

Chantel finally permitted herself to laugh. Faith, what a scene that had been.

"That is not an alliance you should encourage," St. James said in a low voice.

Chantel's laughter died and she stiffened, the reality of the reception and her situation flooding back. "I would not think of encouraging such an alliance, my lord," she said smoothly, anger firing within her. "I find your family top-lofty and rude. And they all possess the same pompous trait; they foolishly imagine that everyone wishes to marry them, when in fact that is the farthest thing from the truth. Now if you will excuse me." Chantel spun from him and escaped before the odious man could say another word to her.

She walked amongst the crowd, trying to act as if she were a happy bride. Those of the St. James clan congregated together, creating a wall of disdain and smugness about them. The townsfolk veered away from them and gladly partook of the food and drink, gossiping and guffawing over the whole affair. Lightly veiled insults and heavy laden comments were the order of the day. Chantel's head was beginning to pound.

Aunt Beatrice approached her and Chantel sighed. Aunt's disapproving expression boded ill for all. "These St. James," she said without preamble, "all snobs. No manners, less sense. Can understand why you were crying during the wedding."

"I wasn't crying," Chantel said, affronted. "I have a cold."

"Hrumph, should be crying," Beatrice said firmly. "Never been so insulted in my life, and they are calling you worse."

Chantel's jaw stiffened. "Indeed. Now if you will

excuse me, Aunt." She turned and walked away. She thought to return to St. James' side as it was the proper thing to do, but as she approached him, she noticed he was encircled by all his kinfolk. They most likely were all commiserating with him upon his misfortune of marrying the nefarious Chantel Emberly.

Chantel suddenly swerved from her course and walked out of the reception room. She found a maid and asked to be led to her room. The maid took her directly to the gold room that she knew so well from her abduction.

How appropriate, Chantel thought dryly. She was back in the cage. Sneezing three times and sniffing once, she ruthlessly dragged the veil from her hair. The pins snagged and hurt her scalp, but as she rid herself of them and allowed her hair to fall unfettered, she felt immensely better. She felt closer to the Chantel Emberly of Covington's Folly who was accustomed to overcoming all the odds, even if they were ten to one. Oh dear, and that was why the St. Jameses did not approve of her. She was riddled, evidently, with the "Covington excesses"!

Chantel's miffed eyes suddenly fell upon a bottle of champagne ensconced within a bucket. Preparation for the romantic evening to come, no doubt. A grim smile cracked Chantel's lips. She walked slowly over to the bucket and hefted the bottle from it, eyeing it with a malicious look. If Lady Esther wanted to see some Covington excesses, then so be it. Chantel had never tasted champagne before, but surely it could help rid her of the miserable headache she had and help her forget her just as miserable situation.

She walked over to the chair and plunked down

within it. As she sniffed, her fingers worked the cork of the bottle. "Well, my lord St. James, the honeymoon has started . . . without you! And without your Mamma, of course." The cork popped loudly and the bottle steamed. Chantel lifted the bottle to her lips and took a full sip.

She closed her eyes as her mouth tingled with bubbles. Even her throat tingled as she swallowed. What a wicked sensation! She suddenly laughed and lifted the bottle high into the air. "Here's to the Covington excesses!"

Richard wearily fielded another snide comment from Cousin Cambric. Bored, he scanned the room as Cambric continued to rate upon the lack of breeding within his new wife's line. His new wife was nowhere to be seen. Richard frowned. Where was that red-headed danger?

He excused himself quickly from Cambric, who was just then delineating the debts of the Emberlys, and went in search of Teddy. "Teddy, do you know where Chantel is?" he asked as he located and approached him.

Teddy pondered a moment and then shook his head. "No, no, I don't. Thought I saw her leaving. Maybe she retired. Would make sense. Big day and all—indisposed, most likely." Teddy flushed as Richard's eyes darkened. "Ah—must be that it was too much for her; otherwise fine reception, fine reception."

"You do not lie well, Teddy," Richard said dryly. "Your sister is not indisposed, she merely deserted her own wedding reception."

Teddy coughed. "Probably best that she did." He

leaned over and whispered, "You wouldn't know, of course, but people are saying unkind things and it ain't in Chantel's line to accept insult well. Now you and me, we're men of the world, we know better than to take snuff. But not Chantel."

"Indeed," Richard said, his brow lowering even more.

"And must warn you, you being my brother-in-law and all, Chantel ain't easy when she's in a pelter. Don't want to rub up against her when she's that way. Best thing that she isn't here." Teddy's eyes were worried and it was apparent he was attempting to soothe Richard, but with every word from the well-meaning Teddy, Richard felt bolts of anger shoot through him.

"Very well, thank you, Teddy," Richard said tersely, and turned on his heel. So the temperamental Miss Emberly thought she did not have to attend her own wedding reception, did she? And she was not to be disturbed when she was displeased, was she? He was to tiptoe around her temper, was he? Well, they would see about that!

Richard reached the door of the gold bedroom in full steam. Miss Chantel Emberly would return to the reception and behave as befitted the Lady St. James. It was not as if he was enjoying himself at the reception, but he did not shirk his duty and run away in a tantrum. He rapped soundly on the bedroom door. "Chantel!"

"Go away," a voice called.

"Chantel, I want to talk to you, now open the door."

"Well I do not want to talk to you, sirrah! Now go away!"

Richard's fist beat a rapid tattoo upon the door. How dare she! "Chantel, open this door!"

"Noooo, I shall not! Begone, my lord!"

"Open the door, dammit!"

"Ohh, such language! Is that a St. James excess?" Chantel's voice trilled from the other side.

The little witch was taunting him, by God. An uncontrollable anger invaded Richard, an anger that he had never experienced before. "O-p-e-n t-h-e d-o-o-r," he enunciated slowly. All he heard was whistling, the very ditty that Chantel had used to entertain his mother.

Red flared before Richard's eyes and without thought, he stepped back and rushed the door, throwing the full strength of his broad shoulders against it. Wood cracked loudly as he burst through. He stumbled into the room, just barely righting himself from the velocity. He quickly grabbed the door that now hung on one hinge, half the jamb still clinging to the handle.

Chantel stood before him, her green eyes impossibly wide, her hair a tumbled flame against the white of her wedding dress. She stood immobile, as if frozen in time, and Richard knew that the vision of her at that moment would be frozen in time within his own memory.

Richard stiffened and tried to present a picture of dignity and decorum, no easy thing since his hand still rested upon the splintered wreckage of his temper. He strove for a controlled tone. "Now, madam, I will not tolerate being locked out of any room within my house." Chantel remained frozen, a shocked expression upon her face. He was beginning to feel like the beast she called him. "I-I promise I will never touch you . . ."

"Promise?" Her voice was quivering, her eyes suspiciously bright. Was she going to cry?

"Most certainly," Richard said stiffly. "I am a man of honor, after all. But I will not tolerate . . ."

"I know—being locked out!" And suddenly, amazingly, Chantel let out a peal of laughter! "Oh my, if you could only have seen your face" she giggled, "as you charged through that door! How funny! Like a bull on the rampage."

Richard glared at her dourly, yet Chantel would not be quelled and she giggled all the more. Her hand covered her mouth, but her twinkling green eyes could not be hidden. Then Richard studied her more carefully. That was when he noted the champagne bottle in her other hand. "By God, you are inebriated!"

"By God, so I am," Chantel said with a mock gasp. Her eyes glittered wickedly and she lifted the bottle high and waved it at him, "Here, Bull! Torro! Torro!"

"Thunderation," he exclaimed. "Give me that bottle!"

"Most certainly." Chantel smiled sweetly and traipsed dutifully up to him. She handed him the bottle, or rather he caught it as she swung it in his direction. "Have it!" she said, her tone magnanimous. She twirled away. "I have another one. 'Tis very medicinal for a cold, I have discovered. It has rid me of my headache! And I don't sneeze anymore."

Richard's brows shot up. His temporary wife was proving a permanent surprise. "What?"

His inebriated bride danced across the room and stopping at a chair, promptly bent over. Richard was welcomed to a view of a trim, satined posterior. She came up, however, swinging another bottle of champagne. "See! I asked the maid for it." Chantel giggled, but then she pokered up, her back ramrod straight. She said, in a perfect imitation of his mother's tones, "I am indulging in a Covington excess, you see. 'Tis something you St. Jameses never ever dooooo. You St. Jameses do not even sneeze, I am sure!" Her tones and face were such a fine depiction of his mother on her high ropes that a laugh escaped Richard despite himself.

"Very good," he said. "You have her down completely, and in such short time."

"Ahh, 'tis because I am such a crafty little minx," Chantel said, wagging her finger at him. "I have nef—nefarious designs upon you. *Ach-chu!*"

"Oh?" Richard could not hide the amusement in his voice.

"Yes," she nodded soundly, blinking. "Your Uncle Bertram said so—said it to your other relative—Cambric, I think his name is. The one with the spots. And you know, Uncle Bertram knows these things!" she nodded sagely. "You can't bamboozle him! No indeed. He knows a doxy when he sees one." She cocked her head to one side in consideration. "Hmm, where does he get such experience, I wonder? And is it truly wise to boast of such experience with the muslin company?" She frowned. "Yes, yes that is the term he used, I believe. Oh well, cheers to Uncle Bertram's experience." Chantel lifted the bottle and attempted to drink. Her face was a study in confusion when she

realized it was still corked. She glared at the bottle
reproachfully and went and sat down in a chair. She
applied herself to the cork exclusively.

Richard sighed and asked, "Would you like me to
do that for you?" His bride was already foxed, and
since there was nothing he could do at this juncture he
might as well let her have her way. Trying to detain her
from more drinking would have been very much like
closing the doors after the cows were out of the barn.
There was nothing to do but sit back and possibly
enjoy himself.

"No, no. I shall overcome," Chantel said slowly, her
eyes and fingers fumbling with the cork. Her expression of severe concentration caused Richard to
chuckle. She tugged and pulled at the cork. Then she
tried to grip it in her teeth.

Intrigued by her machinations, Richard walked quietly over and sat down in the chair next to Chantel's.
Grinning, he sipped from his own champagne bottle.

"Drat," Chantel muttered. She opened her legs and
clasped the champagne bottle between silk-clad knees.

Richard choked on his champagne. Very improper
thoughts suddenly rushed through his mind. "Elegant,
my lady," he observed dryly.

"I am not elegant," Chantel said with a grunt as she
tugged determinedly upon the bottle's cork. "I am a
Covington!" The cork flew off at that moment with an
explosive pop. It bulleted across the room and
smashed into the dresser's mirror, a crack running
along the glass in its aftermath. Champagne fizzled
over the mouth of the bottle. Chantel squeaked and
grabbed up the bottle, capping the neck with her
mouth, attempting to drink the gushing fountain.

Richard fell back against the chair and roared with laughter. "Do you do this often?"

Chantel drew the bottle away and grinned impishly at him as she wiped the champagne from her lips. "I've just started. I would not wish to fail to live up—er down, that is—to your family's expectations of me, after all."

Richard frowned slightly. He drank swiftly from his bottle. "They were at their worst today, I fear." He studied the cracked mirror, then nodded toward it. "Seven years bad luck."

Chantel squinted at the mirror and then giggled. "Or maybe only six months."

"Vixen," Richard said, without heat. The champagne was beginning to course through him, washing out the vexations of the day, shading everything in a more humorous light. Yes, he might as well just enjoy himself. He laughed. "Faith, what a tortuous day. I believe we should go back down to the reception. Our guests are waiting for us."

"Why? I do not care to be their joint of mutton to chew on."

"Mutton? No, no, my dear. You are now a St. James. And we St. Jameses must be considered something better than mutton. We are at least beef."

"And not fowl?" Chantel countered.

Richard's brow shot up imperiously. "You are the chicken that ran from the reception, are you not?"

"And I shall not go back." She sighed, and suddenly fell back against the cushions of her chair, allowing her head to loll casually. Her legs were stretched before her and she clutched the bottle to her side. A part of Richard was slightly shocked at her posture, but another part enjoyed seeing a woman act so comfortably and naturally around a man. "If we stay away long enough, perhaps our kith and kin will kill each other and our worries will be over."

"But the St. Jameses outnumber yours two to one."

"I have the townsfolk on my side," she giggled. "Besides, Aunt Beatrice will be good for at least a dozen or so herself." Then she laughed more heartily. "Faith, perhaps we should go down, I want to see Aunt Beatrice go up against your mother. Won't the fur fly then."

"Oh, Lord, yes." Richard laughed. "It is sure to be a bloody battle—" A female shriek suddenly rent the air.

Richard shot up in his seat and looked to the bedroom door, from whence it arose. A maid stood within the portal's entry, a wide-eyed, shocked expression upon her face. "What the devil do you want?"

The maid's eyes were scared, and he noticed they kept flickering between the door hanging drunkenly on its one hinge, and the bureau with its shattered mirror. "I—I came to see if my lady n-needed anything."

"My lady doesn't need anything," Richard said irately, for the maid was then gaping at the relaxed, sprawled Chantel who hadn't bothered even to look her way. "You may leave us. No, wait. Bring us another bottle . . ."

Chantel did raise her head at that. She shook it in negation, a sparkle in her eyes. She pointed to the side of the chair where she had unearthed her bottle and raised her hand to him, holding up three fingers. Richard's eyes widened and he chuckled. "Never mind. It appears my lady is well fortified and er ... entrenched. We shall not need anything for the rest of the night. You are dismissed."

The little maid gulped and sketched a harried curtsey before fleeing, an expression of shock upon her face as if she had just witnessed a Roman orgy. Richard grimaced, but then his attention went directly back to Chantel. "I see you are a woman of resource, my lady."

"My lady, my lady," Chantel parroted. She looked at him with a droll expression. "Faith, I must practice my top-loftiness." She sneezed vociferously. "Hmm, need more medicine," she mumbled, and drank swiftly from the bottle.

Richard waved a negligent hand at her. The champagne was going to his head, but he found he did not care. "Just employ that imitation of my mother and you will have no trouble. You will be able to stare even the most polished out of countenance."

"Even the king, I would imagine."

"Watch it, my dear, that is treasonous."

Chantel groaned. "Oh no, and that's what got us into this mess."

Surprised, Richard realized that at this moment, this "mess" was not so dreadful. He shook his head; he must be bosky. "Perhaps things won't be as bad as they seem."

Chantel had been drinking from her bottle, and she all but choked. She shook her head and blinked her eyes. She cast him a stern glance as she sat up rigidly. "Oh no?" Her tone changed to that of his mother. "This marriage is a misalliance, do not you know?"

"Ah, but mother doesn't know that you have prospects." Richard wagged a finger at her, wishing to take her mind off the insults of the day. He wanted her happy and bubbly again.

"Prospects?" Chantel's face was totally befuddled. She sniffed. "I have prospects?"

"Yes. You have the Covington treasure," he leaned in and whispered. "That's truly the reason I wanted this marriage. I fooled you, but not Teddy, you know."

Chantel's expression was shocked, and then it shimmered with delighted amusement. "Oh yes, how could I forget the treasure. I am a woman of prospects—a woman of substance. And you, my lord, are a villain . . ."

Richard frowned and Chantel's voice trailed away. They stared at each other. Richard felt a surge of some unknown emotion, an emotion that caused him to want to lean over and kiss the disheveled woman before him. It was the first time she had called him a villain with laughter in her voice and not anger. She was still staring at him wide-eyed. He saw her catch her breath. Lord, he wanted to kiss her. And then she would call him a villain again, but not with laughter. He shook himself firmly and looked away. "Just what, pray tell, is this treasure that I have married you for?"

He heard a small sigh from Chantel. Was it of relief? She laughed then, and he looked at her. Her eyes were a deep emerald green, and glowed. "What? You didn't secure the full information upon it before you married me? Tsk, tsk, very rash, my lord. The Covington treasure is emeralds and diamonds." She rose softly and walked slowly toward him. "It is priceless paintings, silver and gold, satin and pearls. All hidden."

She was spellbinding as she stood before him. "All that?" he asked, finding his voice sounded husky. "How came you to lose such?"

"Lady Genevieve hid it," Chantel whispered, and she knelt down in front of him, leaning her face close his. "They say I look like her. They also say she was a witch!"

Richard stared into her sparkling green eyes before him, her russet tresses tumbling around her shoulders, and he attempted to control his breathing. "I can believe that," he said softly.

Chantel fell back to the floor, laughing. She wore a woman's bridal gown, but she looked very much like a delighted child upon the floor. "Great-great-Grandfather believed it too." Her face was devilish. "But he called Great-great-Grandmama a few names other than that, I assure you."

"I have no doubt," Richard said dryly. He offered her his bottle, totally intrigued by the story. "But why did she hide it?"

Chantel grimaced. "The Covington excesses your dear Mamma talks about. Sir Alex . . . was a gambler, like all the Covington men. Lady Genevieve did not like this, so she took all the treasure and hid it. Hid it somewhere within the walls of Covington's Folly."

"You are roasting me!"

"No. And then she entailed it to only the women in the line."

"So you own Covington's Folly?"

"Yes, I do."

"Faith, I did not know your prospects."

"Ah, but Lady Genevieve . . . this is where the witch part comes in—"

"Strange, I thought it already had."

She cast him a stern glance. "She swore no Covington male would ever find the treasure. Only a Covington woman would, and only after the stain of gambling was washed from the Covington line forever." Chantel leaned over and rested her head upon his knee, her green eyes misty from the effects of the champagne. "Do you gamble, my lord?"

"No," Richard shook his head. "I don't find it entertaining."

Chantel sighed gustily. "Oh dear. 'Tis a shame we aren't truly married. You could be the one to lift the curse."

His hand, of its own volition, lifted and smoothed her hair. It was silky beneath his touch. "But we are married."

"For six months," Chantel said. "That won't fadge. I'd doubt Lady Genevieve would be taken in. She wasn't a fool in her time and I doubt death has made her any less canny."

Richard smiled. "Madam, are you proposing to me?" Chantel's eyes widened and then she hauled off and cracked him on the knee. "Ouch!"

"Serves you right, coxcomb," she said tartly. She crawled away and slowly rose. She swayed before him—was it actually she, or merely his vision? "Besides," she said imperiously, "I do not believe in the treasure." She laughed. "But faith, wouldn't it be grand to find it. Now *that* would tweak your Mamma's nose."

"Indeed. She would hate it."

Chantel's face took on a dreamy expression. "Can you imagine me dripping in emeralds and diamonds?"

Richard smiled as the hazy vision of the woman before him changed. He saw a large collar of emeralds and diamonds upon her neck. Rings of inordinate beauty were suddenly upon her fingers. "Damn," he murmured. He blinked hard. The vision was gone and the rumpled Chantel stood before him awaiting his reply. Very slowly, he set the bottle away from him. That was certainly enough for him. "I fear I can," he said, swallowing.

Chantel laughed and curtsied low to him. Actually it was a wobble, dive, and dip. "Thank you, my lord." She snagged in her hem as she rose, and a deep frown crossed her face. She started to squirm and tug at her dress.

"What is the matter with you?" Richard asked as she unaccountably began to hop around.

"This dress. I don't like it. I want it off!"

She said it in such an imperious tone that Richard laughed. Chantel was now stretching her arm behind her back, gyrating in a frenzied manner. "Stop that!"

"But I want it off!"

"If you don't stop that soon, it will be I that takes it off!"

Chantel halted abruptly and looked at him with hope. "Oh, could you? I'd be forever grateful."

Richard stared at the expectant woman. She was looking at him with large, trusting green eyes as if he were her savior. Richard immediately picked up the champagne bottle. Perhaps he hadn't had enough yet.

"Please. I want it off."

Richard took a hearty swig. Chantel began her hopping again. "All right, all right!" Richard said swiftly. Sighing, he set the bottle down and rose. The room swirled and, with Chantel hopping about, his balance was extremely challenged. "Chantel," he gritted, "stop that and turn around." Chantel stopped dutifully and turned. Richard numbly walked up to her and peered at an infinite row of small pearl buttons. "Gads! You are encased. A veritable citadel. Nothing to do." He turned back to his chair. "You'll have to live in it!"

"But I want it off," Chantel pleaded.

"Oh, very well," Richard sighed, unable to withstand her tone. He turned back to her. Breathing in deeply like a man girding himself for battle, he reached toward the dress with grim determination. He brushed Chantel's hair away from the top button, and the silken skeins snagged upon his signet ring. He tried to loosen it but only entangled his hand all the more.

"Ouch, ouch, ouch! What are you doing!"

"I can't get out of your hair," Richard complained.

Chantel began to giggle. "That does seem to be the truth.

"Ungrateful wench," Richard muttered, still twisting his hand away from her tresses. "Ah ha! Now," he said firmly. His fingers went to the first button. He leaned forward, peering at it. Chantel swayed. "Stay still," he commanded.

"I am still," Chantel said, outraged.

"You are not. You are swaying,"

"Am not," was the vehement reply.

Richard blinked and held the button firmly in his grasp. Chantel swayed. "Dammit, stop swaying."

"I'm not swaying. It must be you. I am standing perfectly still." Suddenly, Chantel hiccupped. "Oh my!"

"Correct," Richard said, feeling well vindicated. He

tried the button again, but the traitorous little thing would not be undone. He was getting a headache. "Can't do it!"

"But I want it off. It's sooo heavy."

Richard glared at the button, deep in concentration. Wait!" he grinned. He was not going to be undone by a button. He gripped the material at the top of the dress and ripped with all his might. Buttons bounced and ricocheted about them.

"Oh! You tore it!"

"You're free, aren't you?" Richard said, pleased with his victory.

"But the dress!"

"It's too heavy anyway," Richard said. He suddenly felt extremely fatigued from his efforts. He turned and went back to his chair.

"Must be nice," Chantel said in a musing tone. She was weaving toward the dressing screen. She disappeared behind it.

"What is nice?"

"That you can rip expensive dresses without com-compunc—com—er—thought."

" 'Tis the pleasure of being an earl, madam." He leaned his head back against the chair cushion. Faith, the furniture was moving itself about. "That is why most women wish to marry earls. They do not whistle at their mothers."

"Well, I do."

"I know." He grinned. "But that's because you have a treasure in your Folly, don't you! 'Course," he said teasingly, "you need to marry a proper man, one who does not gamble." There was silence. "I think you should treat me with far more respect than you have, don't you?"

The screen shook. "Never!"

Richard was thoroughly enjoying himself. "What a girl. You wh-whistle an earldom away and the family treasure, both."

The screen rocked and teetered. "I don't care—I will never marry. Men are—damn—are not worth any—huff—anything. Oh-h-h no!" It was a wail. Then, ominous silence.

"Chantel?" More silence. "Chantel?"

"Could—could you come here, my lord?" It was a small, muted voice.

Richard frowned. "Why must you always call me 'my lord.' My name is Richard."

"Please, my lord?"

"What is my name?"

"Richard, would you please assist me?"

Richard grinned. Faith, he had not expected to have so much fun upon his wedding night. He pulled himself out of the chair and dizziness hit him.

"Please, I—I believe I am going to suff—focate." Her voice was weak.

"Faith," Richard exclaimed, stumbling forward as fast as he could. Was she suffering an attack of some sort? Was she dying while he had been funning and teasing her? He spun around the screen, his heart pounding.

He froze. Chantel was headless, and in place of her were mounds of silk. She had evidently attempted to pull her dress over her head and become stuck. Richard had a view of slim, pantalooned legs and hips, and billowing silk from there on up. "Hmm, this could have possibilities."

"Help!" came the muffled reply. "And don't look."

"Too late for that," Richard said and sighed. " 'Tis a shame I am a gentleman."

"Gentleman, my—"

"Tsk, tsk," Richard admonished, "You need my help, remember. Evidently we men are worth something, madam." He reached forward and searched through the folds until he gained a hold of the dress's hem. He pulled. A moan came from the folds, but the dress did not budge. "Wedged, for sure. You'll have to live in it," he said, shaking his head.

"Help!" came the muffled response.

Richard grasped the folds and said, "Trying again." He tugged; a squeak came from Chantel; he tugged again; an "Ouch" came from her. He gripped the material and jerked it with mighty force. A ripping sound rent the air and suddenly he was stumbling backward at high velocity with masses of silk cloaking his face. He tripped and plummeted to the carpet. Cursing and muttering, he fought with the cloying silk. Was the thing alive?

He could hear delighted laughter through the folds. "That is a fine sight," he heard Chantel say. "To see the very proper Earl of Hartford on the floor with a dress over his head. What would Mamma say now, I wonder?"

Growling, he successfully dragged the dress from his head and heaved a quick, deep breath. "Damn, almost done in by a dress," he wheezed. His eyes narrowed. Chantel, no matter how tipsy, had repositioned the screen again. He could see nothing. "Fine thanks I receive," he muttered.

"Finally, I am free," Chantel's voice caroled. A corset flew over the screen and landed a distance from Richard. Shaking his head, he crawled to a standing position. A petticoat came flying past him. Chantel was indeed divesting herself of her clothes with vigor.

"Remember, old man," he hiccupped to himself, "not a real wedding night." He stumbled to the bed and threw himself upon it. Lord, he wished his head would stop dancing.

"Ohh, I feel much better," Chantel chirped.

"I don't," Richard muttered, forcing himself to ignore his thoughts as another petticoat flew over the screen. "Aren't you finished?"

"I am now," Chantel said, and he heard a deep sigh come from behind the screen. He smiled in spite of himself. "I am coming out now. And don't peek!"

"I won't," he lied most convincingly. Chantel emerged from behind the screen very hesitantly. Richard's eyes widened. She wore the ugliest nightgown he had ever seen. "Faith, I did not order that," he exclaimed, forgetting himself.

"You peeked!"

"No, I am looking, but with that monstrosity it does not matter. I could not have chosen that, forsooth."

"No, you didn't," Chantel said pugnaciously, crossing to the bed. "I did not want to wear the one you sent me. I wanted to wear mine."

"Faith," Richard said, shaken, as she sat down upon the bed. "You'd best find that treasure so that you can dress in something other than that!"

"I dress for myself," Chantel said, "and not for

anyone else—especially a man." She fell back against the pillows.

"Tis evident."

She turned her head to him, and he could tell that she was forcing her eyes to remain open. "This is my bedroom, isn't it?"

"Yes."

"Then this is my bed. You must go and find your own."

Drink evidently did not make Chantel Emberly polite. He thought of his room, way down at the end of the hall. He had purposely arranged it that way, thinking he did not want his room anywhere near hers. Now it seemed a great distance. He groaned. "My bed's a mile off."

Chantel's eyes were fluttering shut. "Oh, a mile. 'Tis a long way. Be . . . st-stay here . . . next time." She sighed. "You find . . . it."

Richard watched blearily as Chantel drifted into sleep. "Good hearted," he sighed, and then shook his head. "What a wedding night." He shifted to a more comfortable position, thought a moment, and reached over to pull Chantel into his arms. Fast asleep, she rolled into them willingly and even snuggled closer with a sigh. He buried his head in her hair, breathed deeply of her light scent, and closed his eyes. The softest of smiles traced his lips. "Yes, what a wedding night."

Chapter Five

Chantel was dancing, twirling around and around in Richard St. James' arms. Only he was a different St. James, one who looked at her with love and respect in his eyes. He and she were laughing. He pulled her close, so very close. He whispered something in her ear. What was he whispering? She could feel his warm breath upon her ear, feel the strength of his arms about her, but she could not hear what he was saying.

That was when Chantel realized she was dreaming. She surfaced to consciousness. Strange, it seemed as if she could still feel Richard's arms about her, his breath upon her ear. Disoriented, Chantel slowly cracked her eyes open.

An onslaught of the most unpleasant sensations hit her. Her mouth felt fuzzy and her stomach . . . Oh my, her stomach! Why did it churn so? And her head, why did it pound so? It couldn't just be her cold. Then Chantel remembered. Oh dear, all that champagne!

An even more shocking realization intruded upon her queasy consciousness. She was not alone in her bed! Richard St. James was with her. He had her back snugly drawn up against him, his large hand spanning her rib cage, fingers brushing just beneath her breasts. Chantel could feel his powerful thighs backing her as they lay spoon fashion. His lips were almost to her ear, his face buried within her hair.

"Move, Chantel," her conscience and modesty demanded. Yet her champagne-laden body did not want to budge. Her head was whirling and her stomach was roiling. She couldn't move. Faith, why did she have to? The only pleasant sensation amongst the horrible ones was the comfort of St. James' arms. Yet her conscience would not desist, nor would it permit her to lie in that haven. It ruthlessly forced memories of the evening before into her reluctant mind. Heavens, she had allowed St. James to help her undress! She had not kicked him from her bed. Even now she didn't really object to his presence, which was not good, for they had an annulment to achieve . . .

That thought finally forced her to move. Chantel slowly withdrew St. James' hand from her ribs. She slowly, painfully pulled her hair from beneath his face and slid out of the bed, literally. She thumped to the floor and quickly squeezed her eyes shut as her world capsized. Shaking, she pulled herself to a standing position. "Oh dear Lord," she prayed, "help me through this terrible torture." But then she thought again. Perhaps it wasn't proper to call on the Almighty when one suffered the aftereffects of drink.

She gazed a moment at the sleeping St. James. Oh, most fortunate of men. He was still blissfully unconscious, while she was not. Chantel sighed and tottered to the armiore. She fully intended to dress herself today. She certainly did not wish for a maid to view

her in this condition or take note that St. James rested
in her bed. It was all too embarrassing! Indeed, it was
positively shocking!

Chantel sat morosely in lone state at the breakfast
table. Her fingers curled themselves desperately
around a hot cup of tea. The warmth of it was the only
benign sensation amongst those assailing her. Platters
of food sat about her, and Chantel felt as if she were
surrounded by an enemy army. The thought of food
was obscene. If she so much as glimpsed the platters,
her stomach churned. In truth, she felt as green as the
willows embossed on the wallpaper. Certainly no Covington would elect to furnish a morning room in
shades of celadon and cream.

She sipped the hot tea and let it trickle down her
throat. Oh, did her head hurt! This drinking business
was a hazardous thing. She would most certainly have
to find a different Covington excess in which to indulge.

The door to the breakfast room opened and Chantel
cringed. Was it the earl? She was not sure she could
face him now in the light of day. She sighed with relief
as not the master, but the butler, entered.

"Your cousin and aunt are here, my lady. Do you
wish me to direct them to the parlor?"

Chantel sighed again. Today was going to be difficult. "No, no, tell them to come here . . . and please
bring them extra settings."

He bowed. "Yes, my lady."

"My lady," Chantel muttered dismally into her tea.
"I'm not a Lady." She groaned. "I'm not even sure
I'm human."

"Chantel, what happened last night?" Chad asked, even as he entered the room. He was meticulously dressed in a fawn jacket and robin's egg-blue inexpressables. Chantel blinked and came very close to hating her beloved cousin at that moment. He looked too darn bright and neat, while the best she could hope for was that she was buttoned correctly.

"Nothing at all," mumbled Chantel. "Why?"

"Why?" said Aunt Beatrice entering, a dark squat cloud behind her son. "Because you didn't come back to your own wedding reception, is why."

"Oh."

Chad took up a chair next to her. "You certainly have them all speculating," he chuckled. "First you disappeared, and then St. James. The St. Jameses were scandalized. They thought you two couldn't even wait until the reception was over to consummate the marriage."

"If you hadn't consummated the marriage before that," Aunt Beatrice grunted, taking up the next chair. "Most just thought it rude."

"Mother," Chad said warningly. He eyed Chantel, who refused to look at him. "What is the matter? You look terrible."

"It's nothing," Chantel said weakly, "I-I'm just a bit indisposed. A cold, you know."

"Indisposed? Humph!" Aunt Beatrice's eyes were sharp upon her. "Looks more like you're suffering the consequences of indulging in too much champagne."

Chad studied her and then his eyes lightened and he laughed loudly. "By Gad! She is!"

"Hush," Chantel said quickly. "You needn't be so loud."

"Oh, excuse me," he whispered wickedly. "Does your head hurt frightfully?"

Chantel glared at Chad, but his knowing smile was too much and she nodded wryly. "Yes, yes it does, you beast."

"Serves you right," Aunt Beatrice said callously. "Drink has led many to ruin . . ."

"Mother, we came to see how Chantel's condition was," Chad chided, even as he winked at Chantel, "not to worsen it."

"Thank you," Chantel said gratefully. "How . . . how was the reception after . . . er, I left."

"Oh, quite jolly, to tell you the truth," Chad said. "Until then the facade of civility was being upheld." Chantel snorted inelegantly. "But with neither you nor the Earl present, they all let it fly."

"Those St. Jameses are nothing but court-cards and coxcombs," Aunt Beatrice said. "All jumped-up nobodies. And that Lady Esther, why she is nothing."

"Mother, don't speak treason," Chad exclaimed. "The St. Jameses are the highest *ton,* and very powerful."

"They don't frighten me," Aunt Beatrice said stoutly.

"And you, Chantel?" Chad asked more seriously. "Do they frighten you?"

"No," Chantel said, her chin lifting.

"Even Richard St. James?"

An image of Richard St. James sprawled on the floor with her wedding dress draped over his head floated before Chantel's eyes. She smiled slightly. "No, no he doesn't. Not anymore."

"No?" Chad asked. It looked as if he wished to

speak, and then Reed entered with a maid. They remained quiet as the extra settings were placed and the maid poured the tea. As they left, Chad slowly stirred sugar into his tea. "Where was St. James last night, by the way?"

"What do you mean?" Chantel asked cautiously.

"When he left the reception, do you know where he went?"

Chantel flushed, not knowing why she should. "He—he came to see if I was all right."

"That was all?" Chad's eyes had darkened.

"Of course," Chantel said swiftly. Never in her life had she felt reticent in telling Chad anything. Yet there was a worry and almost a fear in his eyes. Knowing Chad's feelings toward her, Chantel realized that she could no longer tell him everything. "Now can we talk about something else?"

"You let him seduce you," Aunt Beatrice suddenly said, her tone accusatory.

Chantel's cup clattered to her saucer. "I did not! We . . . we merely had a glass of champagne . . ."

"Got drunk and he had his way with you," Aunt Beatrice said with disgust.

"He did not!" Chantel said, stunned. Her chin lifted. "But if that had happened, it would be my affair and none of yours."

"Of course," Chad said swiftly. "But you can't blame us if we are concerned, Chantel. Richard St. James is far out of your league. Please remember he only married you to protect his name. He would never remain married to you, his family will never support it. St. James can and will look high for his wife, I assure you."

Why was everyone so determined to bully that fact into her, Chantel wondered bitterly. Her head began to pound. She gritted her teeth. "If I have to hear one more person cast me as the ragtag woman who can't even shine St. James' boots, I shall scream. I declare, I should help Teddy find the blasted treasure . . . and then what would you say!"

"I would say bravo," Chad said with a wide grin. "Just remember your poor relations when you do." He held up his tea cup. "Alms, my lady, alms for a beggar."

Chantel laughed and then winced. "Stupid!"

"There isn't any treasure," Aunt Beatrice said, her eyes angry. "You won't be able to catch St. James that way."

"Faith, you are as bad as his mother," Chantel groaned. "I was only funning. I do not wish to be married to St. James. I am only doing this for . . . for honor's sake. That is all!"

Aunt Beatrice looked sceptically at her, while Chad studied her and then smiled. "All right. I just don't want to see you hurt."

"I won't be hurt," Chantel said pugnaciously. "Do you think I will fall in love with a man who—who basically blackmailed me into marriage?"

"Yes," Aunt Beatrice said baldly. "You're like your mother. Don't have any sense when it comes to men."

"Oh, lud," Chantel said, shaking her head. "I have never been like my mother or I would have married the first gambler I came across when I was out of the schoolroom. I would most certainly not be the spinster that I am. Or was . . ."

"You've got your mother's blood," Aunt Beatrice

said, as if decreeing her a victim of the plague. "Know you have."

"Stuff," Chantel said, narrowing her eyes.

"I believe we should go now," Chad said swiftly. "Before Chantel throws you out on your ear, Mother." He rose. "I am sorry, dearest, we didn't mean to come here and harangue you." He looked at Aunt Beatrice, who was still firmly planted in the chair, an angry look trained upon Chantel. "Mother!"

She looked up at him. "What?"

"Come, we are going to leave now," Chad said with finality. He sent a hopeless shrug in Chantel's direction.

"Very well," Aunt Beatrice said, rising. She steamed toward the door. "But she's thrown her hat over the windmill for St. James, and you can't fool me. Nothing but tragedy will come from it."

Chad stared after his mother and turned to look sadly at Chantel, who was staring at her departing aunt with indignation. "Nothing could come of it, Chantel," he repeated softly.

Chantel turned fuming eyes to him. *"Et tu,* Brute? I am going to clear Teddy's name and that is all. Richard St. James means nothing to me. And as for last night . . ." She swallowed. "Nothing happened."

Chad's smile was wry. "Methinks thou doth protest too much, my dear." He turned and left the breakfast room quietly. Chantel dropped her head into her hands. She cared nothing about St. James. She was totally innocent! Why did no one believe her?

It seemed that she had not taken one more sip of her tepid tea when the butler entered again. "What is it now, Reed?" Chantel asked wearily.

"Your brother, my lady."

"Oh, no," Chantel groaned. "Let him in."

"Good morning, Sister," Teddy said exuberantly, bursting into the room. His sister glared at Teddy's cherry pink and chartreuse waistcoat as a multitude of watch fobs clanged at a pitch that, to her troubled ears, could only be compared to an advancing army—one suited in full armor plate, no less.

"What is so good about it?" Chantel asked grumpily. "And please, keep your voice down."

Teddy looked swiftly around. "Why? Who's listening?" he whispered, taking up the seat next to her. His whisper was as loud as his speaking voice, and even more irritating.

"Oh, never mind," Chantel said irately. "I just have a headache this morning."

"Oh," he said. His eyes fell upon the food. "You going to eat that?"

"No, no," Chantel gulped. "Help yourself."

Teddy proceeded to take up Chad's untouched plate and scrape food onto it. Chantel winced, attempting not to watch the proceedings. Teddy shoveled a large spoonful of eggs into his mouth and looked at Chantel in concern. "Will you be all right? What ho, these eggs are grand."

Chantel looked away as Teddy swallowed his mouthful. She was striving not to become nauseated. "What brings you here so early?"

Teddy stopped his chewing, thankfully, but the odd, luminous look in his hazel eyes suddenly caused Chantel even more unrest. "It's happened, Chantel."

"What has happened?"

"I am in love."

Chantel stared at Teddy. He had a silly, bovine, look upon his face. Teddy was not one to be in the petticoat line and to suddenly see him acting the moonling was shocking. "You are?"

"Isn't she the most beautiful, the sweetest girl you've ever seen?"

"Who?" Chantel asked cautiously, praying that she did not know the answer.

"Alicia." Teddy said her name with a reverence that befitted a saint.

"Oh, no," Chantel moaned.

"What? Is your headache worse?" Teddy asked solicitously.

"No, just my life," Chantel said under her breath. She eyed Teddy. "Dearest, you know there is no hope for you with Alicia. Even if she cares for you . . ."

"She does, she does!"

"How would you know?" "

"She told me so last night."

Chantel stared. "When?"

Teddy looked shamefaced. "We—we met in the library when her parents were not looking."

Chantel's cup clattered to her saucer once more. "What!"

"Well, her mother wouldn't let us get near each other, so when no one was looking she slipped out and I followed her, of course."

"I can't believe it," Chantel said softly. The thought was amazing. That Alicia, that shy little mouse, would do such a sly thing, and that Teddy—Teddy—had pursued her. Chantel shook her head, attempting to clear it.

"I know it ain't proper," Teddy sighed. "But when

you are in love—can't do the proper thing. Surprising thing, but you just can't be proper. It just don't work with someone you love."

"I see," Chantel murmured, still befuddled. Her brother Teddy was actually offering her a speech about love!

"But it's grand, Chantel."

"Teddy," Chantel shook her head. "You have just met Alicia, how can you both think you are in love?"

"Don't think, Sister . . . I know," Teddy said, his tone once again sounding mystical. "It hit me just like a thunderclap! Alicia said the same thing. That's how it is."

Chantel stared at Teddy. His hazel eyes shone and his face beamed. "Oh dear," she said sadly. "Teddy, you know Alicia's parents will never permit a match between the two of you."

Teddy's face didn't seem to change. "But I'll find the treasure and then they'll accept me."

"Teddy, dearest, that might take years and years." She reached out her hands to him. "Couldn't you perhaps forget her?"

He shook his head. "Couldn't, not now that I've met her."

Chantel sighed. "Very well, let me think on it. I don't know what to say, but let me think on it."

He beamed. "Knew you'd help. She's the best and she loves me too." He rose. "I'll leave you now. Going to meet with Neddy. He has a new notion for the treasure."

"Fine, just don't tear the house down," Chantel said morosely.

Teddy shook his head. "No, wouldn't do that! And

don't worry, Chantel. Things will work out. I mean, love always works out." With this cheerful and terribly simple comment Teddy bounced from the room.

Chantel dropped her head into her hands once more. She had a cousin and an aunt who didn't want her to have anything to do with the St. Jameses. She had a brother who now wished to marry into the St. James line. They had no finances, and a cloud of suspicion hung over them! Life was becoming much too complicated for her. And oh, did her head hurt!

"I am appalled," Lady Esther said dramatically as she slammed into the library and Richard's presence. "Utterly appalled!"

Richard looked up from the letter he was attempting to read. "What appalls you now, Mother?"

"Your licentious behavior with that trollop," Lady Esther said, alighting upon the chair before him and then pokering up until she looked like a statue.

Richard suddenly remembered Chantel's imitation of her. He smiled, despite his aching head.

"Well?"

Richard frowned, forcing himself back to the present. "What are you talking about?"

"Don't pretend with me," Lady Esther said, her foot tapping. " 'Tis all over the house . . . and the town, no doubt."

"What is?" Richard asked again, attempting not to wince at her tone.

"Your behavior with that hussy! If it wasn't bad enough that you deserted your own wedding reception, then you and that infamous woman have such a scandalous night that it has every proper person shocked!"

"I may be wrong," Richard said mildly, feeling definitely at a loss to understand his mother's conversation, "but I would hazard a guess that the infamous woman of whom you speak is Chantel?"

"Of course!" Lady Esther's eyes were frigid. "Don't try to avoid the subject."

"I am not. I am only trying to understand the subject."

"Well! Evidently you understood your subject extremely well last night." Lady Esther's voice dripped acid.

Richard stilled. "And what does that mean?"

"It means that if you had to bed the Jezebel . . ."

"What?"

"You should not have made such a display. Faith, the door broken, the room in shambles, champagne bottles and clothes strewn everywhere, the wedding dress ripped . . ." Lady Esther closed her eyes. "No, I do not want to even consider what depraved behavior you engaged in . . ." She stopped, incoherent.

"It sounds to me as if you have considered nothing else but that," Richard said dryly. "Faith, I never knew you had such a lurid imagination, Mother."

"Stop it! I am no green girl, even the most naive could tell what happened . . ."

"You are wrong," Richard said sharply. "What happened did not involve my bedding Chantel."

"Please." Lady Esther raised her hand. "There is no need to deny it, for I shall not believe you. I only hope you realize what position you have put the family in. We will now have to pay a great deal to be shod of the woman, and if you have made her with child . . . well, the sum will be outrageous!"

Richard stared at his mother. "Do you truly believe that if I got Chantel with child I would then cast her off? You are mistaken, Mother. I am a man of honor!"

"Men of honor do not align themselves with the likes of Chantel Emberly," Lady Esther hissed.

"Why? Her family is of the peerage and well connected, and yet you act as if she were base born."

"The Covingtons are of the peerage but that does not mean their bloodline is acceptable. The Covingtons have always been wild, undisciplined, dissolute! Their whole history is a scandal."

"Especially since they have no money," Richard said sarcastically.

"They brought that on themselves," Lady Esther retorted. She drew in a deep breath. " 'Tis no matter, it surely must be clear to you that a St. James, and indeed, the head of the St. James house, could never align with an Emberly. You simply must not be drawn into that siren's clutches."

"I am not," Richard said stiffly. "But I will also not allow you to malign Chantel while she is under my roof."

"I beg your pardon!"

"You heard me. You will no longer call her hussy, Jezebel, or anything else. You shall treat her with respect while she is my wife."

"She has seduced you!" Lady Esther rose majestically, shaking with rage. "That you could speak to me that way. That you should defend that . . ."

"Mother," Richard's voice was dangerous, "don't say it."

Lady Esther stood, her eyes shooting daggers. She then lifted her head. "I see how it shall be. Well, I shall not stand by while you cavort with that hussy. You have six months to come to your senses and the duty you owe your family. By then, no doubt, we will have to pay the tart an extreme amount, but it will be worth it. Until then . . ." she paused for dramatic effect, "I am leaving and do not wish to see you."

"Very well, Mother," Richard said softly.

"What!" Lady Esther all but screeched.

"I said, very well," Richard nodded. "It seems you will be unable to treat Chantel with respect. Therefore it is best that you leave."

"That a son of mine . . ." Lady Esther shook her head. She stiffened. "But you will come to your senses. You are a St. James, you know what is proper. Until then . . ." she sighed, and walked toward the door. She turned. "And son, don't think that I will not greet you with open arms again, once you have rid yourself of—of that doxy."

"I am sure," Richard said evenly, unimpressed with his mother's histrionics. "And Mother?"

Lady Esther looked at him hopefully. "Yes?"

"How did you hear about the room and its condition?"

"The maid told me."

"Then I advise you to take the maid with you, for she has just lost her position here."

Lady Esther's eyes sharpened. "You would not! She did nothing improper, 'twas you that—"

"I will not tolerate my servants bearing tales!" Richard's tone was implacable.

Lady Esther drew herself up. "Very well, I will employ her. That you would support that . . ."

"Mother!"

"Oh, very well. I am leaving you now!" Richard said not a word. "You will regret this all." Still Richard did not speak and Lady Esther all but growled, "Get rid of her, Richard. You owe it to the family and the name!" Spinning on her heel, she stormed from the room.

Richard sighed. He rested his head upon his hands. "Get rid of her" echoed in his mind. Not married one day to Chantel Emberly and there was strife within his family, not to mention gossip upon everyone's tongue, and about a St. James yet! It was all over how that blasted room had looked. Richard winced. Indeed, his mother was correct, the looks of it did make one think that he and Chantel had . . . he cursed beneath his breath. Oh, did his head hurt!

Two stiff figures sat at the large dining table, each at opposite ends, with what seemed like miles of polished mahogany and silver between them. Both were pale and distracted. It was very obvious to the meanest eye that neither had totally recovered from their excesses of the night before. The servants bustled about, bringing in the first course. Their eyes covertly flickered from Lord to Lady. It was obvious that tension abounded, yet neither party said a word. In disappointment, the servants left. There was not going to be anything of interest to report downstairs tonight, it appeared.

Chantel glanced across at Richard St. James. His face appeared to be composed of granite. She bit her

lip. It was not as if she had not heard the story of Lady
Esther's storming from his room and then his house in
a grand display. Chantel had come across Lady Esther
in the hall and the woman had cast a look upon her
that should have reduced Chantel into a mere pile of
ashes on the carpet.

"I am leaving now," she had said and had added,
"Just remember, no matter what you do, even if you
are crafty enough to become with child, Richard will
end this relationship. You will never be Lady St.
James. I will see to that!" She had then stormed out.

Chantel looked down at her plate and jabbed her
fork visciously into a carrot, spearing it as she wished
she could have done Lady Esther. The woman was
deranged. And her own family was no better! They
thought she was falling in love with the man. Nothing
could be further from the truth! They all were insane.

She once again looked at the forbidding man at the
other end of the table. She snatched up her water glass
and gulped quickly from it. No, the quicker she could
leave him, the better. And the only way she could do
that was to clear Teddy's name so that the man held
nothing over her. "My Lord?" Chantel asked, shocked
at the weakness in her own voice. "Do you know of
the man who gave Teddy the strongbox?"

Richard looked up as if he had just realized she was
there. "What?"

"The man who gave Teddy the strongbox," Chantel
said more loudly, almost shouting down the length of
the table. "Do you know of him?"

He stared at her. His eyes appeared antagonistic to
the sensitive Chantel. "Of course I know of Louis
Dejarn, do you think me a fool?"

Chantel flushed. No, she didn't take him for a fool, just a fiend. Evidently he did not realize that she hadn't known the man's name. Teddy's mind had remained a blank and Chad had said he was still searching for the man. "And do you know of his whereabouts?"

"Do you not?" Richard countered.

Chantel shivered. His eyes were so cool and distant. It was hard to imagine that the evening before, she and this man had shared champagne and laughter. It must all have been in her imagination, for the man was looking at her as if she were not only a stranger, but a distasteful one at that. "Of course not! I told you Teddy is innocent, and so am I."

Richard St. James shrugged his shoulders. " 'Tis no matter. I just thought we could share our information. You and I both know Louis is still in London somewhere."

"But if he's in London why can't we find him, and find him fast!" Chantel said, irritated. "Then we can get this—all this over with." Chantel's voice petered out as Richard stiffened and gave her an odd look.

"I appreciate your haste in this matter," he said, his tone sharp. "They are my heartfelt sentiments as well. But there are more ramifications here that must be considered."

"What? What ramifications?"

"Chantel," Richard said, his face stern. "I am not going to discuss this with you. Neither Teddy nor you are free of suspicion and I will not divulge the proceedings of this operation."

Chantel's chin jutted out. "But if you do not tell me anything, how am I ever going to clear Teddy's name!"

"You are not going to clear his name. I shall do so."

"You shall do so?" Chantel said sarcastically. "It seems you have done precious little in that respect, and don't try and fob me off with this talk of ramifications. Why have you not approached this Louis Dejarn?"

"For the same reason you have not," Richard snapped.

"I doubt that," Chantel said, not wishing now to admit she had not even known Louis Dejarn's name.

"Madam, you appear to doubt me greatly," Richard said, his voice was low and controlled, "when it is you who are the one under a cloud."

"But will you not . . ."

"Enough, I am doing all I can. Trust me! I will do everything in my power to remove you from my household as swiftly as possible."

"Trust you!" Chantel exclaimed, rage coming to protect her from the odd hurt his words caused her. "No, my lord, I do not trust you. For all I know I shall be removed from your household in chains along with my brother."

" 'Tis not a bad notion."

Chantel's eyes narrowed. "I will not allow that to happen, I assure you." She rose from her chair.

"What are you doing?" Richard asked, his brow arching.

"I have decided I have had enough."

"Chantel, sit down," he ordered, his tone turning ominous and his eyes flashing.

"No," Chantel said sharply, not caring about his anger, "I will not. As everyone has been so determined to remind me, I am not truly your wife, and therefore, I do not have to listen to you."

"I doubt you'd listen to me even if you were my

wife," Richard said. It was obviously not a compliment.

"In that you are correct," Chantel said, "and that is about the only thing you are correct in. But make no mistake, I will clear Teddy's name and then, sir, I will be out of this house . . ."

"Madam, I have no objection to that," he said coldly. "I fear we will not survive six months myself. But why not simply have Teddy confess his involvement and you confess your involvement . . ."

"How dare you! I told you we have no involvement!"

The look he gave her made Chantel want to shoot him. "Then tell me what you do know!"

"I told you I don't . . . oh!" Chantel seethed. She realized they were going around in circles. "Forget it." She turned from him and headed for the door.

"Chantel, come back here!"

She heard him call, his voice thunderous. She kept going . . . fast. She had to clear Teddy's name! She had to get out of this house! She had to get away from the earl before she killed him, or he killed her.

Chantel stood before the groom as he eyed her warily. "I would like a horse," she said resolutely. She hadn't ridden for a long time. But it was morning and she had nothing to do. She had already had her breakfast alone, of course, for the earl was "out on business," she had been informed. Now a day stretched before her within the earl's household and she did not know what to do. Therefore, she had donned her garnet wool riding habit trimmed with brown velvet collar à la Hussar and deep cuffs, which did much to hide the darning on the lace undersleeves that had not made it through the last foray into the equestrian world in one piece.

"Do ye ride much, my lady?" the groom asked her.

"Er, no," Chantel said. "Do you have a gentle mount?"

The groom thought for a moment, his roughened face screwing up with the effort. "Yey, Tob will be the horse for you."

Chantel's eyes widened as the groom brought the horse forward. "The horse for me?" she muttered underneath her breath. Tob was a big horse . . . a big, black horse. His hide looked as if it had already been tanned and his big brown eyes surveyed Chantel as if she were a gnat. Indeed, his size made her feel like nothing more.

"He is gentle?"

The groom shrugged. "The gentlest in the stable. Lord Richard believes in fast goers. Knows his horse-flesh, he does. Now Tob, he's old and slow."

Chantel tightened her resolve. "Very well." She allowed the groom to assist her up onto the large horse's back. Faith, it was a distance to the ground. Chantel directed Tob toward the woods, and to her surprise the large horse obeyed. His was an unsteady amble, and she was not sure if he was heading toward the woods because of her desire or his own.

She slowly began to feel more and more confident, enjoying the wooded scenery that she and Tob were peacefully plodding through. Suddenly, however, Tob stopped with a jerk. How he could jar her bones so thoroughly by stopping when they had been but walking confounded Chantel.

Chantel waited a moment for Tob to proceed. He did not. She prodded him and commanded him forward. He remained frozen. She prodded him again, attempting to dig her heels into his rough hide. Tob ignored her. And then he moved, but only to turn around and head back toward the stables. Chantel gritted her teeth and sawed on the reigns. She did not want to return yet. Tob snorted and shook his head. She sawed even harder and finally Tob turned to the right, but then he continued. Horse and rider went round and round in one circle. It seemed he would not go forward and Chantel would not go back and thus they spun, two stubborn souls.

On the fifth revolution, Chantel thought she caught sight of another horse and a caped rider. "Richard," she called, hoping that it was he and that he would come to her aid. She received no reply. Dizzy, Chantel finally loosened the reins, deciding that Tob could take the lead after all.

Evidently old Tob was just as dizzy, for he stopped, shaking his head and snorting. "Serves you right," Chantel muttered. "Now forward!"

Tob whinnied and, to Chantel's surprise and dismay, lunged forward. She would not have thought the old sack of bones had it in him. They galloped heavily through the woods, Chantel clutching onto the big horse. "Stop, Tob, stop!" Chantel called, all out of breath, for if Tob's amble had been rough, his gait was earth-shaking. "Stop, I tell you!" Chantel shouted, grasping and pulling on his roughened, spotty mane. Tob stopped, smack in a cluster of briars. "Fiend!" Chantel muttered, for briars snagged at her habit.

She reached down to disentangle the cloth from one

tenacious briar that clung to her. She heard another horse snort, and twisted slightly to glance behind her. She glimpsed a large black horse and a large, gray-caped figure. "Richard, help me," she said, turning her vexed attention back to the briar.

A shot rang out. Old Tob started and reared as if he were a young stallion. Chantel, unbalanced, toppled off his back. Her head hit a root as she fell. Bright lights of pain shot before her eyes. Groaning, she closed her eyes, grateful for oblivion.

Richard charged into the house. "Reed," he bellowed. "Reed, what is this I have heard about—" He stopped short as Reed appeared at the top of the stairs.

"Oh, my lord! My lady has had a spill."

"Then it is true. Thomas said Tob had returned an hour ago without Chantel."

"Yes, and then the gamekeeper found my lady. She was unconscious, my lord."

"How is she?" Richard asked, taking the steps in long strides.

"The doctor says that she will be all right. She is sleeping now . . ." Richard strode past Reed. "But she is to be undisturbed." Richard stopped. "The doctor gave her a sleeping draft. She seemed upset and fretful." Richard turned to survey the butler. "She is resting now, my lord," Reed prevailed.

"I would like to see her anyway," Richard said softly. "I shall not wake her."

Reed nodded, a knowing expression in his eyes. "Certainly, my lord." He escorted Richard to Chantel's door. It took all of Richard's patience not to throw the dignified butler out of the way. Reed opened the door and Richard entered quietly.

He walked to the bedside and gazed down upon the sleeping Chantel. When he had heard the story of her fall, a strong fear had seized him. He could not explain why he had felt such a consuming dread, except that it was he who had demanded Chantel enter into this farcical marriage, and if she came to harm because of it he knew he would never forgive himself.

She lay still, a petite, fragile figure. It unsettled Richard, for he had never seen Chantel without fire or emotion flashing from her eyes, or energy coming from her small frame. His fingers clenched.

Chantel stirred, and her eyes opened slowly. They widened slightly as they looked at him, the pupils dark. "Why?"

"Why what?" he asked, feeling absurdly grateful that she was conscious and able to talk. He pulled up the chair and sat down close to the bedside. It seemed that she shrank back from him. He frowned. "What is it?"

"Why did you try to kill me?"

Richard stared at her, stunned. "I didn't try to kill you."

She looked at him reproachfully. "Well, your shot was awfully close and I am not a very good rider."

That odd, overpowering fear that he had experienced when he heard she had fallen from her horse washed over Richard once again. Was she delirious? Was her mind in danger? "I did not shoot at you, Chantel," he said evenly. "You fell off your horse."

"So we shall tell everyone else," Chantel said, sighing like a lonesome breeze. "But I wish you had not shot at me." She closed her eyes, a mar between her brows. "Now I will always have nightmares of you . . ." She shook her head. "You did not have to shoot at me."

Richard took up her hand, clasping it tightly. "Chantel, listen to me," he said urgently. She opened her eyes. They were woeful, green pools. "I did not shoot at you."

"Yes, you did." She nodded, just like a child determined to tell the truth. "You didn't have to. I will leave for Covington's F-folly. I will not be a problem . . . or make you angry again or a-anything." Her voice quivered.

Richard had never seen Chantel teary-eyed. Even though he knew it must be the drug, it frightened him even more than before. Unthinking, he moved to the bed and scooped her up, holding her to his chest. "I didn't . . ."

Chantel squirmed. "Let me go, y-you should not h-hug someone you t-ried to shoot."

He held her firmly, steadily, until her head fell to his shoulder with a sigh. "Listen to me, I didn't shoot at you, Chanty," he said, realizing she must truly be sick since she did not object to the name. "But you must tell me why you think it was me. Tell me what happened."

"Same cloak," she said, her voice a sad whisper. "You wore the same cloak as that night in my room. You could at least have worn a different cloak." Her weak voice was definitely offended.

"I assure you," he said softly, amused despite it all. "If I ever choose to shoot at you I will not be so gauche as to wear the same cloak twice."

"You laugh at me." Chantel tried to squirm from his arms again. "I suppose you wish to kill me now . . . again! Oh, you know what I mean."

Richard held her, denying her escape. Rather than killing her, he put his hand up to her head and gently held it to his shoulder. "I could strangle you for believing it was I who tried to kill you," he said mildly.

"I am suffocating," a muffled voice came from his jacket.

He loosened his hold slightly, but only enough so that Chantel could draw her head back and look at him. His hand slipped into her hair to cup her head. He couldn't seem to help himself, he needed to comfort her, to somehow erase her hurt. "You must believe me, it was not I who shot at you."

A spark of what looked like hope entered her eyes, and then she shook her head. "No, it was you. No one else wants me dead."

Richard sighed in exasperation. "Would you stop that. I don't want you dead either. It is someone else who wants you dead."

Chantel seemed to consider this, her drugged eyes wide. She shook her head. "No. No one else has ever wanted me dead. N-no one else has ever shot at me. It was you—big—gray cloak—yes, it was you."

"Chanty," Richard said. He put his hand to her jaw to force her to look at him. Her skin was so smooth, he couldn't resist running his finger along her jaw line. "You must give it up. It wasn't me. But that means that someone else does want you dead."

Chanty cocked her head like a bemused kitten. "Your mother?"

Richard stifled a laugh. "I cannot lie, she might like

to see you dead, but she would never attempt to kill you. You must believe me."

"Why?"

"Because it is important. It is apparent someone does want you dead. You are in danger. And since someone shot at me also, we are in it together."

She pursed her lips and her green eyes were confused and teary. "I don't know—I don't know who to trust anymore."

"Poor Chantel. You can trust me." And though he said it softly, Richard knew he meant every word of it. Somehow, he would help her. He gently laid her back down upon the bed. "Now you must go back to sleep. Reed will have my head. I wasn't supposed to wake you."

"Yes," Chantel sighed, closing her eyes obediently. "I shall rest, I am awfully tired." She frowned mightily. "I don't like being shot at, you know. If . . . if it was you, could you not do it again. Promise me . . ."

Richard sighed. "It was not me. But I promise never to shoot at you."

"Then you will wait the six months?"

"I'll wait the six months and any time longer you wish, Chanty," Richard said quietly, as he shifted to a more comfortable position beside her.

Chantel did not respond, for she had drifted off to sleep. 'Twas better she had not heard it, Richard thought. He frowned. Her muddled story was confusing, but about one thing Chantel was correct. It was becoming harder and harder to know who to trust.

Chantel awoke late the next morning. She opened her eyes slowly and stared at the ceiling. She must have been dreaming, but she seemed to remember Richard St. James' arms about her. She flushed. She knew it could not be true. Yet it had seemed real and his arms had been so comforting. She frowned. Those comforting arms could also be the ones that wanted to kill her. Richard had sworn it was not he. Yet that gray cloak still haunted her memory. She sighed. It was odd, after all that had happened, but the truth was, she wanted to trust Richard.

Heaving a sigh, she pushed back the blankets and swung her legs down to the floor. She groaned slightly as she stood. Falling off that blasted horse had bruised every part of her body, or at least that was how it felt. She reached for her robe and pulled it slowly over her nightgown. She hobbled like an old woman toward the armoire. Opening it, she reached in and drew out a dress, not caring which one she had.

She considered ringing for a maid. Yet she did not know which maid she would get, or if she would get one at all. The one who was to have been her personal maid had already left with Lady Esther. She grimaced. No, she would prefer to dress by herself at her own pace.

She turned and immediately jumped. Richard St. James was standing in the room, his arms akimbo, a concerned look in his gray eyes. How had he sneaked in on her? "What are you doing here?"

"I came to see how you are feeling."

"I am fine," Chantel snapped, unsettled.

"You look frightful. You should be back in bed."

"No, I shouldn't," Chantel said, flushing. "And I do not appreciate the way you just walked in without a 'by your leave.'"

His brow rose. "I thought we'd had this discussion."

"And you said you would knock."

He smiled a teasing smile that only made Chantel want to hit him. "I forgot. Shall I go back out and do so?"

"You should remember to knock," Chantel said irately, holding the dress before her in defense.

"And you should still be in bed," he returned firmly.

"No, I shouldn't. Now if you would excuse me, I would like to dress."

"No, I won't excuse you," he said mildly. "You are not going to dress, you see."

"Yes, I am," Chantel snapped. "Now, please leave."

He shifted his weight and crossed his arms, studying her. "I am not leaving until you get back into bed. You are not well enough to be up."

"I am," Chantel insisted pugnaciously. With as much dignity as she could muster, she crossed the room toward the dressing screen. She'd not allow that overbearing male to intimidate her into lying in bed for a whole day. As Chantel passed him in her queenly manner, Richard's hand shot out and snatched the dress from her fingers.

Chantel gasped. "Give that to me."

She lunged to grab it, but he held the dress high, over his head and tauntingly far out of her shorter reach. She felt very much like a small terrier jumping about a great Dane, but she nevertheless attempted another leap for her dress. Richard promptly tossed the dress over his shoulder. He now stood between it and she, a devilish grin on his lips and his eyes twinkling.

"How dare you," Chantel panted, for even such light exercise was fagging her.

"I dare," he said, his tone sounding aggravatingly confident to her. Before Chantel could divine his intent, he reached out and clasped the lapel of her robe.

"Let go!" she gasped. He tugged at the lapel and efficiently had it slid off one of her arms before she could react. Chantel clutched her other arm to her in a desperate attempt to keep her robe. Richard merely walked around her and she was forced to circle to keep the robe from sliding off. "Stop that," Chantel wheezed, becoming dizzy.

"No, you stop that," Richard said.

"I want to dress."

"No," Richard said, and catching her on a revolution, he picked her up in his arms. Chantel would have objected but her head was spinning too much and she was sadly lacking anything like air in her lungs. He carried her over to the bed and then sat down, setting her upon his lap as if she were nothing but a child.

"Now," he said, "you are going to promise me to stay in bed for today."

"No, I'm not," Chantel said weakly. The man certainly knew how to take the fight out of a person. "I think you do mean to kill me."

"No, I promised to wait," he said congenially. He smiled all the more when she glared at him. "But I do want to speak about your accident."

"I am too weak to talk to you, I fear," Chantel said spitefully. She shoved at his broad chest, becoming more and more uncomfortable as he held her. His arms remained gentle iron bands and Chantel felt a flush rising within her body. "Now let me go, this isn't at all proper."

He chuckled. "Chanty . . ." She glared. "Hm, you are better. Chantel, ever since I have met you I have seen you in nightgowns, and robes . . . and sheets . . ."

Chantel growled, flushing an even deeper red. "It is because you are always coming into my room unbidden."

"No," he said, shaking his head solemnly. "I distinctly remember that time with the sheet—it was you who was to blame."

Chantel flushed. "I was only trying to escape you. And it is not right how you brazenly walked in here as if you had a right to . . ."

"I do, I am . . ." He halted and then said, "I own this house, after all."

Chantel's eyes narrowed. "Your house or not, this is improper. Whatever would your mother say?"

His laugh was deep and husky, sending an odd current through Chantel. "Considering what she thinks we've done, she'd consider this very decent behavior for us, I'd say. Now would you stop dithering over proprieties . . ."

"I cannot believe I just heard that from a St. James!" Chantel exclaimed, trying to divert her wondering thoughts. He had such a masculine soap and water scent about him.

Richard shook her slightly. "Stop it, Emberly. I am not going to release you until you tell me what I want to know."

"In that case," Chantel said, looking away, "I will

talk . . . if it will expedite this process. What do you wish to know?"

"I want to know every connection you and Teddy have with Louis Dejarn. I want to know every connection you have with any of his people."

Chantel stared. The man still thought her involved. She swatted him ineffectually upon the chest. "Let me go!"

"Chantel!"

"No," Chantel said irately. "You ask me to trust you, but yet you want to know what connection I have with this Louis Dejarn. I told you I do not have any. Teddy's only connection is that he played cards with the man and promised to keep the box safe for him in return for his vouchers being torn up."

It was Richard's turn to stare at her. "Chantel, that cannot be all there is to it. There must be more. Perhaps Teddy has not told you of all his activities."

Chantel cast him a belittling eye. "You have met Teddy. Do you think him capable of duplicity?"

Richard frowned. "No, I don't think so, but there must be something. Somehow you are involved."

"Oh, so now it is me!" Chantel said, enraged. "Now I am the ringleader. Then why would they shoot at me if I am in on it?"

Richard sighed in exasperation. "I don't know. That is why I am asking you to tell me all you know. If you are innocent . . ."

"If! If!"

"If you are innocent then you are accidentally involved in it as is Teddy and someone wants you eliminated before you can give them away."

"That makes no sense!" Chantel said irately.

"Then you tell me what does!" Richard retorted.

Chantel shrugged. "I don't know. Perhaps I was shot at because I am involved with you."

"So we are back to it being me."

"No, I am saying that perhaps this has something to do with your activities and not mine. It may be my involvement with you that has caused it."

Richard shook his head. "All my enemies that I know of would come directly at me, not shoot at you."

"But they shot at you the first time."

Richard nodded. "True."

"Richard," Chantel said seriously, her anger dying as reason asserted itself. "From what I gather of your work, you have more enemies than I have. In fact, I don't have any enemies. Well, I have your mother now . . . and most of your family . . . and perhaps some of the townsfolk . . ."

She frowned and Richard laughed and shook his head. "So far you've named no one dangerous enough . . ."

"Your mother isn't dangerous?"

"Not physically," he amended. He sighed. "It seems we don't have an answer here. But please, Chantel, think of every acquaintance, every occurrence that might be connected, and talk to me. Please confide in me."

"And you do the same," Chantel purred.

Richard laughed. "Very well, I should have known I wouldn't get anywhere. But the one thing I will persist in is that you stay in bed today."

"But I don't want to stay in bed!" Chantel objected. "I'll be bored to flinders."

"If you don't stay in bed . . ." He paused a moment and Chantel looked at him suspiciously, for suddenly the most dangerous smile crossed his lips. "I will simply take the same measures I did last time to keep you here."

"What do you—?" Chantel suddenly remembered, and swallowed. "You wouldn't dare!"

"I wouldn't?" Richard asked, his arms tightening about her in warning. "I'll take every stitch of clothing from here—and from you." Chantel unwittingly squirmed and his grin turned wicked. "Perhaps that's the best idea after all."

Chantel literally hopped from him and this time he let her go. She disliked the glint in his eyes. "No, I—I will stay in bed."

"Promise?" He stood, towering over her.

"P-Promise!" she said, shifting nervously despite herself.

"How unsporting," he said, sighing. "Pity. Hm . . . 'Tis perhaps still the best idea."

Chantel jumped and dived past him to the bed. She swiftly scrambled under the covers, pulling them up to the very tip of her chin. Even then she didn't feel safe. "I'm in bed, see! And I promise to stay here."

"Very well," he nodded, a sweet smile crossing his face. His gray eyes still twinkled. "I'll have breakfast sent up to you."

"Do! Er—now, now I want to rest," Chantel said quickly. She watched Richard with bated breath until he walked to the door.

"Goodbye for now," Richard said.

Chantel didn't let her breath out until he was gone

and the door was safely closed behind him. She fell back and pulled the covers over her head. It was childish, but for just a moment she wanted to be totally hidden from the world, and from the earl.

Chapter Six

Teddy entered the quiet room and tiptoed clumsily up to Chantel's bedside. "Chantel," he whispered. She lay as still as death. Suddenly her eyes snapped open.

"Yikes!" Teddy jumped back, startled.

"We must go to London," Chantel said softly.

"Whew, startled me," Teddy said, collapsing into the chair next to her bed. "Thought you were dead a moment."

"No, just terribly bored," Chantel said, sitting up. "St. James is making me remain in bed."

Teddy stared. "Making you?" It was evident from the dumbfounded expression upon his face that he was experiencing difficulty grasping such a concept.

"Yes, he . . . well, never mind," Chantel said, waving her hand as if swatting at a noisome fly. "We are going to London."

"We are?" Teddy asked. "But you just got shot at."

"I know," Chantel nodded. "And that is why we are going to London."

Teddy turned an interesting shade of red. "Hm,

don't think you want to go to London. Just been there. No, don't think you want to go to London."

Chantel studied him. He wore a look that Chantel recognized all too well. Her voice became stern. "Teddy, what did you do? Why wouldn't I want to go to London?"

"Er, well, you see, I had this grand scheme," Teddy said, his eyes wide.

"Oh, no!" When Teddy had a grand scheme it was basically like a child with a whole cart of tinder and flint. "What did you do?"

"Well, I told you how much I love Alicia?"

"Yes, yes."

"Her parents won't accept me because I have no money."

"Yes," Chantel nodded patiently. "We have discussed this."

"So I thought to raise the wind very quickly," Teddy continued, not meeting her eye.

"Oh, Lord." Chantel called on her Maker, for she could feel the blow coming.

"So I went to the gaming table and staked everything I had."

Which wasn't much, Chantel thought gratefully. "Then you couldn't have lost that much!"

"Lost a thousand pounds."

"What?" Chantel exclaimed, her fingers fairly digging holes in the blanket. "But that is impossible. How could you!"

Teddy reddened. "It was a new gaming table. They—they all accepted my vouchers. And—there you have it."

"What new set of gudgeons are in town?" Chantel

asked angrily. "Just what imbeciles would accept your vouchers for that amount?"

"Ned says these men aren't nice," Teddy confessed. "Said they fleece men and—and do awful things if you don't pay up."

"Oh, faith," Chantel said, rolling her eyes. "As if it isn't bad enough that someone wants to kill me, we now have men that aren't nice wishing to do awful things to you."

"That's only if I don't pay up. They did give me three weeks," Teddy said, hopefully.

"Very well," sighed Chantel, pulling herself together. "We will have to deal with that when it comes."

"You mean when they come," Teddy said glumly.

"But first, we are going to London," Chantel said with determination.

"Why?"

"Because I know who the man is that gave you the black box and we are going to find him and find out what he knows! I have lain in this bed all day and I have thought and thought. St. James is right. Since I know of no one who wishes me dead, my being shot at has to do with that blasted black box. St. James doesn't trust me and won't tell me what he knows. Therefore, we shall find out what it is all about by ourselves!"

Teddy stared at her. "But ain't that dangerous?"

"And being shot at isn't?" Chantel said indignantly.

"But—but—"

"No butts, Teddy," Chantel said sternly. "You will take me to London and help me, or else . . . or else I won't help you raise the money to pay those men."

Teddy flushed. "Very well. But don't think St. James will approve of you going to London."

"You leave that to me," Chantel said, still riding the crest of her great scheme. "Now do go. And please stay away from the tables."

Teddy rose. "Er—will. Was trying to stay away from London . . ." He gulped at Chantel's quelling frown. "But will go, of course."

Teddy left and Chantel sighed. She had to discover who wanted to kill her and at the same time manage to turn up a thousand pounds for Teddy. All this, and St. James wished her to stay in bed!

Chantel arranged the blankets about her for the fifth time. She had stacked two ivory lace pillows behind her head and was sitting up comfortable. Yet her fingers nervously pleated the coverlet of jonquil-colored watered silk shot with delicate gold threads. She had rehearsed in her mind what she would say to Richard. She had sent a message to him asking him to come for tea. She fully intended to be demure and gentle. She would say that he was right and that she was not recovering swiftly from her accident. She would ask him if she could go to London for an excursion, perhaps some light shopping to take her mind off everything. She rubbed her hands together again. She had never practiced subterfuge before, nor used her feminine wiles. She heard the door open and quickly unclenched her hands, attempting a "gentle" pose.

"Chantel, I came the minute I heard!" Chantel's head snapped around when she heard Chad's voice.

"Chad!" she exclaimed, so prepared for Richard that it was a shock to see her cousin.

He rushed toward her, sitting down swiftly in the

chair arranged for Richard. He reached for her hands. "Tell me, dear, what happened?"

"Oh . . . fell off my horse," Chantel said, nonplussed.

"But I heard . . . Teddy said someone tried to kill you," Chad said.

"Teddy should not have told you," Chantel said, squeezing his hand. "I did not want to trouble you with this."

"Why? You know how I care. I will always be here for you," Chad said urgently. "And so will Mother."

"She will?"

Chad finally smiled. "Yes, believe it or not, she will. She would have come to visit too, but I did not think you would be up to that."

Chantel laughed. "Thank you, my dearest of cousins."

"Your only one, you mean." Chad shook his head. "No compliment. But tell me what happened. I can scarce believe it. Did you see who tried to kill you?"

"No, not really," Chantel said, flushing. "He was on a large horse and wore a gray cloak. That is all I can remember."

"I see," Chad said, frowning. His brown eyes pinned hers. "Chantel, come home with me. Leave this place. Leave St. James."

Chantel did not look away. "You think it might be St. James too?"

"So you realize . . ."

"No, I am not sure I believe that. Killing me just because I am a nuisance does not seem like him at all."

"I think you say that," Chad said gently, "because you care about him and are involved with him."

"Would you stop that!" Chantel exclaimed, irrationally exploding. She was greatly aggravated. She would never have thought her cousin could be such a nag over such a ridiculous subject. "I am not involved with him. I do not care what your mother thinks, nor what his mother thinks, nor what the entire shire thinks, nor the entire world for that matter, I am not involved with him and I did not—did not you-know-what."

Chad was stunned. "You truly didn't?"

"Have I ever lied to you?"

"No," Chad said. "But . . ."

"I know, I have my mother's blood in me," Chantel said bitterly.

"No," he said, with a glimmer of a smile. Finally, his expression relaxed. "Thank you, Chantel, for easing my mind. I am glad you haven't let St. James seduce you, if only for your own sake. I do not want to see your heart broken. Nor do I want to see your neck broken." He frowned again and the urgency was back in his voice. "Chantel, please. I do not know what is going on, but please, leave St. James and come with me. You won't be safe until you do. This I know for certain. Come with me . . ."

"Rather crass, isn't it?" a stern voice said from the bedroom door. "To beg a lady to leave her husband while under his roof?" Richard St. James stood within the doorway, his eyes pointedly trained upon Chad's and Chantel's clasped hands.

"Is she your wife?" Chad asked, though he stiffly withdrew his hands from Chantel's.

"My ring is upon her finger, is it not?" Richard's voice was razor sharp.

"For the nonce."

"True, and I will thank you during that time to resist begging her to leave."

"Very well," Chad said, only the tightness of his jaw expressing his feelings. "But I would advise you to have a better care of her."

Richard's smile was unpleasant. "Strange, I'd not think you the one to encourage me to have more of a care for Chantel."

"I mean for her safety," Chad gritted out. "She has never been in danger until she met you."

"I could say the same," Richard nodded. "I was in no danger until I met her."

"I highly doubt that," Chad said, rising from his chair. "You are the type of man who is always in danger. Always playing games. I know your type well."

"You do?" Richard taunted.

"Yes, I do," Chad said, suddenly cool. "But you shouldn't bring Chantel into the games."

The two men's eyes locked. "It isn't a game," St. James said softly.

Chad bowed. "If you say so. I will leave you now." Chad looked to Chantel, who was watching the men in quiet suspense. "Chantel, I will see you later." He turned cold eyes back to Richard and left the room silently.

The look Richard then directed upon Chantel was so accusing, that it caused her chin to raise. "You need not insult my family, my lord. He merely came to see how I fared."

"That, and to ask you to leave here."

She shrugged. "He is merely overprotective."

"He is merely a suitor of yours," Richard countered sternly. "I would thank you to avoid such compromising situations with him until this marriage is annulled. You do know what a compromising situation is?" His tone was withering as he walked over and sat down. "It is being discovered alone in a room holding hands and receiving proposals from a man who is not your husband."

"Faith, how gothic," Chantel scoffed. "I thank the heavens that I am not truly your wife! I pity that poor woman, whoever she might be."

"Don't," he said curtly. "She will be sure to enjoy both my affection and my protection."

Chantel blinked. "Such as I do not," she murmured softly.

"You . . ." Richard stopped. His eyes where fathomless as he looked at her. Then he looked away. "What was it you wanted to discuss with me, madam?"

"I thought," Chantel said coolly now, totally forgetting her intended demureness, "I would like to visit Teddy in London."

"I see." His eyes when they returned to her held cynicism as well as some other undefined emotion within their depths.

"I thought it might help me to forget the accident." Chantel found her voice weakening, for his gray gaze was unwavering. "I—I could go sightseeing . . . perhaps do some shopping!" There was a silent pause and Chantel tried not to squirm under his solid stare.

"I see," he said finally, softly. He rose and walked to the door. He stopped. "Perhaps it is best that you do go to London. I will give you a draft on my bank that should cover expenses . . . allow you to buy some clothes."

Chantel bit her tongue. "Thank you."

"Think nothing of it," Richard said, his voice dry. " 'Tis nothing, after all." He left her.

Chantel glared after him. He made her feel nothing less than a deserting wife and traitor. Well, she was neither, she thought, her chin tilting up to a fighting angle, and she would prove it to him.

Chantel paced the small parlor of the Emberly townhouse. A swish of satin, deep emerald and bold chartreuse satin, mixed with the crisp crackle of her cherry pink, taffeta petticoat, was heard upon every revolution. Even as she awaited a tardy Teddy, she wondered if the paint on her face was too much or too little. What did a lady who frequented gaming hells look like?

Chantel stopped pacing and stalked to the mirror over the mantlepiece. She studied her image. Her red hair was frizzed in a riot of curls, lampblack lined her eyes, and she had dipped heavily into the rouge pot. A great, shocking expanse of white shoulder and chest was exposed by the emerald green satin. As a disguise it was perfect. No one would have recognized Chantel Emberly of Covington's Folly in this overblown woman.

Tonight would be the night she found Louis Dejarn. Chantel could just feel it. She and Teddy had been in town for two days already, but those days had been used taking in the sights and shopping. She had done so to maintain appearances, though as cool as Richard was when she had left him, she doubted it would matter to him what she did.

Chantel heard the door open and she spun around. Teddy, properly dressed in evening attire, followed by his friend Neddy, entered the room. Both halted when they sighted Chantel. Their mouths fell open identically.

"Oh, er . . . hello," Teddy said, bowing. "Who are you? A friend of Chantel's?"

"Shouldn't be, Teddy, she's not a lady," Neddy whispered loud enough to be on stage. A tall, gangling man with a thin, monocled face, Teddy then clamped his mouth shut and stared.

"Teddy, dear, it is me," Chantel laughed. She twirled about for added measure.

"Me who?" Teddy asked blankly.

Neddy's monocle popped from his eye. "It's your sister," he said hoarsely. "She's your sister."

"Chantel?" Teddy asked, peering more closely at her. His freckled face crinkled into a frown. "What are you dressed like that for? Neddy is right, you know, you don't look like a lady. You look like . . ."

Neddy gouged Teddy in the stomach with his bony elbow. "Not proper to mention that in front of a lady."

"But she ain't dressed like a lady," Teddy complained. "That ain't proper either."

"I know it isn't," Chantel said happily, suddenly feeling a new spurt of freedom when she realized they had not recognized her. "But I must dress this way because you are going to take me to that gaming hell . . ."

"Here now," Neddy objected, his eyes bulging.

"Shouldn't use that word, ain't proper, Miss Emberly."

"I know it isn't proper, but if that is where Teddy played cards with Louis Dejarn who gave him that black box, that is where we will be going."

"Louis Dejarn?" Neddy asked.

"That Frenchy fellow," Teddy said. "That we played with at the, er . . ." Teddy leaned over and whispered the name to Neddy, both men keeping a wary eye upon Chantel.

Neddy's eyes widened and he gasped. "Madame Durham's! Ohh, forgive me. But that ain't proper, it is a gaming hell."

"I know it is," Chantel said, beginning to lose her patience. "But I am going there and since I am going there this is very proper attire."

Neddy stepped back and studied her seriously. "Yes, yes," he finally nodded. "You are dressed properly for Madame Durham's. She's dressed properly, Teddy."

"No, she ain't," Teddy said obstinately. "She's my sister. Look at that neckline, it shows . . . well, you can see what it shows."

"But if she is going to Madame Durham's, then she's dressed properly," Neddy persisted. "Me gaffer always says that a man, or in your sister's case, a woman, should always dress appropriately for the function they are attending. Wear a habit if you go riding, what? Wear evening attire for the evening." He nodded to Chantel. "Wear that dress if you're going to Madame Durham's. Ain't proper for a ball, or soirée, or drum, but is proper for Madame Durham's. S'truth, only place she can wear it," Neddy finished in solemn consideration. "Therefore, must go to Madame Durham's."

Teddy sighed. "You are right. Only place she can go. Bought the dress after all."

"Teddy and Neddy," Chantel said, her slippered foot beginning a tattoo upon the carpet. "We do not have all evening to discuss this. We must find Louis Dejarn, remember? Now go and get your pistols."

"Pistols?" Neddy's face turned owlish.

"Ain't got any pistols," Teddy said, scuffing his foot on the carpet.

"What?" Chantel asked, the wind taken from her sails.

"True, madam," Neddy nodded. "See, Teddy don't need pistols."

"What do you mean? Of course he needs them," Chantel said firmly. "We need them for protection."

"You don't need them for protection," Neddy persisted. "See, Teddy can't shoot. Could use them for protection if he could shoot, but since he can't, you don't need them."

"I don't believe it," Chantel said in exasperation.

"It's true," Teddy said, shamefaced. "Last time I tried to shoot, I took off Lord Aimsley's wig."

"Clean off," Neddy nodded. "Was supposed to be after the pigeon, not Lord Aimsley's wig. Aimsley wasn't pleased, mind you. It was one of his best ones, he said. Made Teddy promise never to touch a weapon again or he would prosecute. A public-spirited man Aimsley, what?"

"Then what are we to do if we run into danger?" Chantel asked. The two men stared at her with wide eyes. Chantel pinned Neddy with a direct look that caused his lanky body to break out fidgeting in all different directions. "Can you shoot, Neddy?"

"Can," he nodded. "Not good. But not like Teddy."

"Then you have pistols?"

"Do," Neddy nodded. "In the coach outside. Only proper, you know, for highwaymen and so on."

"Then get them for me."

Neddy nodded nervously, and dragging Teddy with him, left the room. They returned with Neddy gingerly carrying two large weapons before him, very much as if they were smelly, dead fish. "Here they are."

Chantel felt a qualm herself, but she stiffened her resolve and hesitantly reached out for one. "Is—is it loaded?"

Neddy nodded. "Me sire says they must always be loaded. It ain't—"

"No use otherwise," Chantel finished, gulping as she held the large weapon in her hand. She looked at Teddy, whose face had taken on a gray cast. "Neddy, please unload the other one and give it to Teddy."

"But if it ain't loaded," Neddy objected, "then—"

"Teddy can't shoot anybody's wig off," Chantel finished. She set her weapon down carefully. She then put her cloak on and gently picked up the weapon again to slide it into the large side pocket. She collected her reticule and turned. Neddy was solemnly handing Teddy his empty pistol.

"D-don't think this a good idea," Teddy stammered.

"We have got to clear your name, Teddy," Chantel said with resolution. "And this is the only way to do it. Now, Neddy, if you could escort us to Madame Durham's."

"Can leave you off there," Neddy said. "But got another engagement, c-can't go with you."

"I have no doubt," Chantel said dryly. "Now, let us go."

"If you say so," Teddy said weakly.

"I say so," Chantel said, marshaling the two men out of the door and wondering how she was ever to accomplish her goal with only Teddy and Neddy as support. It was a worrisome thought, to say the least.

Teddy coughed and knocked on the polished oak door.

"But this doesn't look like a gaming hell," Chantel exclaimed. "It looks quite proper."

"It ain't," Teddy said sagely.

The door opened and Chantel gulped. The largest, ugliest man she had ever beheld stood before them. His eyes were small and bloodshot, while his muscles were large and bulging. Despite those ox-like muscles that should have protected him from anything and anyone, his nose was so misaligned that it was apparent it had been broken, and several times at that.

"What do you want?" he growled.

"Good evening, Jerrel," Teddy said in a reedy voice. "Thought we might come in and see the play."

"Can't come in, Mr. Emberly. Mrs. Durham gave me orders not to let you in, 'cause you don't have no money."

"I came only to watch," Teddy said, injured.

The large hulk snorted through his abused nose. "You never just watch, Mr. Emberly. Fact, you said that the last time and dropped a bundle, didn't ye?

And now you got those captain sharps after ye. Bet me grandma on it."

Teddy looked down. "Well yes, but I'm going to reform."

"Ain't we all," Jerrel nodded. "Now be off, Mr. Emberly."

Teddy was unconsciously turning away when Chantel spoke up. "I have money."

The behemoth looked down at her and his eyes brightened. "Who are you, love?"

"I am his sis—chere amie," Chantel amended swiftly.

"Gaw, what are you doing with him, sweetings?" He shook his large head sadly. "He ain't got a feather to fly with, nothing to take care of a darlin' bird like you. Now I have . . ."

Chantel swiftly delved into her reticule, pulling out a wad of notes cashed from the bank draft Richard had given her. "See, is this not enough?"

"Whoa, yes it is, duck," Jerrel said, a note of respect entering his rough voice.

She separated a bill. "And this is for you, since you have been so kind. I really wish to play tonight."

"I can see that, sweetheart, I can see that," Jerrell said reverently. He opened the door wide. "Come right on in."

As they passed, the large creature whispered in Chantel's ear, "You do the playing, love, your man can't play to save his arse."

"Yes," Chantel nodded, embarrassed. They crossed through a hall, but when they entered the main room, Chantel halted abruptly. It was filled with men and women playing at tables. Men dressed in fine evening attire played games at all different kinds of tables. Amongst them floated woman, in various states of dress and undress. The colors they sported were even more garish than Chantel's.

"Where did you get the money?" Teddy whispered.

"From Richard," Chantel responded in an undertone. "He thought I was going shopping with it. I fear what I am buying is not what he expected. Now where is this Mrs. Durham?"

Teddy peered through the room and pointed to a woman of forty with a well-upholstered and fulsome figure clad in burgundy jacquard.

"Very well." Chantel nodded and advanced purposefully, weaving through the crowd. "Mrs. Durham," she said without preamble, "I wish to speak to you."

The older woman looked up from the drink she was pouring. Her eyes roved meticulously over Chantel, appraising her as if she were horseflesh. "Looking for employment? Is that hair real?"

"No and yes," Chantel said, taken aback at the woman's opening. "I am looking for a man named Louis Dejarn. I hoped since he has frequented this er—house, that you would know where I could find him."

Mrs. Durham studied her even more closely. "Even if I know where he is, not saying I do, why would I tell you?"

Chantel thought furiously. "Because I have powerful connections."

The woman cracked a laugh. "I know, we all do, ducky." She looked over Chantel's shoulder toward Teddy, who was futilely attempting to hide his large frame behind Chantel's petite one. "Is he your powerful connection? You'll find yourself without a farthing if he is. You'd be a far sight better off in my employ."

"No, I do not speak of Teddy," Chantel said, not only affronted by the employment offer, but also by the woman before her. Indeed, Chantel's red-headed temper was beginning to simmer. "The connection I speak of is Richard St. James, the Earl of Hartford."

"Oh? I see. Well ain't you the lucky one."

"Lucky?"

"To be under his protection."

Chantel considered that a dubious presumption, but refrained from saying so. "Indeed."

"Oh come on, love, don't be so tight-lipped," Mrs. Durham laughed throatily. "Trying to keep trade secrets? You can't bamboozle me into thinking that your life ain't a pleasure with that one."

"I can't?" Chantel asked, trying to figure out how Mrs. Durham would know anything about her life.

She winked. "My friend, Marion, was your predecessor."

"She was?"

"Heard all about the Earl from her. He's a fine lover, she says. Knows his way around in bed. And generous, to boot. No clutchfisted miser is he. When Marion was under his protection she said she felt as if she'd died and gone to heaven." Mrs. Durham shrugged as Chantel stood stunned and mute. "But then he broke the liaison and up and married some little tart."

Chantel's fist balled. "Tart?"

"Ah, think we should be going," Teddy said nervously, plucking at Chantel's shoulder.

"No," Chantel said quietly, her eyes narrowing. "I want to hear why Mrs. Durham thinks I—er, why St. James married a tart."

"Mrs. Durham! Must tell you, St. James married—me sister," Teddy yelped, displaying a rare quickness of mind.

Mrs. Durham smiled blandly and Chantel realized the proprietress had been fully aware of that before her comment. "Ah yes, that is right, isn't it, Teddy? Forgive me. I didn't mean to insult you. But it isn't any secret, is it? That your sister and St. James *had* to get married."

"Yes, they had to marry," Chantel said, trembling. "But not for the reason you think."

Mrs. Durham laughed. "Either way, she caught him right and tight."

"Hmm," Teddy said, coughing desperately, "don't think we ought to talk about this."

"Now don't take me wrong, Teddy dear," Mrs. Durham said. "I respect an enterprising woman like your sister. Though she's got St. James' mother furious enough to burst her stays. She's been squawking about it all over town. Heard the Earl and your sister shocked the fine Lady Esther so much that she high-tailed it back to town, swearing she would never enter his house until the doxy was gone."

"She said that?" Chantel asked ominously. Her balled fist rose a fraction.

Teddy grabbed her wrist. "Well, ain't that interesting, but we really should be going."

Evidently Mrs. Durham was slower than Teddy, for she grinned slyly and tossed off her drink before the quivering Chantel. "She's letting everyone and their aunt know." She eyed Chantel maliciously. "You'll have your work cut out in keeping his attention if Teddy's sister is the little firebrand they say she is."

"Will I? Will I indeed?"

"Dejarn!" Teddy panted quickly, grabbing the other fist as it came up. "Came here to ask about Dejarn, didn't we?"

"Why are you looking for him?" Mrs. Durham asked, distracted. "Knowing you, Teddy, you ought to be hiding from him. Don't you owe him money?"

"No," Chantel said sharply. Teddy's ploy had worked. Her mind was back to the purpose. Or perhaps only derailed, but Chantel did realize that with one more word from Mrs. Durham she would have happily punched her. She flushed. What was the matter with her? She had come very close to a cat fight with a proprietress of a gaming den. She swallowed hard and said, "In fact, Teddy did him a favor and 'tis Dejarn that hasn't paid him."

"Well, Louis wouldn't like it then if I told you where he was, would he? You'll just have to get St. James to find him. Or is he too involved with Teddy's sister to help you?" Mrs. Durham smiled slyly.

Chantel considered that cat fight more seriously. Perhaps it wouldn't be that bad after all.

"Er, we really need to know where Dejarn is," Teddy said swiftly. "Can't you pay her like you did Jerrel?" he whispered in Chantel's ear.

"I'll pay her one," Chantel hissed. Teddy nudged her and Chantel sighed. She reached into her reticule and pulled out a few notes, waving them in front of the amused woman. "Could this help you to withstand his ire?"

Mrs. Durham smiled. "Well now, why didn't you say that in the beginning?"

Why hadn't she, Chantel thought angrily. Now she knew more about Richard St. James and his world than she ever wanted to know.

Teddy and Chantel stood huddled in a grim, dark hall. Voices and odd sounds surrounded them, coming from various rooms.

"You—you think this is the place?" Teddy whispered, peering about as if he expected trolls and goblins to pop out from the grimy walls.

"Mrs. Durham said so," Chantel said with forced confidence. "But she could have lied," she added uneasily. "Well, we are here. Now, let me do the talking."

"Yes, will! Good plan, you do the talking."

Chantel swallowed and rapped upon the battered door before them. It looked as if someone had scored the wood with a knife. There was no answer. Chantel rapped more loudly.

"Must be out," Teddy said quickly. "Shame. Better luck next time," he said, turning.

Chantel grabbed hold of his arm. "Stay," she commanded. She pounded more loudly on the door. "The proprietor thought he saw him come in."

"Yes, after you gave him money. Don't know why you had to give him money too. Giving everybody money when I need it more."

"You also need to be cleared of treason," Chantel said quietly. She pounded again.

Slowly, the door cracked open. Dark eyes peered out.

"Louis Dejarn?" Chantel asked, forcing a smile and

feeling very vulnerable, for Teddy was hanging back, appearing as if he planned to turn tail at any second.

"Yes?" He opened the door slightly. He was a small man, as small as Chantel. His black hair was lank and oiled excessively. He studied Chantel for a moment, his black eyes roving over her satined bosom and tight-fitting dress. They lighted immediately and he actually licked his lips. "Yes, yes I am Louis Dejarn. You have heard of me! I am a great one with the ladies. Come in, sweetings, come in." He swung the door wide and performed a deep bow. Chantel shuddered. He really did look like a little dark spider inviting her into his web.

"Thank you," she said. Gritting her teeth, she sidled into the small room, waving frantically for Teddy to follow. Teddy scooted in quickly and Louis stepped back, his face falling. "But *ma cherie,* why bring this man?" he complained, frowning at Teddy.

"Because I am not what you think I am," Chantel said sharply. "Teddy and I have come to find out what was in the black box you gave him that night at Mrs. Durham's."

"Teddy?" The little man peered quickly at Teddy. "Ah ha! That is who you are?"

"You didn't recognize him?" Chantel exclaimed, shocked.

The little man shrugged. "You must admit, mademoiselle, his is not a memorable face. But yours, now! Ah, one to remember until death!"

"And you just might," Chantel muttered under her breath. "Do you mean you gave him a box and you don't even remember how he looks? Do you know the trouble you have caused him?"

"Trouble! It is I who have had trouble caused!"
Louis said, raising his hands in the air. *"Oui,* very
much trouble. Do not talk to me about this man's
here."

"Why did you give him the box?" Chantel asked.
"Why did you tell him to take it to Covington's Folly?
What was in it?"

Louis eyed her. "Why does such a pretty one worry
her head over such matters? These are things you do
not want to know." He grinned. "Or you could lose
your pretty little head."

"Listen, my brother is—"

"Your brother!" Louis Dejarn exclaimed.

"Yes, Teddy is my brother."

"Mon Dieu," he said, his dark eyes widening. "So
you are the charming Chantel." He suddenly laughed.
"And you wish to know why I sent the box with your
brother?" He shrugged. "I had to rid myself of the box
fast, *nes c'est pas?* They were after me. Your brother—
he is an easy dupe, no?"

"Here now!" Teddy exclaimed. "May be a dupe, but
you shouldn't say it in front of me. Ain't as if I'm not
in the room."

"And why Covington's Folly?" Chantel said, eyes
narrowing.

The little Frenchman studied her and then sighed.
"Why not? Your brother, he talk and talk about this
Covington Folly, he say it hold a treasure."

Teddy paled. "I—I didn't say that!"

"But of course you did!" Louis said scornfully.
"You said your vouchers were good, *non?* You had a
treasure."

Teddy flushed. "Was bosky. Ain't no treasure," he shook his head vehemently. "Ain't no treasure."

"All right," Chantel said, easily ignoring Teddy since she was focused on finding the truth. "Now tell me what was in the box and for whom you work?"

The slight man shrugged his shoulders and Chantel felt like hitting him. "That I can not tell, *ma cherie.* It would be my life!"

"It will be your life if you don't," Chantel said threateningly.

"Ha, you talk big, *non?* But I know you would not shoot Louis here. You are a lady, *non?* But now, you must leave. And do not play with matters beyond your understanding, *ma cherie.*" He said it in such a condescendingly male way that Chantel really did want to shoot him! He promptly turned his back on them to open the door.

"Wait one moment," Chantel said, suddenly remembering that she could indulge her urge to put a bullet through him if she so desired. Grinning rather maliciously, she pulled the Manton from her cloak. "Stop, *mon cher,* or I will shoot you."

Louis turned. When he spied the gun in her hand he merely chuckled. "Such a marvelous thing. Such fire, little lady, but you really should not hold that, it is not at all feminine. Now will you leave?"

Chantel controlled her temper. She needed information from the little gnat. "No."

He shrugged that irritating Gallic shrug. "Very well," he said, "then I will." He calmly turned back to the door.

"What do we do now?" Teddy whispered. "He's escaping."

Chantel's eyes narrowed. She cocked the pistol with unsteady hands, aimed high, and pulled the trigger. The Manton recoiled sharply, sending Chantel halfway across the room with its force. Her ears buzzed from the explosion. The ball hit the ceiling directly over Louis's head. The room's construction was not strong and suddenly half of the ceiling cascaded upon him. "We'll do that!" Chantel replied, when she had regained her balance.

As the dust settled, Louis slowly turned. Shavings and whitewash adorned his head and shoulders, while an extremely comical look of shock plastered his face. His hands were raised instinctively in the air. *"Mon Dieu,* you shot at me, you actually shot!"

"And I'll shoot again!" Chantel said ruthlessly. "Teddy, give me your gun."

"But . . ." Teddy started to object.

"I don't care if it is murder," Chantel said loudly, jabbing Teddy swiftly in the ribs. "I want to kill him."

"But you can't," Teddy wheezed. "Because—"

"Teddy," Chantel growled, glaring at him. "Do not say another word. I want your pistol, now!"

"Very well," Teddy sighed. He pulled the weapon out, its muzzle inadvertently pointed at Louis's heart. "Ain't no use . . ."

Louis swallowed with a noisy gulp. "No, no, please," he pleaded, hopping nervously from one foot to another. "Watch what you do!"

"What?" Teddy asked. His grip on the gun weakened and the muzzle drifted lower upon Louis's form. The little Frenchman realized its strategic and delicate target and he instantly froze, emitting one terrified squeak.

"I know it's no use if I kill him without getting the information," Chantel shrugged in a fair imitation of Louis. "But I want to kill him anyway." She swiftly grabbed the pistol from Teddy, for Louis's eyes were beginning to roll back in his head.

"Mon Dieu," Louis breathed. "Please do not kill me."

Chantel cocked the pistol. "Then tell me what I want to know!"

"Mother of God, you are a woman," Louis murmured. "You do not understand, I—I cannot tell you. I would be killed."

"But if you *don't* tell me, you will be killed," Chantel said.

"Yes," he wailed. "But—but you do not understand, if—if my employer kills me, it will be most terrible."

Chantel's hand trembled. Her ploy was not working. She forced a cold stare upon him. "Dead is dead." She shook the gun at him.

"Wait—" he pleaded. "Wait! Let me think for a moment!"

"Let him think," Teddy nodded. "Reasonable thing. I always have to think."

Louis cast him a grateful look. "I—I cannot tell you and have—have my employer after me . . . but," he looked pitifully hopeful, "but if you could give me money—then I could tell you. I could tell you and then escape to France, before he found out. Only think, *ma cherie . . .*"

"Call me that one more time and I will shoot you," Chantel gritted out.

"No, no of course not *ma belle—*"

Chantel rattled the gun. "Or that either!"

"No, please, I won't," he stammered. "But . . . what do you think? If you could give me the money, I would tell you all I know and I could escape to France. We would both be happy . . . and both alive," he added weakly.

Chantel made a grand display of considering his offer. "Oh, very well," she said, shoving the pistol into Teddy's lax hands. Both Teddy and Louis squeaked.

She dug for her reticule in her cloak. Delving into it, she withdrew the remainder of the money she possessed. "Will this be enough?"

Louis, with one wary eye on Teddy, cast the other upon the bills she held forth. He shook his head nervously. "No, not enough."

"Here now, that's a lot of money." Teddy objected.

"Not enough to escape to France." Louis said. "I will need another two hundred pounds."

Chantel thought furiously. "If you will come to my house two days hence in the morning, for St. James is always away then, I will have it, plus another hundred," she added magnanimously, knowing she needed an added enticement if she was ever to see the Frenchman again.

Louis smiled, his black eyes brightening. "Ah, you do a fine thing Ma . . . mademoiselle," he substituted quickly. "You see, I am no longer of service here, no one will hire me since—since the black box. But if you will give me this—I will tell you who employs me. This I swear."

"Very well," Chantel nodded briskly, excitement coursing through her. "Now we shall leave you."

"But—but you must promise me something in return," Louis said hesitantly.

Chantel froze. "I need promise you nothing."

"No, you must promise me that you will tell no one of this agreement of ours," he said. "Else I will be dead."

Chantel studied him. "You mean I must not tell St. James, don't you?"

"Oui," he nodded. "And everybody else you know. Everybody. No matter who. This must be completely secret. You must promise."

He looked desperate and Chantel nodded solemnly. "Of course, I promise."

"Merci," he breathed.

"Now we must leave," Chantel said, anxious to depart before anything could go awry.

"Please, please do," Louis said swiftly.

Chantel grabbed Teddy by the arm. Louis sidled out of their way and gratefully allowed them to pass him. As the door closed and they entered the dank hall, Chantel whispered, "We will have our answer within two days."

"But how are we going to get the ready?" Teddy whispered back. "We ain't got three hundred pounds."

"Just leave that to me," Chantel said with a wave of her hand as they strode down the dark corridor.

"What are you going to do?"

"I don't know," she replied vaguely, still too pleased with her efforts to consider such small, nagging details. "But I'll think of something, I have no doubt."

Chapter Seven

Richard studied the two men who sat in the library chairs before him. He wished he could level the one who was just then speaking. It was not because he did not like Jameson or believe him an excellent man, it was because of what the man was saying.

"And then the Lady St. James and her brother went to Mrs. Durham's. My lady was dressed—er—flamboyantly."

"Was she?" Richard asked, forcing an attitude of nonchalance.

"Had a green dress on," the second man, Brett, said grinning stupidly . . . or so it seemed to Richard. "It was—" He evidently caught Richard's look, for he coughed before continuing. "It was—er—green."

"Yes, my lord," Jameson concurred. "Then they met with Louis Dejarn."

"What?"

"They went and met with Louis—"

"Are you positive?"

"Yes, my lord. They were rather easy to follow. They kept greasing everybody's palms as they went."

Richard growled. "And I funded it, I have no doubt. What happened when they met with Dejarn?"

The man shrugged. "They came out looking extremely pleased with themselves."

"They did?" Richard said, bewildered.

"Do you think they are in on it, then?" Brett asked.

"I cannot say," Richard replied noncommittally. "Either they are or they are merely idiotic enough to believe they can uncover the traitor. Knowing Chantel, she would think she was being clever. She has a strong sense of protectiveness toward her brother."

"God," Jameson breathed, "she evidently doesn't know who she's playing with."

"But neither do we," Richard sighed. "Thank you, men, for doing this service for me."

" 'Twas nothing," Jameson said, rising. Richard glared at him and he swallowed. "I mean . . ."

"I know what you mean," Richard said dryly. He shook his head. "As if I don't have enough trouble, now I have that little shrew playing sleuth. Very well, I thank you. You men have done an excellent job. When you return to London I wish you to take a missive to Edward."

"That will be no problem," Jameson said, nodding.

"No problem at all," Brett repeated.

The two men left. Richard sat down once again in his chair. His fingers drummed the polished wood of the desk and he frowned deeply. Just what was that little minx up to now?

"Ooooh miss, you do look a treat," Betty, the newly acquired maid said, stepping back. Chantel liked her far better than the one that St. James's mother had absconded with. "My lord isn't going to be able to take his eyes off you."

"Let us hope so," Chantel said breathlessly, peering into the mirror. She once again wore the green dress, minus the cherry petticoat and chartreuse furbelow; and, though she did not wear face paint or frizz her hair, she thought she looked seductive. "You truly think I will attract my lord's attention?"

"His attention?" Betty was a wholesome country girl and giggled. "You'll attract more than that, I'm a-thinking." A broad smile crossed her dimpled cheeks. "My lord won't be denying you nothing once he catches you in that dress."

"I hope you are right, Betty," Chantel said, unwilling to admit to the butterflies that were fluttering in her stomach. She fully intended to seduce Richard St. James tonight. It was the only thing she could do. She needed money to give to Louis Dejarn. She needed to protect Teddy and clear the family name.

Chantel drew in a deep breath. No, there was no other way. She would be the sacrifice upon the altar of her family. She had thought and thought about it. She knew that St. James would not simply give her the money straight out. She had almost despaired, but then the memory of Mrs. Durham had entered her mind.

Mrs. Durham made a living by seducing men, and a rather plush living at that. Chantel knew that St. James was an easily seduced man. Mrs. Durham had said as much. He had alliances with that other kind of woman. Chantel's lip curled slightly. She could not respect St. James for it. Indeed, every time she thought of it, an angry sick feeling settled within the pit of her stomach. Her sense of decency was offended.

Chantel sternly forced her attention back to the moment. Her eyes narrowed. Tonight it wouldn't be any doxy receiving his attentions, it would be her—all for the sake of the family, of course. "Very well," she nodded shortly to her reflection in the mirror. "If you think I will do, Betty, I must go down to dinner."

"Yes, miss," Betty said, beaming. Then she started. "Ohhh, I just remembered something. Ohh, do wait a moment!"

"Why?" Chantel asked in alarm.

"I've got one last thing you need," Betty said. "I'll be back in a winking." She dashed from the room and Chantel fidgeted. She would be late for dinner. She looked in the mirror again and wondered if she should perhaps use the face paint. After all, she could not afford to fail tonight. She must seduce Richard into giving her the money.

"Here it is," Betty said, rushing back into the room, all aglow and breathless.

"What is it?"

"It's called Eau De Passion," Betty said. "I use it and my Tom goes wild." She uncapped it and liberally dashed Chantel with it. Chantel sniffed. It seemed a heavy scent.

Chantel smiled weakly. "Thank you." She rose. The butterflies in her stomach seemed to have multiplied. "Wish me luck."

"Luck!" Betty snorted. "Don't you worry, you'll have the master eating out of your hand before the dinner's halfway finished!"

* * *

"That is a very . . . stunning dress," Richard said softly.

"Do you like it?" Chantel asked, almost shouting down the table. She had forgotten that dining at the formal table did very little for the project of seduction. Richard was far down the length of the table. They'd both need eye glasses soon if they continued dining here.

"Why, of course I do." His smile was more puzzled than besotted, Chantel thought nervously, but then she really didn't know what a man looked like when he was enamoured of a woman. "Is that one of the new dresses you bought while in London?"

"Yes."

"And did you buy more like that?"

"Why do you ask?" Chantel countered suspiciously. There was a note of amusement in his voice. Did this bode well?

"Oh, only because I approve, of course," Richard said.

"Good," Chantel said, beaming.

"Indeed, I hope you bought a dozen like that."

"You do?" Chantel asked, surprised. She herself thought the dress brash and crass, but it only went to show that men's tastes were different. And then a great inspiration hit her. "I am so glad you approve. For you see, I fear I er . . . went overboard in my spending spree."

"You did?" Richard again seemed amused.

Yes, yes, this was certainly the right tack. "Yes," Chantel nodded. "It seems that I-I will need more er—ah—money."

"You will? And how much more money do you need exactly?"

"Exactly?"

"Yes, exactly."

"Three hundred pounds," Chantel blurted out. "And I need it by tomorrow morning."

"Three hundred by tomorrow!" Richard said, sounding stunned. He took a sip of wine from his glass and then said, "Well, what can I say? It seems a rather large figure and that you would need it so soon . . . but then to have you well dressed, it is going toward a good purpose. It is not as if it is going toward a bad purpose, is it?"

"Oh no, it is definitely going toward a good purpose," Chantel nodded vehemently, feeling flushed with pleasure. He was falling right into her clutches. She took a large gulp of wine. She, Chantel Emberly, was successfully seducing Richard St. James. "I will pay you back, of course."

"You will?" Now he sounded curious. "And how will you do that?"

Here it was! The time had come to use her feminine wiles. Chantel battered her lashes inexpertly and leaned forward. She only hoped he could see her from the distance. "Why, I am sure I will think of a way that will please you."

Richard's eyes widened. "I see. And must you truly have it by tomorrow?"

"Oh yes," Chantel said firmly. "Or perhaps tomorrow evening at the latest."

He looked at her speculatively. "So I have only tonight to decide if I will give you this money?"

"Yes, but tonight . . ." Chantel attempted to imbue

her voice with a sultry tone, "will be all the time you'll need to decide. For I will do anything to persuade you."

"Indeed," Richard said, and suddenly, stunningly, he grinned. It was a grin that made Chantel catch her breath. He was such a good-looking man when he wanted to be. "Then let us enjoy our dinner and you can tell me more."

"Yes," Chantel nodded. She swiftly drank from her wineglass, her mind racing. Tell him more what? What should she do next? How was she to further this seduction?

"What else did you do in London?" Richard asked.

"What?" Chantel asked, still pondering her quandary.

"Ah, I see you cannot hear me," Richard said, raising his voice. "It is the table, it is far too long, far too distancing."

"Yes," Chantel agreed heartily.

"You know, I can hardly hear you," Richard said with an odd tone to his voice.

"You can't?" Chantel asked, raising her voice.

"No, I can't." Richard then leaned back and surveyed her. His look was expectant, as if he thought she should do something. Chantel stared back at him in confusion. Just what was she supposed to do? Richard looked down at his plate, a slight smile playing about his lips. "Er, don't you think it would be better if you were to come and sit by me—rather than all the way down there?"

"Oh yes!" Chantel said enthusiastically. Things couldn't be working out better! She jumped up quickly, picked up her wineglass with one hand, grabbed hold of her chair with the other and approached Richard. She halted, dropped her chair next to Richard, and sat down swiftly. "Oh yes," she said, delighted with her ploy. "This is much better."

Richard laughed, and then he stopped, sniffing. "What scent is that?"

"It is Eau de Passion," Chantel said happily. Betty was right. He had noticed that special touch. And by the expression on his face he was most definitely affected. "Do you like it?"

"Superb," Richard said. He looked at her and smiled a warm smile that suddenly made Chantel's bones feel as though they had liquefied. "You did not bring your plate, Chantel." His voice was low.

"No, no, I didn't," Chantel said breathlessly. "But I am not hungry," she added, her own voice becoming husky as her throat dried up. She resorted to a fast sip of wine. There was something to this seduction business that made one extremely thirsty.

"Oh, but you should eat," Richard said. "I wouldn't want you hungry tonight . . ." He broke off a piece of pastry and held it just before her lips. "Here, we can share mine."

Shocked, Chantel felt her mouth fall open. He brushed her lower lip with the pastry and swiftly popped it into her mouth. She closed her mouth immediately and chewed on the morsel, unable to tear her eyes from Richard's face. His gray eyes glowed. "You left a crumb," he said, and reached out to touch the corner of her lips with his thumb, so very lightly.

"Is—is it gone?" Chantel asked weakly, for she was feeling such odd sensations.

"Hm, no," he said softly. "Come here."

Mesmerized, Chantel leaned toward him and he toward her. He placed his lips just on the corner of her mouth. Chantel's breath caught, but she did not draw back. She remained motionless, a slight shiver racing along her skin. And then Richard's lips lightly kissed her cheek, her temple, just below her ear. Chantel closed her eyes, feeling a tantalizing warmth drug her.

Richard's lips slipped to the hollow of her throat, and without thought Chantel lifted her head back, welcoming his kiss. The slightest sigh of satisfaction escaped her lips. Feather light, Richard's lips slid to the very hollow between her breasts, running along the fabric of her tight decolletage. Chantel trembled. A deeper, surprised moan rose from her throat.

She thought she heard him whisper her name and suddenly he stood. She opened her eyes in confusion, bereft of those warm lips upon her skin. But then Richard clasped her hand and pulled her up along the length of him.

The moment her body came up against the hard strength of his, Chantel's thoughts, needs, and emotions solidified into one purpose. She wanted. She wanted Richard St. James. She reached up and drew his head down to hers. She kissed him, loving the firmness of his lips, the silk of his hair beneath her fingers, the scent of him in her nostrils. His hands splayed across her back and then he was lifting her into his arms. His lips never left hers even as he began to carry her from the dining room.

A shocked, hazy thought flitted through Chantel's mind. She had lost control of the situation. Heavens, she didn't even have control of herself, let alone the situation. But the wild heat coursing through her was a need that Chantel instinctively knew Richard could satisfy. It was a desire that he must satisfy for her or she thought she might go crazy.

Richard's lips found her earlobe and she moaned. Family honor be hanged. She wanted this man and it had nothing to do with monetary gain. "Oh," she sighed, shivering. "I'll think about the money tomorrow." She was so entrapped within the grip of the raw emotion passing between she and Richard that she hadn't realized she had murmured the words aloud. Her thoughts were only for the magical sensations Richard's lips were creating.

It seemed Richard flinched and faltered. Yet he still kissed her and Chantel did not consider it. Indeed, she had not considered their progress at all. She really didn't care where he was carrying her, didn't care that he had turned around and had walked back to the dining table, didn't care . . .

"What!" she exclaimed as Richard dumped her unceremoniously onto the table, amongst silver, heirloom crystal, and Limoges china, as well as a remove of roasted capon and candied pears. Brussels sprouts met Brussels lace. A glass toppled and Chantel could feel liquid seeping through her dress. Her mind and body warred with each other. Strong, hot desire for Richard still coursed through her, yet her physical discomfort in sitting amongst dinner dishes demanded her attention as well.

"The bedroom is too far," Richard said in a low tone. His voice wasn't filled with passion now, it was more like anger. "We can do it here on the table."

"What!" Chantel squeaked. Reality won out and all her ardor was doused. Richard made to approach her.

"No," Chantel said frantically. She picked up the nearest thing she could find, a plate of butter, and held it up threateningly. "Stay away from me!"

"But don't you want the money?" Richard taunted. "Three hundred pounds is quite a sum. You should be willing to be tumbled anywhere. Faith, it would take a year on the streets of London to make what you intend to in one night."

Chagrin, rage, and frustrated passion flooded through Chantel. "Beast!" she cried, and flung the dish. Richard dodged it easily. "Fiend!" A glass went flying. "Cad!" She sent a bowl sailing. "Ohh!!"

Richard dodged all missiles deftly and when she halted her throwing, panting and out of breath, he looked at her for a moment. Then suddenly, horribly, unforgivably, he began to laugh. "You should see yourself," he roared, doubling over in laughter.

"Don't laugh," Chantel said furiously. She lifted the wine decanter threateningly. She froze, however, as Richard straightened and caught her eye.

"I wouldn't if I were you," he said, all humor gone and a dark, dangerous look on his face. "You've already been warned."

Chantel slowly lowered the decanter. "I hate you."

His gray eyes were almost black. His back was stiff and he looked like the powerful man he was. "Let this be a lesson to you. The next time you seduce me, don't seduce me for money."

"There won't be a next time," Chantel said, her eyes tearing, her voice not only angry, but desperate.

It seemed as if a look of deep pain crossed Richard's face. Without another word, he walked from the room.

Tears fell down Chantel's cheeks. "There won't be a next time," she whispered sadly, with regret. "There won't be a next time."

Chantel sat in the parlor. A deep, depressing numbness prevailed. She doubted she had ever felt as awful as she did now. Her mind continuously replayed the humiliating scene from last night over and over again. Hot mortification flushed her as well as another feeling, a feeling as if she had just lost something very special, very important.

She shook her head to clear it. What was she thinking? There was nothing for her to lose when it came to the earl, for there was nothing to possess with him. He had never respected her, so her humiliation last night had changed nothing. He was an honorable man, one who did not deal with families like hers, families that had enough skeletons in their closet to fill a graveyard. He was also an experienced man who didn't fall for the ploys of inexperienced redheads with no seductive powers. He had experienced mistresses to enthrall him. What had she been thinking when she had come up with the bacon-brained notion of seducing him?

The door opened and Richard's butler entered. "Mr. Chad has arrived."

"Excellent," Chantel said, grateful for a diversion from her thoughts. Chad would cheer her. Oh, how she needed a friendly face.

Chad entered, meticulously dressed as usual. "I received your message that you wished to see me," he said. "You said it was urgent?"

"It seems I am always sending you urgent messages these days," Chantel said wryly.

Chad sat down comfortably next to her. "I don't mind. Though I would rather you sent messages saying that you were fine, but that you desired my company all the same."

Chantel touched his hand briefly. "I am sorry. But one day it will change."

"In five months, perhaps?"

"Yes," Chantel nodded, forcing a smile. "And then I will invite you with nary a trouble on my mind . . ."

"Since when has there not been contretemps in our family?"

Chantel sighed. "True, due to the Covington curse no doubt."

"Now tell me, what is bothering you?" His face tightened. "You have been safe? There have not been any more attempts—"

"Oh no! Of course not," Chantel said swiftly.

He frowned. "I visited last week and St. James said you were in London. Of course he was as cool to me as he could stare. Was he telling the truth, or just turning me off?"

"No, I went to London with Teddy," Chantel said. "It was a rather quick decision on my part. I-I did not think of notifying anyone."

He laughed. "You don't have to explain, my dear. You are free to do as you wish. If it made you happy, that is all that counts."

"I thought to find you in London," Chantel said, "But you were not at home."

Chad smiled wryly. "I was away on business, of sorts. Now tell me what I can help you with?"

"I fear I have a great favor to ask you," Chantel said hesitantly.

"Ah, great favors, good," Chad said, rubbing his hands together. "Finally, I am to perform a great favor for you."

"Silly," Chantel said, laughing despite herself, for Chad's expression was comically eager. "I fear that I wish to borrow a great sum of money from you."

His brow rose. "You do?"

"Yes, three hundred pounds."

His other brow rose. "My!"

"I will pay you back," Chantel said worriedly.

"No, no, 'tis not that, the sum is not that much in my view. 'Tis only that I wonder what would cause you finally to break and borrow from me. Is it Teddy?"

"No, not at all," Chantel said. She rose and walked away from him. "I-I promised not to talk to anyone about this."

"Then it is St. James," Chad said positively. "He seems to have an extreme yen for secrecy."

"No, it isn't St. James," Chantel said. She turned. "The only thing I can tell you is that I am using the money to—to gain some information that shall clear Teddy of the charges of treason."

Chad stared at her, open-mouthed. He rose swiftly, crossing to her. "Chantel, are you doing something dangerous?"

"No, no of course not," Chantel prevaricated. " 'Tis a simple transaction, but I need money for it."

"Then you have it, and don't you ever think to pay me back," Chad said sternly. "This is to help the entire family. If you can free it of the suspicion of treason it will be worth every farthing." He raised his hand to her cheek. "Poor Chantel, you take too much upon yourself. Please, I can help, you know. I truly can, if only you would come to me more often."

"I will," Chantel smiled, feeling a weight fall from her shoulders. She wasn't alone after all. Furthermore, Chad thought her a heroine, not some hussy bent on getting money.

"Good. Now when do you need the money?"

"I'll need it by tomorrow."

Chad whistled. "Then I must act quickly." He smiled. "Don't worry. I will bring it this afternoon."

Chantel threw her arms about him, hugging him in gratitude. "Oh thank you, cousin dearest."

"Any time." Chad laughed happily. "Now I best leave before St. James finds me here and spends his time glowering at me."

Chantel nodded, neglecting to tell Chad that she was certain Richard wouldn't care what she did now. She was sure he felt too much disgust of her for that. Thank the Lord she still had Chad. He still respected her. He had come to her rescue.

Yet a tiny voice within her cried out at the thought. Why couldn't Richard St. James have been the one to help her? Why couldn't it have been Richard St. James she could have trusted?

"Madam," Reed said with dignity. "There is a person who wishes to speak to you in the library." He looked slightly offended. "He would not state his business and is of a certain foreign persuasion."

Chantel smiled in excitement. "That is all right. I was expecting him." She rose from the table, leaving her breakfast untouched. Louis was early. As she grabbed up her reticule, it crackled with the money Chad had lent her. "Thank you Reed, that will be all."

She hurried out of the breakfast room into the foyer and across it to the library. She was sure Teddy would be disappointed not to be there, but Dejarn was early and she would have to take care of the business herself. It had worked out as she planned, for Richard was out upon errands and would not return for another two hours. Everything was going perfectly.

Chantel entered the library and closed the door firmly. A nervous tingle ran down her spine. What would she discover from Louis Dejarn? She turned to discover him sitting at Richard's desk.

"Mr. Dejarn?" Chantel kept her voice low. "I have the money."

He did not answer and she walked up to him. "If we could proceed . . ." Chantel's voice petered away as she stood before Louis Dejarn. His eyes were shut and his face had a bluish tint. "Are you all right?" Chantel asked urgently, reaching out to shake Dejarn. He toppled forward onto the desk.

The man was dead! She had a dead man lying on Richard St. James' desk. Chantel suddenly noticed a fine white cord wrapped around Dejarn's neck. No, not just a dead man, but a murdered dead man!

Chantel looked frantically about. Whatever was she to do with a dead Louis Dejarn? If Richard found him here he would believe Teddy was the murderer. They'd clap him in irons and drag him away for certain. She turned a stern, angry eye upon the dead Dejarn. "Well, you can't stay here and ruin it for Teddy."

Chantel resolutely pulled the chair back from the

desk and secured a hold on Dejarn, dragging him from the chair. He fell to the floor and Chantel grabbed up both his hands. She began to drag him toward the door. He was not going to be found in the library, or anywhere in the house for that matter, or her name was not Chantel Emberly. She had enough to do to protect the family honor, what little there was left of it, without having incriminating dead bodies on her hands as well.

Chantel opened the library door and peeked out. The foyer was clear. Not a sound could be heard. Chantel swung the door wide and dragged Dejarn through it and out across the black and white marble tile floor of the foyer, counting the squares as she tugged and pulled. Thank heaven Dejarn was such a small man or she would have been in the suds. She had reached the center of the foyer when she heard footsteps approaching from the back of the house. With trepidation, she gazed about and down at Dejarn sprawled across several squares of floor, feeling that her burden resembled a piece upon a chessboard. The question was, which direction to move in order to avoid checkmate.

"Drat!" she muttered, panting. She picked up speed and dragged Louis to the closest door, which led to the breakfast room. She tugged him along the Aubusson carpet to the table, and flipped up the lacy flounces of its cloth. She had just managed to roll him underneath the breakfast table when Reed entered. She dropped the cloth swiftly and scrambled to seat herself at her place. "Yes, Reed?" she said as innocently as she could, taking up her teacup with a shaking hand.

"Madam, there are contretemps within the

kitchen," Reed said with a sigh. "Cook and House-keeper are in a wrangle and are all but at each other's throats."

"Not them too," Chantel said distractedly. "They had better not kill each other. I already have one body—er one problem on my mind," Chantel said, stunned at what she had almost said. She realized shock was overtaking her.

"They are both saying they shall give notice and leave," Reed said as Chantel remained anchored to her chair.

Chantel sighed deeply. As if it wasn't enough having a dead body under her breakfast table, now she had servants giving notice. "Very well, I shall come," Chantel said. She couldn't face it if Richard came home and found no cook or housekeeper. Pity! What she wanted gone wouldn't leave, and what she wanted to stay, was leaving. She rose, and with a hasty look back at the table to ensure Dejarn was not visible, she left the room.

Teddy entered the front door, neither knocking nor waiting for Reed to come. He was feeling very stealthy, very daring. Tiptoeing, he went from room to room, peeking into them. He found no one.

When he looked into the breakfast room, he at least discovered food awaiting him on the table. Wondering where Chantel was, he crossed to the table and sat down. The kippers looked particularly tasty. He was filling his plate with a heaping serving when his foot kicked something below the table. Frowning, he looked down, wondering what it could possibly be. A hand was sticking out from under the pristine table cloth. Teddy's kippers flew in the air. He squawked and sprung from his chair.

"Who's under there?" he cried. There was no response. "All right, don't play games, come out from under there." Still no response. The hand remained, taunting him. Teddy frowned and then his expression cleared. "Dejarn, that you? Why are you hiding under there?" He knelt down, lifting up the tablecloth. He peered closely at the still body. It took him a moment of staring and then he exclaimed, "Gadzooks, you ain't hiding, you're dead!"

Teddy sprung from his crouch. "Why's he dead?" he asked the room at large. "Why's he under the table, who would kill a man under a breakfast table? Queer thing to do."

Then Teddy's brain worked fervidly in an attempt to reason it all out. "Under the table . . . Chantel's food is here. Oh no, oh no, Chantel killed him." He started pacing in a circle, his hands flapping out. He looked very similar to a distraught hen. "What am I to do? Sure she had a reason, but what to do now. Anyone can find him here. I did. Anyone can. St. James won't like this, not one whit." He stopped abruptly, coming to a decision. "Got to hide him, that's what."

Teddy tore from the breakfast room and returned in a few minutes, a proud expression upon his face. He ran to the breakfast table, knelt down, and flipped up the table cloth. "Got the perfect place, Dejarn, they won't find you there."

He tugged the body out from under the table. Once again Dejarn crossed the breakfast room's carpet, out into the hall to cross the foyer's marble floor, and was once again . . . dragged into the library.

Teddy, an intent expression upon his face, dragged Dejarn to a large wall cabinet. He opened the cabinet door and began tearing out the rows of books it housed. Panting, he knelt down, grabbed Dejarn beneath the armpits, and lifted him into the cabinet. "Tight fit," Teddy grunted. "Lucky you are small," he informed the dead man. Teddy bent and scooped up two armfuls of books, with which he attempted to conceal Dejarn. "There we are. All finished," Teddy muttered approvingly. Wheezing from his exertion, he slammed the cabinet doors shut. "Got to find Chantel," he told himself. Stumbling over the remainder of the books that he had not been able to force back into the cabinet, he ran from the room.

Richard entered the front door, a determined set to his jaw. He was going to confront Chantel. Ever since last night, he and Chantel had been maneuvering to ensure neither saw the other. He would stay away on errands, she would have her meals in her room. It was enough! They had to talk.

He really didn't know what he could say, however. How to apologize for his ungentlemanly behavior? He had actually toppled a lady onto a dining table! He had never behaved so shabbily toward any woman, and especially not a lady!

Yet he had been so full of passion for Chantel at that moment. All he had wanted to do was carry her to a bedroom and make love to her. He had been so full of need for her. Then she had murmured neither sweet nothings nor endearments into his ears, but only talk of the money she so desired. He had simply seen red. In truth, he had seen every other color as well!

No, it was time to talk. Time to find out what game Chantel was playing. Time to put the cards on the table and see what they turned up. In deep contemplation, he entered the library. He would finish his books for the day and then he would find Chantel.

He had not made it across the room to his desk when he noticed that a goodly number of books were strewn upon the floor. They must have fallen out of the cupboard and no one had replaced them.

Frowning, he crossed and opened the cupboard. "The devil," he muttered. A cascade of books tumbled out, revealing the body of Dejarn. Richard's thoughts flew immediately to Chantel and her need for money. Had Dejarn been blackmailing her? And when he, Richard, had so callously refused to give the money to her, had she been forced to kill Dejarn?

No, Richard didn't believe it. Staring at Dejarn's lifeless form stashed in his book cabinet, Richard suddenly came to both a decision and a revelation. He believed in Chantel. No matter the extremely incriminating evidence before him, he believed in Chantel. In some way, she was innocent. He would have to discover the truth from her, but until then, he needed to rid them of the body.

Richard pulled Dejarn out from his cubbyhole and onto the library floor. He then dragged him onto the library's Oriental rug. He pulled the chairs off it and proceeded to roll Dejarn up in it. He went to the window to open it, only to find it already ajar. He scanned the landscape carefully . . . there was not a soul in sight. Richard went back, hefted the carpet roll up, carried it over to the window, and dumped it out.

Dejarn was at least now safely out of the library.

Richard fully intended to transport the body off the
estate, but he would wait until nightfall for that endeavor. Until then, Dejarn would have to be hidden in
the barn. Richard left the library and strolled through
the foyer and out the front door.

Chantel came from the back of the house. She
thought she had heard the front door open and shut,
but when she entered the foyer, there was no one in
view. She trod stealthily to the breakfast room and
entered, grimly shutting its doors.

Teddy, still looking about nervously, walked cautiously down the stairs. He had not found Chantel
upstairs. Shaking his head in bemusement, he went
back into the library to reevaluate the hiding place of
his dead charge.

Silence fell upon the house. Then a shriek arose
from the breakfast room. A shout came from the library. Both library and breakfast room doors flew
open. Teddy thundered out of the library. Chantel
charged from the breakfast room. They collided in the
middle of the foyer.

"He's gone!" Chantel cried, clutching at Teddy for
balance.

"I know," Teddy exclaimed, grasping her.

They both froze and eyed each other suspiciously.
Slowly they released one another and stepped back.

"Who are you talking about?" Chantel asked cautiously.

"I don't know," Teddy stammered. "Who are you
talking about?"

Chantel swallowed. "Louis Dejarn."

Teddy nodded his head so vigorously that by all

rights it should have fallen off his shoulders. "That's who I'm talking about. That's him. Ah . . . you know he—he isn't exactly alive?"

"Yes," Chantel sighed. "I know. But where is he?"

"Don't know. He's not in the library."

"Of course not," Chantel said irately. "I moved him from there. I put him in the breakfast room."

"You put him in the breakfast room again!"

"What do you mean, again?" Chantel looked at him in confusion.

"Well, I mean, I put him in the library," Teddy said, nonplussed.

"You mean the first time?"

"What first time?"

"When—when you killed him," Chantel said gravely.

"Me! Killed him!" Teddy squeaked, aghast. "No, didn't do any such thing."

Chantel's look was piercing, then she sighed. "Thank heaven. But you put him in the library the first time?"

"What is this first time?" Teddy asked in frustration. "I put him in the library after you killed him in the breakfast room."

"I didn't kill him!" Chantel said offended.

"You didn't?"

"No, of course not. I took him from the library because I thought you had killed him."

"Oh, then that's why he's not in the library," Teddy said in great relief.

"But he's not in the breakfast room either!" Chantel said angrily.

Teddy looked at Chantel. Chantel looked at Teddy.

"What are we going to do?" Teddy asked, his voice jittery. "He's gone."

"We've got to find him. Dead men just don't disappear."

Teddy's eyes bulged. "Are you sure he was dead? Maybe—"

"No, he was dead. I am positive of that."

Teddy looked suspiciously at Chantel. "Are you sure you didn't kill him?"

"Of course I am," Chantel said indignantly. "One doesn't forget something like that."

"Well, just thought since you were so positive that he was dead that—"

"Teddy, would you stop it, he was positively, irrevocably dead. And I did not have to kill him to know that," Chantel said, frustrated. "Now where could he have gone?"

"Don't know, best start looking for him again," Teddy sighed heavily. "Wonder where he took off to?" He peered suspiciously at the side table in the foyer as if it could be shielding Dejarn.

"Teddy, you can't believe he'd be there," Chantel objected as her brother then turned his eye to a chair and bent under it to study it as well. "He is too large for . . . Richard!" she finished as she spied the door open and Richard entering. "You are back!"

"Yikes, St. James," Teddy cried, his face washing thirteen different shades. He stood up swiftly, wringing his hands before him. "You're back!"

"So I am," Richard said calmly. "Is there anything odd about that?"

"No, no," Teddy stuttered quickly, his eyes bulging. "Er—nothing odd, everything normal, nothing out of the ordinary, everything just the usual, everything—"

"I understand," Richard said, holding up his hand. "Everything is normal."

"Yes, yes, that is what I meant," Teddy nodded, gulping in air.

"Teddy has to leave now," Chantel said, casting Teddy a warning glare and shoving him in the direction of the door.

"Yes, yes, must run." Teddy jumped at Chantel's suggestion like a drowning man to a lifeboat. "Yes, can't stay. Must run. Not that I'm running from anything, mind you," he added anxiously. "Only thing is, got an appointment. Common for me, nothing—"

"I know, nothing out of the ordinary," Richard interjected, smiling kindly. "But I would like a moment of your time, and Chantel's as well." Brother and sister faltered and stopped. "We could have a drink. Perhaps we could go into the library . . ." Richard suggested.

"No! Not the library!" yelped Teddy, shaking his head in alarm.

"The library is fine," Chantel said as calmly as she could. She glared at Teddy.

"Oh, yes," Teddy said. "Forgot, the library is fine now."

"No, no," Richard said politely. "Since you seem averse to the library, let us have our drink in the parlor."

"Er . . . yes, very well," Teddy said, casting a suspicious glance around the foyer. Chantel pinched him on the arm as unobtrusively as she could.

"Ouch!" Teddy jumped.

"Is anything the matter?" Richard asked, brow raised.

"No, of course not," Chantel said, smiling as demurely as possible. "If you would care to lead the way?"

Richard nodded and walked toward the parlor door.

"Shouldn't let him in first," Teddy whispered to her as they followed behind. "Haven't checked that room yet."

"Stop it," Chantel whispered back, worried that Richard would hear. "He wouldn't be in there. Now, be quiet."

Richard went directly to the decanters on a sideboard. "What would everyone like?"

"I'll have a sherry," Chantel said absently as Teddy and she sat down upon the settee. Teddy promptly jack-knifed over and peered beneath the settee.

"And you, Teddy? . . ." Richard turned to catch him in that rather interesting position. "Teddy?"

Teddy straightened. "Hmm?"

"What would you like to drink?"

"Oh, er, brandy," Teddy said nervously.

"Brandy? Hm, that decanter is almost empty." Richard said with a frown. He looked about. "Now, where is the extra supply? Ah, yes, it is in this cabinet." He reached for the handle of a large cabinet.

"No, don't!" yelped Teddy suddenly, springing up. "Let me check first!" He sprinted over to the cabinet. Pushing Richard aside and shielding the cabinet door, he opened it cautiously. He looked in warily. Chantel could do nothing but drop her head and pray for survival. "Ain't here!" Teddy sighed in relief. "It's all right." Beaming, he left the cabinet and returned to sit down next to Chantel again. Chantel kicked him out of sheer vexation. "Ouch!"

"But Teddy, you are wrong," Richard said, peering into the depths of the cabinet.

"What! Oh God!" Teddy gasped, blanching visibly.

"What?" Chantel exclaimed.

"It is here," Richard smiled, pulling a bottle of brandy from the cabinet.

"Whew," Teddy said, drawing a cuff across his perspiring brow. "Thought for a moment you had—"

Chantel frantically slapped her hand on his knee and squeezed so tightly that Teddy didn't have the breath to cry out. "He meant he really did want that brandy," she said with a stiff smile, her teeth gritted.

"I see," Richard said. He poured the drinks out and brought them over to Teddy and Chantel.

"Thank you," Chantel said, trying to ignore the fact that Teddy was still running his eye about the room as if he expected Dejarn's body to slip out from under a piece of furniture at any moment.

"Cheers," Richard smiled, sitting on a chair across from them. Before Chantel could stop him, Teddy lowered his head as if to look under Richard's chair. "Teddy, did you lose something?"

"Hm, what?" Teddy asked as he straightened, stunned.

"It seems you are looking for something," Richard said mildly.

"He's not," Chantel said at the same time as Teddy said, "I am."

Richard looked back and forth between brother and

sister. "Well, what is the verdict? Are you or are you not looking for something you have lost?"

Chantel sighed. Teddy looked at her nervously and sputtered, "No, no, I am not looking for something."

"Pity," Richard said. "For I am very good at helping people find things they lose."

"That's all right," Teddy said. "Wouldn't want you to find this one anyway."

"I beg your pardon?" Richard said, raising both brows.

"What Teddy means," Chantel said swiftly, "is that if he had lost something, he wouldn't want you to worry yourself about finding it."

"Oh, it would be no trouble," Richard said sweetly. "I have a knack for finding things. In fact, you wouldn't believe what I did find."

"What?" Chantel asked, a terrible premonition shaking her.

"I have in fact found a body . . . dead, of course. Could either of you tell me why I found Louis Dejarn in my book cabinet in the library?"

"Ain't there any more," Teddy said glumly. Then his eyes widened. "What-ho! Did—do you know where he has gone off to?"

"Well I know where his body is, but where he has gone off to? That is a philosophical question to consider, but I would hazard a guess that Louis did not go to heaven."

"Where is he? The body I mean?" Chantel asked, excitedly.

"We will talk of that only after you tell me why Louis met his comeuppance within the walls of my house." He looked to Chantel, his expression now deadly serious.

"I—I don't know why he was killed," Chantel said, "or who killed him."

"You don't?"

"No, I don't," she said defensively. "I suppose you think it was me?"

"It wasn't," Teddy said before Richard could even speak. "I thought the same thing at first. I mean, Chantel has a temper and all, but she didn't kill him. She told me so."

"And you, Teddy?" Richard asked quietly. "Did you kill him?"

"Me!" Teddy jumped. "No, of course not. Waved a gun at him once because Chantel told me to after she shot at him, but never killed him. Never killed anyone in my whole life. Er . . . ain't in my line."

Richard's brow rose and he looked to Chantel. "Just when did you shoot at Louis Dejarn and make Teddy wave his gun at him?"

Chantel clamped her mouth shut and steamed. But since she knew, no matter how civil Richard was being at this moment, that he held their future welfare in his palm, she replied, "I shot at him when we were in London."

"I see. Please explain it all."

"We went to London to find Louis Dejarn. When we found him he promised to tell us who the man he worked for was, but only if we could give him enough money for him to escape to France."

"So that is what you needed the money for?"

Chantel flushed deeply. "Yes. If only he could have told us who the traitor was."

"What were you going to do this morning when you didn't have the money?"

"I secured funds from Chad," Chantel said, squirming. She saw Richard's jaw clench and for some reason she did feel like a traitor. "It is our family that is under suspicion. He was glad to help me."

"I have no doubt," Richard said coolly. "And did you offer him the same incentive as you did me?"

Chantel stiffened and she felt as if she had been slapped. She swallowed a sudden painful lump in her throat. "I did not have to. Chad would help me without anything else involved."

Chantel and Richard glared at each other. She thought she was going to scream until Teddy said, "Shame Louis stuck his spoon in the wall before we could find out who the traitor was."

"I could have told you that Louis would be killed before he could tell you that," Richard said firmly, his eyes still on Chantel. "The man you are playing with is very deadly."

"The man?" Chantel asked. "But didn't you think it was me?"

"No," Richard said. "I have come to the conclusion that both you and Teddy are innocent." Chantel felt the cold hard knot within her suddenly dissolving. He believed in her innocence. Her innocence of treason that was, a small voice cried back. Richard looked away from her. "Did it ever occur to you that I had not approached Louis Dejarn because I knew he would be silenced if I did? I had hoped to keep him alive until I had found enough evidence against the traitor, and then I'd have used Louis as a witness."

Teddy frowned. "Pardon?"

"Don't worry over it Teddy," Richard said kindly. His eyes darkened. "Something I wish your sister would have done as well."

Chantel lifted her chin. "I did not know you had a reason for not searching out Dejarn. You never see fit to tell me anything that is transpiring. Do you think that I will just sit and do nothing while Teddy and I are in danger?"

Richard sighed. "No, I should have realized that you would not do what a normal woman would do." Chantel's eyes narrowed. "No, don't fly out at me, I did not mean that as an insult. Furthermore, we have other important things to consider . . . like Louis's body if it is found on these premises. Since everyone knew that you visited him in London—"

"What do you mean, everyone knew?" Chantel exclaimed. Then she gasped. "You knew!" she accused.

"Yes, I knew. My men followed you in London."

"Your men followed . . ." Chantel stared at Richard. "That means you knew when I came home . . . and you knew that night when I—when I—oh, I should kill you!"

"No," Teddy cried, alarmed, "already got one body on hand. Don't need two."

Richard laughed and turned a taunting eye to Chantel. "Really, Chantel, what are you thinking? Besides, if you kill me you won't know where Louis is," he added, apparently recognizing that Chantel was on the brink of violent mayhem toward him. He had allowed her to make a fool of herself trying to seduce him when she had returned, all the while knowing that she had seen Louis Dejarn. Chantel glared at him in impotent rage. "Now, we will wait until it is night and then we all will go and retrieve Louis Dejarn and take him somewhere else.''

"Why?" Chantel asked suspiciously.

"Because," Richard smiled, "that way none of us can singly be caught with his body. Not just one can be accused of murder. And in your two cases, that will be an advantage." Richard rose. "Now I believe I will try and do the work I intended to do before this whole issue arose.''

Richard walked from the room and Teddy looked to Chantel. "He's taking it rather well, I think."

"So he is." Chantel gritted her teeth. "I'd like to kill him, I truly would.''

Teddy sighed. "Wish you'd stop talking about killing people. Don't like dealing with dead people, don't like dealing with them one jot.''

The night was clear, the moon thankfully low, as three figures slipped from the back of the earl's house and walked across the yard toward the barn. The last figure, more portly than the others, tripped and fell. The other two turned with a hiss as the third muttered an oath. The figures disappeared into the barn. A night lantern was finally lit. Teddy's frightened face glowed in the light as well as Chantel's concerned one and Richard's composed one.

"Damn," Teddy said, "never knew it could be so dark at night without a candle about.''

"Where is he?" Chantel whispered to Richard, ignoring anything but business. She was still annoyed with Richard for his duplicity in having her followed and then luring her into making a fool of herself that night. She feared he could see her red face even in the meager light.

"He is over there," Richard nodded. "Buried beneath those bales."

"Very well, let us get to it," Chantel said, straightening her shoulders and marching to the stack of hay that Richard had pointed to against the far wall. She was attempting to hide the fact that she was not thrilled about the idea of delving into the hay after a dead body.

"After you, St. James," Teddy nodded, his eyes blinking nervously. "You know where you put him, after all."

Richard's smile was amused. "So I do." He followed Chantel over and bent to assist her. "I buried him deeply."

Chantel nodded silently. Teddy finally joined them with a shiver and began to pick hesitantly at the hay. Five minutes later Chantel leaned back, her glare directed at Richard. "Just how deeply *did* you bury him?"

Richard stopped, a frown upon his face. "Not this far down."

Teddy stood, wiping perspiration from his brow. He looked about. "Maybe you forgot, buried him over there perhaps." He pointed across the barn, and immediately headed toward a new stack.

"No, Teddy," Richard said in exasperation. "I did not forget where I buried him."

"Could have," Teddy said, "Might have got confused, I do it all the time."

Chantel looked at Richard suspiciously. "Are you confused? Or are you making a May game out of us?"

Richard's brow rose. "Have you ever known me to perform practical jokes?"

Chantel looked at Richard, her eyes widening. He nodded grimly. Both turned at the same time and attacked the pile anew. Hay positively flew. Whereas before Chantel was cringing at the thought of unearthing the body, now all she wanted was to grab hold of a part of the troublesome Dejarn. "Where is he?" she asked angrily, as she reached the last handful of hay in the stack.

Richard was right beside her. "I don't know, Chanty, I don't know."

"Well, he ain't over here," Teddy said from a hole he had burrowed through. Dusted in hay, with sprigs sticking out amongst his red locks, he was sitting flat on the barn floor. "That Dejarn certainly is a slippery fellow."

"In death as well as in life," Richard sighed, rolling to a sitting position as well.

Chantel gave up and joined them upon the floor. "Where could he be now?"

"Never seen a dead body that moved around as much." Teddy shook his head glumly. "But then, never seen a dead body at all before."

"Someone's taken him," Richard said, shaking his head.

Chantel shivered with fear. "But who? Do you think it is the authorities?"

"Authorities!" Teddy cried.

"I don't think it could be," Richard said. "If it had been, they would already be at our house questioning us."

"But then who took him?" Chantel asked.

"I don't know," Richard said. "We'll just have to wait and see what happens." He rose and stretched out his hand to her. "Come. Evidently somebody has already seen to Dejarn."

Chantel took his hand and allowed him to help her up. "But who? Who in the world would take a dead body away without a reason?"

Richard shook his head. "It is a mystery to me."

"Well, whoever the chap was," Teddy said rising and dusting himself off, "it was damn decent of him."

"Decent of him?" Chantel asked.

"Yes," Teddy nodded. "Dejarn's off our hands now."

Richard looked at Chantel and Chantel looked at Richard. They began to laugh. "He's right, you know." Richard said, chuckling.

"He is," she nodded.

Teddy was already heading for the door. "Tell you what, I'm glad it's over with. Don't want to deal with another dead body ever again. Can't trust them. Always moving about when they shouldn't. Glad this one is off our hands, what?"

Chapter Eight

"Madam, you have a visitor," Reed announced the next morning while Chantel was diligently attempting to eat her breakfast.

Chantel set her teacup down. What was the point? It seemed as if she hadn't eaten for days. In fact, ever since she had arrived at St. James's abode there was one upset after another that always seemed to deny her the morning tradition of breaking fast.

Her stomach lurched. Yesterday was indeed the worst "upset" to date. Then she cringed inwardly. Perhaps she shouldn't say that until she discovered who or what now awaited her outside the breakfast room doors. "Who—who is it?" Chantel asked, trying not to choke on her question.

"My lord's cousin, Lady Alicia," Reed said, a note of fondness entering his voice. "She is in the blue salon."

"Oh? Very well," Chantel said, surprised but delighted that it was no one threatening, such as the law in search of one Louis Dejarn. She rose swiftly. "I will go directly to her, Reed."

Chantel noticed Lady Alicia's maid sitting properly in the foyer. Chantel nodded and passed her, entering the blue salon; the room was so called for its collection of ancient vases in all shades of blue, from the robin's egg-blue of the Limoges to the cobalt inlay on a rare Etruscan urn. Eighty-two vases were catalogued. With the sunlight from a row of floor-to-ceiling bay windows dappling through the myriad of blues, the room had the restful quality of an underwater grotto. Lady Alicia was perched on the edge of a teal striped satin Louis XV chair. She presented a fretful face when she saw Chantel. "Oh, Lady Chantel, I am so glad you would see me."

"Of course I would see you," Chantel said, walking forward and sitting down across from the clearly upset woman. "Why ever should I not?"

"Oh, I—I don't know," Alicia said, her small hands twisting in her lap, crushing tiers of rosebud-dotted muslin flounces. "But Teddy told me you had advised him to forget about me."

Chantel smiled as warmly as she could. She wished she could throttle Teddy for passing on such information. "I told him that only because I know how strongly your parents disapprove of Teddy."

"Then, if my parents approved, you would have nothing against me personally?" Alicia asked, her brown eyes widening.

"No, of course not."

"I am so glad, for I decided I simply must talk to you. I—I am desperate," she announced. "Very desperate."

"You are?" Chantel asked hesitantly.

"I—I am worried over Teddy." Her eyes were large

and dark. "I realize I have no right to ask, but do you know where Teddy is?"

"Not exactly," Chantel answered cautiously. Alicia's look turned frantic. Chantel could not remember when an eligible female had ever inquired of Teddy's whereabouts with any semblance of interest, let alone with urgency. "Why do you ask?"

"I am worried," Alicia said, rising. She paced back and forth in front of Chantel. "He did not . . . he failed to meet me at the appointed hour last night."

"You had a tête à tête with him!"

Alicia halted, flushing. "I know it is quite an improper thing to do. But—but," she drew herself up and looked at Chantel defiantly, "but when a woman meets a man as wonderful and as magnificent as Teddy, she cannot listen to the dictates of propriety—can she? Would you?"

"Er, no," Chantel stammered, bemused. She could find no hint of irony in Alicia's statement. The woman was sincere! She shook her head to clear it. "You think Teddy wonderful?"

"You are his sister, you must know he is."

"Oh . . . indeed yes."

"Then you must realize what a torment it was to me last night when he did not keep his assignation," Alicia sighed, throwing herself down upon the settee. Her face turned pale of a sudden. "Is—is Teddy seeing another woman?" She looked pleadingly at Chantel, reaching out her hands. "Please. You can tell me. I will be strong. At least, I think I will be strong."

"No, he wasn't seeing another woman," Chantel said, clasping Alicia's hands in reassurance. Then she thought, and said honestly, "Well, yes, he was in a way." Alicia moaned and all but wrung the blood from Chantel's hands. "But the woman was me," Chantel added swiftly.

"You?" Alicia asked wide-eyed.

"Yes, it was very important family business," Chantel said, certainly not intending to go into the details. She tried unobtrusively to recapture her hands. "I—I wish I could tell you about the matter, but I cannot. Indeed, you wouldn't wish to know."

"I see," Alicia said, nodding and letting go Chantel's hands. Her expression turned tranquil. "He was doing something dangerous, wasn't he? You don't have to tell me. He is such a mad, dashing fellow."

"He is?" Chantel asked, stunned.

Evidently Alicia hadn't noticed Chantel's interrogative tone. She frowned at Chantel. "I am sure you are accustomed to him being so. But I have told him he must reform if Mother and Father are ever going to accept him. They simply do not understand his daring, devilish nature. And I must own, I do not approve of his gaming either. It is simply no good."

"No, it isn't."

"But I truly do not believe gambling is in Teddy's blood as Mother and Father claim," Alicia said consideringly. "I cannot believe that anything can be in one's blood if one is not proficient at it. Why, it is quite unnatural to wish to do something that one does not do well."

"And Teddy does not do well at gambling," Chantel agreed fervently.

"No, he makes a mull of it every time." Alicia sighed heavily. "He was not cut out to make his living at the tables, I fear. That is why," she continued, as she turned suddenly determined eyes upon Chantel, "that why it is so very important that the Covington treasure is found."

"Oh, Lord." Chantel rolled her eyes toward heaven. Teddy had instilled belief in yet another person as to the existence of the Covington treasure—she could see it in the sudden glow of Alicia's eyes. She attempted to be gentle. "Alicia, Teddy believes in the treasure and indeed it has been a family legend for quite some time, but I fear that Teddy will never find the treasure."

"Well, of course not," Alicia said stoutly.

Chantel sighed in relief. Evidently Alicia was not totally lost to reality. "I am so glad you understand."

"Of course, I understand," Alicia said, patting Chantel's hand. "It is you that must find the treasure."

"What!" Chantel all but yelped.

"I know it is hard for Teddy to accept, but after all, Lady Genevieve said that only a woman of the line would find it." She leaned forward and said conspiratorially, "Men never like to acknowledge such details. They never like to think a woman can do what they cannot, but you and I both know it must be you who will find the treasure."

"We do?" Chantel asked weakly.

"We do," Alicia nodded positively. "Now Teddy has told me that you refuse to look for the treasure, which I think is . . ." She halted.

Chantel eyed her warily. "Is what?"

"Well, I think it slightly unkind," Alicia said gently.

"Unkind!"

Alicia flushed. "Oh dear, my mother is always saying I speak my mind when I should not. I do not wish to upset you. All of us are unkind at one time or another."

"Why do you think me unkind?" Chantel asked, feeling unfairly condemned.

"Well, the only course that I can see for Teddy to escape his difficulties would be for you to find the treasure," Alicia said with a mar to her brow. "But then you refuse even to search for it. Is that not a tiny bit selfish?"

"Alicia, I wouldn't be able to find the treasure—"

"Now don't be disheartened," Alicia said, interrupting before Chantel could tell her she couldn't find the treasure since there wasn't one. "I know you could find it if you would only make a push to do so."

"You do?" Chantel asked dryly.

"Oh, I am positive," Alicia nodded fervently. "I know you haven't wished to look for the treasure, but if you would only reconsider, since the curse has now been lifted from the family, you should be able to find it without any difficulty."

"And why do you think the curse has been lifted from the family?" Chantel asked, intrigued despite herself.

"Because Teddy has promised never to gamble again," Alicia said simply.

Chantel choked. "And you believe him?"

"Oh, yes," Alicia smiled. "You see, Teddy didn't realize that he was the reason you haven't been able to find the treasure . . . that he was prolonging the curse. I do hope you won't hold it against him."

"I still don't understand," Chantel said, shaking her head.

"Well, I pointed out to Teddy that Aunt Genevieve

was very strict about the importance of the curse being lifted from the family before the treasure could be found. By gambling, a thing that Lady Genevieve abhorred, Teddy has been detaining you from finding the treasure. How can Lady Genevieve know it isn't truly in Teddy's nature to gamble if he is always gambling?"

"So you have made him promise to stop?"

"Oh yes. The minute Teddy realized the importance of it, he was quite willing to give up gambling."

Chantel stared at Alicia. She wasn't certain if she was sitting with a young innocent woman or a female Machiavelli. Yet Alicia's eyes were sincere. Chantel took a fortifying breath. "I am quite glad you have helped Teddy to see the . . . ah, importance of changing his ways."

"But don't you think it only fair, if Teddy is doing his best for the sake of finding the treasure, that you should at least look for it in return? You do not want to discourage Teddy, do you? Besides," Alicia sighed, "once you find the treasure, my parents should have no reason to deny Teddy my hand. And I do love him so."

"Alicia," Chantel said as firmly as she could, "I do not believe in the treasure."

"Couldn't you at least look for it?" Alicia pleaded. "Please! Teddy will be in a fix if he doesn't acquire funds soon."

"Alicia!"

"Please?" Her brown doe-like eyes were pleading.

Chantel sighed. She couldn't believe what she was about to say. Yet, at the same time, she didn't want to be the one who sent Teddy back to the gaming tables, not if Alicia had truly lured him from them with the carrot of finding the treasure. Nor did she care to have Alicia going about saying she was unkind. "Oh, very well."

Alicia clapped her hands together. "Oh, famous. I knew you would not fail us."

"Alicia, I don't want you to get your hopes up. I truly do not believe there is a treasure, but if you wish me to try and look, I shall."

"We will find it," Alicia said with naive faith. Her eyes began to sparkle. "Oh, do let us begin looking for it now. You know Teddy only has a short time before those men come for their money."

"You wish to look for it now? This very minute?"

"Yes, now!" Alicia said excitedly. Her eyes were like an eager spaniel's.

Chantel laughed. In truth, some of Alicia's excitement was rubbing off on her. Why shouldn't they go and look for the treasure? Admittedly it would be a wild goose chase, but it would be a far sight more entertaining than sitting in this house with nothing to do but muse and ponder about the macabre incidents of yesterday. Hi, ho, one day it was hunting for bodies, and the next day for treasure. She could not claim a hum-drum life. "Yes, we can start now," Chantel said decisively. "But if we are going to do it we must hurry, for Richard shall be coming back soon and it would be better if we were gone before that."

"Oh, yes," Alicia nodded. "Where is he?"

"He is out trying to discover where . . ." Chantel stopped. She didn't want to say he was out trying to learn who had snatched a body. "Ah, he is out upon business."

"Good," Alicia approved. She sighed. "Cousin

Richard is the best man imaginable. But he will not think we should look for the treasure. Which I do own is not kind of him."

"It isn't?" Chantel was glad to know she was not the only unkind one in Alicia's book.

"Just because he is wealthy does not mean he should deter others from becoming so as well."

Chantel laughed. She couldn't wait for Alicia to show Richard the error of his ways. "How right you are. You should remember to advise him of it." Chantel thought for a moment. "Does your mother know you are here?"

Alicia flushed. "Oh, no. She believes I am at the lending library."

"For the entire day?"

"Oh yes, I often spend the day at the lending library. I do so love to read."

"You do?" Somehow Chantel could not envision Alicia as the bluestocking.

"Oh yes! Aren't Mrs. Radcliff's novels thrilling?"

"Indeed," Chantel smiled. Alicia's bookishness was explained. Also Alicia's easy acceptance of the Covington curse and treasure; the books she read no doubt made such things seem an everyday occurrence. "Where do you propose we should look first?"

Alicia's eyes widened. "Why, we must go to the attic of Covington's Folly, of course! Heroines always find treasure in attics."

"That, or dust and spiders."

"Sometimes they find ghosts," Alicia said knowledgeably. She hesitated and asked in concern, "You won't be frightened if Lady Genevieve visits us?"

"Of course not," Chantel said solemnly. "Why ever would I be? She would be a relative, after all."

"Wonderful," Alicia approved.

Chantel controlled her amusement. "And what happens if we don't find the treasure or a ghost in the attic?"

Alicia considered for a moment. "Then we'll search for a secret door, or a hidden priest's hole."

"My, you certainly have all this planned out."

"Yes." Alicia nodded. "I have been researching the matter for an entire week now. It is Teddy's only hope, you know."

Chantel sighed. The saddest truth was that in all likelihood Alicia was correct. They had as much chance of finding the treasure and pulling their coals out of the river tick as they had of encountering any other solution. Since the chance of a treasure's even existing was close to nil, it didn't leave Teddy's future, or hers, very bright. She shook herself to clear her mind of such a depressing thought. "Very well, let us hunt for the treasure."

Alicia rose. "Let us go," she whispered.

"Very well," Chantel found herself whispering back. She rose. "But I must tell Reed—"

"Oh, no!" gasped Alicia, stopping. "This must be a secret. How could you think to tell anyone?"

"Why shouldn't I?"

"You never know when some villain could overhear and try to stop us from finding the treasure."

"Villain?" Chantel barely stifled her laughter. "Oh, yes, of course."

She watched Alicia tiptoe to the door and open it softly. Chantel followed behind in amusement. They entered the foyer and Alicia ran to her maid. "Sarah," she whispered.

The maid looked up. "Yes, mum?" she whispered back.

Alicia looked swiftly around. "We are going to search for the treasure now."

The maid's eyes widened. "Ohh, mum, do be careful. It could be frightfully dangerous!"

Chantel couldn't believe it. Alicia's maid was not only privy to Alicia's plans, but she entered into them as wholeheartedly as her mistress. That there could be two such fanciful women amazed Chantel.

"We are going to Covington's Folly," Alicia whispered. "Tell no one of this on pain of death."

The little maid did not laugh as Chantel would surely have. She shook her head vehemently, and said, "Oh miss, you know I wouldn't. Not even if they poked out my eyes or put me on that there rack that would stretch me out a mile."

Alicia grabbed up her maid's hand. "I couldn't live without you, Sarah. Now we must go."

There was a sudden rapping at the door. Both Alicia and her maid jumped into the air with a squeak. "Who could that be?" Alicia asked with just the proper touch of fear.

"I hope it is not a villain," Chantel said teasingly, crossing to open the door. The dark figure that stood upon the step caused Alicia to clutch at her maid and her maid at her. Both women screeched.

"Why, hello, Aunt Beatrice," Chantel said pleasantly. "What brings you here?"

"What do you mean?" Aunt Beatrice steamed past Chantel into the foyer. "Came to pay you a visit, anything wrong with that?" She stopped as she viewed Alicia and her maid, both staring at her as if she were a frightful sight. "Hm. You're that Lady Lillian's daughter, ain't you? The one Teddy's mooning over? What are you doing here?"

"Alicia and I are going for a ride," Chantel said swiftly. Alicia was turning extremely pale and appeared close to swooning. Chantel shook her head wryly. Here Alicia had talked about meeting Lady Genevieve's shade without qualms, yet she did not possess the fortitude to face the sight of Aunt Beatrice.

Aunt Beatrice turned to study her. "A ride, you say? Hm. That sounds fine. I will go along."

"Ah, I didn't mean that kind of ride," Chantel prevaricated quickly. Aunt Beatrice's sharp eyes were upon her. "I—I mean we are going out on our mounts."

It was Aunt Beatrice's turn to pale. She detested horses. But then again, the four-legged creatures detested her just as fervently. "Er, no, then I shall not join you."

"I am sorry," Chantel said, attempting to sound regretful as she held the door open. "But I thank you for visiting."

Aunt Beatrice looked stunned. Then her baleful eye swerved and surveyed Alicia, who immediately turned a crimson red. "Hmph," Aunt Beatrice snorted, treading ponderously from the house.

Chantel was swift to close the door behind her. "Well, I am glad that is over."

"Chantel, you were wonderful," Alicia said with awe. "Why, she looked at me and I thought I would die of fright."

"Aunt Beatrice has that effect on people . . . horses, too," Chantel laughed. "But don't think me clever. Aunt Beatrice knows that I was gulling her. Neither you nor I are dressed for riding. But no matter. Let us give Aunt a few minutes to leave and then we can . . ." she lowered her voice to a secretive hush, "go fortune hunting."

Chantel stood, dusty, hot, and flabbergasted. "I cannot believe it. I just cannot!"

"But I told you we would find a secret door," Alicia exclaimed in delight as she and Chantel peered into a dark opening, musty with stale air.

The two women stood at the very back corner of the attic, the attic which they had rooted through from stem to stern. They had crawled across every inch of oak floorboard, swiped at every cobweb, and picked through every Covington cast-off. Stacks of rotted hatboxes and wood crates had been delved through to no avail. They had rifled through bins of mildewed papers only to learn of the extent of tradesmen bills owed by previous generations of Emberlys. What Chantel found was that even the Folly's attic was threadbare and down to its last prayer.

Then Alicia had begun her thumping and tapping and knocking at every panel of water-stained wall. Chantel had joined in, attempting to be a good sport. And then this! With one knock from Chantel on the right spot, an entire section of wall had suddenly swung out at her. Chantel lifted her candle high, excitement rising within her. "Well, let us see what is in there." She peered closer. "Why, it is steps!"

"It is?" Alicia exclaimed, directly behind her.

Chantel gingerly trod down the stairs, which were just barely wide enough for a person to travel single file upon. The side walls were of mold-covered brick, chunks of mortar jutting out here and there as the steps curved and spiraled. Chantel lost her sense of direction. All she could be certain of was that they were descending.

Finally the steps led into a room, a room that more than lived up to the descriptions used in Alicia's prized gothic novels. Both woman's candles were needed, for the room was small and airtight. Alicia squeaked in alarm as her wavering candlelight spread to catch a shape, much like that of a human form. Chantel checked sharply. Lady Genevieve was floating before their eyes within the candles' glow.

After a suspended moment, both exhaled in relief. "Why, it is only a portrait," Alicia breathed gratefully.

"Yes, yes it is," Chantel nodded, finally stepping forward to the painting that rested upon a large easel encrusted with gold papier-mâché bows and cherubs, many now missing arms and limbs as time had chipped away at the intricate molding. "Why, 'tis the same portrait as the one that is downstairs in the drawing room."

Alicia came to stand behind Chantel. "Th-that is Lady Genevieve?"

"Yes it is."

"It is eerie," Alicia whispered. "She looks exactly like you."

Chantel quirked her head and studied her great-great grandmother. "Perhaps. But then, in truth, *I* must look like *her.*" Chantel remained staring at the picture, entranced by her ancestor's features. She had always been thus entranced, though she would never have admitted it to anyone. She frowned then, looking more closely at the portrait. "It is exactly the same picture. Now why would she commission the same pose to be done twice?"

"Perhaps it was a first attempt," Alicia suggested, still in a whisper. Clearly the atmosphere of the room affected her.

Chantel glanced around at the brick walls which ascended to bricked vaulted arches along the ceiling housing a network of entwined spider webs, diaphanous in the candlelight. Surely, with the addition of iron chains and manacles, this would be the perfect setting for the *The Wicked Marquis* or *The Dungeon of Despair*.

Chantel turned back to the painting. Studying it, she shook her head slowly. "No, 'tis as finely made as the other canvas." She drew her eyes away from the portrait with an effort. "Most likely Great-great-Grandmama Genevieve was simply vain and wanted two of herself . . . That, or she wanted to gall Sir Alex with it."

"Chantel, look!" Alicia's whisper was loud, harsh in its excitement. "A trunk!"

Chantel turned. Alicia stood over an extremely large, ornately carved brass-banded oak trunk, which was secured by a large brass catch in the shape of a gargoyle's face. Even in the dim candlelight her brown eyes were large and glittering. "This could be it!"

"Perhaps," Chantel smiled without any true interest. She walked over and stared down at the trunk with Alicia.

"Open it," Alicia breathed.

"Very well," Chantel said. She bent, released the

catch, and lifted the lid very easily. Shimmering gold brocade met their eyes, but not emeralds and diamonds.

"Oh no, it isn't the treasure," Alicia said aloud in disappointment.

Chantel was silent. With a strange thrill entering her, she set her candle down and bent to lift up the heavy material. She gasped in delight. "Why 'tis Lady Genevieve's dress, the one she wore in the painting."

"Just look," Alicia murmured, reaching out to touch the dress. "It is so finely made and expensively fashioned."

"The Covingtons were rich at that time," Chantel mused, her eyes still on the dress she held. An inexpressible warmth passed through her. She was actually holding her great-great grandmother's dress. One that she had worn, and danced in, and lived in. She held it close to her, feeling suddenly linked to the long-dead woman, the woman who had always hovered in her memory and life.

"Oh, and look," Alicia gasped. It took a moment for Chantel to shake out of her trance. Alicia was rooting through the rest of the contents of the trunk. She lifted up a delicate fan for Chantel's inspection. "It is made of chicken skin, and the scene upon it is delightful."

Chantel spun to view Lady Genevieve's portrait once again. It still seemed unearthly. "It is part of her costume in the painting."

"Yes, yes," Alicia nodded. "And her shoes are here, and . . ." Alicia giggled, "And all her undergarments . . . only look at this hoop!" She fell back with a sigh. "But there isn't a treasure here." Suddenly she perked up and reached back into the trunk, thumping on its insides. "No, it is all wood . . . not even a secret compartment."

Chantel found that she was now clutching the dress to her. "It is enough, Alicia, this dress is a treasure to me in itself."

"We must be missing something," Alicia muttered. She lifted her candle and picked up Chantel's as well. She began peering at the walls while Chantel gently, reverently, lowered her great-great grandmother's belongings back into the trunk.

"There is nothing here," Alicia declared finally.

"Evidently not," Chantel said mildly, her attention still upon the dress and trunk. She couldn't explain the deep satisfaction she was feeling—as if she had discovered something important to her. "I believe we must hunt elsewhere."

"But it makes no sense," Alicia said, clearly peeved. "I mean, the secret wall, the winding stairs, the hidden room. By all rights we should find the treasure now."

Chantel's smile was wry. "Perhaps Genevieve was more clever then we thought. This could be a false lead prepared on purpose."

"But in all the books this is always where the heroine finds the treasure."

"But Lady Genevieve wasn't merely fiction," Chantel smiled. And suddenly she realized why she was feeling such a deep, happy glow. Lady Genevieve really hadn't been fiction.

"Well, I suppose you are right," Alicia sighed. "But I think it was terribly unfair of her to so mislead us."

Chantel was finding out very quickly that Alicia, as mild and unprepossessing as she appeared, had a clear sense of what was right and wrong and what a person should and should not do. "I think she's been misleading many more than just us. Indeed, she's been doing it for generations now."

"Yes, you are right," Alicia sighed. "Let us go and look somewhere else."

"We will take this with us," Chantel said in an imperious tone.

"Yes, but let us go and look—"

"No, we shall take it now! Do you hear me, young miss?" Chantel said sharply—so sharply that Alicia jumped. Chantel was startled herself, for she did not know why she had spoken so and in such a voice.

"We can if you wish," Alicia said, wide-eyed.

Chantel gulped. "I do."

"Let us take the trunk between us, then," Alicia said rather soothingly, her look wary.

Chantel forced a smile. "Very well."

The two women, slowly, and with great effort, picked up the trunk. They were forced to leave their candles and use both hands. Between the wood of the trunk and the heavy material of the dress within, it was a back-breaking effort. As Chantel tugged it up the first step, Alicia stopped pushing and panted, "I don't believe it will go up the stairs, they are frightfully narrow."

"It will, now stop whining and push, gel."

Alicia all but fell back in shock. "Chantel, are you feeling all right?"

Chantel blinked, surprised at herself. "Of course I am. But I am certain that the trunk will go up the stairs." Alicia gave her a nervous look. Chantel smiled weakly. "After all, it must have come down the stairs, must it not?" She hefted the trunk up and began pulling it and the now leery Alicia up the stairs. The trunk was a smooth fit—as if it had been fashioned to be just a quarter of an inch thinner than the stairs.

"Er, of course," Alicia said warily.

After that the women were silent, for it was a difficult task. At every turn they thought the trunk would not fit, but each time it would clear a corner with but a quarter of an inch room to spare.

Chantel breathed a sigh of relief when she felt her backside hit up against the stairtop wall. "Thank heaven," she gasped. "I doubt I can tolerate this dark tight space much longer." Her hands full, she threw her back and derriere up against the door to open it. She almost threw her spine out. The door would not open. Indeed, it would not budge.

"*Ooff!* What is the matter?" Alicia grunted as the reverberations of the collision went through her.

Chantel froze. "Alicia, do you remember closing the wall?"

"No," Alicia said. "D-did you?"

"No, of course not."

"Oh, my Lord," Alicia breathed.

"Oh, my Lord is right," Chantel said.

"What if we are trapped in here? What if—"

"Stop it, Alicia," Chantel said swiftly. "We aren't trapped. We just have to push harder on it. I am sure we will have this open in a minute. See if we don't!"

Richard entered his home approximately at four o'clock tea time. He halted in the foyer as a peculiar sight greeted him. His entire household staff surrounded a lone, unknown maid, who was pinned against a chair. His staff had the wild look a mob gets before burning a heretic at the stake. Reed's hands were clenched to his side, while the cook and house-keeper, two such dignitaries that they never emerged from the back of the house, were unbuttoning the cuffs of their service uniforms. Tears streamed down the maid's face.

Richard's heart sank. He never doubted that the cause of the impending battle before him would some-how trace itself back to one Chantel Emberly-St. James.

"Are ye going to tell us where they are or are we going to wring it from ye?" the cook barked. She turned up her right cuff.

"They went for a ride," the maid said in a watery voice. "That is all I can tell you. They went for a ride."

"We can see that, my girl," Reed said. "They took the pony cart. But where did they go? Why didn't Miss Alicia take you and why didn't they take your car-riage?"

"They've gone out," the little maid repeated, and then straightened and said with the look of a Joan of Arc in domestic service, "and you can't make me say different. You can put me on the rack and I won't say nothing."

"I'll rack ye one," the cook growled.

Richard deemed it was time to intervene, for cook's left sleeve was now completely rolled up. "Reed, could you please tell me why this individual is being threat-ened with the rack in my foyer?"

The participants had been so deeply immersed in their discussion that no one had noticed him. "My lord, I am so glad you are here," Reed exclaimed.

"Lady Alicia and Lady Chantel went out just before luncheon and have not yet returned. This . . . young person will not tell us where they have gone and we are quite worried."

"Yes, it looks like it will come on to rain," the cook said with dire import. The little maid let out a loud sob.

Richard's brow snapped down and he suddenly glared. "Will you cease that wailing!" She froze in mid-sob. He looked to Reed. "Exactly who is this watering pot?"

"She is Miss Alicia's maid, my lord. She says the ladies went out for a ride. But they have not returned. We have searched the entire area and there is no sign of them. They took only the pony cart, my lord, so they had to have a purpose of some sort."

"Most likely fell," Richard muttered under his breath. He turned dark eyes upon the maid. "Now tell us all you know about where your mistress went and what she intended to do."

"I can't," the little maid shook her head wildly. "Even if you torture me, if you put me in boiling oil, or use those—those thumb screws . . ."

"I will have Lady Lillian turn you off without a reference," Richard interjected smoothly between the items on the grisly list of what she was prepared to withstand.

The maid gasped, turning wide eyes upon him. "But—but that would be worse than torture."

Richard nodded solemnly. "Yes, it would. Only think . . . Lady Lillian."

The little maid blanched. "That would be frightful.

Miss Alicia wouldn't expect me to withstand that, would she?"

"Of course not," Richard. "No one would."

The maid bit her lip. "Miss Alicia said to tell no one on pain of death. But turned off with no reference . . . that ain't death. That's worse."

"Far worse," Richard agreed.

Very well," she said swiftly. "Lady Chantel and Miss Alicia went to Covington's Folly. They have gone to . . ." Here she stopped and said shyly, "I cannot tell everyone, please come here."

Richard obligingly leaned over and she whispered the special news. He jackknifed up. "Oh, my God! I cannot believe it! What a skimblewitted start! I am going to—to—"

"You're not going to use the rack on them?" Sarah gasped.

Richard looked at her. The chit had a positive penchant for that item. "No, I am merely going to kill her."

The household staff all exclaimed and proclaimed at once.

"Sir!" Reed objected.

Richard sighed. "Oh, very well, I shan't. Now you all may return to work. I will go and retrieve Miss Alicia and Lady Chantel. Reed, please send a message to Lady Lillian saying that I met Alicia in town and have asked that she may stay over with me this eve." With that, he spun on his heel and strode from the foyer.

Chantel leaned against the wall and half-heartedly thumped upon it. Hours had passed and they had felt more like centuries. Gruesome images flitted through her mind of she and Alicia exhaling their last breath behind the infernal wall. There were no servants left at Covington's Folly; Richard had demanded from the beginning that none be permitted to stay until he discovered whatever subversive activities were afoot there.

She sighed. It might only be their deaths afoot now. She shook her head. She was allowing her imagination to run amuck. But why had the wall closed up all on its own? It was not as if a wind could have closed it, no, not even a breeze or a draft could have. And it was not as if she hadn't left the wall wide open. Her fingers were raw from trying to find a lever to open the wall. Oh Lord, would they die in this small, stifling stairwell? No! She was sure Richard would force Sarah to tell him where they had gone. If anyone could force something from someone it was Richard. Once he knew, he would come to the Folly to find her, but would he look in the attic? More importantly, would he think to look for secret walls?!

She shook herself again. Why was she worrying? Richard would come and save her. If only so that he could inform her of her stupidity. She thwacked on the wall again, "Help! Somebody help!" she cried hoarsely. Her throat was raw. "Alicia, shout," she croaked.

"Please don't make me," Alicia whispered just as weakly. "Who would come to the attic anyway?"

"Richard will," Chantel said with a small smile as she leaned her head against the trunk that was wedged between she and Alicia. "He has a knack for finding me in embarrassing positions, and this certainly qualifies as one." Chantel reached over and thumped on the wall with renewed vigor. "Help!"

She heard a low rumble. "Wait," she whispered. "Do you hear something?"

Another muffled rumble sounded.

"Yes, yes!" Alicia squeaked. "Someone is out there."

Suddenly there was a loud crash and they could feel a reverberation throughout the building. "It must be God," Chantel sighed. "There is a storm outside, evidently." Then she thought for a moment. "Of course, it could be Richard in a pelter."

Alicia laughed weakly. "You know Cousin Richard never loses his temper."

"No?"

"Of course not." Then Alicia moaned. "Oh, I am so hungry."

"Don't mention food," Chantel said severely, for her stomach suddenly strangled her backbone at the mention of the word. "Help!" she called in a gravely voice, thumping on the wall. "He-e-e-lp!"

Her call petered out as the wall she was leaning against promptly slid open. Caught unaware, Chantel tumbled forward onto the attic floor. Sneezing from the dust, she looked up. "Oh, hello Richard," she said, rasping each word.

He stood over her like an avenging God. His candle must have been set somewhere behind him, for the glow surrounded him. His gray eyes were like molten lava in his chiseled face. His hands were on his hips, his legs spread in a belligerent stance. "So that was you rumbling," Chantel murmured.

"Hello, Cousin Richard," Alicia called from the enclosure. "I am so glad you found us. Could you help me with this trunk?"

Richard's first action was to reach down and drag Chantel up from the floor. He held her close for a fraction of a moment and then set her back and gave her a swift shake. Chantel felt very much like a rag doll. "What the devil do you think you were doing!"

"Cousin Richard, I can't get out unless you move the trunk!" Alicia called.

Chantel looked into Richard's angry eyes. "We were fortune hunting," she said, knowing she was skirting death but feeling fey about it. She was just so happy to see Richard again. "Alicia said it was our only hope."

"Hope! You little fool!" Richard shook her slightly but Chantel didn't notice. In truth, she felt so weak that it was only Richard's hands on her arms that kept her standing. There must have been less air in that stairwell than she'd thought. "What would have happened if . . ."

Chantel blanched and reached out to clasp Richard's lapel. "Don't say it! Just don't say it! Now will you please help us with this trunk!"

He stared at her for a moment and then shook his head. He withdrew his hands from her and she almost did fall. He peered into the enclosure. "Why do you have this trunk?" he asked, even as he reached into the tight stairwell and dragged it forth.

Alicia was directly behind it. Her smirched, begrimed face beamed in the candlelight. "We found it! It has Lady Genevieve's clothes in it."

Richard's brow rose and he looked at Chantel. "That is the treasure?"

"It is to me," Chantel said tartly. The attic reverberated again with the sound of thunder.

"Come," Richard said swiftly, moving past her and picking up his candle. "The storm hasn't burst yet. At present it is only thunder. We can try to reach home before we get too drenched."

"We must take the trunk," Chantel said swiftly, urgently.

Richard turned and stared. "I beg your pardon?"

"We must take the trunk . . . and the painting that is still in the secret room."

"Painting? Secret room?" Richard's tone became ominous. "What the devil are you talking about now?"

"There is a painting of Lady Genevieve down there that we must take," Chantel persisted.

"Oh, we must?" Richard said quietly.

"You—you'd better, Cousin Richard," Alicia said. She lowered her voice. "Chantel—Chantel gets a little strange over the painting and trunk. She truly wants them."

"Well, we do not have the time to take them now. I will send someone to pick them up later."

"No," Chantel insisted, her hands going to her hips. "We will take both the trunk and the painting now. I don't know why that door closed on us and I am not taking a chance that—"

"Oh, for God's sake, Chantel," Richard barked. "Are you insinuating that someone would actually want those things?"

"I don't know about someone else wanting them, but I do," Chantel said fiercely.

"Please, Cousin," Alicia said. "Let us take them before Chantel starts calling me "gel" again . . ."

Chantel turned surprised eyes to Alicia. "Alicia, what are you talking about?"

Alicia flushed. "Never mind. Let's just get the painting."

"Oh, very well," Richard growled. He headed toward the stairwell in a rage. "Come on."

"I—I'd better stay and guard the door," Alicia said quickly with alarm. "We—we wouldn't want it to close again."

"Yes," Chantel nodded.

Richard turned and looked at Chantel. "You want to help her, I suppose."

Chantel looked to the stairwell where she had just been a prisoner for over three hours. She gulped. "Yes, please."

"Women!" Richard exclaimed angrily as he disappeared down the passage.

The ladies waited silently, very silently, for Richard to return. Chantel sighed when she heard movement and then a curse. Richard emerged, half lifting, half dragging the large frame.

"Doesn't Lady Genevieve look like Chantel?" Alicia said.

"I didn't look," Richard gritted out, still dragging the painting past them. "We don't have time. Now will you two women follow quickly!"

Alicia looked in bewilderment at Chantel. "I have never seen Cousin Richard so surly."

"I have," Chantel grinned. A sudden warm feeling passed through her as she heard Richard hit something and growl as he carried the portrait for her. "I have."

Chapter Nine

Chantel sank deep into the tub, eyes closed, reveling in the hot water. The tub was set before a crackling fire in her bedroom, the sound of which soothed Chantel all the more. She slightly opened her eyes. Lady Genevieve's portrait was perched upon a chair next to her bed. The large trunk rested beside it.

Chantel sighed in satisfaction and again closed her eyes. All was well in her world now. Indeed, having both the portrait and trunk in her possession had been hard won. Richard had cursed and complained all the way through Covington's Folly as he carried the painting. The trunk had been no easy feat for Alicia and she to tug, drag, and carry.

By the time they had loaded it all onto the dainty pony cart and covered it, the rain had begun to fall. Richard had been silent and dangerous all the way back to the manor. His anger had been as monumental as the storm. When they had entered the hall, three dripping, freezing waifs, to be greeted by all the worried servants, he had barked out orders for baths in a furious voice and then had coldly left them all.

She heard the room's door open and lazily opened her eyes, expecting Betty, her maid. Richard stood within the frame of the door, dressed in a lounging jacket and wearing an arrested expression upon his face.

Chantel sucked in her breath and submerged herself further into the tub. How much of her had been exposed? From Richard's face, a goodly amount. "Couldn't you try knocking just once?" she asked, water up to her chin. His startled expression still did not change.

Suddenly it was all Chantel could do to hide the feminine smile that wanted to tug at her lips. What was the matter with her? She should be embarrassed and enraged at his unannounced entry. Instead, the expression on Richard's face warmed her more than either the bath or the fire behind her.

"I . . ." He cleared his throat. "I wanted to see if you were all right."

"I am in heaven," Chantel admitted truthfully.

A smile played on his lips and his gray eyes lightened. "Then I imagine you do not need anything as mundane as food."

"Food!" Chantel sat up in excitement and then submerged again as Richard's eyes widened. "Yes, I would very much like something to eat."

"Then if you will get dressed I will bring you a tray," Richard said rather gently. He closed the door, and Chantel stared after him. Was that the same man who had ranted and raved all the way home? Was that the mighty St. James offering to bring her food? Food! Her stomach growled in anticipation. Chantel rose from the tub in haste, rushing for her towel and robe.

Chantel was sitting upon her bed, towel-drying her hair and considering Lady Genevieve's portrait, when there was a knock at the door. Could that be Richard actually knocking? "Come in," she called rather breathlessly.

Richard entered, carrying a food-laden tray before him. The firelight glinted off his mahogany hair as he set the tray down upon the bedside table. He was such an attractive man. Attractive! At that moment, he was divine. Chantel forced her eyes to the tray. "I am famished."

"I thought you might be." His voice was softly amused. He turned and reached out a hand to her. Chantel's brows rose. "If you give me your towel I will dry your hair while you eat." Chantel was too amazed to do anything but hand him the towel. "Now come and sit next to the food." Chantel, still stunned, shifted down the bed to be near the food. Not knowing what to say, she reached for a piece of bread and cheese.

" 'Tis simple fare," Richard said. "But cook was in such a dither over your absence she had not considered dinner. I told her not to bestir herself, and that this would be acceptable."

Chantel bit into the bread greedily. "Oh yes." Her agreement was slightly muffled as she swallowed her first piece of food since breakfast. No, she hadn't eaten at breakfast, she remembered. "This is fine," she reemphasized as she then bit into the cheese.

Richard walked over to stare at the portrait of Lady Genevieve. He was silent and then he turned to look at Chantel, who was happily devouring another piece of bread. "It is uncanny. She looks just like you."

Chantel grinned. "You mean I look like her."

He turned and looked again at the picture. "I have not seen this painting before, have I?"

Chantel shrugged. "You might have seen the one at the Folly. It is exactly like this one."

Richard shook his head. "No. I would have remarked it. No, what I remember is our wedding night, I remember seeing those jewels . . ." Again, he shook his head. "Never mind. Suffice it to say she looks like you." He turned and came and sat down next to her. True to his word, he took the towel and began to dry her hair. Chantel was truly in heaven. The rain poured down outside, while she was snuggled indoors, a fire crackling, food within her hand, and a smiling, gorgeous husband drying her hair.

Suddenly the bread became dry in her mouth and she choked. It was all make-believe. This wasn't her husband, nor was this her snug home. "Why are you being so nice?" she asked weakly after swallowing that bitter thought.

Richard remained silent, still toweling her hair. "Perhaps as an apology."

"Pardon?" Chantel asked, wide-eyed.

He smiled as he drew the towel away. He rose restlessly and stood looking down at her broodingly. "Is it so shocking that I would apologize?" Chantel was silent for a moment. Yes, it was shocking that he would apologize. Richard stepped closer and ran his hands through her hair, massaging her scalp. "It is almost dry," he said quietly. Chantel instinctively closed her eyes with pleasure. "I should not have been so angry with you."

"Yes," murmured Chantel, more in assent to his actions than his words. Her scalp was tingling.

"I—I reacted that way because I felt you were in danger."

Chantel opened her eyes then, a fear shooting through her, displacing her sense of well-being. "Yes," she said softly, "I thought and felt the same." She shivered and looked up at him. "I don't know why, but I think someone closed that wall on purpose." A loud crash of thunder sounded, and lightning illuminated the room. They stared at each other.

Richard muttered a curse. His hands reached to curve the contours of her head and, without conscious thought or will, Chantel rose. Their bodies met with the next clap of thunder. Their lips met with the wildness of their hidden fears. Chantel clung to Richard, clung to him with the need to feel his life as well as her own. She stretched in his arms, willing his hands to move across her.

Richard growled and they toppled to the bed, their bodies intertwined. Chantel's hands brushed his hair, followed the column at the back of his neck and settled upon his shoulders, the feel of corded muscle beneath her palms.

"I thought I had lost you," Richard whispered.

"No, I'm here," she murmured.

"I don't ever want to lose you," he said, burrowing his head into the hollow of her neck. He kissed that tender skin.

"No," she said, dazed, holding him all the closer, kissing his head, breathing him in. "I'm going to live. I promise you."

And then suddenly Richard stiffened. Chantel could feel it infinitesimally. But she had experienced this before. Her nails dug into his back. "No, don't . . ."

she began, even as he withdrew from her. She let him disentangle himself from her arms and watched as he rose. What was the matter with the man? Was he made of stone? How could he retreat when only a minute ago . . .

"Yes," he said softly, his eyes unreadable. "You are going to live." He looked at her with a rather dogged expression. "I must apologize once more."

"Apologize?" Chantel asked, stunned. She didn't want apologies. She wanted him back in her arms and in her bed. Heat and desire still coursed through her like a tidal wave. "Apologize for what?"

"For taking advantage of this situation," he said roughly.

"What situation?" Chantel asked, bemused and a little desperate. She needed him to be with her tonight. She needed him to comfort her, to hold her, to chase away her fears. "What are you talking about?"

"Fear can often act as an aphrodisiac," he said coolly, just like a doctor speaking to a patient. Chantel flushed, for it was as if he had read her thoughts. "When one's life has been threatened, a person often—often . . ."

"Wants to make love?" Chantel whispered, not able to look at him.

"Yes," she heard him say softly. "Now you must rest." He quietly left the room.

Chantel didn't look up as she heard him leave. What could she say? Yes, she did want him to love all her fears away. Yes, she had needed him to assure her that she was alive and safe. Her nails dug into the blanket and she finally looked up at the door from which Richard had departed. There was only one hitch to it all. She hadn't wanted to make love to him for just those two reasons. She had wanted to make love to him because she loved him! He should have been in her bed tonight for that reason. He should have been her husband tonight. For whatever time they had left together before their marriage ended, Richard St. James should have been hers.

Chantel closed her eyes in pain. He should have been hers. At least for a moment, because she was his. It was a painful realization; but, she was his. Her eyes roved desolately about the room and fell upon the portrait of Lady Genevieve. "What am I going to do, Lady Genevieve? I love him." She lay back down on her lonely bed and stared up at the ceiling. "What am I to do? I want him as my husband in every way."

Richard all but stumbled back to his bedroom. Need and frustration were literally a pain within him. He was a fool! He wanted Chantel Emberly, deeply and completely. Yet, if he took her tonight, he would never want to give her up. He had been so rash as to tell her that he never wanted to lose her. Luckily she had been so overcome by fear and passion that she hadn't really recognized what he was saying . . . but he had.

She had merely said she would live. Indeed, she would live—and without him. She might have gladly given herself to him tonight, but what of tomorrow? Or at the end of the next few months? She would have left him. Their marriage was not real. She was not promised to him for life.

Richard slammed into his room. His nerves and body were strung tight. He was a damned fool. He had wasted all the time since he met her, doing everything to stay clear and detached from Chantel. He had harangued her and accused her of everything under the sun, when in truth, she was the woman he wanted as his wife.

He had such a short time to turn things around, to overcome the obstacles that surrounded them and make her wish to stay married to him. He sat down on his bed and his mind raced. What should he do first?

His urge was to walk straight back to her room and make mad, passionate love to her. He shook his head and lowered it into his hands. No, that was not the way to win the lady to wife. It was the way to have her perhaps, but not to win her past one night. He wanted her free spirit as well as her body. He stood promptly, poised. What should he do?

It seemed as if he had no control. He was walking back toward the door. He was opening it. He remembered the passion in Chantel's eyes as he had left her. He needed to go to her. He stopped. No. He had to win Chantel for life. He closed the door again. To do so he needed to clear her name and protect her life. When it was all over he could woo her, make love to her. Damn, there was that thought again!

Richard, with the greatest determination, went to his armoire and withdrew a valise. It was apparent to the meanest intelligence that he wouldn't be able to stay in a house where Chantel's room was but a few yards from his. He withdrew some cravats and threw them into the valise. He was going to be honorable! He threw more clothes within the valise. He was going to win his wife! He threw toiletries on top of it all. He was going to escape to London before he went back into Chantel's room, that's what he was going to do!

Chantel meandered through the house, deep in thought. It had been three weeks since Richard St. James had departed the house. More like, escaped the house in the middle of the night. The cad! Chantel sighed. She wanted her cad to come home. How was she supposed to turn him to her way of thinking if he wasn't around for her to persuade? Time was running out. Soon it would be the appointed annulment date.

Chantel shook her head as she half-heartedly went toward the drawing room. Why had he departed so precipitately, leaving her with no consolation? She swung open the door. Alicia sat upon the settee, sewing a neat stitch into a sampler. Chantel smiled wryly. Now, there was somber consolation. Richard had evidently managed to talk Lady Lillian into permitting Alicia to remain as her companion until his return. Chantel well remembered the note she had received the very next morning:

Madam, I must go to London. Will arrange for Alicia to stay with you. Please refrain from fortune hunting or any other dangerous activity.
    Yours,
    Richard

It was rather pitiful how she wished she could believe the word "Yours" literally, rather than have it be the most common of partings. Chantel entered the room and took up a chair across from Alicia. She appeared rather distracted and Chantel noticed that she merely played with her needle.

"Alicia, what is the matter?" Chantel asked, confused. Alicia had been in bloom these past weeks. Teddy visited her every day without fail. The two made a rather strange Romeo and Juliet, but there was no mistaking that their emotions were as strong. Their mooning and romancing had only darkened Chantel's mood. Where was her Romeo to go on picnics with and walk through the garden with and receive flowers from? She sighed. Her Romeo was in London performing espionage feats and could not waste time on such mundane activities as courting and romance.

"Oh Chantel, I do not think I can bear it any longer," Alicia said in a stricken voice, dropping her sewing into her lap.

Chantel dragged herself back to the point at hand. "What can't you bear any longer?"

"Being with Teddy and loving him so much and knowing," her chin began to tremble, "that there is no hope for us."

Chantel felt concern. For all of Alicia's histrionics, she was not one to cry. "Now, Alicia," she said helplessly, "perhaps it will turn out."

"How? My mother and father are against it." Alicia was beginning to sniff. "Teddy is such a sweetheart that he has no worry that we will be together. He thinks he will find the fortune, or fall into money, or have some miraculous thing happen so that my parents will suddenly agree to our marriage. He is always so trusting and believing. But I—I know now that our love is destined to fail." Alicia began to cry in earnest.

Chantel's eyes started to sting. What was the matter

with her? She was not a woman to cry either. "Perhaps something will happen?"

"I do not think I can live without my Teddy," Alicia said brokenly.

Chantel rushed over to her and put her arm about her. "Now, now, d—don't cry," she said, blinking hard.

"But I love him so!"

"I know!" Chantel said in a watery voice, thinking about her own ill-fated love.

"Oh, Chantel!" Alicia turned into her shoulder. "I wish I had never fallen in love."

Chantel gave in. She began crying as well. "I know," she nodded, tears streaming down her face. "It is terrible, isn't it?"

The two clung to each other, crying their hearts out. "Oh why, why?" sobbed Alicia incoherently.

"I don't know," Chantel sobbed back.

Suddenly the door opened and Reed entered. He froze on the spot when he discovered the two woman hugging each other and sobbing. He cast a harried look about. His expression was that of someone who had just been shoved into a lion's cage.

Chantel caught his look and suddenly laughed. "Reed, do come in," she said, withdrawing from Alicia.

"Oh, yes," Alicia said, sitting up straighter. "Pray, do not pay any attention to us."

Reed's face was paling. He actually began shifting from foot to foot like a small boy. This was Reed, their indomitable butler. "I am sorry, my lady, I only came to see . . ." he gulped, "if you desired tea this morning."

"Oh, yes," Chantel smiled through tearing eyes and clogged throat. "Tea is exactly what we need."

"Yes," Alicia said, looking down.

Chantel began looking frantically about. "And handkerchiefs. We—we don't have any."

"No—no," Alicia said in a trembling voice. "I never carry one. I—I don't usually have the need."

"Very well." Reed bowed. He resembled a streak of lightning as he exited.

Alicia, her eyes red-rimmed and her face tear-stained, looked at Chantel. A small, slight smile twitched at her lips. "Did you see how we frightened him?"

Chantel nodded, knowing she looked no better. Crying was such a ravager of one's looks. "I know. He looked ready to faint."

Suddenly both women began to laugh. "Oh dear," Chantel said, brushing her hands across her wet face, "what gooses we are." She rose to cross to her original chair. She was determined to regain her composure before Reed returned.

"It is ridiculous," Alicia nodded. "I—I don't generally cry."

"Neither do I!" Chantel nodded, surprised that she felt much better none the less. "What is galling is that love has reduced us to this."

"I know," Alicia said sheepishly.

Chantel sat up. She truly was feeling better. "And it is about time we stopped allowing it to." The door cracked open hesitantly and Chantel noticed it. "Do come in Reed, it is all right now."

Reed, having been caught trying to sneak in, straightened and entered with as much dignity as he could. "Madams, your handkerchiefs," he intoned as he presented a silver tray with a neat stack of lace centered upon it, accompanied by a delicate crystal decanter of rosewater.

The ladies fell upon the handkerchiefs as if they were bonbons. "Oh, thank you, Reed," Chantel said.

"Indeed," Alicia nodded, sniffling into hers. Reed coughed, bowed, set the tray down, and once again left the room in record time. "What—what do you mean, we should stop allowing it?"

"Well, you and Teddy love each other. There is no obstacle there. You are both of the same mind. The only thing you must do is overcome your parents' objections. Correct?" Chantel was beginning to marshal her thoughts, as she discarded another sodden kerchief.

"Correct," corroborated Alicia, as she grasped the rosewater, as if reaching for a lifeline.

"And in my case I need to make the man I love, love me."

Alicia smiled. "You do love Cousin Richard, then?" she asked as she set a kerchief sprinkled with rosewater against her flushed cheeks and neck.

Chantel blushed. "Yes, yes I do," she said shyly, as she too reached for the rosewater.

"I think you are just perfect for him," Alicia said happily. She frowned slightly. "Though I never knew he could be so overbearing and have such a temper. Truly that is not common for him."

Chantel sighed. "I know, but I fear it is because I have a temper too. I just wish I could sit your parents down and have a good talk with them." She laughed. "And then do the same with Richard."

"I know," Alicia agreed.

Chantel looked up. "Alicia. We are going to do it!"

"Do what?"

"We are going to bring your parents here."

"How? They permitted me to stay here because Cousin Richard asked them, but they haven't come to visit."

"No matter." Chantel waved her hand. "They are going to come to my ball."

"Your ball?"

Chantel's eyes brightened. "My masquerade ball! Then I can wear Lady Genevieve's dress. I've been wanting to ever since we found it. Oh yes, it will be perfect."

"It will?" Alicia said hesitantly.

"Your parents will attend and Richard will attend . . ."

"He will?"

Chantel nodded. "He would never fail in his duty . . . and that would be to stand by his wife at their first ball together."

"Yes, yes, you are right," Alicia said excitedly. "And my parents will deem it their duty as well to support the family image."

"Yes, yes!" Chantel's smile was wide. "And then, Alicia, see if we don't turn this situation around. We mustn't give up the battle so quickly."

"No," Alicia nodded stoutly. "We mustn't. What do you think I should go as . . .?"

Reed entered hesitantly into the room with the tea. The ladies, however, rather than crying and sniffling as they had only minutes before, were deep in excited conversation. They did not even notice when he set the tray down, though both delved in immediately, chattering all the while. He quietly removed the tray of crumpled lace and the half-empty flacon of rosewater.

Reed left, shaking his head in perplexity. The fairer sex was a marvel! They could be crying fit to rend a poor man's heart to pieces the one second and be in high alt the next. They had stamina, the fair sex. They truly had stamina. Given a supply of linen and lace and scent, they could take on Hannibal's army. Whereas, he was fair exhausted from the experience, and would be all day!

Richard and Edward trod silently down the hall of the small inn. Neither man spoke. Richard could barely control his excitement. They were going to meet an operative who had written that he was close to discovering who the traitor was and would have the information for them this evening. Soon this would be over and he could go home and look to the business of securing his faux wife's affections enough to make her into a real wife.

Richard and Edward stopped and knocked on the agent's door. There was no response. They rapped again and waited.

"Something must have detained him," Edward said softly. "Shall we return later?"

Richard frowned. Rollins was one of the most reliable agents he knew. "No, let us enter and wait for him."

Edward shrugged. "Very well." He knelt and applied himself quickly to the lock. In a moment he was swinging the door wide. The men entered the room. They discovered Rollins sleeping on the bed.

"Hey, Rollins, you slug-a-bed," Edward chided, walking over to the supine agent. Edward stopped in his tracks when he stood next to the bed. His eyes flew to Richard's "He's dead."

"I was afraid of that," Richard said softly, having sensed it the moment they opened the door. He walked over to stand by Edward. He looked down at the agent. "Rollins must have discovered who our man was."

"Why do you say that?"

Richard nodded toward the body. "Our traitor's signature. He killed Rollins personally."

"What?" Edward asked, still confused.

"See that small white cord about Rollins' neck?"

Edward peered closer and whistled. "Neat, very neat and clean, our man."

"Yes," Richard said meditatively. He looked slowly about the room. "Poor Rollins. We must search the room. Perhaps there will be a scrap of evidence."

The two men meticulously combed the room. Edward suddenly exclaimed as he performed the difficult task of searching through Rollins' pockets. "Be damn, here is a note." Richard strode over and took it from him. "It doesn't make much sense, though."

Richard scanned the note: "This one you must dispose of yourself."

Richard crumpled the paper. "It makes sense. He is becoming rather arrogant."

"He is?" Edward asked, not having been told anything about Louis Dejarn and his disappearing body. He shook his head. "There is nothing else in Rollins' pockets. He's clean."

"I have no doubt," Richard said softly. "He wanted to make sure we knew this note was from him."

"Why?"

"He is warning us off."

"How do you figure?"

Richard shrugged. "He's letting me know how close he is."

"And how close is he?"

"Too damned close, it appears," Richard said, pocketing the note. "Too damned close."

Richard and Edward sat quietly in Richard's town-house library. The men nursed their brandies, quiet and solemn after taking care of Rollins.

"Damn," Edward murmured and took another healthy swallow of his drink.

Into this somber atmosphere entered Richard's butler. He held an envelope within his hand. "My lord?"

"Yes, what is it?" Richard asked in distraction, his mind still attempting to unravel the events of the day.

"Your wife has sent a missive. A messenger waits to return your answer."

"My wife?" Richard asked, suddenly liking the sound of the words, when before he had only tensed over them. He reached out his hand and his butler gave him the envelope. He opened it. He quickly read the note, then stared at it, perplexed.

"What is the matter?" Edward asked. "Is there an emergency?"

"I cannot say," Richard said. He looked up. "Chantel is inviting me to a masquerade ball that she is hosting as my wife."

"What!"

Richard's lips began to twitch. "I wonder what mischief she is brewing."

"You don't want to know," Edward said positively. "You aren't going to go, are you?"

Now Richard smiled all the more. "Yes, I do believe I shall."

"But we are so close to our man now . . ."

"You mean he is so close to us, do you not?" Richard said, musingly. "So close, I would hazard that if my countess is hosting a masquerade ball, he will be there."

"Why do you say that?"

"Because Chantel is still involved in this, somewhere and somehow, even if unwittingly. Besides, we are going to give our man an incentive to be there," Richard said, his eyes narrowing.

"What kind of incentive?" Edward asked suspiciously.

"We shall offer him a chance to steal information that no right-thinking traitor would ever deny himself."

"A trap?"

"Most definitely."

Edward grimaced. "And what if he doesn't take the bait?"

Richard shrugged and smiled widely. "Than we shall merely have an enjoyable time at the masquerade and I shall find out what my unpredictable lady is up to."

Edward snorted. "You call that enjoyable?"

"Yes." Richard's eyes were bright. "Oddly enough, I do. Now we must consider closely, we have but two short weeks in which to arrange it. Chantel must not know anything about this, for if we do not capture the traitor I do not want our superiors believing she was involved in tipping him off."

Edward shook his head and swallowed the last of his brandy. "You appear very happy for a man who is playing with fire."

Richard laughed. "To whom do you refer? The traitor or Chantel?"

"Both, my man." Edward frowned deeply. "Both."

Chantel stared into the new dressing table mirror that had replaced the old dresser in her bedroom. A stunned, almost unreal feeling was overtaking her. It resulted from the fact that while she saw herself in the mirror, a flame-haired woman in a golden gown, directly behind her she saw exactly the same image in her great-great grandmother's portrait. "We do look terribly alike," she breathed. "I mean, tremendously alike," she amended, in case it had sounded like an insult. Lady Genevieve had become somewhat of a confidant to Chantel of late. It was ridiculous, but her ancestor no longer felt distant to Chantel, or dead for that matter, not since she possessed her dress and personal articles.

Chantel turned about slowly, as not to overset herself in the large panniers that fanned out from her slim waist. "Our fashions are more comfortable," she told Lady Genevieve's portrait. She turned back to the mirror and perused herself. She leaned over and picked up Lady Genevieve's fan. She fluttered it before her, holding it in the same position as the painting's. She tilted her head imperiously, feeling grand. "But yours were most definitely more stately."

Chantel then studied the delicate fan she employed. "And, more provocative, too," she murmured. The fan was of a soft rose hue, a romantic scene of a gazebo in a lush setting intricately painted upon its skin. "And so wealthy," Chantel sighed, finding it hard to imagine buying an accessory that was so delicately wrought as to be a piece of artwork in itself, as well as a tool of flirtation.

She set the fan down upon the dressing table and crossed to her ancestor's portrait, practicing walking in the shoes which fit surprisingly well. Her eyes became brooding. "If Richard doesn't come I will just die," she said softly. The masquerade ball was tomorrow eve and Richard had still not appeared. He had sent a message assuring her that he would be at her masquerade. But that had been two weeks ago. Why wasn't he home yet? And would he truly be there tomorrow, or would he fail her?

Sighing, Chantel turned and began to carefully remove the dress. Everything was prepared as well as she could imagine for the masquerade ball. All the one hundred invitations had been sent out and accepted, the guests including Alicia's parents. She set the dress aside and wiggled out of the wide hoop and petticoats. She wasn't sure what to do for Alicia and Teddy tomorrow, or whether speaking with Alicia's Montague parents would help, but she intended to do so.

She pulled her cotton nightgown over her head and crawled into bed. Sighing, she leaned over and blew out the candle. She doubted she could sleep since she was so tense and impatient over the coming day, but she was determined to try. She would be hosting a ball for a hundred members of the *haute ton* tomorrow night. She would need to look her best. Chantel thought of all the money she had spent, all the effort she had put forth. Why, why had she done it? She grimaced. She very well knew why. "He had better come," she murmured, even as her eyes closed.

At first she was counting sheep, and then money, and then masked revelers that were twirling madly about her, all calling out her name. She held her hands to her ears, trying to block out the clamor. She was spinning about, looking desperately for something. And then she saw Richard. He was far, far across the dance floor. She could only see glimpses of him as the dancers spun and intertwined. She tried to go to him. The dancers in the crowd stopped her. The wide panniers of Lady Genevieve's dress dragged at her. She cried Richard's name out over the laughter, but nothing could be heard . . . and still everyone called her name, "Chantel, Chantel, Chantel . . ."

Then the ballroom and all the revelers were dissipating into a fog. The scene misted and turned gray. Still she heard her name being called, "Chantel, Chantel, Chantel . . ."

Suddenly she was back in her bed, dressed in her nightgown. She sat up in bed slowly, very slowly. She looked, as if in a trance, toward the picture of Lady Genevieve. "Chantel, Chantel, Chantel . . ." rang in her head.

The portrait began to glow, actually glow as if someone had lit a thousand candles from behind it. Chantel gasped. Lady Genevieve was taking on human form within the picture, rounding and shaping to three dimensions. And then she moved. She snapped her fan shut with a brisk click.

Chantel shook her head, even as Lady Genevieve picked up her skirts and emerged from the painting, stepping down from the canvas onto the chair as one would step down from a high carriage. The painting's scenery remained the same; there was merely no evidence of Lady Genevieve in it. Chantel swallowed as Lady Genevieve pointed at her. She had a rather admonishing look in her eyes. She began to move slowly toward the bed. Chantel could hear the rustle of her skirts. "Chantel, Chantel, Chantel . . ." the voice still called to her in her mind.

"No!" Chantel shouted, and suddenly woke up. She had only been dreaming. She stared into the dark, wet with perspiration. Slowly she turned and looked toward the portrait of Lady Genevieve. It was but a dark shadow in the dark room. "Thank God," Chantel muttered, sitting up and running a shaking hand through her hair.

Knowing she was being childish, Chantel threw back the covers and scampered over to the painting, slowing as she approached it. The dream had been so very real that even now she trembled from it. Swiftly, and with great determination, she grabbed up the frame and turned the image of Lady Genevieve away from her.

Nodding in satisfaction, she rushed back to her bed and jumped in, pulling the covers up to her chin. She nestled down, hugging her pillow close. She must sleep, she told herself. It had only been a dream and nothing more. She had to sleep. She sighed. It was going to be one of those nights when the dawn wouldn't come soon enough. She stared at the ceiling until she finally drifted off once again.

Chapter Ten

Chantel peered once again into the dressing table's mirror. This time Lady Genevieve's picture was not reflected behind her. That good lady's image was still banished from Chantel's sight. The back of the canvas was the only visible thing. She had not yet forgiven or forgotten the dream of the night before.

Yet the very first ball she would ever host would soon be in progress. Was there enough champagne? Enough food? Would the people like the musicians she had employed? Would Alicia's parents come? Would Richard ever arrive? Where in blazes was he? Would he humiliate her in front of all these people and not attend?

She shook her head and frowned at herself in the mirror. "Stop woolgathering and dress yourself," she admonished her reflection. She wore only her petticoats and one of the frilly, sheer robes that Richard had given her. It was true she had sworn never to don the clothes he had given her, but a lady needed every support she could find on an evening like this one. The sheer, feminine garment made her feel as if she could face anything . . . and perhaps, seduce any*one*.

Chantel picked up the face powder from the dresser. Suddenly a movement flashed from behind her. She glimpsed it from the corner of her eye. "Oh, Lord," she murmured, dropping the powder back to the table. She trembled, reliving her nightmare from last night. Had Lady Genevieve truly stepped from the picture this time?

With fear clutching at her heart, she spun on her chair. A large, gray-caped man stood behind her. His hair was of mahogany, his eyes water-gray. "Thank goodness it's only you," Chantel breathed in relief. Another emotion crowded in directly behind that . . . desire . . . and excitement. Chantel flushed in embarrassment and turned back to her mirror. "What, pray tell, do you want, sir?"

"You turn your back on a masked man awfully quickly, madam," Richard said with a growl. She peeked up to catch his mock frown.

A smile slid across her face. All the fear and anxiety were melting away, being replaced by a warm, evanescent glow. Richard had come! He was in her room, a warm, teasing look in his eyes. Chantel feigned a delicate yawn. "Oh, but I am so accustomed to masked men entering my boudoir, sir . . . and to men who do not knock for entrance."

"Men, madam?" Richard quizzed. "As in plural? You had best make that singular," he said, walking slowly up to stand directly behind her. His cloak brushed against her back. "I should be the only man entering your chamber without knocking."

His tone was teasing and Chantel returned just as

lightly as her skittering heart would allow, "Why ye
now that you have mentioned it, you are the only ma
that rude." A low, warm laugh sounded from behind
her. It tingled through her and she hid her pleasure a
she added teasingly, "And what do you want now
sirrah? I no longer have the black box."

He was silent for a moment and Chantel's eyes ros
quizzingly to his in the mirror. " 'Tis simple then
madam, you have but the last two choices I offere
you that night." Chantel's brows rose even higher. H
smile became wicked. "Your virtue or your life, m
lady."

Chantel returned her eyes to the dresser and th
articles upon it. She toyed with the silver brush. "A
cording to your mother I have no virtue or honor, yo
know."

"No, you have both," Richard said softly with
smile. His hand lightly, gently, brushed the back of he
neck. " 'Tis an unfortunate combination."

"Unfortunate?" Chantel asked, her eyes lightin
"Do my poor ears deceive me? Could a St. James, or
of the most respectable, truly be suggesting that ther
is something better than honor and virtue?"

He bent and placed his lips upon the very skin h
hand had just caressed. "Yes," he whispered, "that
what I am suggesting."

Chantel sat confused for a moment. She said cau
tiously, lest she misunderstand him, "But this ma
riage was solely created for the protection of you
honor."

Richard knelt down so his words were but a war
breath upon her ear. "Hang my honor. I find I do n
care for it anymore." His arms slid about her wais

nestled in her curves as if they belonged there. "Decide, madam. Which is it to be, death or dishonor?"

Chantel closed her eyes to the sensations coursing through her, hid them that Richard might not discover her deepest feelings. "Death can be very unpleasant, I have heard."

"While dishonor can be very pleasant," Richard's chuckle teased, enticed. His one hand drifted from her waist and drew back the collar of her frothy robe. He kissed her exposed shoulder.

Chantel shivered. She was so glad she had worn the inviting creation. One never knew when one was going to be accosted by a masked man . . . She tried to commandeer her straying thoughts. "But isn't virtue to be rewarded?"

His lips lifted from her sensitive skin and he remained silent for a moment. Chantel's eyes sought his in the mirror. His were suddenly blazing gray. "I fully intend to reward it, my dear. But never mistake it, you would be mine, Chantel, and mine alone."

Chantel shivered. Was not that what she had wanted? Yet now when he presented the offer, and in no uncertain terms, she faltered, afraid. It was he and not she demanding a commitment. The light flirtation was over. "I—I . . ."

"Oh, my stars," a voice exclaimed from the bedroom entrance.

"Damn," Richard muttered as both he and Chantel turned to discover Betty standing within the doorway, eyes wide and gleefully intent.

"Another one who does not knock, my lord," Chantel said, forcing a merriness, grateful for the timely interruption.

"I am very sorry." Betty bobbed a curtsey as Richard stood stiffly. "I didn't mean to interrupt like, m' lord, but you and my lady will be required downstair soon for the ball and all."

"Yes, yes." Richard nodded without enthusiasm.

"I've come to help my lady dress," Betty persisted "The guests will be arriving at any moment."

"Yes, I must dress," Chantel added quickly. "It i late."

Now a smile was crossing Richard's lips. He looke to Chantel. "But my dear, I could help you dres: Have I not been of service in that department before Though it was in undressing—"

"Richard!" Chantel exclaimed, blushing.

Betty giggled. "You best let me help her, sir."

Richard turned to Chantel, who lifted her chin an attempted not to appear rattled. "I will see you dowr stairs, my dear. What or who shall you be coming a: so that I do not waste a moment in finding you?"

Chantel smiled. "You will recognize me withou difficulty." His brow rose. "I shall be coming as Lad Genevieve."

He laughed. "Ah, the witch!"

"And the last famous Covington," Chantel nodded

"Oh no, Chanty," Richard said softly. "You ar that . . . you have surpassed your great ancestor . . . He grinned.

"How dare you, sir! I take exception to that!" Char tel exclaimed in mock anger. "I am no witch."

"I meant that you are bewitching," Richard mur mured with a wry eye. He was out the door befor Chantel could retort.

* * *

"You are certainly in a jubilant mood," Edward commented, looking up as Richard entered the room. He was lounging at Richard's desk in the library.

"That I am, Edward," Richard said cheerily. "Is everything set?"

"It is," Edward nodded. "The packet is in the drawer." He nodded back. "Roth and Perkins are in place."

"Hello, Roth and Perkins," Richard said as if to thin air.

"Hello, my lord," a curtain said.

"Yes, my lord." A voice arose from behind a patterned jacquard sofa.

"You may have a long watch," Richard said. "I am not sure when our man will attempt to steal the documents."

"Don't worry, my lord," the curtain said. "We're the patient sort."

"Yes," the settee agreed, "we'll nab the devil whenever he tries to lift the documents."

Edward frowned. " 'Tis unseemly that we must go and miss it all."

Richard shook his head. "No use mourning the fact. You and I must be out circulating at the ball. If we don't stay obviously in the open, our thief might not attempt his theft."

Edward rose. "Then let us get on with it."

"Yes." Richard turned toward the door. "Let the hunt begin. Tonight is the night."

"It will be if we catch our traitor," Edward agreed, following him.

Richard chuckled. "He is not the only one I am thinking of catching tonight."

* * *

Chantel stood just inside the entrance to the ballroom, sipping champagne and awaiting any tardy guests. She surveyed the room very much as a queen would her dominion, and just as smugly. Her ball was a definite success. Couples of every shape, form, and facade danced upon the floor merrily and noisily, reveling in the superb champagne, and titillated by the daring decor of the St. James ballroom.

The room was festooned with ivory muslin so transparent as to intensify the light of hundreds of candles in huge candelabra set atop tall Grecian columns. Each column was entwined with vines of ivy, which here and there swung in an arch to be clasped in the chubby fists of gold cherubs suspended from the ceiling as if floating amongst the clouds of muslin. The theme of Mount Olympus was proving to be a success.

Richard St. James was circulating amongst the guests across the room from her. Yet he had whispered as he parted from her that after social duty had been satisfied, he would return and she had best be ready to dance with him and no one else. His expression had been so demanding that Chantel still flushed at the thought. Unwittingly, she raised Great-great-Grandmother's fan to her face and waved it with more vigor than decorum.

Forcing herself away from the heated memory of Richard's gaze, and the thought of what she should and should not do this very night, she noticed a portly Harlequin shoving a blushing milkmaid across the floor. His was a bovine expression, and the lady, rather than misliking the manhandling, was smiling at him in an infatuated manner.

If Teddy and Alicia did not exercise more discretion her mother would be down upon them soon, Chantel thought with a frown. It was a feat in itself that Lady Lillian and Sir Thomas were in attendance, but as for talking to them in any serious manner, that had been well nigh impossible.

Chantel scanned the room quickly and discovered Lady Lillian. She was standing on the edge of the dance floor, a vulture's look in her eye. She was dressed in the medieval mode, and the long conical headdress she wore did nothing for her thin, horsy face. It also did nothing for the surrounding crowd that was in danger of losing eyes every time the lady turned her head. Since her head was jerking back and forth, very much like a frustrated viper unable to pin its prey, this was no small threat.

Sir Thomas had poured his rotund form into some old chain mail and armor. Chantel giggled behind her fan. He did not look much like a knight to save a lady fair from a fire-breathing dragon. But then his particular lady fair could ably scare off any dragon deluded enough to try and attack her. She'd simply breathe her own fire in return.

Chantel was so immersed in the study of the people about her that she was quite stunned when she heard what sounded like a bellow, or perhaps a war cry, directly behind her. She spun, champagne sloshing from her glass, her fan held up before her in defense. Her eyes fell upon a squat, armored, horned, Viking woman. The long fake golden braid about her head clashed horribly with her complexion.

"Aunt Beatrice?" Chantel asked, choking. Aunt Beatrice's costume fit her personality all too well, if not her form and figure. Her Aunt stood stock-still, eyes transfixed upon Chantel, in a face gone ashen gray. "What is the matter?" Chantel asked worriedly.

Chad, dressed as a corsair, stepped forward. "Chantel? My God, you look exactly like Lady Genevieve. You could easily be her ghost."

Chantel suddenly understood. She laughed and curtsied cautiously in her wide panniers. "Thank you, kind sir. Or at least, I think I thank you."

He bowed. "You know I always respected that grand dame."

"Where . . . ?" Aunt Beatrice stuttered. She clapped her mouth shut. Color was returning to her face and she tried again. "Where did you get the dress?"

"Oh, I found it," Chantel said. "I—I was hunting in the attic . . ." Suddenly she did not want to admit to hunting for the treasure. Chad would roast her forever. "Looking for something for the ball, and I found this."

Chad whistled. "No wonder it looks so authentic."

Chantel smiled with delight. "It is Lady Genevieve's dress indeed." She sighed in mock regret. " 'Tis a shame I didn't find the jewels to match the outfit as well."

"A sheer misfortune," Chad grinned.

A choking sound came from Aunt Beatrice. Chantel realized she had truly frightened her aunt. Who would ever have thought that such a prosaic, gruff woman as Aunt Beatrice could even think she was a ghost? She turned apologetic eyes to her aunt. "I am sorry if I frightened you, Aunt, but I could not resist wearing the dress for the masquerade."

Aunt Beatrice's eyes scanned the costume with meticulous care. "Wasn't frightened. No such thing." She snorted. "Why didn't you get a proper fan for it?" Aunt Beatrice was returning to her regular form of finding fault with everything.

"What do you mean, a proper fan for it?" Chantel asked, slightly miffed. "This is the proper fan."

"No it isn't," Aunt Beatrice said pugnaciously, most definitely back to her normal self. "The fan should be blue."

"Blue?" Chantel's eyes were narrowing.

"What's the matter with you, girl?" Beatrice gruffed. "The fan should be blue. Haven't you looked at the portrait in the parlor? Probably not," she said with obvious disdain. "That's why it is never cleaned as it should be."

"This fan . . ." Chantel began, but was not permitted to finish for she heard her name being called in desperate tones.

"Chantel, help us, she's after us!" Teddy came galloping off the dance floor, the bells on his hat and shoes jingling in alarm. Alicia finished a breathless second behind him.

"Mother has spotted us," she said urgently.

"Has she?" Chantel asked, quickly looking out across the floor. Lady Lillian was steaming across the dance floor with eyes snapping, her mate chugging and clanking behind her.

"Don't know how she saw us," Teddy gasped.

"Anyone can tell it is you, you simpleton," Aunt Beatrice barked.

Teddy's face fell. "Thought I was pretty clever."

"I don't think you will win the costume contest," Chantel said gently. "And you won't win Lady Lillian's regard this way either. Now Teddy, you must leave. Alicia, you stay here."

"Can't do that," Teddy objected. "Won't leave Alicia here alone to pay the toll."

"Please leave," Alicia said urgently, even as Lady Lillian swatted a capering Pan out of her way. "She's coming."

"Very well," Teddy bleated. "Do anything for you. Will meet you later in our special place." He spun on his heel and rushed away in such a frenzy that he knocked into both a waiter and a potted laurel tree before he secured the exit.

"Isn't he wonderful!" Alicia sighed.

"Wonderful?" Chad asked, mystified.

"He always does what I ask him to," Alicia said simply. "He cares for my wishes."

Chad looked at Chantel and she at him. Both were laughing when Lady Lillian finally stood before them. "So, there you are, you deceiving minx."

"Are you talking to me?" Chantel asked quickly, since Alicia had immediately cowered behind her.

"No, I am talking about my daughter," Lady Lillian said, her eyes trained upon her errant offspring.

"Oh, I am so glad you don't think me a deceiving minx," Chantel said happily.

"I do," Lady Lillian snapped. "I have no doubt my daughter's misbehavior is due to your unhealthy influence."

"What unhealthy influence is that?" Chantel countered, working to draw Lady Lillian's fire toward her instead of the shaking Alicia.

"Yes, what unhealthy influence?" Aunt Beatrice asked roughly, apparently misliking Lady Lillian enough to deny all the faults she usually applied to Chantel.

"I told Alicia she was not to dance with, nor fraternize in any manner with, that Teddy of yours."

"But that wasn't Teddy," Chantel exclaimed, deciding a lie might be for the best. She widened her eyes and attempted an honest demeanor.

Lady Lillian pinned Alicia with a glare. "Alicia, you won't lie to me. Was that or was that not Teddy Emberly?"

Alicia paled. "I—I don't know who he was, Mama."

"Well, I know he wasn't my cousin," Chad said firmly. "I would have noted it. But I do hope, Miss Alicia," he smiled, directing his gaze toward Alicia, "that you will recognize me, since this is our dance."

"Oh?" Alicia's mouth formed a perfect O. "Ah, yes," she said gratefully. "I will be glad to dance with you." Alicia instantly clutched Chad's proffered arm.

"Alicia, you are to stay here and explain yourself," Lady Lillian said harshly. Her words were said to empty air, for Chad had whisked Alicia away with a swiftness most excellent.

"Do you have an objection to her dancing with my son?" Aunt Beatrice inquired, her face becoming mottled.

"He is of the Covington line," Lady Lillian returned witheringly. Her fury immediately focused upon Aunt Beatrice, since she was denied her daughter's attention.

"Now, ladies . . ." Chantel began, as both woman squared off. "Let us calm down."

"Calm down!" Lady Lillian gasped. "You have my

daughter disobeying her parents and dancing with bounders and cads."

"My son is no bounder." Aunt Beatrice's chest swelled so much that Chantel was sure her warrior chest plate would pop off.

"I was talking about Teddy Emberly!" Lady Lillian snapped.

"Teddy is no bounder either," Aunt Beatrice barked. "He is a want-wit, but no bounder."

"He's a Covington and that is enough for me," Lady Lillian exclaimed. Both ladies were now standing within spitting distance and Chantel really began to worry.

Just as she opened her mouth to attempt mediation, she felt a strong hand upon her shoulder. "Come," a voice whispered in her ear. "Retreat is the better part of valor."

Chantel spun around, and immediately found herself in Richard's arms. "But Richard . . ."

"Do not destroy their pleasure," Richard said. He took her champagne glass promptly from her nerveless fingers and dropped it on the recovering waiter's serving platter as he stumbled by. "Nor mine." He directed her swiftly toward the dance floor and swung her into a dance.

"I had hoped to soften Lady Lillian's attitude toward Teddy tonight," Chantel fretted. "Not to worsen it."

"Ah, is that the reason for this affair?" Richard asked. "I had wondered at your purpose in throwing this ball. You wish to play Cupid."

"Well, yes," Chantel flushed, still unsettled and distracted. "It was the second of my purposes. Alicia had begun to sink into a blue migraine over it all and I thought that if I could meet her parents in this social atmosphere and perhaps persuade them . . . but now Teddy and Alicia have only aggravated her, and once she is trounced by Aunt Beatrice, Teddy won't have a prayer of a chance." Both she and Richard looked over to where the two ladies were standing. They were shaking their fingers under each other's noses.

"Cheer up, perhaps Aunt Beatrice will kill Lady Lillian for you."

Chantel sighed. "No, Aunt Beatrice never does anything to oblige me."

Richard laughed. He swung her close. "And what was the second purpose?"

"Hmm?" Chantel murmured, suddenly distracted in a new direction. The strength of Richard's arm about her waist was causing her to think of other matters.

"What was the first purpose of this ball?"

"First?" Chantel looked up, alarmed. How could she say it was not match-making, but mate-catching that was her first purpose for this masquerade? "I-I don't know why I said that. I only had one purpose."

Richard looked skeptical. "You are hiding something from me again."

"No, I am not!"

"Yes, you are," Richard said firmly. Chantel suddenly noticed that they were picking up speed and that Richard was pushing her across the dance floor very much as Teddy had Alicia.

"Richard, could you slow down?" Chantel asked breathlessly. Much more petite than he, she was unable to keep up with his long steps. Her panniers rocked alarmingly.

He suddenly shoved her toward the balcony doors. Before Chantel could exclaim, she was outside them and standing alone with him in the cool night air. "Now," he said, "You will tell me what you are keeping from me." He faced her and his broad body shut out any avenue of escape.

"I am not keeping anything from you." Chantel stepped back. She realized, for all her planning, that she was not yet prepared to tell him of her love. "Honestly."

"You aren't hiding any dead bodies anywhere, are you?" he asked, still crowding her. She felt the bones of her hooped skirts bending, so close did he stand.

"No, of course not," Chantel said, retreating. Her backside hit the cool stone of the balcony's wall.

"You haven't been searching for the treasure again?" Richard asked. He stepped even closer. Chantel was sandwiched between Richard's body and the stone wall. It was a position she rather enjoyed.

"No," Chantel shook her head. It was becoming hard for her to speak. She peeked up at Richard and swallowed. Her eyes were focusing themselves upon his lips.

"If you don't tell me your purpose for this ball," Richard said, "then I shan't tell you mine." His arms were on either side of her now.

"You had a purpose?" Chantel asked bemused.

"Yes," he said softly. "And it has everything to do with you," he murmured. Chantel's heart leaped even as he bent and kissed her. It was a quick, thorough kiss. He drew back, studying her.

Chantel flushed. "Did it? I must confess . . ."

"Confess what?"

"That was my first purpose in this ball, too." She melted into him, kissing him with a fervor of her own. He had come home for her! She had confessed she wanted him and he had not drawn back! She kissed him even more deeply.

Chantel was drowning in the sensations of Richard's kiss when suddenly a shrill voice called out, "Chantel, Chantel!"

"Damn," Richard muttered, drawing back. "Can I never be alone with you?"

"It is a ball," Chantel murmured.

Suddenly Alicia was upon the balcony. "Chantel!" Her voice was shrill. "Chantel, come quickly."

Chantel could hear the sigh of exasperation as Richard withdrew from her and stepped aside. Chantel's euphoria was swiftly doused when she saw Alicia, whose eyes were tear-stained and ravaged. "What is it?"

"They are taking Teddy away!"

What do you mean?"

"Men—men who say they are government agents. They—they have him chained."

"Oh, my Lord." Chantel paled. "Where?"

"They—they were in the library."

Chantel lifted up Lady Genevieve's skirts and ran into the ballroom. She could hear Richard calling to her urgently but she did not stop. She dodged through the dancers, hearing certain ones call out to her. Still she ran. She burst out of the room and down the hall. She could hear Alicia running behind her. She reached the foyer and checked in frozen fear. It was a nightmarish scene. Two men were ruthlessly dragging Teddy from the library.

Teddy clutched at the door frame with manacled hands. "Let me go, I didn't do anything."

"Ye were after the documents," one of the men growled. "We caught you red-handed, ye traitor."

"I only wanted some paper to write a sonnet, only looking for paper," Teddy jabbered. "I didn't know that paper was important."

"Let him go," Chantel shouted, enraged. They were tugging on him. She charged forward, slapping at the men. "Let him go, you beasts!"

"Here now, miss, step back or you'll get hurt," one man cried even as he attempted to ward off Chantel. She punched him in the eye for that. "Ouch!"

"Let him go," Chantel cried again, swinging broadly at the other man. Suddenly, strong hands grabbed her from behind. Even as she landed another shying blow she was being hauled away from the men. "Let me go," she shouted, and spun to attack her captor. She landed Richard a blow to his cheek before she realized it was him. "Richard, I am so sorry," she cried, realizing that she could barely see through the tears in her eyes. "They are trying to take Teddy away, stop them!" She clutched his lapel and leaned against him as his arms came about her comfortingly. "Stop them!"

"Please, Cousin Richard," Alicia pleaded.

Suddenly Chantel realized that they were not alone. Alicia stood behind them as well as her parents and other onlookers. Frightened, Chantel scanned the crowd. Chad and her Aunt were there as well.

"We caught him, my lord," one man said proudly. "We waited, and waited. He sneaked into the library just as you said he would. Went straight to the desk and then the drawer. He's a swift one."

"I wanted to write a poem," objected Teddy. "I was going to meet Alicia and wanted to write a poem."

"He's bluffing you, my lord," the other man said. "He found the packet right off. Looked at it and pocketed it in a winking. It's still there."

"No, he was meeting me," Alicia said frantically, wringing her hands. The onlookers murmured in excitement at that. "Honestly, Cousin."

"Alicia," her mother said shrilly. "Come here immediately and allow justice to be done."

"He's our man, my lord," the other man said. "He stumbled into your trap just as you planned."

Chantel drew stiffly back from Richard, looking wildly into his eyes. "You—you planned this?"

Richard looked at her for one long, solemn moment. "I planned to catch the traitor, yes."

She backed away from him, shaking her head, unable to believe it. "But Teddy is no traitor. You know he isn't. You can't let them take him away."

Richard's eyes had suddenly become opaque, unreadable. "He was caught with the evidence. There is no denying that."

"But you can't let them take him away," Chantel whispered in horror.

He looked away from her toward the guards. "Take him to the local gaol tonight."

"Yes, my lord," the one nodded.

"But I am innocent," Teddy wailed, even as they began to drag him toward the outer door.

"No, you can't!" Alicia cried and ran across the

foyer, flinging herself at Teddy and clutching him about the neck. "You can't!"

"Alicia, stop that." Lady Lillian was directly behind her. "Thomas, take care of your daughter!"

Sir Thomas came and, with surprising gentleness, disentangled his sobbing daughter from Teddy "Come, Alicia," he said, pulling her away. "You must let them take him. We will go home. You are becoming hysterical."

Chantel watched numbly as father directed weeping daughter out of the door. Her eyes went to Teddy's They were anguished. "You must take care of her, Chantel."

"I will," she said, choking on her tears.

"I-I'll be going with them now," Teddy said, his face white, his freckles standing out in relief. "Only wanted to write a poem," he sighed.

"Take him away." Richard's cool, sharp voice came from behind Chantel, who flinched. The pain hurt so much it felt as if someone had stabbed her in the heart She could not watch as the men took Teddy out. She focused her eyes upon the floor, willing this all to be untrue.

Everyone in the hall was silent. Chantel felt some body by her side and she looked up, ready to fight. I was Chad, his eyes full of sympathy, understanding, "Chantel, we will do something," he said softly, ever as his hand went out to her shoulder.

"Don't touch her, Tabor!" Richard's voice was a cracking whip. Chantel's eyes flew to his, in anger and almost hate. But only almost hate. God, she loved him and he had betrayed her. His eyes were ablaze as he looked at her. "If you want to help, Tabor," he said never taking his gaze from her, "you will clear all these people out of here. Now is not the time."

Chad withdrew his hand. His voice was cold. "No, now is not the time. I will see you tomorrow," he said softly to Chantel, and then walked to the observing crowd. "The excitement is over. Everyone return to the ballroom, please."

Chantel stood frozen, as did Richard. Their eyes were locked in battle. Slowly all the sounds of people faded and they stood alone. Chantel felt very alone. "Foolish me, you said you came to this ball for me. I thought . . ." Chantel's voice faltered, hoarse through tightened vocal cords. She blinked away tears. "I didn't know that what you meant was you wanted to entrap my brother, to destroy my family."

"I did not," Richard said softly, stepping toward her.

"Don't," she cried, lifting her hand in a warding gesture. "Don't come near me."

He stopped. "Chantel, I was not out to get your brother. I set a trap for the traitor, but Teddy sprung it. You must believe me."

"Believe you?" Chantel looked at him, stunned. "I will never believe you again. You have been nothing but torment and destruction to me."

"Don't say that," Richard growled.

Chantel lifted her head, her eyes frigid. "I will say anything I wish. You have done your best to destroy my family, destroy my very life. But you shall not succeed, that I swear to you." Richard stood, tall and proud himself, as she swept by him. She walked to the stairs.

"Chantel," Richard called. She stopped at the first

step. He turned to her, his eyes solemn. "I am the only one you can trust. I want your life . . . but only so you can live it with me. When you realize that and can truly believe it, come to me."

"Come to you?" Chantel asked amazed. She shook her head. "No, I will never make that error." She walked up the steps as if her feet were lead. She knew her heart was.

As she reached the top of the stairs she heard Richard call out once more, "When it is all made clear come to me, Chanty."

She walked slowly down the corridor to her door. Tears streamed down her face. Richard St. James was either insane or he was the devil. She opened the door. He had to be the devil, she thought, but she would never fall to his temptations again.

Chapter Eleven

It was late morning as the two men sat in the parlor taking tea. The clock ticked loudly upon the mantle. Other than that, silence prevailed.

"Has she come down yet?" Edward asked in a hushed voice.

"No, not yet," Richard said, shaking his head ruefully. "She is probably sitting up there trying to think how to disembowel me."

Edward did not laugh, for he personally thought that was exactly what Chantel was doing. "In truth, I do not quite understand why you allowed Teddy to be taken into custody either."

"Why?" Richard's brow rose. "First, I believe it is time we give the true felon some extra rope to play with. If he believes we are settled upon Teddy and are no longer after him, perhaps he will become more active, and less cautious."

Edward frowned. "I hadn't thought of that." He grinned. "We could only hope he would make another mistake like the black box."

"I'm not so certain that was a mistake. It effectively set us on a wild goose chase."

"And now we have Teddy Emberly in gaol." Edward sighed. "I'd say we bungled it."

Richard shrugged. "All we can do is make the most of it. I couldn't let Teddy be set free last night anyway. Everyone would have believed that I had used my power to do so and that I was protecting a traitor. Teddy must go through a trial so that he is totally cleared of suspicion."

"It's a shame that Chantel can't see it that way."

"I hope that after she calms down she will," Richard said. Edward looked at him to see if he was joking. He appeared totally serious. Edward shook his head. He doubted Chantel would ever calm down.

The two men sat in silence then and drank their tea. The door suddenly opened upon them and Chantel walked into the room. Edward caught his breath. She wore a stunning gown he had never seen before. Of celadon green watered silk trimmed in russet ruched velvet, it set off her complexion and accented the titian glints of her hair. Her eyes were a-glitter in a hauntingly pale face.

"You look most well in that dress, Chantel," Richard said calmly. Edward giggled, for it was an understatement. "I knew when I chose it for you that you would."

Edward choked. Chantel was finally wearing one of the gifts that Richard had given her? What was he purpose?

"Thank you, my lord," Chantel said evenly. "I am leaving to return to Covington's Folly this morning.

have packed all my belongings and sent a message to Chad. He should be arriving shortly."

As an opening salvo it was good, Edward mused. Now he knew why she wore a dress that she had refused to wear before. It was her battle flag. Chantel did not wait a moment for the men's reactions. She turned and promptly vanished. Edward realized he was hearing a low rumble in the room. It was coming from the respectable Richard St. James. Richard sprung from his chair and walked toward the door, very much like an aggravated panther on the stalk. Edward's cup clattered to the cart as he dropped it in his hurry to see the upcoming fray. He reached the door and halted. A slow, appreciative whistle escaped his lips.

Valises, boxes, satchels, and bundles littered the marble foyer. The hall was strewn with cordovon leather, brushed tapestry, worsted wool tartan, belts, buckles, latches and brass bandwork . . . a display to do a Coventry shop owner proud. Chantel must have packed all night to have achieved such effect. Reed was standing at the apex of the mountain of paraphernalia, with a startled expression upon his dignified face. Richard stood upon one side and Chantel upon the other. A maid was just then descending the stairs, yet another valise in hand.

"Betty, stop!" Richard's voice cracked through the foyer. "Return that to your mistress's room."

Betty dutifully halted and turned to go back upstairs.

"No, Betty," Chantel exclaimed, her voice furious. Bring that valise down to me." She turned and glared at Richard. "Betty will be going with me to Covington's Folly."

Betty stopped and nodded. "Right, my lady." She turned around and proceeded down the stairs again.

"Is she?" Richard's face darkened. He glared at the intrepid Betty, who was still advancing. "Reed," he suddenly exclaimed. "You are in my employ, take this," he reached over and snatched up a box, "and return it to your mistress's room. She will not be leaving."

Reed caught the box in obvious surprise and dismay. The fine old butler did not debate that toting boxes was not in a butler's duties as Edward had half expected he would. Rather, Reed proceeded to carry the box up the stairs in a stately manner.

"Oh, you are a beast," Chantel exclaimed to Richard, hands on her hips. "I will not stay under the roof of the man who has incarcerated my poor, innocent brother."

"He was caught with the papers . . ."

"As if that means anything. He was going to write a poem for goodness' sakes, not sell government secrets!" Chantel fumed. Reed was just then passing Betty upon the stairway. "Reed, stop. Return that valise to me immediately. If I am your mistress, you must listen to me!"

"Betty," Richard called swiftly. "You are not out of my employ yet, return that valise to your mistress' room."

Both employees froze. Like the changing of the guards, they spun and reversed their directions.

"How dare you! I am leaving this house . . . No, no, Betty, bring that valise down," shouted Chantel.

"You are staying! Reed, take that box up!"

The two harried servants twirled and then stopped upon the stairwell. Edward stifled a chuckle. They looked like human spinning tops.

"I'm getting dizzy," Betty announced. She looked to Reed for support.

"And I am too old for this," Reed said, panting.

"Betty, bring that valise here!" Chantel said, still glaring at Richard.

"Reed, take that box up!" Richard persisted, his face dangerous.

Both servants looked to their feuding employers, glanced at each other, and in accord, sat down upon the stairs. They cast their master and mistress exhausted looks. "Once ye decide it, I will do it," Betty sighed.

"I will be all too glad to serve you, my lord," Reed said kindly as only a long time retainer could, "once the matter is settled."

Edward held his breath. What next? Chantel was studying Richard with narrowed, furious eyes. Richard's face was stern and forbidding.

"Very well," Richard said slowly, "then I will carry it all upstairs myself." He glared at the servants. They but leaned back, clearly showing that they would neither hinder nor help him in his endeavor. The lord of the manor was forced to pick up a satchel.

Chantel pounced. Like lightning she was across the hall, snatching at it. "No, I am not staying, I tell you!"

They tussled, with both Richard's and Chantel's hands upon the coveted satchel. Suddenly both froze. They stood but inches from each other. Edward blinked. The raw energy that emanated from them when they looked into each other's eyes was stunning. It was of such a passion that Edward turned his eyes away, for he felt as if he was observing something both primal and infinitely private.

"I told you I am leaving," Chantel said, a small figure beside the impressive height of Richard.

"No, you will stay until it is all settled," Richard said, his voice a liquid metal. "You will not run. You will not disgrace either my house or yours. And you will not hurt Teddy's chances for release. And I guarantee you, you will hurt his chances if you leave."

"Is that a threat?"

"That is a fact. You will stay here if you mean to help Teddy. You will stay if you mean ever to gain anything from me—including an annulment."

"I will get the annulment without you."

"Don't try to go up against me, Chantel," Richard warned softly. "You will lose, and lose greatly."

Chantel emitted a wail and dropped the satchel. She fled across the foyer and charged up the stairs. Both Reed and Betty scrambled to remove themselves from her furious path.

"Hell and confound it," Richard cursed. He threw the satchel down and turned.

Now it was Edward's turn to scurry and retreat into the room before Richard slammed into him. Richard did not look at him but walked directly to the liqueur cabinet. Edward started as Richard poured himself a tall brandy. Richard was not a drinking man!

"I want Chad Tabor followed," Richard growled, turning a dark eye upon Edward.

"Followed . . . why?" Edward asked, nonplussed. "Do you think he is involved with our man?"

"I don't know and I don't give a damn," Richard said, tossing down a great dose of brandy. "But he will not help Chantel to leave this house."

"You mean you think she will try to do it anyway!"

"Of course." Richard's smile was grim. "I know she shall."

Edward shook his head, amazed. He couldn't imagine a woman who would try and brook Richard St. James after that scene. He almost felt sorry for Chantel. "Why don't you let her go back to Covington's Folly—just until this is all settled?"

Richard turned away, his back stiff. "She is my wife. I want her here."

"But—but she isn't," Edward stammered. "Not really."

"She will be." Richard's tone was implacable. Yet there was a thread of pain within it. Edward shook his head. Now he wasn't sure who to feel sorry for. When Richard turned, his eyes were unreadable. "Just see to it that Chad Tabor doesn't help her escape."

Edward nodded, bemused. He could tell by his friend's face that Richard was not only deadly serious, but that he, Edward, dare not fail in the commission. He swallowed. "I think I'll have one of those brandies myself, if you don't mind . . ."

"He will not let me go," Chantel said in pain. She looked up at Chad, who stood by the fireplace.

Chad turned. "What do you mean, he will not let you go?"

"He says that if I try and leave he will not grant me an annulment. What kind of man is he? He wants to imprison me as well as Teddy."

Chad was immediately by her side, a comforting arm about her shoulders. Chantel, exhausted and tormented, laid her weary head upon his shoulder. "My poor Chantel," Chad said softly.

"Why?" she asked. "Why is he doing this?"

"Because he is a man of power and cannot tolerate anyone who countermands him."

"But surely he knows Teddy is innocent."

"Teddy's innocence doesn't matter to him," Chad said, shaking his head sadly. "They have been after the traitor for so long that they must find someone to be the traitor."

Chantel drew back, fear in her eyes. "You mean Teddy is to be the sacrificial lamb?"

"I'm afraid so," he sighed. "St. James's image is being damaged the longer he fails to find the traitor."

"Oh, my Lord," Chantel gasped. "Then Teddy will have no chance."

"Don't say that." Chad shook her gently. "Don't give up. You must fight for him."

Chantel grabbed Chad's hand up in a vise-like grip. She needed his strength. "How? How am I going to fight for him?"

"Run away with me." Chad said simply.

"What?" Chantel couldn't believe his words. "But—but how will that help?"

"Escape St. James," Chad said urgently. "You know I love you. You know I want to marry you. I will take care of you always. And once you have escaped St. James, once you are out of his power, then I can fight to clear Teddy. I can do it, Chantel."

"But—but how could you do it?" Chantel shook her head.

Chad's eyes were sincere. "I have the money, Chantel. I also have connections you don't know about."

"Connections?"

"Yes," Chad said. "St. James is not the only powerful man. I simply do not care to flout my power. But you must come with me. I could never allow myself to wage this war with you under his roof. Why do you think he is forcing you to stay here? You are his security."

"I am his pawn." Chantel sat stunned.

She was swirling in a vortex of emotion. To run away with Chad. To never see Richard St. James again. It was insane! She didn't want to run away from him! Richard was trying to destroy her and her family; yet, her heart rebelled against the thought of leaving him. She just didn't want to believe that he was doing this to her. Yet he was. Dear God, she would have to run away. For if she stayed, loving St. James as she did, she would be lost. She would be yielding all control to a man who only held her out of pride and for power. Not only would she be lost, but Teddy would be lost. She looked in anguish to Chad. "Do you really believe this?"

"Yes, I do, Chantel," he said. "Run away with me. Escape."

"But won't he follow?"

"Not if we travel to Europe. Once the gossip is out he will not follow you. His pride will not permit it. He will grant you the annulment and you can marry me."

Then it would be final, a small voice cried in Chantel. She would never see St. James again. Yet, if she did not run away with Chad, Chad could not protect Teddy. Chad could not protect her. Chantel closed her eyes. What a bleak life she had to look forward to. But she was a woman with no money, no options. She could stay with a man who had incarcerated her brother, or flee with a man who loved her and wanted to help her. She nodded. "I will run away with you. If you truly believe it will help Teddy."

"It will," Chad said with a positive, joyful voice. "I have the connections, Chantel. And once we are on the Continent I will show you the kind of life you should always have had. The one I've always wanted to give you. I promise you, you will want for nothing."

Chantel nodded and forced a smile. "Whe—when should we do this?"

Chad stood, drawing her up. He put his hand to her chin and tilted her face to him. She had been trying to hide her eyes, but she looked at him with what she hoped was an honest gaze. "It will take me a week or two. I must do certain things first." He smiled. "Get all my business in line as it is. Then I will come for you."

"Yes, yes," Chantel nodded. She had a week still, maybe two. "But you must leave now, before St. James comes."

Chad shook his head. "I am not afraid of St. James. Not now." He hugged her and Chantel was grateful that he did not try to kiss her. Perhaps he knew how confused she still was. "I will leave you. But I will return, I promise you. Don't even worry about packing. I will buy you a new wardrobe. I will take care of it all."

Chantel forced another weak smile and nodded. She walked with him to the door and said goodbye. She watched Chad ride away. What was she doing? What she must, no doubt. Yet her heart was crying out at the cruelty of her fate. She shook herself and closed the door. She would survive it all. She always had. She always would.

Chantel returned home from seeing Teddy. She was in a numb daze. Teddy seemed to be taking it well. He had told her that the food was decent and the gaolers seemed pleasant fellows who even wanted to play cards with him.

Chantel shook her head. Even in gaol a Covington would find a way to game. But when she had admonished him on that he had looked offended. "Ain't playing for money, Chantel," he said, shocked. "Told Alicia I wouldn't. We won't ever find the treasure if I game. Lady Genevieve don't like it." Then he frowned. "But playing for nothing ain't gaming do you think?"

Chantel was forced to admit that it wasn't and the interview had proceeded along. Teddy's only pain was that Alicia had not come to see him. Chantel had said as gently as she could that she doubted her parents would permit her to.

Teddy had nodded and said that until he was free he imagined that would have to be the way of it. Until he was free . . . Chantel had not been able to tell him what she planned to do to free him. To speak the words would have been too concrete, too painful.

She walked up the stairs to her bedroom. Her head was pounding. She would lie down and rest for an hour. Perhaps the persistent pounding would lessen . . .

She was running from gray, shapeless forms, nameless monsters. She had to run away. She kept shaking her head. She didn't want to. She didn't want to! Then out of the dark void a brilliant scene burst upon her. She was at her masquerade ball again. Aunt Beatrice in her ridiculous Viking costume was before her. "You don't have the right fan, it should be blue. You don't have the right fan, it should be blue, it should be blue . . ."

The scene swirled about her and suddenly she was standing in a large portrait gallery. Two paintings of Lady Genevieve hung on the wall before her. She peered at them both. "Aunt Beatrice is right," Chantel thought. The fan was blue, in one of them. In the other the fan was rose. Such a small difference in the vast portraits.

Suddenly, as Chantel studied the portraits, the figures of Lady Genevieve began to dance and pirouette within their frames, both waving their unfurled fans. Yet the Lady Genevieve with the blue fan suddenly disappeared, leaving the portrait's background in place and nothing else. The Lady Genevieve with the rose fan froze into place. Chantel looked from the portrait with the figure to the one without.

Chantel awoke. Drat, why had she? She had wanted to study the portraits in her dream some more. There was something that confused her. She rose swiftly, going to her dressing table. She picked up the rose fan that was still lying there. She unfurled it and studied it. There was the bucolic scene of a gazebo in a plush green setting. She set the fan down and went to the portrait. She turned it around to view it once more.

Something was teasing her mind, nagging at her memory. Chantel closed her eyes to remember the portraits in her dream. Her eyes snapped open wide. It was the background behind Lady Genevieve! When Lady Genevieve had disappeared from the one painting, the background had been of a garden setting at eventide. Chantel had never considered the background of the painting, and she doubted many people had. The figure of Lady Genevieve in her splendor was all too consuming, while the background had been impressionistic and muted.

Chantel closed her eyes again. A garden at eventide. She opened her eyes and ran to pick up the rose fan. It was a garden in daylight. In one Lady Genevieve held the focus, in the other, a gazebo held the focus. But the actual setting was the same. She stared at it and remembered it in her mind's eye. She studied the trees and land contours so delicately depicted upon the fan.

"Why, I've played there," Chantel murmured. It had been a childhood haunt of hers at the Folly. The trees and bushes did stand in a circle about a clearing. A gazebo could have been there. But had never been.

She frowned. No, not ever in her memory had she heard of a gazebo on that spot. And her mother had recounted endless stories about the Folly in its grander days. But she recognized the mulberry bush to the right, she recognized the curve of the path and the way the hill rose behind it.

"That's it." Chantel snapped the fan shut with a grin and held it close. What a very dainty, feminine treasure map. She giggled. Indeed, Lady Genevieve did intend a woman to find the treasure if there was one. For what man would consider the details of a painting, let alone those of a fan. In the painting all they would see was the brilliance of the Covington's jewels and in the fan, merely an article for a woman to employ. "Lady Genevieve," Chantel laughed, "you *were* a witch."

Chantel donned her oldest work dress and sun bonnet the next morning and slipped out of the house. She proceeded to the gardener's work shed and rummaged through it until she found a serviceable shovel. She threw the shovel onto the pony cart that she'd had the groom hitch up, and she was off.

It was a lovely day and she reached the Folly and the appointed spot at mid-morning. She was humming when she began to dig in the center of the clearing. The mulberry bush was to the right side and the copse of trees surrounded her like sentinels. She was totally involved in her digging, a task that was far more difficult than she had expected. She was no expert with a shovel. But her dreams kept her going even as she became hotter and dirtier. Blisters began to form on her hands but she was thinking of how she was going to employ the fortune she would find. Such a treasure could surely buy Teddy the best services. Why, she'd take the treasure to Prinny himself and offer it to him for the release of her brother. He was always looking for funds, always granting knighthoods and waivers for the aid of his coffers.

Perhaps there would be enough left for her, even. She wouldn't have to run away with Chad. Indeed, she would never be beholden to any man. She could thumb her nose at St. James if she so chose. Play his game against him. But then she might be so wealthy that his family would demand he remain married to her. Of course, he wouldn't remain married to her because of the treasure. Not in her dream. He would remain married to her because he would realize that she was his equal and the perfect mate for him.

Chantel's digging slowed as her blisters began to surface. However, another sensation crept into her consciousness. She felt as if she were being watched, as if she were not alone. The hairs on the back of her neck rose, despite her mind telling her that she was imagining things.

Chantel looked up from the hole she was now standing in and surveyed the area. She listened carefully. All was silent, but the creeping, crawling feeling still persisted. A bird flashed through the trees and she jumped at the movement.

"Hello?" she called. She gripped the rough wood of the shovel tightly. She was not alone. She knew it. She could sense it. What had she been thinking, to come here all alone? Maybe it was the caped man who had shot at her, or the person who had closed the secret door and locked she and Alicia in, or—

A distant whistling came to her. After a moment, Richard St. James appeared, riding lazily through the trees. He drew his horse up a few feet from her, and eyed the hole she was standing in. "Having fun?"

"Yes," Chantel returned, forcing a frown. In truth she was simply grateful to have Richard St. James with her. It hadn't been the caped man or anyone else. "What are you doing here? You almost scared me out of my wits."

"I hope I did," he said, dismounting. "It was foolish of you to come out here by yourself."

Chantel remained silent, not willing to admit that she had just come to that same conclusion minutes ago. Richard strolled over and peered into the hole she had dug. "Found it yet?"

Chantel attempted a nonchalance as she swiped a damp curl from her face. "Found what yet?"

Richard grinned. "China, of course."

"I'm not digging to China."

"Looks like it," he said amusedly. "But perhaps you will find the treasure before that." He quirked his brow. "That is what you are doing, I hope. This isn't a grave for anybody, is it? Not hiding any more corpses, are you? I really could not encourage you in that habit."

Chantel flushed. "No, I am not." She determinedly returned to her digging, attempting to ignore the grinning man. She had just remembered she hated him. "But perhaps that isn't a bad idea." She looked up. "Exactly how tall are you?"

He laughed. "You must dig it much deeper and wider than that, darling, if it is to suit me."

Chantel almost dropped her shovel at his use of an endearment. She eyed him suspiciously. "Just exactly what do you want?"

His smile did not waver. "I thought you might be hungry." He went back to his horse, and Chantel noticed a basket upon the saddle.

"How did you know that I was here?"

"It was no great secret. The whole staff came to the same conclusion. You rode out with a shovel and a pony cart and dressed in that delightfully antiquated frock. It was rather obvious that you planned to indulge in some treasure hunting." He pulled a blanket from his saddle bag. "Cook sends her best wishes, as well as some sustinance while you hunt your fortune."

Chantel's chin jutted out and she glared at him. "Don't laugh at me."

Richard was spreading the blanket out upon a level patch of ground. He looked up. "I am not. I was merely explaining." His face took on an all too knowing look. "I wanted to ensure you didn't think I was spying on you. I wasn't."

"Oh," Chantel said, nonplussed. That was to have been her next accusation. She turned away and jabbed the shovel into the soil again, once again attempting to ignore Richard.

"The food is ready," he said a moment later. Chantel looked up. He had the blanket covered with a veritable picnic. There was chicken, bread, and some assorted cheeses and pastries. It looked inviting. Her stomach growled promptly at the tempting sight. Chantel sniffed and lifted her nose, however. "I do not choose to eat with a man who sent my brother to gaol." She plunged the shovel fiercely into the ground.

"Chantel," Richard called. She resolutely ignored him, keeping her eyes focused on the soil she was turning over. "Chantel." His voice was closer but she kept digging. "Chantel!" His voice was directly in her ear. Jumping in surprise, she spun, almost teetering over a mound of dirt.

Richard was standing directly behind her in the hole. He reached out and caught her before she toppled.

"Unhand me!"

"Not until you come and eat with me," Richard said congenially. His large hands were firm and warm upon her waist. Chantel swallowed and refused to look at him. "Now we can stand here all day," he said, "which means you will never finish your digging or find the treasure—or you can come and eat lunch with me. Then, I promise you, you may return to your digging." His hands stealthily inched toward her hips and around to the small of her back. "Of course, I wouldn't mind staying in this position."

Chantel forced herself not to lean into him. "Very well," she said, even as he drew her closer. "I will dine with you."

Richard laughed, releasing her swiftly. Despite herself, Chantel was a little miffed that he had kept his word. She had enjoyed that position as much as he. Embarrassed, she followed Richard out of the hole and sat down upon the blanket.

She had her eye upon a tasty-looking chicken breast when she noticed Richard reaching into the basket once more. He withdrew a bottle of champagne.

Her eyes widened. "Champagne?"

"Of course," he said, smiling and popping the cork. "In case you had found the treasure, I thought we could toast your success."

"Very amusing," Chantel said as she watched him pull out two glasses and pour the frothy drink into them.

"Not amusing . . . hopeful," he said. He handed her a glass. She took a sip. "And if you don't find the treasure, I thought it could be our last drink together before you run off with Chad."

Chantel swallowed her champagne in a painful gulp. Her eyes flew to his, which were sparkling gray, like sun on the water. He lifted his glass silently to her and then drank. "How did you know?"

"How couldn't I? You are not the woman to remain

where you believe you have been betrayed. When do you plan to run off with him? This week or next week?"

He said it so urbanely that Chantel felt guilty. "I am sorry."

"Don't be." Richard looked her levelly in the eye. "I won't let you succeed."

Chantel gasped, for then he winked at her. She stared at him. Yet, suddenly, she returned his smile. She lifted her glass in salute to his audacity. "You are an odious man, you know," she said, laughing.

He chuckled and they drank their champagne. It tasted light and bubbly, very much the way Chantel was beginning to feel. Richard had taken all of the subterfuge out of the situation. There would be no running off without his knowing it. She could not betray him if he already knew her plan.

"Now, eat some food," Richard nodded. "The chicken is delicious. So are those meat pastries."

"Yes, it does look good," Chantel said, reaching for the piece of chicken she had noted.

"You know, dear . . ." Chantel lifted a brow, but Richard continued, "I have not betrayed you, not one whit."

"No, you have merely sent Teddy, who is innocent, to gaol," Chantel said, biting into her chicken.

"You never permitted me to explain why I allowed Teddy to be taken."

Chantel swallowed hard. "You and I both know that Teddy bumbled into your trap. He was merely looking for some paper to write upon."

"Yes, you and I do know that. But other people don't. In fact, they will find it hard to believe that such a thing could happen. They don't know Teddy like we do." Chantel remained silent, for Richard was unfortunately correct. "I own I had not considered such an event. I must apologize for that. When I set the trap, I forgot Teddy would be about. All I can say is that I was distracted when I created the plan and put it into action."

"You were?" Chantel asked, amazed.

"Hunting for a compliment?"

"No." Chantel flushed. "It is simply that I have come to believe that you never make mistakes. You told me that the first night when you came for the black box. I thought you told me that to intimidate me. But now I have come to see that you were telling the truth."

Richard laughed wryly. "No, that was before I met you and your family." He shook his head. "Teddy was not supposed to be caught in that trap. But once he was, I couldn't simply set him free. No one would have believed his innocence. He needs to go to trial in order that he may be proven innocent. Otherwise this cloud will be over his head for the rest of his life."

"Oh," Chantel said weakly, wondering why she had never thought of that.

"That is why Teddy is in gaol. And I confess I want to keep him there." He lifted his hand swiftly to stop Chantel from screeching at him. "I need to find the real traitor so that Teddy can be cleared. With Teddy in gaol, it looks like we have settled upon him."

"That's what Chad told me."

Richard's brow rose. "He did?"

"Yes. That you plan to make him a sacrificial lamb."

Richard's mouth turned grim. "I thank you for that confidence, but I would please ask you not to tell Chad all the things I say in return."

"Why not?" Chantel asked suspiciously. "He is family."

Richard smiled once again. "He is also my competition."

"Competition?" Chantel asked, confused.

"You plan to run off with him, do you not?" Chantel remained silent. Richard shook his head with a sigh. "But I cannot deny that I want Teddy to stay where he is for now. We must flush the traitor out, and fast. Otherwise I don't know how to spring Teddy." He frowned. "It is a gamble, I own . . ."

"I thought you never gambled."

"I told you, your family is having a dire effect upon me."

She glared at him. He grinned unrepentantly. Squinting up to look at the sun, he said, "Hurry and finish your champagne."

"Why?"

He stood. "From the look of it, we will have only a few more hours of digging time."

"What do you mean, we?"

"It would be ungentlemanly of me not to aid a lady in finding her treasure." He reached a hand down to her. "Come, I promise that if we find it, it is all yours. But I will not leave you here by yourself and neither can I sit and watch you do all the work yourself. So come. Let us find the treasure so you can send me to the rightabouts."

Chantel gave him her hand and allowed him to pull

her up. "Laugh now. But when I find it, you won't be laughing."

Richard went and pulled a shovel from his saddle. "I won't?" He walked over and stepped into the hole, expertly plying the shovel. "Why wouldn't I want a rich wife?"

Chantel picked up her shovel. "I'm not your wife," she said tartly as she entered the hole.

"I know." He grinned. "But if you find the treasure I'll just be forced to keep you."

"Hmph," she said, hitting the dirt with her shovel. "You aren't going to have a choice."

He refused to answer that. "I thought you didn't believe in the treasure," he grunted as he lifted another shovelful.

"I do now."

"Why?"

"It's all in the fan."

"I beg your pardon?"

Chantel was digging steadily and so was he. She proceeded to tell him her theory. He was an attentive listener and another hour passed. The hole was growing apace and they were both standing waist high in it.

"Enough," Richard suddenly said. "I believe we need a refresher."

Chantel straightened, wiping her hand across her damp brow. She turned to him to agree and checked. Richard, at some point in time, had rolled up the sleeves of his shirt, pulled it from his pantaloons, and unbuttoned it. The slight breeze played with the cloth, flapping it about his lean waist, lifting it from his broad chest.

"I would certainly like something to drink," she

wheezed. Her stomach clenched for no good reason. The sun glinted off the mahogany hair that matted his chest, as it did his ruffled hair. She looked swiftly down.

"I'll get it," he said easily. Chantel was grateful, since she still couldn't seem to marshal her thoughts. She pulled in a deep breath. She could object to his improper dress, she knew; but the truth was that the sight of him pleased her as much as it ensured his comfort.

Richard returned with bottle and glasses in hand. He stood smiling down upon her and Chantel thought it was a sin. The man did something to her senses that she couldn't control. She returned his smile unwittingly. She gazed at the disheveled, sweaty male and shook her head in amazement. When she had been forced to marry the earl she had never thought he could be anything but the imposing, powerful, Richard St. James, the man who was always in control, always on the winning side. But today, as he smiled and offered her a glass and bottle before jumping into the hole they had dug, he was simply a flesh and blood man. And she adored that man.

Richard turned, looked at her, and laughed.

"What?" she asked, bemused.

"You look exactly as you did the day you were doing your wash."

"You don't," Chantel murmured as he took the bottle from her to pour.

His brow lifted. "What do you mean by that?"

She shrugged. "First of all, that day you were furious with me."

"Yes, I was. I must apologize."

"No, it's more than that," Chantel said, aware that she was going to confess exactly what she was thinking. "It is more. You are so different today. You bring champagne, you call me darling, and you don't even keep your shirt buttoned." She looked at him at a loss. "Why are you being like this?"

He silently reached out and tugged a damp curl away from her forehead with a frown. He said, "If it is to be the last day for us to be together, I don't want to waste time being anybody but the man I want to be when around you." His smile was quizzical. "A man can be many different men. I've lived in a world where one cares for propriety, consequence, and position. But whenever I am around you, propriety falls by the wayside. I don't worry about image. I merely want to be."

"I see," Chantel said quietly. She understood, for that was what she wanted when around him. She sighed. Life wouldn't allow it to be, however. She shook her head in regret.

"You are tired," he said briskly. "Let us stop for the day. We can return tomorrow." He smiled. "You will just have to wait one more day to give us all our comeuppance."

She smiled. "All right," she agreed. He would be with her again tomorrow. Richard helped her out of the hole and they picked up the food and blanket. She drove the pony cart and he rode beside her. They were companionably debating the possible whereabouts of the treasure and why digging had not uncovered it as they drove lazily back from Covington's Folly. They were interrupted by a shout from down the road.

"Richard, hulooo!"

Richard and Chantel looked up to find Edward riding toward them at a spanking pace. "Richard—I must talk to you!" He waved his hand as he came closer.

"Wait here," Richard said and prodded his horse forward. He met Edward halfway and the men talked while their horses pranced. Then Richard turned his horse and was galloping back toward her.

"What is it?" Chantel asked in alarm as he pulled up beside the cart. She could not read Richard's expression as he dismounted. "For heaven's sake, what is it, Richard?"

"We have a lead on our traitor, and this time we will be able to get him." He reached out his arms for her. "Please come here a moment."

"Why?" Chantel asked in confusion. She reached out and allowed him to lift her from the cart. "Richard, what is it?"

He bent swiftly and kissed her passionately. He pulled her up against his sweaty body. She reached instinctively for him and drew up against his smooth, warm chest. Richard drew back so quickly from the kiss that Chantel was left blinking in shock.

"I must leave for several days. Promise me you will not run off with Chad during the time I am away."

"But . . ."

He kissed her again, thoroughly and warmly. Chantel's senses were reeling when he pulled back. "Promise me, Chanty."

"But Richard . . ."

This time his kiss made her toes curl. She was clinging to him when he drew back. "Promise me!"

"I promise," Chantel gasped out.

"Good." His grin was blazing. Chantel had a hard time standing on her watery legs as Richard stepped back and mounted his horse. "Remember, you've given me three days, madam."

She nodded mutely as he turned his horse and galloped off toward Edward. Chantel remained in a daze, watching the disappearing figures. He'd said three days. But what could be accomplished in three days?

Chapter Twelve

Richard and Edward sat silently outside a disreputable inn, derelict to the point that if it hadn't been for the sturdy walls of fieldstone, it might well be wondered if it would not collapse in on itself. As it were, crumbling wood beams could be relied on only to roost assorted farmyard fowl. Located on the outskirts of London, the hostelry, which was reached by a narrow, pitted road, saw few visitors. This night was different. Richard and Edward had their horses well hidden within a copse of trees while they kept their eyes upon the inn's yard. There had been very little human activity for the past few hours.

Finally a dashing equipage pulled up into the yard, scattering the chickens and cats that meandered across it. A slim, well dressed man alighted from the gleaming vehicle. He entered the inn with a casual confidence. Not fifteen minutes later, he returned. He gave his coachman the order, entered the vehicle, and it was off.

"There's the transfer. Let's go," Richard said softly. He spurred his horse forward. Edward was but a minute behind him as they entered the yard. The chickens and cats once again scattered with squawks and hisses.

Richard dismounted and ran toward the inn. He burst through the door, searching the room. He found no one in the common room but the proprietor, apparently enjoying a tankard of his own watered-down ale. Yet, Richard caught the flash of a dark cloak disappearing through the door to the back.

"There he goes," Edward exclaimed from behind Richard.

Richard moved swiftly across the room, toppling stools and benches. He raced through the back door. It led into the kitchen. The proprietor's scrawny, slatternly wife stood at a cutting table, a slab of beef in one hand, a knife in the other.

"Where did he go?"

She looked at him with uncaring eyes and pointed the knife toward the exit door. Richard nodded curtly and crossed the small, rancid-smelling kitchen in a flash. He ran out the rear door, his eyes scanning the area. A bullet suddenly whizzed by his ear and he sprang to a crouch behind crates of rotting corn husks. He saw nothing, but soon could hear the sound of diminishing hoofbeats.

"Dammit!"

"Where is he?" Edward gasped as he joined Richard.

Richard stood, his face dark. "He's gone."

"Can we catch him?"

"Why? He'll only lose the evidence before we can get to him."

"What shall we do?"

"Wait until next time. We now know who he is. It

won't be long. I want you to go back to London and report to the department." Richard turned back toward the door.

"But where are you going?" Edward asked.

"Home to Chantel."

"Are you going to tell her?" Edward asked quietly.

There was a moment's silence. "Yes, I am going to tell her."

Edward shook his head. "It won't be easy."

"No," Richard sighed. "It won't."

"Madam, you have a visitor," Reed announced.

Chantel looked up eagerly from her stitching before she realized it could not be Richard, for he surely would not have had himself announced.

"Who is it?" she asked with less enthusiasm.

"Your cousin, my lady."

"Chad! So soon!" Chantel exclaimed, blinking. It had not been a week since she had promised Chad she would flee with him. It had only been two days since she had promised Richard that she would not flee with her cousin. It seemed she would need a calendar and chalk if she were to keep up with her promises. "Er . . . please admit him."

Reed bowed and departed. Chantel gripped the frame of the sampler she was attempting to embroider and waited.

Chad entered, dressed in a midnight-hued cape draped in tiers of wool with the top of the cape rimmed in sable. He hadn't even bothered to hand it over to the butler. Chantel forced a smile. "Hello, Chad. Why have you come back so soon?"

"Things have been moving more swiftly than I expected." He smiled, crossing to her with purpose in his brown eyes. Suddenly he stopped, and those eyes widened. "Do my eyes deceive me or are you actually sewing something as useless as a sampler?"

Chantel attempted to hide it from his quizzing gaze. "I've made a botch of it, I fear. 'Tis amazing, I have sewn seams and patches for years, but to embark on petit point—I cannot. However, it is as much as I dare without the entire household staff falling into a decline because I do the maid's work." She grimaced. "I fear I am not much of a lady of the manor."

"My poor Chantel." Chad shook his head as he sat down beside her, his arm coming around her shoulders in comfort. "Do not worry, you will fare much better as my lady."

Chantel clasped her hands together and drew in a breath. "Chad, dear, I—I am sorry, but I am not—I am not going with you."

Chad's arm reflexively tightened about her. Then it eased. "Why not?"

She bit her lip and found it hard to meet Chad's questioning gaze. "I—I promised Richard that I wouldn't run away with you for three days."

His brows curved down. "Why ever would you promise him such a thing?"

Chantel shrugged uneasily. "Somehow he divined that I would run away with you and he asked me to give him at least three days before I did so."

"Three days? Why three days? Is it biblical or something?"

"No, he just said he needed three days to prove himself to me."

"Prove himself! How could he do that?"

"He intends to find the real traitor, Chad." She reached out her hand to his. "He says he is only keeping Teddy in custody until he can find the real traitor to take his place. He said that is the best way to prove Teddy is innocent. In fact, it might be the only way."

He clasped her hand firmly. "And do you believe him?"

"I think it only fair to give him a chance to prove himself."

"I see," Chad said softly. He disentangled himself from her and walked away to stare out of the window. "Which means you want to believe him." Chantel remained silent. He turned. "Which day is this you are on, may I ask?"

Chantel flushed. "This is the second day."

"Where is St. James then?"

"London, I assume. Edward had come with news that they definitely had evidence as to who the traitor is. Richard said he must leave, but asked me to give him three days. He seemed confident that he would have the traitor by then."

"Did he?" Chad's smile seemed wry. His eyes darkened. "But if he doesn't come back with any evidence tomorrow, will you go with me then?"

"No," Chantel shook her head sadly. "He asked for three days, but I'd give him a lifetime."

Chad stiffened as if he had been hit. Then he seemed to throw it off, and shook his head. "You have fallen in love with him, haven't you?" Chantel nodded mutely, unable to say it. Chad crossed softly and laid a gentle hand on her flushing cheek. "Now how am I ever to prove myself to you?"

Chantel looked swiftly and fiercely at him. "You

have proven yourself to be my best friend and confidant. Is that not enough?"

"Not compared to having your love," he said softly. Then he forced a smile, and his brown eyes lightened. "Well, enough of that. Do say you will at least come and see my new coach. Teddy would say it is bang up to the nines. The interior is in satin and the finest leather."

Chantel laughed, grateful that he'd brought the mood back to lightness. She reached up and withdrew his hand from her cheek, holding it tightly. "You wouldn't be trying to bribe me into running away with you, cousin mine?"

"Satin and leather," Chad tempted, tugging on her hand. "And Madam, the clothes that could be yours. There are trunks of them atop the coach. They outshine anything St. James has ever given you. Indeed, they make his presents look paltry." He grinned. "Come Chantel, you simply must see it all."

Chantel allowed him to pull her to her feet. "You sadist. You wish me to see it only so that I may be sorry I won't run off with you."

He laughed, dragging her toward the door. "How right you are. Perhaps once you see it all, you might reconsider this insanity of remaining with St. James and not coming with me. Think of the stifling, proper, dull life you must lead if you remain with him—and he with you. And his family, forsooth! Do you truly want to live with that disapproving, priggish lot? Only think of his mother! She'd be your mother-in-law! That is if she didn't kill you first."

"And what of your mother?" Chantel retorted.

He halted with a comical look of dismay. "I object.

My mother would welcome you to our family with open arms. Indeed, that is all she's ever wanted."

"I didn't mean that, and you know it."

He grinned. "Ah yes, but I was going to take you to the Continent, remember? Wouldn't that have been far enough away from any mother-in-law?"

"You have a point," Chantel was forced to admit.

"Come on," he said, jerking upon her hand again. "I want you to see this coach and the horses . . . six matched bays."

They sped out of the parlor door and across the grand hall. Both were laughing and Chantel felt as if they were children again and he was dragging her out to see his new pet retriever.

Chad flung open the door and all but shoved her out. Chantel froze. A magnificent coach gleamed with burgundy enamel trimmed with narrow scrolls of gold on mother-of-pearl door panels. The coachman atop did indeed hold a team of six gorgeous bays in check. They were restive and frolicsome. "Oh, Chad! It is beautiful. And, oh, the horses! They must be fast goers."

"Prime ones," Chad nodded, running down the steps and opening the door to the coach. He waved a beckoning hand at the stunned Chantel. "Now, come and see the inside, my reluctant Cinderella."

"It must have cost you a fortune," Chantel breathed, shaking her head. "No matter what, you shouldn't have done this."

"Only the best for you."

"Oh, Chad, I am sorry."

"Don't be," he said, and beckoned again impatiently. "Now do come and see the detailing of it."

Chantel shook her head again, tears stinging her eyes slightly. She did love her cousin. She ran down the stairs and up to the coach. "Oh Chad," she laughed as she peered in. He had not lied. The seats were in cream leather and the interior was of ivory ruched satin. "It is in satin. How decade-e-ent!"

Her words ended in a wail as Chantel found herself boosted none too gently into the coach. Her face hit the coach floor and it seemed Chad couldn't hear her muffled exclamation, for he jumped into the coach as well. "Chad, what is the matter?" she asked, scrambling to right herself. She heard him shout, "Spring them," and then heard him slam the coach door shut.

"Chad what on earth . . ." Chantel gasped, attempting to crawl to a less ignoble position. She fell back as the coach lurched into motion. "Oh, for heaven's sakes," she cried, disgusted. "What the devil is going on?"

"I am abducting you," Chad said cheerily as he lifted her with strong hands to the seat beside him.

She nearly slid off again. "Abducting me?"

"Yes, abducting you. Meaning you are going with me to France whether you want to or not."

Chantel gasped, looked into Chad's determined eyes, and immediately dove toward the door. Chad pulled her back swiftly, wrapping powerful, restraining arms about her. She had never thought of Chad as strong before now. "Don't try it. You'd hurt yourself, Chanty."

In that one moment, Chantel knew that unfortunately Chad was odiously right, for the coach was picking up tremendous speed. Indeed, considering the bouncing they were doing even in such a well sprung vehicle, the coachman must have been driving those six matched bays like a demon. She began to struggle against Chad. "Let me go! Damn it!"

"Very well," Chad said. He lessened his restraint. Chantel plunged away from him to gain the seat across from him. She indignantly righted herself and cast him a fuming glance. Then she yelped. "What!"

Chad had a very deadly looking pistol leveled at her. "Now behave. Unlike poor Teddy, I know how to use this."

"You—you wouldn't shoot me," Chantel said aghast.

Chad's brown eyes were far too knowing. "No. But I don't intend to have you kill me before your temper cools."

Chantel almost growled. She sat back upon her seat and clasped her hands together. "Do you mind telling me what this is all about, Chad?"

"I told you, I am abducting you." He said it in very much the manner he had always used with her; except, now he had a gun trained upon her. "I fear I am forced to flee to France and I wish you to go with me. I won't leave you behind. I love you too much for that."

"I see," Chantel murmured, attempting to marshal her thoughts. She couldn't believe she was in a satin-lined coach going at breakneck speed with her beloved cousin Chad telling her he loved her while he pointed a gun at her. Her mind was awhirl with confusion and questions. "But why must we go to France?"

"Because of your charming St. James. Everything had been famous until he came into the picture. I've never seen such a determined man. Nor such an intelligent one. It is amazing how very few intelligent people there are in the world. Thank God I've had you to help me stay in front of him."

He sighed. "But if what you say is true and he's known who the traitor is for these two days then we simply must leave England."

Chantel shook her head. "I must be one of the unintelligent ones, but why must we—you, leave England? Once he finds the traitor, Teddy can be . . ." Something seemed to ring in Chantel's mind. "Oh no!"

"Oh, yes," Chad nodded. "Teddy would go free, but I'd be in gaol. Merely a swap of Covingtons."

"You are the traitor!"

Chad's eyes were gentle as he nodded. "Yes, Chanty. I have been for a long time."

"But . . . but why?"

He smiled wryly. "The Covington curse, I fear."

"But the curse has nothing to do with treason. It is only gambling," Chantel said irately. "And drinking and, and licentiousness I suppose . . ."

"All of which my father indulged in," Chad nodded.

"He did?" Chantel's eyes widened. "But we all thought he was proper. How did we never hear of it? I mean—"

"He didn't gamble with cards, he liked to gamble in a business-like manner," Chad said patiently. "He liked to gamble on the exchange."

"And he lost, of course" Chantel muttered, knowing how the story went when it involved a Covington. She looked at him. "Did Aunt know this?"

"Not all," Chad said, shaking his head. "One of her greatest prides is that she did not marry a here-andtherian gambler like all the rest of the Covington women had."

"Like my mother had."

"Like your mother."

Chantel thought for a moment and she narrowed her eyes. "So your father was like the rest of the family, but that still didn't mean you had to resort to treason to save the family funds."

"Yes, it did."

"No, it didn't."

"Yes, it did," Chad nodded firmly. "It wasn't only the Covington curse at play, I fear it was the Covington excesses as well."

"What do you mean?"

"I didn't like being poor," Chad said simply. "I didn't like living under the hatches. You always have to wear the worst clothes, eat the worst food, and put up with insults and slurs. Money is just too enjoyable, Chantel, as is the power that comes with money."

"But treason," Chantel persisted. "Why didn't you try cards, for goodness sakes? It is at least legal!"

Chad laughed. "Forgive me, dear, but I find cards a dead bore. But espionage? Ah, now there is a game of chance worth the risk. There is so much more involved than watching the turn of a card or the roll of the dice." He shrugged. "The stakes are far higher."

"That's because they are life and death."

He nodded. "Yes, they are life and death. It's the ultimate gamble, and always exhilarating."

"But you have killed people!" Chantel exclaimed.

"It's all part of the game," Chad said, as a gentle teacher to a novice student. "You simply must rid yourself of the low cards."

He said it so reasonably that Chantel clamped her mouth open and shut before she finally said, "But why be a traitor to England? Couldn't you have been an agent for her? It would have served the same purpose and it would have been legal."

Chad shook his head. "This unswerving fixation you have with legality. Really Chantel, it doesn't befit you. St. James has tainted your mind." He then looked her straight in the eyes. "I offered my services to His Majesty. But I was categorically rejected. I was a Covington, and none would trust me because of the family and our background."

"Oh, I am sorry," Chantel said sadly. "It's the blasted Covington curse." But then she shook herself. "What on earth am I saying? Chad, you are a villain." He laughed. "You truly are. You must not abduct me . . . you mustn't!"

"I fear I must. I love you too much, you see. I have as much as St. James has to offer. Perhaps even more, because I won't always be losing my temper with you; nor will I be requesting that you behave like a proper little lady. And then there is Mother . . ."

"Your mother!" Chantel exclaimed, irritated. "What does she have to do with this?"

Chad hesitated and then he smiled. "She really wants you as her daughter, Chantel."

"Faith!" Chantel rolled her eyes. "What kind of villain are you, to worry over your mother's wants?"

He shook his head wryly. "Even villains have mothers, Chantel . . . and I love her . . . and I love you."

"Love me?" Chantel was indignant. "Chad, how can you say you love me when the simple fact is you have almost had me killed—and more than once!"

"You were never truly in danger," Chad returned firmly. "I would never have let anything happen to you. The operation at the Folly went smoothly and safely for years without you ever being disturbed once by it." A glimmer of a smile tipped his lips. "Except for Teddy's thinking we were Lady Genevieve's ghost, of course."

"So it wasn't Teddy. It was you thumping and bumping down in the cellars?"

"The cellars were an excellent hiding place and, as for storage, they could take shiploads. You'd be amazed at the labyrinth beneath the Folly."

"I suppose I would," Chantel muttered. "I'm surprised we weren't all murdered in our beds."

"Chantel, stop it. No one, but no one, would dare to risk my wrath. Even Dejarn didn't intend to set the dogs on you. He was merely stupid and scared when he gave Teddy the box to bring to the Folly. He was afraid to be caught with the information, but afraid to lose it and come to me empty handed." He frowned. "I really should have killed him immediately, but I thought I still had some purpose and use for him." He shook his head. "That he would truly think to inform on me—and to you yet. Gads, the audacity!"

"You are the one who killed him!"

"Yes," Chad nodded. "I apologize for the discomfort and additional effort it caused you. I did remove him from the premises as soon as possible." Once again a smile lurked in his eyes. "That is, after you three stopped moving him about so. It was rather hard to keep up with it all."

"Chad, I can't believe it," Chantel shook her head. "I just can't believe it was you."

He lifted his brow. "Be reasonable, Chantel. Do you mean to tell me you would have enjoyed it if Dejarn had told you I was the traitor? And think if you had then been forced to tell the high and mighty Lord St. James that your family numbered a proven traitor as well as all the other skeletons in the closet. I simply eliminated such an unpleasant possibility. Or, is it that you object to my transporting Dejarn from the premises? Did you truly wish to dispose of him yourself?"

"Well, no," Chantel admitted. "But still . . ."

"There isn't any but still," Chad persisted. "I protected you from it and for that you must give me credit."

"Then why did they find that incriminating evidence in the Folly?"

"An oversight." Chad sighed. "Truly, Chantel, it's a maze down there. I had ordered the men to clear it all out the minute you told me about St. James. They must have missed one of the rooms. And, it is not as if I didn't remove you from the house while I was undertaking such action."

"You mean when you invited me to your mother's it was to get me out of the way, rather than out of concern?"

"I am trying to tell you it was out of concern. I was planning only one more information exchange at the Folly before locating my operations elsewhere. But then you suddenly decided to attend the ball and return to Covington's Folly. I did not wish to spoil your pleasure, so I called the drop off. Which, I must own, was a streak of luck in itself, as St. James raided the Folly that night and would have caught me if I hadn't."

"Lucky for you, perhaps. He thought it was me who had informed to you," Chantel said angrily.

"Could I help it if he jumped to the wrong conclusions?"

"Yes, you could." Chantel's eyes suddenly widened. "Oh God! He's going to jump to another wrong conclusion!"

Chad sighed. "You've just realized that?"

"He'll think I chose to run off with you!" Chantel clenched her fists tight. "He'll think I broke my promise!"

Chad nodded. "Yes, he will."

"Ohh, I swear I—"

Chad raised the gun and waved it at her. "Now calm down, Chantel."

She contented herself with a fierce glare. "I do hope St. James kills you when he catches up with us."

"No, you don't. And he won't catch us."

"Yes, he will. He'll come after me." Chantel said, lifting her chin.

"If he comes, it will be after me for treason. That is why he made you promise not to leave with me. He must have learned by then that I was the traitor and didn't want you to escape with me. Indeed, the way it looks, he'll most likely think you my accomplice."

"Don't say that! Don't you dare!"

"He will think you broke your promise and betrayed him," Chad said firmly. "Now, you will be beneath his contempt. You're a Covington, Chanty, and St. James won't have you after this. Just like England wouldn't have me. You'll be better off with me, I tell you."

"That's not true," Chantel fumed. Gun or no gun,

she thought she'd like to take a punch at Chad. Suddenly, a shot rang out. A muffled cry could be heard outside and the coach was finally slowed to a rough stop. "That's Richard!" Chantel said in excitement. "Now, we will see!"

Chantel rushed to the window and leaned out. Indeed, Richard St. James was flying from his horse at that moment to jump the coachman, who was escaping on foot. Winged from a shot levied by St. James, the coachman evidently desired nothing so much as to flee in the opposite direction till apprehended by the earl.

Chantel applauded with glee. "He's attacked your coachmen. You know you have a very disloyal coachman, Chad," she added maliciously.

Richard leveled the coachman with a jab to the jaw.

"He's got him!" Chantel cheered.

"And I've got you," Chad laughed, suddenly grabbing her about the waist tightly. Cold steel nuzzled her ear. Chantel gulped. "Now open the door slowly."

Chantel didn't even bother to nod, but reached for the door and swung it wide. St. James was standing straight and tall, his own pistol trained upon the coach.

"Watch it, St. James, or I will kill her," Chad called out. "Now get out, Chantel, but slowly, and with me." The two crawled out in tandem. Chantel's eyes flew to Richard's. His were stern and unreadable.

"Hello, Richard," she choked out, attempting to ignore the metal point at her ear. It was giving her a headache. "I am glad to see you."

"Are you?" he asked, his brow arching up maddeningly.

"See," Chad whispered. "Tell us, St. James, who have you come for? Chantel or me?"

"Both," Richard shot back.

"I told you so," Chad murmured. Chantel thought there was never anything worse than someone who said "I told you so," but there was. Someone who chose to do so while holding a gun to one's head.

"If you want Chantel—alive, that is—you will have to let her and me go," Chad ordered.

Richard's eyes glittered. He snorted. "You wouldn't shoot her. She's your accomplice."

"Accomplice!" Chantel sputtered.

"And you thought he loved you," Chad murmured. "Accomplice or not, St. James, I don't think you'd want your wife's death to be on your hands. Think of the scandal. Think of the family pride. Now, drop your gun, St. James."

Richard's jaw tensed. "You won't get away, Tabor."

"I'll take my chances. I have a feeling I'll lay far more on the table than you would ever dare to." Chad laughed. "Now throw down your gun. Don't make me shoot Chantel."

"Shoot her and you'll have to find another partner," Richard retorted.

"I hate you both," Chantel declared, even as a shudder ran through her.

"Throw it down," Chad said in a tone that Chantel realized was frighteningly honest. "If you force me to shoot Chantel, I will kill you, St. James. I swear I will."

It all came into focus for Chantel at that moment. She didn't hate them both, she loved them both. And

the simple truth was that for Chad to escape, he would
be forced to kill Richard. Chad couldn't merely take
her and leave St. James. Richard was a card Chad
would want to discard from his hand. Richard moved
to throw down his gun.

"No!" Chantel shouted. She bucked against Chad
and twisted in arms slackened in shock. She grabbed
at Chad's gun hand.

"Chanty, don't," Chad commanded, even as they
struggled for control of the gun. Chad swiftly raised
his free hand and slapped her sharply across the cheek.

Chantel staggered. She heard a roar from behind
and she was ruthlessly pushed aside. She fell to the
ground. She finally mustered the strength to lift her
ringing head from the dirt. Her pain-blurred eyes
cleared enough that she could see. Chad and Richard
were fighting, fist to fist. The blows they delivered to
each other seemed to resound in Chantel's head. They
were going to kill each other! Chantel sat up and frantically scanned the ground around her. Where was it?
Her eyes spotted Chad's pistol not five feet away from
her. She crawled toward it, continually watching the
men. Her fingers contacted the metal, and she
snatched it up.

She dragged herself to a standing position. She had
the gun, yes, but what to do with it exactly? She
couldn't be expected to hit any specific thing. The men
were bobbing blocks, ducking furious punches and
taking on vicious blows. Chantel shrugged to herself.
If you couldn't use a thing one way, try another. She
reversed the gun in her hand, so the butt was directed
outward, and crept cautiously up to the battling men.
She raised the weapon and waited, praying every mo-

ment for a break in the fighting and a chance to incapacitate one or the other. Her moment arrived when
Richard, dodging a swing, stepped on the fallen coachman and tumbled backward. Chad hesitated for a split
second, and before he could move, Chantel cracked
him sharply over the head with the butt of his pistol.
He crumpled to the ground.

Richard lay upon the fallen coachman. His breathing sounded like a bellows and he had a large shiner
coming on over one eye. "Chantel . . ." was all he
could wheeze as he scrabbled off the coachman.

Chantel backed up. "Don't you 'Chantel' me!" She
shook the gun butt angrily at him. "How dare you
think I was Chad's accomplice. How dare you!"

"I only said that to confuse Chad," Richard said as
he gained his feet. He grimaced. "I didn't truly believe
it."

"Yes, you did," Chantel accused. "Don't you come
near me!"

"Woman, it's time you start believing me," he
growled. Before Chantel knew it, Richard had
grabbed the gun from her and thrown it over their
heads. He grasped her now-weaponless outstretched
hand and pulled her to him. Chantel opened her
mouth to screech and he covered it with a fierce, demanding kiss.

With the rush of sensations and needs that instantly
struck Chantel, she forgot it all: the betrayals, the
shocks, the fears. She reached up to clutch Richard
close. A soft moan escaped her lips as Richard's hands
roved over her possessively.

Richard drew back, a fierce look in his eyes. "Do

you believe me now? Don't you know how much I want you!"

"Hmm," Chantel murmured dazedly. Her eyes were on his lips and her mind focused on another kiss. "You want me," she repeated dutifully.

"Lord, woman," he said, his voice gravel. "You could have been killed."

Her eyes slid from his lips and flew to his intent eyes. She started shaking her head. "No, oh no." She backed away from him. "It's that aphrodisiac thing."

"What?" His brows snapped down. "What are you talking about?"

"You are kissing me and wanting me only because of the danger," Chantel sputtered.

"Oh, for God's sake."

"You said it yourself. That's what it was last time. That's what it is this time. And the minute you feel safe—you—you're going to leave like you always do."

Richard just looked stunned. "Chantel, you have it all wrong. That was different. And I only told you that because . . ."

"Richard," Chantel shrieked. "It's Chad, behind you!"

"Damn," Richard growled. He spun swiftly. Chad was attempting a halting weave toward him. Richard delivered a jaw-breaking right hook and Chad crumpled again. Richard spun and glared at Chantel.

"D-don't look at me," Chantel gulped.

"Oh, Lord." Richard rolled his eyes toward heaven. "Come on. Let's take Chad into custody. We'll discuss this later."

"Much later," Chantel nodded. She looked to the fallen Chad and sighed. "He was the last one I would have thought was the traitor. But then, I never seem to be able to judge men."

Chantel paced the small confines of what was the local gaol. It consisted of one outer room and two cells within the next room. The facility had never seen such excitement as it had in the last few weeks. It was common to house drunks, thieves, and poachers here . . . but never had it housed traitors.

"Why can't Teddy be released immediately?" Chantel said on a swift revolution. "It's been over three hours."

"They couldn't release him until Squire Peterson signed the release," Richard said. He lounged against the only desk in the room.

Chantel forced herself not to look at him. His face was bruising, and a cut marred his forehead. Strangely, all she wanted to do was kiss away his bruises. She refueled her waning anger. The man had thought her an accomplice to Chad. He had not trusted her, and had only kissed her because of the danger. She shouldn't feel one jot of tenderness toward him.

"It shouldn't be much longer now that we've got the release."

The door to the cells opened and Teddy came through the opening. The two local wardens followed behind him. "Teddy!" Chantel exclaimed. "Are you all right?"

Teddy blinked. "Am fine. But do you know they have Chad in there? He looks frightful. Someone knocked his lights out. Seems he's just coming around." Teddy looked more closely at Chantel.

"Truth to tell, you don't look in high force either. What's that on your cheek?"

"Er, it's nothing but a scratch," Chantel said. "I'll explain it to you later."

"But we can't leave Chad in there," Teddy said, his hazel eyes bulging.

"I fear we must," Richard said. "Your cousin has been the traitor all along, Teddy."

"Chad? The traitor? No, Chad's a good chap." Teddy looked to Richard in shock. Then his eyes widened even more. "Gadzooks, you look as bad as Chad."

"I'd prefer to think he looks worse," Richard suddenly smiled.

"But . . ." Teddy began, "How could . . . ?"

The outer door suddenly burst open. Aunt Beatrice stood within the opening. Her face was dark, her eyes wild. "Eeks!" Teddy jumped. "Er, hello, Aunt Beatrice."

Beatrice entered the room, not even looking toward Teddy. Her eyes were sharp upon Chantel. "What is this? I have a message that says Chad has been imprisoned."

"Message?" Richard asked sharply. He directed a stern look at Chantel.

Chantel shrugged. "I sent it while we were waiting. Aunt Beatrice has a right to know."

Aunt Beatrice turned her burning eye upon Richard. "Why have you incarcerated my son?"

"He is being held under suspicion of treason."

Aunt Beatrice stared at him for a full moment. No one spoke. "Tommyrot!" She suddenly barked.

"Nothing but a pack of lies. The message said as much and it's all fustian. I must see him."

Richard nodded. "Of course. Thomas here will show you to him."

All were silent as Aunt Beatrice trod past them. Teddy jumped to escape her path. The warden, Thomas, seemed to tremble as he escorted her through the door to the cells.

"Whew," Teddy breathed. "She's in a pelter. Pity Chad if he's come round."

"Gore, you can say that," the remaining warden said. "Now we just need some more papers signed."

"More!" Chantel exclaimed, exhausted and distressed to the breaking point. "How many papers do you need, Geoffry? Faith, not even Whitehall would have this many."

The warden reddened. "Sorry, Miss Emberly—I mean, my lady, but we've got to be official-like about this."

"Let us get to them, then," Richard said calmly.

Both he and Teddy walked to the desk and began looking at the papers that Geoffry presented with due pomp and ceremony. Chantel resumed her pacing. Only minutes had passed when the door to the cells opened again. Aunt Beatrice steamed out. Her face was ashen.

Chantel ceased her pacing of the floor. "Aunt, are you all right? I am terribly sorry."

Aunt Beatrice glared at her. Her jaw quivered with suppressed emotion. "You! I told you you had your mother's blood in you. Told you nothing but pain would come from it all." Her venomous brown eyes sliced to St. James. "How could you take my son from me?" Beatrice walked across the room and was gone. The slam of the door resounded.

"Poor Aunt," Chantel said, swallowing hard.

"Poor Chad," Teddy said, shaking his head.

"No, not poor Chad," a voice, very similar to Chad's, said from behind them. Everyone turned to the voice. It was Chad! He stood in the doorway to the cells. He also held a wicked-looking Manton pistol.

"Evidently not poor Chad," Richard said softly.

"Now, let's not make any of you a poor, 'dead' one," Chad suggested. "No sudden moves. Raise your hands high above your head. Geoffry, I suggest you rise from that desk very, very slowly."

"But where did you get the gun?" Teddy asked as he raised his hands high.

"I had it hidden."

Teddy shook his head. "You always were a knowing one. Wish I had thought of hiding one of those when I was here."

Chad laughed. "Teddy don't worry over it, you weren't cut out to be a villain."

"You couldn't have had it hidden," Chantel exclaimed, her hands high, her eyes narrowed.

"I want you all to come this way. I believe you may have my sleeping quarters for the night. Now move."

It was a very obedient crowd that filed through to the two cells. Perhaps it was because Richard and Chantel had already barely escaped Chad's sending them on to the Almighty, while Teddy wouldn't dream of countermanding his cousin, and Geoffrey was downright terrified.

"Geoffry, you need to join your friend in this cell," Chad directed. A crumpled heap could be seen upon its floor. "Thomas might require your assistance. He shall most likely have a terrible headache when he wakes up."

"Thomas," Geoffry exclaimed, speeding into the cell and kneeling by his partner. Chad slammed the bars shut behind him and turned the key in the lock.

"Now, my dear family," Chad said, turning, "You must occupy this cell."

"How did you get that gun?" Chantel persisted as the three filed into the cell.

"Yes, must have hid it very well," Teddy nodded.

Chad cast a silent eye towards Richard as Chad slammed the barred door shut and locked it. "Any suggestions, St. James?"

"Why yes, quite a few," Richard said dryly.

Chad laughed. "Now, now, there is a lady present!" He turned and smiled at Chantel. "How did I get my gun? As I said before, dear, even villains have mothers. I am sorry, Chantel. Despite my wishes, I must leave. But in case you are interested, I will not be going to France."

"You won't?"

"No, I won't. Your determination that I should employ the Covington excesses legally has rather appealed to me. I did not lie when I said I cared about you. Therefore, there is but one place for my talents."

"Where is that?" Teddy asked.

"The Colonies. I have heard that America is quite open for er—gamblers of my sort. It is wild and unbroken and perhaps that is where I always should have been."

Chantel clasped her hands together. "Oh yes, Chad, that would be perfect. I hear it is terribly dangerous, and risking life and death against the savages is the common occurrence. Oh yes, you should enjoy that."

Chad cast a discerning look toward St. James. "Does it meet your approval? I swear I shall never return to England, or France for that matter. Do not discount my oath merely because I am a Covington."

"No," Richard said. He looked at Chantel with a glint in his eyes. "A promise is the one thing your family takes very seriously." His eyes were solemn when he returned them to Chad. "You have my approval."

Chad bowed. "Thank you, cousin-in-law." He looked at his fob watch. "You should have approximately the night to wait. Thomas told me there will not be a change in guards until then."

"The whole night!" Chantel exclaimed.

Chad's eyes were still upon Richard. "I did pretty well at convincing her that you do not care."

"So I have noticed," Richard said.

Chad laughed. "But I have given you the night. Consider it reparation." He looked at Chantel. "Dearest, don't be too difficult."

"Difficult!" Chantel exclaimed. "I am no such thing."

Chad shook his head ruefully and lifted a brow toward Richard. "I suppose you'd not let me escape if I took Chantel with me?"

"No," Richard said politely. "I fear I would have to hunt you down and kill you."

"Right," Chad sighed. "Well, though it galls me to say so, if I have to leave her, at least I am confident I am leaving her in capable hands. And they will have to be capable if you plan to take care of the Covingtons."

"So I have seen," Richard nodded, his gray eyes finally lighting. "But I will do my best."

"I don't know, it is a hard task for one not born of the line," Chad said, shaking his head sadly. "But I do not wish to frighten you off, for I want you to take care of them. Now I must leave."

Chantel ran to the bars. She knew she would never see her cousin again. She knew the proper thing to do would be to despise him for his actions, but she could not hold on to that coldness at the moment. She would miss her friend. "Chad, do you think you might write? Tell us how the Covingtons fare in America?"

He laughed. "That I shall. Goodbye, Chanty." He nodded toward Teddy. "I suppose it's left to you two to find the treasure, Teddy. Me, I'll just have to build one." He blew Chantel one last kiss and disappeared through the doorway.

"Goodbye, Chad," Chantel said softly, gripping the bars tightly.

"Come, Chantel," Richard's voice was soft from behind. "We have until morning, let us get some rest."

She turned. Richard was sitting upon the sole cot within the cell. Teddy had slid to sit on the floor. "I don't want to."

"Yes, you do," he laughed softly. "You are merely in a temper."

"Think you ought to rest," Teddy added with brotherly concern. He squinted at her. "You look fagged to death."

"See, even Teddy wants you to rest," Richard laughed. He patted the space beside him. "Come here."

She crossed her arms about her. "No, you and Teddy can have the cot."

"You mean share?" Teddy said, his face reddening. "Here now, Chantel, men don't do that kind of thing. It ain't proper. Someone might think they were . . . er . . ." He swallowed. "Well, never mind. You can share with St. James . . . but he and I can't . . . and you and I can't. That's the way it is. It just ain't done."

Chantel could tell that Teddy had the protocol well worked out within his mind and there would be no changing it; besides, she was beginning to ache in every muscle of her body.

"Oh, very well," she said none too graciously. She crossed over and plopped down upon the cot next to St. James.

A long arm snaked out and pulled her close. "Don't open your mouth," he advised her. "Merely close your eyes and go to sleep."

"Can't wait for tomorrow," Teddy sighed, shifting. "Don't like this place. Mean, Thomas and Geoffry are nice, but don't like it anyway." His eyes closed. "I miss Alicia. Now that I'm free, perhaps I can see her. Will have to find the treasure first, of course."

Suddenly Richard began to chuckle. Chantel shifted slightly in order to look at him. "What are you laughing about?"

"Not more than one minute after being designated head of the Covington clan and I am already spending the night in jail."

"You think you are head of the clan now?" Chantel said, attempting a haughtiness, though her body was relaxing against Richard even as she spoke.

"Yes," he said, a slight smile upon his lips. "And sooner or later you will agree with me."

"I doubt it," she said, laying her head back against his supporting chest. Despite herself, a smile was curving her lips. "Now, didn't you say we should get some sleep?"

"Yes." Richard's breath was soft upon her hair. "But one day you'll have to believe in me and believe that I want you."

"I know you do," Chantel said. "But only when we are in danger."

"No, it will be when you are not in danger as well," Richard said firmly. He chuckled. "But with you Covingtons that seems a rare occasion."

"No," Chantel said. "Chad is gone now—there won't be any more danger."

"Nor shocks or alarms?"

"None," Chantel said sleepily.

"Then, my lady," Richard's words were just a breath, "you will see that I am right, and you will come to me."

"No, never," Chantel murmured, even as she snuggled closer into the shelter of Richard's arms and fell deeply asleep.

Chapter Thirteen

The Earl of Hartford and his lady, as well as one
Teddy Emberly, were released from the local prison
the following morning by one extremely surprised day
guard. His mouth had slacked open when he arrived to
discover that the gaol housed such noble clients. A
sleepy Lady St. James and a very jovial Earl had accepted his stammered apologies once he discovered
from his other confined cronies the amazing story behind it all. Their pace upon leaving him was leisurely.
Teddy Emberly, the original confinee, however, was
anything but leisurely in his departure. To be exact, he
tore from the building. "Like a man possessed,"
Geoffry noted as they watched his portly frame speeding away.

While Richard and Chantel returned to their home,
Teddy made his way, post haste, to London. He did
not stop at his establishment; neither did he visit his
clubs or his friends. Rather, he dashed to the lending
library.

Now any of his close acquaintances would have
laughed at the thought of Teddy discovered in a read-

ing establishment. The notion of combining Teddy
Emberly and the written word in one space was too
similar to the idea of mixing oil and vinegar. The light
liquid would always float to the top; and, indeed,
Teddy was "light" by one oar or more. However, the
ladies commanding this erudite establishment noted
nothing unusual when Teddy bounded through the
door. They had become quite accustomed to him in
the past few months. They had often remarked on his
eclectic taste and wide range of reading interests, for
he borrowed every imaginable book, from the mundane to the infinitely elevated. They could not know
that he merely rambled the shelves and pulled out an
assorted variety without regard to title or theme. Nor
could they know that the books he borrowed were
often employed as door stops and window props instead of as tomes of education.

Today, Teddy did not hesitate at the sciences . . . nor
the maths . . . not even the sporting section! He galloped toward the shelves of gothics. He chased down
the aisles very much like a hound upon the scent. He
turned the corner of the third row and halted abruptly.

"Alicia," he shouted, then shuddered and looked
nervously about.

Alicia turned about in surprise. "Teddy? Oh,
Teddy," she breathed, clasping the *Count of Ugliano*
to her breast. "Is it really you?"

"Yes," he nodded, a silly grin crossing his broad
face. "I was sprung just this morning."

Alicia dropped the *Count of Ugliano* in obvious ela-
tion, and reached out her hands towards her Lothario.
"But how, Teddy . . . how?"

Teddy rushed forward to clasp up her hands. He

stood so close that he stepped upon the Count's binding. "They found the real traitor. So they let me go." He looked about quickly. "Need privacy to tell you the rest."

Teddy then pulled the clearly infatuated Alicia through the aisles of books until he came to the multitude of translations of ancient Greeks. "Bound to be private here," Teddy nodded with confidence. He tightened his hold upon Alicia's hands. "Must tell you. The real traitor is my cousin, Chad. He say's he's been doing it for years."

"Oh, Teddy, no," exclaimed Alicia, her face falling. "If my parents hear of this, they will never let us wed."

"I know," Teddy nodded solemnly. "Chantel says that I shouldn't worry, because they have not proved Chad a traitor, and fact is, he escaped last night. Locked us all up in his place. But it means they can't try him, since they ain't got him. But . . . well, it don't matter, I didn't like prison—didn't like being away from you." Teddy suddenly hunkered down upon one knee and looked up at her with pleading eyes. "Alicia, run away with me to Gretna Green. Let's do it before I'm nabbed for something else. You know I don't mean to fall in the briars all the time, but somehow it always happens."

Alicia was silent for a moment, her big brown eyes wide. Then they welled with tears. "Oh, Teddy, I never thought you would ask me."

"But I told you I wanted to marry you." Teddy looked both concerned and confused.

"Yes, but I never thought you would ask me to elope with you . . . to marry me out of hand! It is such a desperate, romantic thing to do."

"I know it ain't proper," Teddy said worriedly. "But I can't live without you. I love you."

"You are such—such a wild, madcap man," Alicia said tearily. "Are you sure you can settle down?"

"Am sure, very sure," Teddy said, nodding his head vehemently. "I know I'm not the best . . . ain't very top notch in the think box . . . but I love you, and I don't want to wait. Please, let's go to Gretna Green. Want you to be my wife as soon as possible!"

"Ohhh, Teddy," Alicia sighed. She promptly fell down upon her own knees and flung her arms about him, kissing him wildly.

Teddy returned her favors with fervor. Both, quite forgetting their tenable positions, lost their balance and toppled over, rattling the shelves as they did so. Socrates, Aristotle and Aristophanes, in all their various translations and languages, were ruthlessly shaken from their perches to fall down upon the kissing couple. It was the wisdom of the ages meeting with young lovers—and such wisdom was duly left strewn upon the floor as the two lovers finally picked themselves up and wandered away, creating schemes for their impending flight.

A full moon overlooked London that night, spilling its luminous white light liberally over the city. A lone hack trundled down the fashionable streets of Mayfair. From the vehicle's erratic progress, it was clear that the driver was either terribly inept or four sheets to the wind. It was fortunate that mankind, as a whole, was safely home in bed and not wandering about. Stray cats and dogs were forced to run for their furry lives as the equipage careened along the row of tonnish residences.

It halted before a particularly elegant town house. The driver cautiously tied off the reins and jumped down from the hack. He did not proceed to the front door of the home, but rather to the side of the building, stopping below the only window that still showed a light within. He did not turn to note the two riders that had followed silently behind, or see that they had dismounted only yards away.

"Alicia!" Teddy called in a low, long howl, a very unlikely wolf.

The sound of a sash being swiftly opened was heard. "I'm here, Teddy! I am here!" Alicia's voice called from the second story. A ladder, made of bed sheets knotted together, snaked its way down the length of the building.

Teddy jumped at it until he held it fast. "Got it, Alicia."

"Good. But Teddy, you must catch my things first," Alicia called. "I will send them down!"

Teddy dropped the rope and looked up. He dutifully stretched out his arms and awaited Alicia's first parcel. He jumped when he heard a gruff voice hiss from behind him, "You Teddy Emberly?"

Teddy swung about, his arms still outstretched. "I am sorry, Sir Thoma—" He froze and his eyes bulged. "Hello, I don't know you."

Two men stood within the shadows. The one closest to Teddy was all of six-foot-two, with a dirty, fierce face. The other was a small, wiry man with a toothsome, evil grin.

"Yeh? But I know you, Teddy boy," the tall one

said, smiling nastily. "Yer the flash cull who owes our clients a debt. Now, our clients are gentleman and have waited long enough for you to hand over the dibs. You do remember ye played with them at Madam Durham's? It's been long past three weeks and we are here to collect fer them."

"But . . . but I will pay you in a week or two," squeaked Teddy, backing up and flattening himself against the building's wall. "Don't have it now. Been working on it, though. Been working on it."

Six Footer stepped closer. "I ain't interested in you working on it. I wants it now or my clients told me to rearrange yer phizz fer them."

"But . . . I don't have it yet. And—and I've got to make it to the border, I'm eloping tonight. Couldn't you wait just one more week? I'll pay you then—"

"Don't try and bamboozle me," the thug growled, reaching out a large fist. "Ye've had enough time, and you ain't going nowhere on no honeymoon, cause I'm goin' to break yer bones as a sort of interest payment." He grabbed hold of Teddy's neatly arranged cravat and shook him.

Suddenly a heavy valise plummeted down from above and conked the villain upon his thick skull. The ruffian gurgled in shock. He stood stunned for a few seconds, his large fist wrapped about Teddy's collar, and then he crumpled to the ground.

"Did you catch it?" Alicia's voice called down.

"Almost," Teddy shouted up, with a hasty glance to the sprawled, cumbersome man at his feet, the huge satchel lying inches from his head. "Almost!"

" 'Ere now, you bleeding cove, stop right there." The scrawny one sprang forward from the shadows.

He held a knife that glinted in the bright moonlight. "Ye hurt Big Mike. I'll have to slash ye fer that," he hissed between rotten, uneven teeth. "And I'm the best at it."

"I—I didn't mean to," Teddy stammered, his back hugging the wall again. "But, I told you, I must go to Gretna Green. Am in a hurry and can't wait."

"In a hurry to meet yer Maker is wot I say," Rotten Teeth said, swiping his knife in the air a few times to reduce Teddy into gurgles. "Yer going to be sor—" A large iron bird cage sailed down from the dark night above and smashed into him. "Owee," he howled, as the massive iron structure struck his slim shoulder and felled him. The large cage landed a foot away from him, a crumpled frame. From out of its tangled mass of wire hopped a white turtle dove, cooing, its feathers ruffled.

A disoriented Rotten Teeth sat up, shaking his head as if he saw stars before his eyes rather than in the sky above him. "Why, you bastard," he muttered, still rattling his head about, "I'll get ye fer this . . ."

Once again, a missile from up above came careening down. This time a huge satchel thudded upon him. Rotten Teeth valiantly struggled to remain sitting up, but his head was wobbling alarmingly. When two bandboxes directly followed, he groaned and plunged backward, stretched out upon the ground next to his nefarious mate.

"That is all of it, Teddy," Alicia's voice called. "Is it too much?"

"No, just right, dear," Teddy called up, glancing at the two sprawled bodies before him. He rubbed his hands together and grinned. "Just right, by Jove."

He turned then and awaited his true love's alluring progress down the rope ladder. He held out his arms as Alicia reached the ground. Alicia did not enter them, however, but gasped and went to peer at the two fallen thugs. "Teddy, what are these two men doing upon the ground? Are they dead?"

"No, no. Thank God. You don't want to deal with dead men, Alicia, trust me. Tricky, dead men are." He flushed. "Er, these were sent by the men I owe the money to. Neddy told me they were not nice men and they aren't. One said he would stab me if I didn't pay . . ."

Alicia rushed toward him, throwing her arms wildly about him. "Oh Teddy, what a brave man you are to fight off two ruffians like that!"

Teddy's arms went strongly and eagerly about Alicia. "Well, truth is that I didn't—"

Suddenly Alicia pulled back. "Teddy! Where is King George?"

"King George?" Teddy asked in severe confusion. He frowned. "I suppose he's residing in London still. Ain't quite certain. Might have him somewhere else. Heard he's dicked in the nob. That's why Prinny—"

"No, no," Alicia said urgently. "He is my turtle dove!"

"Oh, well now," Teddy said, blinking, and looking about himself. "There he is," he pointed in excitement. King George had made his perch upon the comatose Rotten Teeth's nose.

"King George, you get off that nasty man and come here," Alicia admonished her pet. King George cooed, lifted his tail feathers, and promptly left a memento.

"King George, you shameful bird," Alicia scolded. "He is a nasty man, but that was still uncalled for!"

She immediately went to chase her pet. King George hopped away as Alicia grabbed at him. The flat-footed bird, cooing in disgruntlement, swiftly scurried over the ground and across Six Foot's recumbent chest. Alicia, crawling over Rotten Teeth, grabbed at him just as one of the bird's claws caught in Six Foot's clothing. King George squawked frightfully and his feathers flew. Yet Alicia only garnered another handful when she tried to catch him. King George was off again, cooing and squawking.

"Teddy! Help!"

Teddy ran to help his love. But King George was in a royal fuss and hopped up and down, scrabbling over the two fallen men, always one inch in front of Teddy's and Alicia's snatching hands.

"King George, what is the matter with you?" Alicia asked, dropping a fistful of down as King George once again ruffled his tail feathers and splattered Six Foot's chest.

"He's scared, is what," Teddy said knowledgeably. "Makes a chap have—er, dietary indiscretions." He crawled out of his four-limbed position, a rather pale look upon his face himself. "Thinkin' he might be right. Best get yer stuff and leave before we get caught again."

"Oh yes, what a goose I am being," Alicia said, swiftly rising. She frowned down at the recumbent men. King George rested upon Rotten Teeth's belly, his fat chest heaving as he emitted exhausted coos. "Whatever should we do with them?"

Teddy went and tugged at the rope ladder, frowning

in severe concentration. The makeshift rope fell upon Teddy. He grabbed the length into his hand and looked up in inspiration. "We can tie them up with this! Don't want them to wake and follow us."

"Oh, Teddy," Alicia said, her eyes bright in the silver moonlight, "You are such a fine man. What a wonderful thought. I am so proud to be running away with you."

Teddy beamed proudly, his chest puffing up as much as King George's. Teddy and Alicia went about their business of securing the men and they even dragged them to the front of the building so that the two rogues would not be overlooked come the dawn. And whereas King George was not as proud as Alicia to be running away with Teddy, when it came to leaving, he was dutifully back in his cage, his head tucked under his wing, sleeping off his excitement.

It was a cozy tea that Chantel and Richard enjoyed two days hence. She was laughing at a story he had told her while she poured tea into his cup. In the past few days Richard had treated her with an easy, teasing manner and a gentle chivalry. At times she would accidently catch a passionate look upon his face that would make her flush with heat, but he would always dispel it before she could say anything. He was not pressing her, only giving her each day to know him more. She had known she deeply loved him, but now she was growing to like him as well.

The door burst open upon this domestic scene and Sir Thomas charged in, a disgruntled, pugnacious look upon his face. "Richard, do you know where that bloke Teddy Emberly is?" he barked, forgoing both greeting and manners.

"Why no," Richard said, his brow rising mildly. He looked to Chantel. "Do you know where he is, dear?"

Chantel flushed, for Richard had grown accustomed to calling her by that endearment. She found she was growing accustomed to him addressing her so as well. "No, we haven't seen him since our—er, his release from prison."

Sir Thomas growled and put his hands upon his hips. "And why didn't you think to tell me the bounder was free from prison, St. James?"

Richard shrugged. "Why, I hadn't thought you cared so much about his welfare."

"I don't," Sir Thomas all but shouted. "But I do about my girl's. If I had known that addlepate had been released, I would have watched Alicia far more closely. As it was, didn't know anything until I found the two thugs tied up in bed sheets!"

"Thugs? In bed sheets?" Chantel asked, looking at Sir Thomas and wondering if he might be bosky. "Whatever would bed sheets have to do with Teddy?"

"They have everything to do with him," Sir Thomas barked, glaring at her. "Or they will, if the clunch ever succeeds in making it to Gretna Green."

"Gretna Green!" Chantel exclaimed. Her cup clattered to her saucer, while Richard's hung suspended in midair. "Never say Teddy eloped to Gretna Green with Alicia."

"Blast it, that is exactly what I am saying!" Sir Thomas growled, looking outraged.

"I can't believe it," Chantel said, shaking her head in surprise. "Teddy actually eloped with Alicia." Then she frowned. "But I still don't understand what thugs and bed sheets would have to do with Teddy's elopement."

"Perhaps you would like to have a cup of tea, Sir Thomas," Richard said kindly. "Then you can tell us all of it."

"Tea!" Sir Thomas's face flamed a deep red. "My daughter's run off with the greatest noddy in England, and you would have me take a cup of tea?" He glanced scornfully at the tea cart. Then his eyes wavered and seemed to rivet themselves upon Cook's special biscuits. "Oh very well, might as well. Have lost the young rapscallion somewhere anyway." He threw himself down into a chair, expelling air like a bellows. "When I get my hands on that clothhead, I am going to kill him."

"Biscuit," Chantel offered quickly.

"Thank you," he said, grabbing up three in one swipe. "Been over all of England chasing the blasted boy." He turned accusing eyes upon Chantel. "Do you know that damn fool brother of yours can't even make his way to Gretna Green correctly?"

"In truth, I am still trying to accustom myself to the notion that he has eloped," Chantel confessed. "I'd never have thought he would have had the wherewithal to do so."

"He hasn't," Sir Thomas said, cramming a biscuit into his mouth. "That's what I've been telling you. Hasn't made it to Gretna yet. The addlebrain keeps taking the wrong turns. Ain't got any sense of direction. I've been following him and I swear I have seen more of the damn countryside than I ever care to see again. Nothing but cows, sheep, and peasants. But

now I've lost the blasted simpleton." He cast a fierce
look at Richard. "And don't tell me what that makes
me, for I know it." He sighed, and munched morosely
upon his biscuit. "They're probably touring the Neth-
erlands by now."

"I wouldn't think so," Chantel said soothingly.
"They'd not honeymoon until after they are properly
married, I am sure. Teddy may be irregular, but he is
not lost to all sense of propriety."

Sir Thomas looked at Chantel as if he intended to
disagree, but Richard said swiftly, "If I know Teddy,
he probably thinks he's being clever and giving you the
slip."

"No such thing," Sir Thomas said glumly. "He's
been asking at every post the directions to Gretna. All
of England knows he's out looking for it. Ain't bad
enough that he's run off with Alicia, but then he goes
and misses the mark for two days! Won't be able to
show my face in the clubs without being laughed out
of them," Sir Thomas sighed. "Not to mention him
leaving those two fellows tied up in front of the house.
That really sent Lillian into a swoon."

"Are these the ones with the bed sheets?" Chantel
asked excitedly. "Good. I was hoping you would explain about them."

"Don't be too certain about that, madam," Sir
Thomas said. "That great gabby of a brother of yours
evidently tied these two men up in a rope made of bed
sheets. Seems a queer thing to do. Why didn't he just
use real rope?" Sir Thomas mused over his cup of tea.
"Of course, queerer thing was, the chaps were covered
in feathers and bird droppings. They were a hellish

mess. Not the sight you want greeting you when you walk out of your front door."

"But why ever did Teddy tie them up?" Chantel frowned. "Teddy is not a violent sort at all. And who were these two men anyway?"

"Said they were there to collect on Teddy's gambling debts."

"Oh no, the two thousand pounds," Chantel exclaimed, her hand flying to her mouth. "With everything going on I'd forgotten about that."

"Well, the men he owed evidently hadn't," Sir Thomas grunted. His hand reached out and snared two more biscuits. "Told the men to send their employers around to me and I'd pay them."

Chantel smiled and exclaimed, "Oh, how very kind of you!"

Sir Thomas flushed. "Well now, couldn't have those ruffians hanging about anymore. Ain't good for the neighborhood. Or for my little girl when she comes home." His face darkened. "If she ever does come home."

"She will be ruined." A shrill voice suddenly cut into the conversation. It came from the door.

"Oops," Sir Thomas said, dropping his biscuits in alarm. "Forgot to tell you, Lillian came with me. Another reason I ought to kill the young bottlehead." He turned toward the door, as did Chantel and Richard. Lady Lillian stood within the frame, haughty and enraged. Her pose was very much the same as a Greek tragedian actress's would be.

"Your brother has shamed and ruined my daughter," she repeated in a voice that was almost a scream. She stalked into the room.

"Er, feel more refreshed dear?" Sir Thomas asked solicitously.

"No, I don't," Lady Lillian snapped. Her eyes shot daggers at Chantel. "Your brother has destroyed my Alicia's reputation."

"But he intends to marry her," Chantel returned, attempting to be conciliatory. "Sooner or later Teddy is bound to find Gretna Green and then it will be all right."

"All right!" shrieked Lady Lillian. "It will not be all right! That my daughter would align herself with such a cad and bounder." Her eyes narrowed. "I have no doubt you were in league with him."

"No, I was not," Chantel said, her chin lifting. "This was strictly Teddy's notion and I am as surprised as you are. But I will not say I am not glad of it. Teddy and Alicia truly love each other."

"Love! Fustian," Lady Lillian said. "The simple truth is, you wanted them married so that another Emberly could sap the St. James's coffers and squander the St. James's funds."

Chantel stiffened. Yet before she could open her mouth to defend her brother and herself, Richard spoke. "Aunt Lillian, I am aware you are overset, but I will not permit you to speak to Chantel in such a manner. I advise you to apologize to her."

"Apologize? To that money-grubbing tramp?" Lady Lillian shrilled. "She may have tricked you, but she hasn't me. You'll not be shod of her, ever. She has no intention of giving you an annulment, I declare."

"I can only hope she doesn't," Richard said softly. "And as my wife, you shall show her full respect. Now, you need to apologize to her, and swiftly."

"I shall not," Lady Lillian said, glaring at him. "That a St. James would have to apologize to a penniless Covington!"

Richard unbent his frame and rose. "As head of the St. James household I suggest you apologize to Chantel, Aunt Lillian, or 'tis you who will suffer, I assure you."

"Well, I never," Lady Lillian huffed. Her chin quivered slightly. "Sir Thomas, are you going to allow him to threaten me like this?"

"Well, Lilly, they are family now," Sir Thomas said, rather blandly. "Best you bury the hatchet before you get cut with it."

"Oh—Oh—Oh!" Aunt Lillian spun and stalked from the room.

Sir Thomas snatched the last biscuit from the plate. "Sorry about that. Lilly always was the one for kicking at the barn door after the cows were already out." He looked at Chantel and his eyes were suddenly gentle. "Hope you don't take her rantings much to heart. She's just overset, you know. Always planned for Alicia to make a grand marriage, but then me, I've never been certain Alicia was cut out for being a grand dame, she ain't got the manner for it, too tenderhearted I suspect." He frowned. "But Lilly's got one thing correct. What is the boy supposed to do to support Alicia? I mean, we don't want him to look like a total barnacle."

"It will be simple," Richard said, and Chantel knew his eyes were upon her. She refused to look at him. "I will find him a post with the government. With my recommendation he'll get one."

Chantel's eyes did fly to his then. "You will do that?"

Richard nodded, his eyes warm. "It will be quite easy. I daresay Teddy will be no less expert than any others employed there."

"Well, that settles it," Sir Thomas said, dusting off his hands and rising. "Now I best go see to Lilly. She'll be down to apologize to you shortly."

Chantel flushed. "You don't have to make her do so. It really isn't necessary."

"Yes, it is," Sir Thomas said. "If we're going to be family, we're going to be family." He turned and walked toward the door. "That is if the young dolt ever gets my girl safely to Gretna," he grumbled before exiting.

"Well, Chantel," Richard said softly. "Will you be able to accept Aunt Lillian's apology? And mine? She should never have said such things to you."

Chantel blinked. The sudden memory of her wedding flitted through her mind. She remembered Richard as he had lectured her upon her rudeness to his family. Now he was apologizing for them. And he was also including her as one of the family. She blinked again, as an odd warmth seeped to the core of her soul. She was finding an acceptance she had never expected. She was also close to making a fool of herself by crying.

Chantel jumped up. "Of course," she said quickly, looking away from him. "Now I must go . . ." She sped across the parlor toward the door.

"Chanty," Richard called, causing her to halt. "I can't change my family any more than you can yours. If I could, I would. But just as you have gamblers and a traitor in yours, I have snobs and shrews in mine. It would make a fair exchange, wouldn't you say?"

Chantel looked at Richard. His gray eyes were gently teasing, but with an underlying seriousness, even perhaps a fear. "I really must go, Richard," she said, and then smiled. "I must make arrangements for Aunt and Uncle, they'll want to stay for dinner, I am certain, and most likely the night."

Richard's eyes widened, and then he leaned back with a relieved grin. "Yes, Aunt and Uncle will most likely do so."

Chantel grinned and left her very satisfied husband stretching out in his chair. Yet as she rushed across the foyer toward the back of the house and to the kitchen, she realized that he was not the only satisfied one. She was deeply satisfied herself, amazingly so.

Chantel made ready for bed that evening lost in a strange emotion that she could not define. Lady Lillian and Sir Thomas had remained for dinner as well as to spend the night before they returned to the hunt for Teddy and Alicia. Lady Lillian had indeed apologized. That she did so in a very stilted and cool tone mattered not one jot to Chantel. What mattered was that the supper had gone smoothly and the talk was over the best course in aiding the new couple back into what would be a disapproving society. It seemed once again that a Covington would scandalize the *ton*. The St. James's sat at the table and like major strategists arranged a campaign to bring society back to accepting Teddy and Alicia's *faux pas*.

Chantel was grateful for it. Still, even as she warmed with the feeling of being a member of the family, Aunt

Lillian's accusation that the Emberlys had married into the St. James family for money still nagged within her mind. Chantel's chin lifted as she told herself fiercely that it wasn't true. She knew, however, that the rest of the world would see it as Aunt Lillian did. She would always be a poor beggar who had snagged Richard, and he would always be the duped man, married for his money. The thought stung, cutting at her pride and her heart.

She sighed, and crawled underneath the covers. Not a short while ago, she had been prepared to do anything to seduce Richard to her bed and gain his love. Yet now as her love for him grew, thoughts of the consequences of it if he did truly take her to be his wife crowded to the front of her thoughts. Would their love be enough to battle the cutting words and attitudes of society? Did she even want to force Richard into such a position? Suddenly his pride and dignity were very important and precious to her. Now, when he claimed his consequence mattered not to him, it mattered to her deeply.

Chantel closed her eyes tightly. There was no use trying to think it all out tonight. She was only giving herself a headache. It was something she would have to ponder upon before she could decide what would be right and best for Richard. Once she decided, then she would do what was right for both of them, no matter if it hurt her or not. She fell asleep, feeling the weight of her thoughts and fears. Thus she tossed and turned, dreaming fitfully.

Close to morning she dreamed she was in gaol once again. Chad was saying goodbye. He said, "You'll have to find the fortune yourself." He started repeatng it and repeating it, louder and louder. Suddenly, as only in dreams does it happen, Chad's voice evolved into Lady Genevieve's. It was Lady Genevieve who was saying these words in an irritated, imperious tone.

Even as Chantel looked at her through the bars of the cell, the room elongated and stretched until it opened up into countryside. Now Lady Genevieve was standing at the hole that Chantel and Richard had dug that day. She was standing with her arms crossed, her face a picture of impatience, her foot tapping imperiously in the dirt. "You'll have to find the fortune yourself! You'll have to find the fortune yourself!"

Chantel's eyes suddenly snapped open. She was wide awake, as if she had not been dreaming. "I'll have to find the fortune myself," she said in surprise. Then she smiled in the dark. Yes, she would have to find the fortune. And she would.

The next morning Chantel feverishly waited through breakfast for Uncle Thomas, Aunt Lillian, and Richard to finish. She knew she would be free and clear to hunt for the treasure afterwards, for all three intended to depart and search for the errant elopers. Therefore, she smiled and chatted throughout, forcing herself to keep her attention upon them.

She was grateful when she was finally able to wave goodbye to them. Richard had cast her a suspicious look before leaving, asking her if she were all right. She had laughed and said that she was feeling fine. Apparently she had satisfied him, as he had finally left with his relatives.

Chantel promptly turned and charged back into the house and up the stairs. She needed to change out of

her favorite blue muslin morning dress trimmed i
white eyelet flounces set with tiny enameled button
painted with yellow daisies. She would need to chang
to her designated "treasure hunting" frock, now sadl
worn and darned along a large tear caused by a mis
directed shovel during her last expedition to search fo
Lady Genevieve's legacy.

As once before, she found a shovel from the ga
dener's shed and took a loaded pony cart back towar
the Folly. This time the cart was loaded to the gill
with every imaginable item Chantel could think woul
aid her in her quest. She had ladders, rope, trowels
flint and candles. She was determined to be prepare
for any event this time. No longer was it a game t
please Alicia. Now it was for real, and Chantel full
intended to uncover the treasure.

When she arrived she went directly to the place sh
had dug at before. Lady Genevieve had tapped he
foot at the very spot within her dream. Chante
jumped into the hole and began shoveling the dirt wit
vigor. Half an hour into her digging, her shove
scraped against a hard surface. Could it be the trea
sure? She thumped again with the shovel. Meta
clanged upon metal.

Excitedly, she threw the shovel down and knelt. Sh
brushed dirt away until she discovered a large meta
rectangle. Disappointed it was not a treasure chest
Chantel uncovered the metal plate even further. Sh
realized then that it was of a goodly size and that
metal ring was attached to one side.

"Oh dear, it is a trap door." Chantel fell back on he
heels, dusting off her gritty hands. "Why does it hav
to be another door?" she muttered, as her mind flev

back to the last hidden door and being trapped behind it in that dank, stifling stairwell.

She shrugged fatalistically then. Faint heart would never win gold and jewels. With a grunt she leaned over and tugged on the large, rusted ring, lifting up the iron door with severe difficulty. Chantel peered into a dark abyss, steep stone stairs leading down into total darkness. She swallowed hard. Her first instinct was to turn tail and run.

"No, you'll have to find the fortune yourself," she admonished herself.

Determined, she turned away and stalked toward the pony cart. She grabbed up a candle and flint from her supplies. She returned to the trap door. Taking a deep, steadying breath, Chantel lowered herself down to reach the steps. It was a dark tunnel she traveled down and through. When she had gained her balance and lost the outside light, she lit her candle. She was reluctant to touch the sides of the tunnel walls, for they seemed to be covered with mold and seeping residue. She followed the tunnel and expelled a breath of relief when it leveled off and opened up into a room. Three corridors fanned out from the room, each presenting a confusing and dark possibility.

"Oh dear, three choices," muttered Chantel, biting her lip and looking at the corridors with indecision. "Which one, Lady Genevieve? Which one? Wait, don't answer that," she added quickly, looking about her eerie surroundings with a wary eye. "Please don't answer that. I'll find it myself," Chantel said, finding that speaking aloud calmed her nerves, for it cut the muted, dense silence about her. "I'll try the middle one." She moved toward the center corridor and followed along it. She began humming to herself slightly, merely to keep her lagging spirits afloat. At the very end of the corridor she discovered a door, a wood bar against it. Excitement leaped within Chantel even as the candle flickered, creating strange shadows upon the corridor's walls.

Chantel found the wood bar easy to lift. She swung wide the door and raised her candle high as she entered. It was a room. A perfectly empty room. Not even a pebble lay upon its stone floor, nor a cobweb clung to its plastered walls. "Drat," muttered Chantel. "Lady Genevieve, you had an odious sense of humor, I fear."

Chantel shook her head and turned back toward the door. She screamed. A dark, squat shadow stood within the threshold. Chantel's candle shook in her hand. The shadow's features took on definition.

"Aunt Beatrice?" Chantel stammered. She heaved a sigh of relief. "Thank heaven it's only you. You scared me out of my wits." Aunt Beatrice stood mute. Chantel could hear her heavy breathing. She had an odd, glazed look upon her face, even as her eyes glittered in Chantel's candlelight. "Aunt Beatrice, why are you here?" Chantel asked with sudden hesitancy.

"So you thought you would find the treasure?" Aunt Beatrice said, her voice strangled. "That treasure is mine, do you hear?"

"But I thought you didn't believe in the treasure!"

"I'm not like that fool Teddy," Aunt Beatrice snorted. "Telling everyone about it. Letting others know about what should be mine." She stepped into the room.

"Oh, Lord," Chantel said. Aunt Beatrice held a

knife in her hand. "Is—is that meant for digging, Aunt?" Chantel asked the question hopefully, yet the odd light in Aunt Beatrice's eyes was like that in a mad dog's and Chantel didn't expect a positive answer.

"I would have shared the treasure with you," Aunt Beatrice said. "But you should have married Chad. Then we three would have shared it." She lifted the knife high. "But you married St. James instead. Did you really expect me to allow you to find the treasure and have it pass on to another family, when it should be in the Covington family and the Covington family alone?"

"I—I hadn't thought of it much," Chantel said in what she hoped was a soothing voice as she backed away from Aunt Beatrice. She knew there was no escape but the door that Beatrice blocked, and nothing in the room to use as a weapon. "But perhaps we should discuss this more."

"Discuss it!" Aunt Beatrice shouted. Her knife slashed through the air. "What is there to discuss now? St. James married you despite my warning him not to."

"You're the one who shot at him!"

"I could have killed him if I had wanted to. I thought he'd get the message and stop. But no. He married you anyway. And then you, you silly twit, fell in love with him. Just like your mother, marrying where she oughtn't. She never had a care for the Covington name. Never!" She raised the knife again. "I should never have let you live this long. But that fool I hired missed you."

"You're the one who hired the man in the gray

cloak!" Chantel exclaimed. "But I thought that Chad . . ."

"Chad." Aunt Beatrice's face crumpled. "My boy, my boy has left me." Pain, anger and insanity emanated from Aunt Beatrice's eyes. "It was all because of you, you ungrateful wretch! He kept telling me how you would marry him and we would all share in the treasure. He kept telling me how happy we would all be together living at the Folly. But you betrayed him and married St. James."

"Did—did Chad know that you had tried to kill me?" Chantel asked, a pain flashing through her at the thought.

"What kind of mother do you think me?" Aunt Beatrice said indignantly. "I'd not tell my boy such a thing. He wanted you. And against my better judgment I allowed you to live because he wanted you. He even made me promise to take care of you when he went away." Her eyes became piercing lights of hatred. "I'll take care of you now, the way you deserve to be taken care of. There is nothing to stand in my way now. My boy has gone. We will never live together at the Folly." She began to sob loudly. "We will never share the treasure, never, never!"

Aunt Beatrice, with a wail like a banshee, lunged at Chantel with her knife. Chantel dropped her candle and grabbed desperately at Aunt Beatrice's arm before she could bring the knife down. Aunt Beatrice was squat, but sturdy-framed and strong with insanity. Chantel realized in fear that she could not overpower her. She leaned forward and sunk her teeth into Aunt Beatrice's knife arm. Aunt Beatrice roared, but dropped the knife. Chantel immediately kicked at the knife, and saw it skitter away. Beatrice delivered a fist to Chantel's jaw. She reeled back just as the candle guttered out upon the stone floor. Chantel heard Aunt Beatrice's guttural growl in the dark. Two strong hands circled her neck. Chantel grabbed at them, tearing desperately at them. She was choking, growing faint. Aunt Beatrice's insane laugh rang through the buzzing in her ears. She could feel herself slipping, weaving to the floor. Still she could not shake the iron vice at her throat. She closed her eyes and prayed one last prayer.

"Chantel!" she heard Richard's voice calling. Through blurring eyes she saw a light appear. Suddenly the killing hands were no longer upon her throat. The air actually hurt as it rushed back into her deprived lungs. She fell to the floor, gulping air in greedily, despite the pain.

Chantel looked up and saw Richard rushing at her through a haze. "No," she croaked. "Go after her." He knelt beside her. "Please! She's insane."

"I'll be back," Richard said, and was gone.

Chantel lay there but an instant, drawing in the air, regaining her senses. Then she crawled to her feet. She must follow Richard and Beatrice. She walked toward the door with an urgency born of fear. She staggered down the corridor, seeing a glowing light far before her. When she caught up with it she was back in the large room. Richard stood in the center, his candle high, his body tense and waiting.

"Richard," she whispered through raw vocal cords. "Where is she?"

"Chantel!" He turned and held one arm out. She stumbled to him, clutching at him even as his strong arm wrapped about her. She buried her head in his shoulder, breathing in his scent. It comforted her. "She's in one of the corridors. But I don't know which one."

Chantel shivered slightly. "She's mad, Richard."

"It's her grief, Chanty," he said softly. "But we must find her."

"Yes," Chantel nodded, holding even more tightly to him. "Yes, we must."

They stood quietly then, listening intently for any sound that would tell them which corridor to travel. A sudden shriek rent the air. Aunt Beatrice came pelting out of the right corridor. She looked back over her shoulder, fear stamped upon her face. As she skidded to a halt and saw Richard and Chantel she cried, "Lady Genevieve, it's Lady Genevieve!" She turned and pointed to thin air.

"Lady Genevieve?" Chantel asked. She shook her head. "Aunt, I don't see her."

"Tell her, Chantel," Aunt Beatrice cried. "Tell her to leave me alone."

"But Aunt, I don't see her. Where is she?"

"There!" Aunt Beatrice pointed to no phantasm that Chantel could see. "There. Tell her to leave. Oh, God," Aunt Beatrice shrieked. She turned and ran three steps. Suddenly she stiffened, clutched at her heart, and crumpled to the ground.

Richard exclaimed and rushed to her. He knelt, turning her over and leaning down to her. He looked up, his gray eyes almost black in sadness. "She's dead, Chantel. She must have died from a seizure."

"Oh, no," Chantel murmured. Then Chantel did something she had never done before in her life. She rolled up her eyes to the ceiling and promptly fainted.

Chapter Fourteen

The next few days were a painful haze to Chantel. She did not remember how she got home, nor how Richard got her to her room. She remembered a doctor coming and looking at her and him whispering to Richard that she would be fine, she just needed to recover from the trauma of it all.

For those next few days, Chantel believed she would never recover from the shock. Learning that one's aunt wanted to exterminate one, and all because of a treasure that she had sworn she never believed in, was not an easy thing to swallow. Watching that same Aunt rave of ghosts and immediately topple over dead did not help either.

So Chantel took to her bed just as the doctor had ordered her to do. She slept around the clock, and woke only to pick at the food Richard would bring her. Then Chantel would turn over, close her eyes, and succumb to the safety of sleep again. What was the purpose of getting back into life when it was such a wild and unpredictable affair?

At the end of the week, however, Chantel was finding that sleep no longer comforted her. Indeed, she was starting to become heartily bored with it. And whereas before she had been impatient when Richard interrupted her sleep and forced her to eat, now she wanted him to stay. Yet he never did, leaving her after half an hour, urging her to rest some more. Chantel would clean her plate of food, wondering all the while why Richard was being so distant. Didn't he know she needed his comfort and solace?

Desire for life was creeping back into Chantel, whether she willed it or not. Indeed, she realized it was of no use to feel sorry for herself. Everyone had their difficulties, and if her aunt had been driven insane by greed and jealousy, it was nothing Chantel could change. Nor could she change the fact that her aunt had passed on to her rewards in such a startling fashion.

What she could change was her nightrail, and she did. She changed it from the simple cotton she wore to one of Richard's more fetching and feminine ones: the ombre rose smocked with taupe silk ribbons across portrait sleeves designed to rest off the shoulder. She smiled as enticingly as she could when Richard entered, and thanked him for his kindnesses. She tried to hold him in conversation but he always seemed overly conscientious of time. He also appeared restless and would often leave her abruptly.

Chantel was sitting up in her bed on the sixth day, mulling over Richard's behavior. Was it that he did not love her anymore? Yet as reasonable as that notion was to explain his behavior, Chantel found she didn't accept it. She realized that she had come to trust in Richard, to believe that he was a steady man and that his heart would be faithful. She frowned. Then why would he not remain in the room with her? The doctor had said she must rest this whole week and though Chantel was attempting to be dutiful, it fretted her that she could not chase Richard down.

"Yet why can't I chase him down?" she murmured to herself.

The door opened at just that moment and Chantel looked hastily to it in embarrassment. Her expression changed to one of joy. "Teddy!" She stretched out her hands. "And Alicia," she said as they both entered. "You are finally here!"

Teddy said sheepishly, "Had a little difficulty, you see."

"Oh, Chantel, he showed me the world," Alicia said, rushing forward. Her mild brown eyes were no longer mild; they sparkled and snapped.

"Well, most of England," Teddy amended. "Didn't mean to, but there you have it. Didn't know going to Gretna Green was such a hard thing to do. They should post it better."

"Oh, but it was very exciting," Alicia giggled, sitting down upon the chair. "Our dash to the border. We thought we'd be caught at any moment."

Chantel laughed for the first time in days. "Did you? Well, Sir Thomas made a gallant effort to find you. He even had Lady Lillian with him."

It was Alicia's turn to look sheepish. "I do feel dreadfully sorry for that. I never dreamed that Mama would wish to go with him. Mama is not the best of travelers, you see."

Chantel reached over and patted her hand. "Well, you are married now and . . ." She stopped and looked

at them cautiously. "You are married now, aren't
you?"

"Oh yes," Alicia nodded, blushing. "And it is quite,
quite delightful."

Teddy turned a beet red and shifted upon his feet.
He coughed and an idiotic grin crossed his face. "Yep,
done the trick. Married right and tight. Best thing in
the world—to be married."

"I am so glad," Chantel said, attempting not to
laugh at the guilty-looking lovers. "And what are your
plans?"

"We intend to do the Season in London," Alicia
said. "Mother and Father say it is imperative that we
present ourselves to society as a couple. Else we will
never be able to enter it again."

"I am not sure of that," Chantel said with a frown.
"Though Lady Lillian is the best to know what to do
about society and so on. Perhaps you should listen to
her."

"But after the Season, we thought we might like to
. . . to repair to Covington's Folly," Teddy said hesitantly.

"Would you mind dreadfully?" Alicia asked swiftly.
"Teddy is truly reformed, but I thought—I mean we
thought—perhaps he should stay away from London."

"And the tables," Teddy added without the delicacy
that Alicia was striving so very hard to achieve. "Am
tired of losing at them anyhow. Did you know Sir
Thomas paid my gaming debts?"

"Yes, I did."

"It was good of him, but can't have my step-father
footing the bill for me like that any more." Teddy

decreed it with such a sternness that Chantel found it difficult to recognize her own brother.

"And also," Alicia blushed again, "we would like to have a lot of children and—and I am not quite certain that Town is the best place to raise them." She straightened. "I know it sounds strange, and Mother says I am impossible, but that is how I feel."

Chantel could suddenly see the Folly with little Teddys and Alicias running about it. She shook her head wryly. Well, the Folly had withstood the ravages of countless Covingtons before, surely it could withstand Teddy and Alicia's brood. "I think that would be wonderful." And then she hesitated. "You do know what happened to Aunt Beatrice?"

"Yes," Teddy nodded solemnly. "Always thought she was slightly off beam." Then he brightened. "But I also always told you that it was the treasure the killer was after, didn't I?"

"Yes, Teddy," Chantel said approvingly, "You did and you were correct."

"Teddy is sometimes very brilliant," Alicia nodded. "Though not everybody realizes that. We have also thought . . ." She looked at Teddy.

"Er, yes," Teddy said, his hazel eyes darkening. "Don't think you should look for the treasure any more, Sis. Mean, we'll all make by without it."

Chantel was stunned. Recovering, she said with attempted lightness, "But aren't you going to need it for all those little Covingtons you intend to rear?"

"Oh, as to that," Teddy said, "Sir Thomas said that if he got grandchildren from this all, he'd help out. Said they'd be of the St. James family and he wouldn't allow his grandchildren to be little beggars—or was it bergers?" Teddy frowned. "Wasn't sure I heard him straight on that."

"Chantel, we had never considered how dangerous it was for you to look for the treasure," Alicia said in a rush, putting her hand out to her. "We have since realized that it was a very selfish thing for us to ask of you."

"And we thought we'd rather have you than the treasure," Teddy said, nodding.

After all the trauma of the past weeks, Chantel was forced to blink back silly tears. "Well, thank you. But there was no possible way we could have known that Aunt had—had taken it all to heart so."

"But still," Teddy said, sighing. "Should have thought of it."

"Teddy, dearest," Alicia said gently. "Could you please leave us ladies alone for a moment? We would like to discuss some private matters."

"We would?" Chantel said surprised, finally regaining her composure.

Teddy straightened, puffing his chest out. "Of course, of course, you ladies need to talk between yourselves." He walked to the door and left, still strutting a little.

Alicia giggled. "He is such a dear." She turned to Chantel then, her brown eyes serious. Chantel was beginning to learn that when Alicia became serious it was usually uncomfortable for the other person. "I truly do want to know if you object to us repairing to the Folly."

"No, whyever should I?" Chantel asked, confused.

"I didn't know your plans, and it is your house after all," Alicia said hesitantly. "And I worried that you might not want us there if you are living there as well."

Chantel stared and then flushed. "I—I hadn't thought of that. But—but if I do return to the Folly I would most certainly wish you to live with me. I—I fear I would grow dreadfully dull if you didn't."

"Oh, Chantel," Alicia said, sighing. "Marriage is truly wonderful. Don't you think you might see your way to reconciling with Richard?"

"Reconciling?" Chantel asked, shocked. "What do you mean, reconciling? I am not against the marriage. It is Richard. He's been avoiding me."

"But I do not understand," Alicia said, frowning, her brown eyes troubled. "When we arrived, Richard was in a frightful fit of the sullens. Reed says he's paced the whole house every day since you've been recovering."

"He has?" Chantel asked, amazed. Then her eyes narrowed. "Why were you talking to Reed?"

Alicia giggled, and a most mischievous smile crossed her face. "Oh, Chantel, being married has made the world of difference to me. I am my own mistress now and I find I am asking and doing exactly what I wish. Not at all like when I was at Mama's."

"Alicia, you are incorrigible," Chantel said, Alicia's spirits becoming contagious. "And what else does Reed say?"

"He said that Richard remained constantly by your side for the first few days and that he actually haunts this hall outside your door."

"But I never see him. He comes only to bring me food, and then he'll only stay for half an hour. Why won't he spend more time with me?"

"I asked him that," Alicia said, nodding.

"You what!" Chantel exclaimed, appalled, yet curious.

"I asked him that," Alicia repeated. "And he said something about you not being recovered yet and he didn't want to press you."

"But that is ridiculous," Chantel said, outraged. "These past few days I've been wanting nothing but for him to . . . well, I've been missing his company."

"Do you think you could tell him that?" Alicia asked. "I know the staff would appreciate it. Reed says that Cousin Richard is biting everyone's heads off. And though he, Reed, believes you will stay, Cousin Richard is not so sure."

"He isn't?" Chantel asked, stunned.

Alicia looked swiftly about as if ensuring they had privacy. Then she leaned over and whispered in a confidential tone, "Chantel, I know that men are very strong and brave, but I have found that sometimes they have to be told what is there before their very eyes. They aren't as quick as we've been taught."

As wife to Teddy, Alicia's words were an obvious understatement, and Chantel stifled an amused laugh. Yet then she frowned. She had laughed, but perhaps there was some truth there as well. Maybe Richard wasn't as quick as she had thought him. Chantel flushed suddenly. Or perhaps she was the one who wasn't so quick. Richard had told her more than once that he would wait for her to trust him enough to come to him.

"Oh dear," Chantel murmured, her hand flying to her warm cheek. "Alicia, I am going to have to go to him."

"Will you?"

"Yes," Chantel nodded. "I must go to him."

"Oh Chantel, I hope you do!" Alicia almost jumped out of her chair. "Then this means you will be my cousin as well as my sister-in-law?"

"If all goes well."

Alicia giggled. "Oh, it will go well. I just know it. And Chantel, you will love marriage. It is so delightful." She colored again and stood. "Now I best leave and permit you to rest. Richard told me I was not to tire you."

"Tire me!" Chantel's eyes narrowed. "I am not tired and he's going to find that out very shortly, I assure you!"

It was all very well to boast to Alicia that she, Chantel, would approach Richard and settle matters, but when it came right down to it, Chantel found her courage as fickle as a weathervane. One minute she was prepared to march down to Richard and tell him she wanted to be his wife in every respect, and the next she merely wanted to remain hidden in her room.

She tried to reason why it would be so difficult to tell Richard that she loved him and wanted to be with him forever. When she practiced the words, speaking them aloud, they came out easily and smoothly. Yet when she thought of saying them directly to Richard, her heart quivered and her throat became dry. If she approached Richard with her love and he turned away as he had before, she imagined she would just curl up and die. Chantel shook her head softly. No, the risk was just too high.

"Oh, come on, Chantel," she muttered to herself. "So it's a gamble. Where's that Covington spirit!"

Chantel suddenly jumped out of bed. Yes, where

was the Covington spirit? She had much to lose, but if she didn't risk the play, she'd not win either. It was but noon, where would Richard be? She dashed to the bell pull. She'd call Betty and get dressed. Then she would find Richard and tell him immediately. It was time to put the cards on the table. Her hand froze upon the bell pull. But which ones did she intend to lay down? "Get rid of the low cards," Chad had told her. Chantel's hand drew slowly back and her eyes narrowed in a frown. She very well knew which cards were her low ones, which cards she'd turn in for a better chance if she could.

She walked over to the picture of her great-great grandmother. She placed her hands upon her hips and said, "I want that treasure, Lady Genevieve. And I know it's in the right corridor. Now you and I have come to know each other rather well, so if you want to appear to me you'll just have to do so. I warn you, though, I'm not going to be frightened off one whit. I want that treasure!"

Chantel went back to the bell pull and tugged sharply upon it. She would need Alicia to cover for her while she was away. She had no doubt that Alicia could do it successfully. Chantel next crossed to the armoir and pulled out her favorite fortune hunting dress, newly pressed and repaired for the next expedition. She pulled off her robe swiftly.

"Beware, Richard St. James," she said, a determined glint in her eye. "I'm going to come to you. And it will be with some very high cards to play!"

Chantel stood quietly in awe. She held her candle high. It flickered dimly, but with every muted shift of light there was a flash of silver or gold. She breathed out a soft sigh. She had naively been expecting a trunk that would hold the treasure. There was not trunk. There was an entire roomful!

Softly Chantel moved through the room. Pictures of great artistry ranged along a wall. An array of glittering silver covered what appeared to be an exquisite Jacobean carved mahogany banquet table. Delicate china pieces sat amongst the silver heirlooms like so many bouquets in a garden. Tapestries woven with precious gold metal thread from Russia, waist-high Ming vases set with jewels of jade and carnelian, screens carved of Chinese turquoise, alabaster candle sconces, each vied for attention among rolls of Turkish carpets. Gold-encrusted frames, wider than a handspan, housed works by the masters; each painting qualified to be hung in a museum as an example of the greatest artistry. A tall tigerwood tree set in an engraved bronze planter spread branches bearing leaves of carved emeralds.

Chantel set her candle down slowly, for it had begun to shake in her hand. The scene before her was overwhelming. She picked up the nearest item and stared. Had Lady Genevieve actually eaten off the gold plate? And drunk out of the gold goblet beside it? Her eyes widened. Indeed she must have, for there were another twenty place settings in gold. Faith, that was an excess!

Gulping, she picked up her candle and continued through the glistening room. She came to a cabinet at the far end and opened it. She blinked as not only silver and gold flashed at her in the candlelight, but also the rays that could only emanate from the cut facets of diamonds and precious stones. The cabinet was full of jewelry. The most magnificent jewelry Chantel had ever seen. Yet in the center position lay the most brilliant of all, the famous Covington collar of emeralds and diamonds. Chantel reached reverently to touch the glorious necklace.

"Thank you, Great-great-Grandmother," she whispered softly. "Thank you so very much."

Richard slipped his robe on and tied it. He looked at his bed, which was already turned down, and wondered if he'd even manage to sleep in it tonight. He grimaced. Most likely not. He'd probably pace the floor again, just as he had the night before, and the night before that. He sighed. He hadn't even been allowed to see Chantel this afternoon. Alicia said that Chantel had been feeling unwell again and had not wished for company. When Richard had gone to take Chantel her meal, Alicia was there before him, tray in hand, saying that she would take it to Chantel.

Richard went and sat down upon his bed. He stared into the flame of the candle that sat upon the night stand. Would Chantel ever recover? She had lost both her cousin and her aunt in such a short time. How could she bear it?

He punched the mattress beneath him. He felt so helpless. What could he do for her? Richard knew she needed time. He also knew that her trust in him was a fragile thing. He dare not shake it or press her. Yet every time he was around her, he was overcome with a desire to take her in his arms and kiss her wildly until she consented to come to his bed. Richard sighed. Where was the man of control that he had once been?

Richard heard the door open and then the whisper

of a soft movement. He lifted his head, wondering which servant was entering so stealthily. He froze. He could feel the blood draining from his face. Lady Genevieve stood before him. Her titian hair flamed in the candlelight as brilliantly as did the jewels about her neck. But none could outdo the glitter in her green eyes. Richard remained transfixed.

"I have come to you," she said softly.

Richard's heart stopped. It was Chantel's voice that spoke, warm and husky. He rose slowly. "Chantel?"

"Yes," she nodded.

"I thought you were Lady Genevieve's ghost."

"No, it is me. In flesh and blood. It's only her dress . . . and her jewels." Then she grinned that grin of hers that always seemed to twist his stomach a little. "You told me not to try and seduce you for money." She shrugged her shoulders elegantly and the collar of emeralds and diamonds sparkled. "It won't be for money this time. I have more than enough."

A slow grin crossed Richard's face and he walked slowly across the room, still afraid she was just an apparition. He came to stand within inches of her. Chantel looked up into his eyes, hers steady, unwavering. He placed one hand on the curve of her waist. "Will it be for life, sweet witch?" he asked huskily.

She leaned into him, a rustle of silk. He drew in his breath as he felt her slim body against his once more. "Are you sure, Chantel?" He could hear the rasp in his voice, but could not contain it.

She wrapped her arms about him, gazing at him with trusting, loving eyes. "I am sure."

They met then in a wild, passionate kiss. Chantel's was open, demanding. Richard felt the tremor run through them both. He kissed her just below her ear, loving the sweet scent of her hair. He ran his lips down the column of her neck, reveling in the smoothness of her skin. When his lips brushed the stones of her necklace he pulled back for a moment. He couldn't stop his smile. "It will kill my mother, you know?"

Chantel giggled, stretching like a purring, satisfied feline within his arms. "I know. Isn't it marvelous? And Richard, it's a whole room! Not just a trunk or so."

"Is it?" he murmured, not caring one whit for what she said, but delighted at the joy and passion within her eyes. He bent and claimed her warm and willing lips once more. He heard her slight moan, and his arms went to encompass her. His fingers discovered an open dress back and bare skin beneath. He drew back, shocked. "Chantel, you aren't buttoned and you don't have anything on . . ."

She grinned impishly. "I know. I really didn't think we dare rip Lady Genevieve's dress, not after she was kind enough to let us have her treasure. And also . . ." here she looked hesitant. "I—I didn't want to give you a chance to draw back again."

Richard laughed loudly. With a swift movement he scooped her up within his arms.

"Richard!" Chantel exclaimed, her arms going about him in surprise.

He carried her toward the bed with purpose, just as he had been waiting to do all along. "Madam, beware, I'll never draw back again. Ever." Richard hesitated a moment, looking into the green depths of her eyes, a challenge in his. "Do you think you can withstand it, Chanty?"

The challenge leaped into her eyes and she laughed, throatily and temptingly. "I am a Covington. We have been known to handle great excesses, my lord."

"Remember those words, my lady," Richard laughed, laying her gently down upon the bed. "They may very well be your misfortune."

"Oh, no," Chantel whispered, holding her arms out to him with a confident smile. "I only have fortune now, only fortune!"

Betty, the maid, entered her mistress's room the next morning, only to halt when she did not find her. The bed was not only unslept in, but the room was in shambles. Now Betty, being a healthy country girl, did not go off half-cocked. Before she raised the alarm, she thought it wise to check one other spot for her mistress's whereabouts. She trod softly down the hall to the earl's room.

She cracked the door open and peeked in cautiously. Lady Genevieve's gold dress lay discarded at the foot of the bed. The hoops to it were tossed upon a chair. Lord St. James' robe rested a distance from there. Two figures slept soundly in the bed, each entwined with the other. Bare skin showed here and there amongst the sheets. The expressions upon the slumbering couple's faces were the same, that of complete contentment.

Betty giggled softly. "Looks like there won't be any more talk of an annulment now!"

She silently closed the door and tiptoed away. Betty couldn't wait to tell the rest of the staff that they would finally have both a master and a mistress for good. Of course, that was all Betty would tell them. She'd not be silly enough to lose her job by blabbing to everyone how she had discovered the room with clothes strewn all over the place. Or that her mistress slept in nothing but her necklace—and what a necklace it was. One of the largest and grandest ones she ever did see, she'd be bound!

ZEBRA'S REGENCY ROMANCES
DAZZLE AND DELIGHT

A BEGUILING INTRIGUE (4441, $3.99)
by Olivia Sumner

Pretty as a picture Justine Riggs cared nothing for propriety. She dressed as a boy, sat on her horse like a jockey, and pondered the stars like a scientist. But when she tried to best the handsome Quenton Fletcher, Marquess of Devon, by proving that she was the better equestrian, he would try to prove Justine's antics were pure folly. The game he had in mind was seduction — never imagining that he might lose his heart in the process!

AN INCONVENIENT ENGAGEMENT (4442, $3.99)
by Joy Reed

Rebecca Wentworth was furious when she saw her betrothed waltzing with another. So she decides to make him jealous by flirting with the handsomest man at the ball, John Collinwood, Earl of Stanford. The "wicked" nobleman knew exactly what the enticing miss was up to — and he was only too happy to play along. But as Rebecca gazed into his magnificent eyes, her errant fiancé was soon utterly forgotten!

SCANDAL'S LADY (4472, $3.99)
by Mary Kingsley

Cassandra was shocked to learn that the new Earl of Lynton was her childhood friend, Nicholas St. John. After years at sea and mixed feelings Nicholas had come home to take the family title. And although Cassandra knew her place as a governess, she could not help the thrill that went through her each time he was near. Nicholas was pleased to find that his old friend Cassandra was his new next door neighbor, but after being near her, he wondered if mere friendship would be enough . . .

HIS LORDSHIP'S REWARD (4473, $3.99)
by Carola Dunn

As the daughter of a seasoned soldier, Fanny Ingram was accustomed to the vagaries of military life and cared not a whit about matters of rank and social standing. So she certainly never foresaw her *tendre* for handsome Viscount Roworth of Kent with whom she was forced to share lodgings, while he carried out his clandestine activities on behalf of the British Army. And though good sense told Roworth to keep his distance, he couldn't stop from taking Fanny in his arms for a kiss that made all hearts equal!

Available wherever paperbacks are sold, or order direct from the Publisher. Send cover price plus 50¢ per copy for mailing and handling to Penguin USA, P.O. Box 999, c/o Dept. 17109, Bergenfield, NJ 07621. Residents of New York and Tennessee must include sales tax. DO NOT SEND CASH.